THE COMPLETE CASES
OF CASS BLUE, VOLUME 1

John Lawrence

THE COMPLETE CASES OF

CASS BLUE™

VOLUME 1

JOHN LAWRENCE

INTRODUCTION BY
ED HULSE

ILLUSTRATIONS BY
JOHN FLEMING GOULD

ALTUS
PRESS

BOSTON • 2014

EDITED AND DESIGNED BY
Matthew Moring

PUBLISHING HISTORY
"The Ten-Cent Sleuths: *Dime Detective* Revisited" appears here for the first time. Copyright © 2014 Ed Hulse. All Rights Reserved.

"The Bloodstone" originally appeared in the November 1932 issue of *Dime Detective* magazine.
"The Corpse Was Cold" originally appeared in the October 1, 1933 issue of *Dime Detective* magazine.
"The Corpse Control" originally appeared in the June 1, 1934 issue of *Dime Detective* magazine.
"Calling All Cars!" originally appeared in the August 1, 1934 issue of *Dime Detective* magazine.

THANKS TO
Joel Frieman, Paul Herman, Ed Hulse, Everard P. Digges LaTouche, Rob Preston & Daniel Sanders

TABLE OF CONTENTS

THE TEN-CENT SLEUTHS:
DIME DETECTIVE REVISITED
ED HULSE

J **OHN LAWRENCE** was still relatively new to fiction writing when in 1932 he sold a story titled "The Bloodstone" to New York-based Popular Publications, whose recently launched pulp magazine *Dime Detective* was considered a comer. The former stockbroker had previously placed two yarns in Popular's new sheet. "The Torso Trap" (October 1932) introduced detective Sam Beckett, whose exploits Lawrence would chronicle in eight more issues. His third contribution appeared in the next number and brought forth New York-based private investigator Cass Blue, a morally flexible tough guy who backed up his hard-boiled rhetoric with frequent applications of the blackjack he carried in a hip pocket.

Lawrence related his hero's adventures in the first person, guiding his protagonist through a maze of conventional plots and innumerable gunfights. What the Cass Blue series lacked in polish and innovation, it made up for with vigorous action and the tough-as-nails attitude that gave *Dime Detective* the distinctive flavor that made it a favorite of Depression-era readers. He surely didn't know it at the time, but John Lawrence was participating in the Golden Age of American crime fiction.

When Street & Smith launched *Detective Story Magazine* in 1915, they probably didn't realize they were also launching an entire genre of rough-paper magazines—one that would eventually encompass more than 150 titles published over a period of 45 years. Some of the crime/mystery/detective pulps came and went quickly, being unimaginative simulacrums of more successful predecessors. Others thrived and settled comfortably into what eventually became a well-defined niche. After a shaky start, *Black Mask* during the Twenties evolved into an outstanding pulp and, under the editorship of Joseph T. Shaw, gave voice to the pioneering writers of what became known as "the hard-boiled school"—Dashiell Hammett, Raymond Chandler, Carroll John Daly, and Frederick Nebel among them. During the Depression years *Black Mask* was widely imitated, but only one pulp-wood periodical offered serious competition. And for a time, that magazine—*Dime Detective*—dominated the genre.

Henry (sometimes referred to as Harry) Steeger and Harold S. Goldsmith started Popular Publications in 1930 with $10,000. They launched four titles in the fall of that year—one of them the short-lived *Detective Action Stories*—but only *Battle Aces* made any money in those early Depression days. At 20 cents each, Popular's pulps were luxury items to many potential readers. The following year, Steeger and Goldsmith began a line of ten-cent titles with *Dime Detective*, which almost immediately generated profits for the company.

Although Steeger later claimed he wasn't specifically going after *Black Mask's* readership, it was probably no accident that Cap Shaw's most popular writers at the time—Daly, Nebel, and Erle Stanley Gardner—were induced to write for Popular's new magazine. They were joined at the outset by J. Allan Dunn, T.T. Flynn, and Oscar Schisgall, all old hands at the game. Steeger's strategy was simple: he paid higher rates than his competitors. Four cents a word was the ceiling for detective-story writers at that time, and Steeger paid it cheerfully to get the genre's big names on his covers.

In the beginning, *Dime Detective* published mystery-horror hybrids as well as straight, hard-boiled action stories. Possibly Steeger was influenced to a degree by A.A. Wyn's *Detective-Dragnet Magazine*, which had introduced a weird-menace strain into its yarns a year earlier. The cover story of *Dime Detective's* inaugural issue, Dunn's "Shadow of the Vulture," established an eerie atmosphere in the first chapter when two policemen and a butler discovered a brutally dis-figured corpse in a darkened street:

> The three looked at the body of a man, poorly dressed. His hat had rolled into the gutter, and his pate showed bald, surrounded with gray hair. A common face, made no more prepossessing by the fallen jaw, the staring eyes and the look of utter dismay that death had not yet effaced.
>
> His shabby clothes were disarrayed. Something had ripped them apart, had torn the flesh on his chest and sunk deep into his entrails. He lay in a puddle of his own blood that was steadily enlarging.

A witness claimed to have seen the shadow of the killer: a man-sized bird of prey with a large, sharp beak. Dunn expends some 20,000 words before "The Vulture" meets grisly death after being exposed by "famous criminal investigator" Guy Livingstone, who graciously allows police to take credit for unmasking the fiend.

More conventionally hard-boiled fare was offered up by *Black Mask* émigrés Nebel and Gardner. The former introduced blunt, tough-as-nails private eye Jack Cardigan of the Cosmos Detective Agency in "Death Alley," while the latter wrote of unorthodox shamus Snowy Shane in "Snowy Ducks for Cover." Gardner, whose many series characters never quite duplicated the appeal of his Lester Leith (in *Detective Fiction Weekly*) or Ed Jenkins, the Phantom Crook (in *Black Mask*), failed to make Shane sufficiently distinctive to impress readers, and his first case chronicled in *Dime Detective* was also his last. In fact, of the half-dozen or so heroes Gardner featured in his 27 stories for the magazine, only Paul Pry, created in 1930 for Popular's *Gang World,* aroused much interest.

The other two stories in *Dime Detective's* November 1931 number, T.T. Flynn's "The Pullman Murder" and Edward Parrish Ware's "The Devil's Jackpot," were routine offerings. But the magazine was an instant hit and almost single-handedly relieved the financial pressure on the fledgling company. The early issues continued to exhibit a bias toward mystery-horror yarns; mad scientists and homicidal maniacs abounded, both on the covers and in the fiction. Cover artist William Reusswig pioneered the vivid, startling look that became Popular's corporate trademark. Steeger's early reliance on vignette covers with white or pale pastel backgrounds gave way to a preference for bold colors and liberal use of red, yellow, and black—to his eyes, the most striking combination. Before the title was two years old it was being published twice monthly, on the 1st and the 15th.

Every now and then, a big name pulp writer appeared in the pages of *Dime Detective:* Edgar Wallace (June 1932), Arthur B. Reeve (October 1, 1933), Max Brand (October 1, November 1, and November 15 of 1934). But for the first three years Steeger and editorial director Rogers Terrill pinned their hopes on the small but efficient roster they had assembled. Nebel's Cardigan, a clone of his "Tough-dick" Donahue still appearing in *Black Mask,* was the book's star. Carroll John Daly, still peddling Race Williams yarns to an increasingly dissatisfied Cap Shaw, came up with several new characters for *Dime Detective:* Marty Day (who fought a mystery villain named "The Reckoner"), Clay Holt, and the clear favorite, Vee Brown, whose day job as investigator for the Manhattan District Attorney enabled him to moonlight as a composer of pop tunes known on Tin Pan Alley as "the Master of Melodies."

True *Dime Detective* aficionados know that the magazine's peak period began in 1934 and continued throughout the decade and into the early Forties. Editor Kenneth S. White (a second-generation pulp editor: his dad was Trumbull White, *Adventure's* original blue-pencil man) gradually shifted the magazine's focus away from mystery-terror to straight hard-boiled action. It took him a couple years to do so, but the effort was apparent early on. By 1934 John Newton Howitt and Walter Baumhofer were doing the covers, and while distressed damsels still showed up, the screeching skulls and drooling madmen receded into history.

White recognized the value in recurring characters and actively encouraged his stable of writers to develop them. Frederick C. Davis, a facile storyteller who would become one of the mainstays of Popular Publications, first offered private eye Oak Oakley but hit paydirt with psychiatrist Carter Cole, who handled seemingly supernatural cases that turned out to be anything but. Cole's first adventure, "Case of the Crimson Claws" (August 1935), was probably his best. Davis had a flair for detective yarns with weird-menace trappings, and while plotting was his strong suit, he proved equally capable of crafting darkly atmospheric prose. And he kept coming up with series heroes: After Cole there were Keyhole Kerry, Bill Brent, and Thackeray Hackett.

Others who earned favor with *Dime Detective* readers in the mid-Thirties included Fred MacIsaac's peripatetic crime reporter, Rambler Murphy ("Alias Mr. Smith," April 1, 1933), William E. Barrett's Needle Mike, the sleuthing tattoo-parlor proprietor (first appearance: "The Tattooed Corpse," January 1, 1935), John K. Butler's Tricky Enright, a special state investigator posing as an ex-con ("Seven Years Dead," January 1936), and Barrett's newspaper columnist Dean Culver ("The Blue Barrel," March 1936), created several years earlier for *Strange Detective Stories*. It was during this period that John Lawrence chronicled the exploits of Cass Blue and two other hard-boiled dicks—Drago and Sam Beckett. His major contribution to the magazine, the Marquis of Broadway series, began later in the decade.

Dime Detective hit its stride in 1935, a year that saw many outstanding issues. It also saw publication of "Murder in Wax," the second of Cornell Woolrich's 31 yarns for the magazine and arguably his first great crime story. Submitted as "Angel Face" (the nickname of its female protagonist), it told the suspenseful tale of Bernice Pascal, the first of several Woolrich women who attempted to rescue the men they loved from death in the electric chair for murders they didn't commit. Ken White recognized in Woolrich a writer of uncommon talent and gave him free rein to submit offbeat tales that didn't play out along typical hard-boiled lines. In fact, Woolrich was the only major contributor to *Dime Detective* who never created a recurring character. Arguably his most important contribution to the magazine was his 1942 yarn "It Had to Be Murder," the basis for Alfred Hitchcock's classic thriller *Rear Window.*

The September 1935 number is a key issue in the magazine's history and should be at the top of every *Dime Detective* collector's want list. To begin with, it included the first of 21 Race Williams thrillers submitted by Carroll John Daly following his break with Cap Shaw and *Black Mask.* The split was a long time coming; the Williams series was too flamboyantly melodramatic for Shaw, who preferred the gritty naturalism of Hammett and had tried to make all his contributors write along the same lines. The trigger-happy Williams was, to be honest, far better suited to *Dime Detective.* Ken White hadn't done any poaching of *Mask* characters, but Daly's departure from the *Mask* (which proved temporary) gave the editor access to newly commissioned yarns featuring the original hard-boiled detective.

Some detective-pulp aficionados believe Daly's Race Williams stories for *Dime Detective* actually improved upon many of those which appeared in *Black Mask.* For one thing, the Popular pulp didn't run serials; Race's adventures there were novelettes or short novels, although some storylines overlapped. Daly's plotting seemed a little tighter and his prose a little more polished. (It's possible, however, that the extra gloss was the result of editorial revision.) "Some Die Hard," lead story for the September 1935 issue, portended better things to come. But it wasn't the only memorable tale in that number. Spider scribe Norvell W. Page, making his only appearance in *Dime Detective,* revived Ken Carter, the sleuth he had created a couple years earlier for A.A. Wyn's *Ten Detective Aces,* for "Satan's Sideshow." Woolrich supplied another of his early classics of nail-biting suspense, "The Corpse and the Kid," in which a loyal son, believing his missing father has killed his stepmother, wraps the body in a carpet, sneaks it out of the house, and is nearly caught while trying to dispose of it. "Crimson Jade," an Erle Stanley Gardner yellow-peril yarn, made exciting reading and rated the cover (which sported one of Baumhofer's most unusual *Dime Detective* paintings, a torture-by-fire image). Even the issue's weakest story, O.B. Myers' "The White Mask," was above the average found in many of *Dime Detective's* competitors.

The November 1935 number boasted another superb Baumhofer cover, this one featuring a black-clad surgeon preparing to operate on a naked blonde bound in white straps strategically placed to conceal her naughty bits. The scene illustrated "The Devil's Scalpel," a nifty Norbert Davis entry in the mystery-horror sweepstakes. But the issue's standout story was Daly's "Dead Hands Reaching," a Race Williams novel that reintroduced fans to Race's female co-star, The Flame. John K. Butler's "The Stairway to Hell," a taut installment in his Rex Lonergan series, finished a close second.

More notable issues from this period include January 1936 (with Vee Brown, Jack Cardigan, Carter Cole, and the first Tricky Enright story), April 1936 (with Woolrich's unforgettable "The Living Lie Down with the Dead," Race Williams, Rambler Murphy, and Cardigan), and November 1936 (the fifth anniversary issue, with contributions by every major writer from *Dime Detective's* first five years: Nebel, Gardner, Daly, MacIsaac, Flynn, Barrett, John Lawrence, and Leslie T. White). The latter, which added extra pages to celebrate the magazine's birthday, featured "The Tongueless Men," a short but curiously flat novel written round-robin style.

Raymond Chandler, annoyed by Cap Shaw's abrupt dismissal from *Black Mask*, switched his allegiance to *Dime Detective* the following year with "Mandarin's Jade," the first of seven tales he sold to Ken White. It was the second, "Red Wind" (January 1938), whose opening became possibly the most frequently quoted passage in hard-boiled history:

> There was a desert wind blowing that night. It was one of those hot dry Santa Anas that come down through the mountain passes and curl your hair and make your nerves jump and your skin itch. On nights like that every booze party ends in a fight. Meek little wives feel the edge of the carving knife and study their husbands' necks. Anything can happen. You can even get a full glass of beer at a cocktail lounge.

All but one of the seven featured as its protagonist private eye John Dalmas, whose "voice" was essentially that of Philip Marlowe, whom Chandler created for his first hardcover novel, 1939's *The Big Sleep*, much of which was cobbled together from bits and pieces of his earlier pulp stories. At the time, Chandler's arrival at *Dime Detective* wasn't really a big deal; his meticulous approach to writing (which involved repeated rewriting) prevented him from being a top producer like Nebel or Gardner, and at that time he still hadn't seen print in hard covers or sold a story for Hollywood adaptation. Today, Chandler issues of the magazine in even average condition routinely sell for hundreds of dollars.

White's editorial savvy kept *Dime Detective* flying off newsstands. Early 1938 saw back-to-back publication of exceptionally fine issues: February, with the first installment of T.T. Flynn's long-running series starring Mr. Maddox (a race track tout with a knack for getting involved in murder investigations) and yarns featuring the Rambler, Needle Mike, and Lawrence's Marquis of Broadway, the marginally honest police detective whose beat was the Great White Way. March sported a striking Baumhofer skeleton cover and included Chandler's frequently reprinted "The King in Yellow" along with novelettes starring Daly's Race Williams and Frederick Davis' Keyhole Kerry, yet another crime-solving newspaper columnist.

Deliberately antagonistic, wheelchair-bound Inspector Allhoff, the D.L. Champion creation that *had* to have anticipated Raymond Burr's TV show *Ironside*, made his debut in "Footprints on a Brain" (July 1938). This taut tale was the first of 30 Allhoff novelettes published in *Dime Detective* between 1938 and 1946. His are among the most memorable adventures in the magazine's 274-issue run, and we recommend them heartily. Allhoff is a fascinating character—bitter, brilliant, and sadistic. He takes special delight in verbally abusing his aide Battersly, who as a rookie cop turned coward during a police raid and thus failed to keep a thug from crippling Allhoff by shooting his legs to pieces with a machine gun. The interpersonal dynamics of these stories are often more compelling than the plots, although Allhoff is portrayed as a super-sleuth who regularly solves intricate puzzles.

Ken White kept *Dime Detective* fresh by printing stories about offbeat characters such as Allhoff. While other detective pulps published hundreds of clichéd yarns starring processions of interchangeably two-fisted, hard-drinking private eyes, White's magazine boasted a string of quirky, colorful protagonists. Future Hollywood scriptwriter John K. Butler, having exhausted the possibilities of his earlier characters Rex Lonergan and Tricky Enright, hit paydirt with playboy-cum-cabbie Steve Midnight, "the Hardluck Hacker," who often turned gumshoe reluctantly to get himself out of trouble. The series opener, "The Dead Ride Free" (May 1940) set the pattern for this excellent series, which ran to nine entries in a two-year period, after which time Butler left pulps for more steady work at Republic Pictures, where he ground out screenplays for dozens of "B"-grade Westerns and mysteries.

"Strangler's Kill" (August 1940) introduced the almost impossibly erudite Dean Wardlow Rock, whose encyclopedic knowledge and ratiocinative skill was matched by his physical toughness and willingness to use violence when necessary. The Dean, as he was nicknamed, plied his trade in 19 novelettes printed in *Dime Detective* between 1940 and 1945. They were penned by Merle Constiner, one of Popular's most reliable mystery writers during the Forties. During the same period Constiner contributed to *Black Mask* a series featuring Memphis-based private investigator Luther McGavock, whose cases often took him to small Southern towns vividly and evocatively described.

Dime Detective's February 1941 issue alone offered two new series characters: Frederick Davis' lonely-hearts-columnist-cum-detective Bill Brent and Peter Paige's private dick Cash Wale. This particular number, by the way, is also collectable because it contains the only *Dime Detective* story penned by veteran Western writer Luke Short.

Norbert Davis, forced to keep his puckish sense of humor in check while writing for *Black Mask* under Cap Shaw, gave *Dime Detective* two highly engaging characters in shady, seedy detective Max Latin (who secretly owned a cheap restaurant) and William "Bail Bond" Dodd (the nickname tips off his occupation). Davis, who sadly committed suicide in 1949, was a terrific storyteller, and his early Forties yarns for *Dime Detective* rank among his very best pulp stories.

By this time the magazine had settled into a pleasant if predictable groove. During the wartime years there was very little difference between Ken White-edited issues of *Black Mask* and *Dime Detective,* the two best detective pulps. Both magazines relied heavily on popular series characters. Both magazines favored novelettes over longer or shorter stories. Novelettes generally ran to 12,000 words and up, with very few exceeding 20,000 words. Working in these lengths, the regular writers streamlined their plots and rarely included more than three suspects in any whodunit. The onset of American involvement in the Second World War manifested itself in detective pulps with an increase in the number of stories with espionage underpinnings; seemingly run-of-the-mill murder mysteries were now often peopled by collaborators, black marketers, and Fifth Columnists.

During the early War years, Cornell Woolrich continued to supply his special brand of suspense yarns, which provided welcome contrast to formula-driven whodunits featuring the magazine's popular series characters. "The Body in Grant's Tomb" (January 1943) is narrated by its protagonist, a middle-aged spinster who stumbles over a corpse while visiting one of New York City's famous landmarks and decides to play detective. "Mind Over Murder" (May 1943) takes Woolrichian terror to new heights as a dissatisfied wife, acting on the advice of a female friend, plots to murder her husband and make it look like an accident.

The majority of *Dime Detective's* early- and mid-Forties covers were painted by Rafael De Soto, who succeeded Thirties artists Reusswig, Howitt, Baumhofer, and Malvin Singer. De Soto rarely illustrated scenes from stories; generally he submitted cover ideas to Popular art director Aleck Portegal, who okayed the concepts from pencil roughs. Occasionally, White commissioned stories to go with the covers. One of the most interesting from the wartime period: Hugh B. Cave's "This Is the Way We Bake Our Dead" (June 1943), which was not only his last for the magazine but among his last rough-paper yarns as well.

In 1944, the price of *Dime Detective*—indeed, of all Popular's Dime titles—rose to 15 cents. Unfortunately, the increase coincided with the beginning of a gradual diminution of quality across the board. The thing to remember is that issues of any *Dime* titles bearing 15-cent price tags represent magazines in decline. There are individual numbers worth having, to be sure, but for all intents and purposes, *Dime Detective* began to slump once its price contradicted its title.

The mid and late Forties saw additional series characters introduced, but the new ones didn't have as much snap as the older ones. D.L. Champion's Mariano Mercado, and Frederick C. Davis' Thackeray Hackett, Dale Clark's "High" Price, Richard Dermody's Doc Pierce, and Robert Martin's Jim Bennett lacked the appeal of such flamboyant recurring heroes as The Rambler, Needle Mike, and the Marquis of Broadway. A few "old timers"—Race Williams, Bill Brent, Mr. Maddox—popped up from time to time, but *Dime Detective* was clearly on the downswing when Ken White left Popular Publications in 1948. Under new editors the one-time champion limped along until August 1953. By then it was priced at 25 cents and, except for isolated stories by superior writers like Fredric Brown and John D.

MacDonald, bore little resemblance to the upstart pulp that once challenged the mighty *Black Mask* for supremacy in the detective-pulp field.

Dime Detective printed just over 1,500 stories in 274 issues published over 22 years. The ten-cent sleuths of Popular Publications still have loyal adherents: both the original magazines and reprint collections are avidly sought after today by pulp fans who weren't even born when the title was in its heyday. John Lawrence is not by any means the best-known contributor to this classic rough-paper periodical, but he played an important role in its development. And while the Cass Blue stories don't necessarily show him at the top of his game, they certainly deserve this long-overdue revival from Altus Press.

THE BLOODSTONE

IT WAS A HOUSE OF HORROR
WHERE THE KYLE FAMILY
DWELLED. MURDER STALKED
FOR NO APPARENT REASON,
STRUCK AT RANDOM FROM
THE SHADOWS. YET BEHIND
ALL THESE KILLINGS WAS
A BLOOD-RED MOTIVE. AND
THE ANSWER COULD BE
READ ONLY IN A DEAD MAN'S
PALM!

CHAPTER ONE

THE MYSTERIOUS MR. KYLE

THERE WAS a picture of me in *The Sentinel,* and a nice little blurb, giving me a hand for knocking off Joe Cirofici, as dirty a gun, incidentally, as had prowled New York for some time. I was giving the item my undivided attention when my office girl—Tam Cotter her name is—came in and laid the card on my desk. "He's old, and he looks like money."

I fingered the card. The *Mr. David Kyle* was engraved. "Send him in," I said.

He had on expensive clothes, and two diamonds. One in the tie, and one on a skinny, shrunken hand. He had a limp, and a stick to work it with. His face was wrinkled skin, tight over razor-edged cheek-bones; his lips were moist and vermilion, like a girl's and his little red tongue kept licking them. His frame looked as though it had shrunk. His eyes were brown, but there was a red smoldering light behind them. Dirty white hair stuck down over one eyebrow. He didn't take off his hat. There was a folded newspaper in his free hand. He looked at it, then at me.

"If you're Cass Blue," he cracked suddenly in a harsh voice, "this don't look much like you."

He had *The Sentinel* too. I said these half-tones never look much like a person. His eyes kept darting up and down, all over me. "All right," he snarled finally, "I've been swindled by every other crook in town. You might as well have your cut," and sat down.

I warmed up under the collar right away. Things were breaking just about right for the Blue Inquiry Agency at this point. I couldn't see where this drooler got a call for language. "If you've got something to say, suppose you get going on it," I said. "I've not got much time."

His eyes got narrow. "Oh, you've got time all right!" he snapped.

I

"Shoot me and I'll fall on this plunger. Better not, Blue!"

"I've got the money to pay for your time. Listen—there's a man—maybe more than one—trying to murder me!"

I said was that so?

"He's an Italian. Name's D'Aguido. He's in New York now. I live out at Pine Lake. He's trying to find me to kill me."

"Why?" I said.

"That's none of your business, is it?" he blurted—and I got him then. He was frightened half out of his wits, and trying to bluff it out. "You don't have to know that, do you?"

"Depends. What do you want me to do?"

"Find him! Arrest him—have him deported! Anything—only keep the devil away from me!"

"How do you know he's here?"

"I saw him!" The bluff wasn't holding up. His face was strained and a vein was bulging in his forehead. "I saw him in the—in the street."

"What's he look like?"

"He's an Italian?—a lag man, an enormous man—with brown eyes. And black hair. He's always snarling."

"Well," I said, "there's probably not over twenty-five or thirty thousand Italians in New York would fit that."

"But this man's name is D'Aguido!" he raved. "He's been after me for fifteen years! Everywhere I go, he pops up. I see him everywhere— snarling, showing his teeth at me, like—like a dog!"

"There's no law against that."

"But my God! He's going to kill me!"

"Do you live alone?"

"Alone!" He laughed gratingly. "Alone but for my family and any alley cats they can drag in!"

I was getting a little fed up with this. "You want a bodyguard. I'll supply one for twenty-five dollars a day, and—"

"No! I don't want a guard! I want you to find this man, keep him away from me—arrest him!"

"For what? If he's been in the country for fifteen years, you can't deport him. And in the first place, unless you can give me a far better description, I couldn't find him anyway. If he's looking for trouble, as you say, he won't be using his own name. What am I supposed to go on? How many people are there in your establishment?"

"That doesn't matter. Ten maybe, but—"

"Does he know where you live?"

"He'll find out! He always does. Now, mind you, I'm willing to pay, Blue—pay well."

I shrugged. "I'm just as willing to be paid, but there's nothing to it, unless you'll hire a bodyguard. If you're certain you're in danger, you can watch yourself, and with your family around—"

He got up. "It so happens," he said in a hollow voice, "that I can expect anything but protection from my family. They—but that's something else. I've told you what I want. If you won't do it, someone else will. Will you or will you not, look for this man for me? For a substantial—"

"I will not," I said disgustedly, "and if I were you, I'd hire a psycho-analyst, not a detective."

"Oh," he showed broken teeth again in a snarl. "So you think I'm crazy!"

I shrugged again. "I didn't say so. The fact remains, I'm not going to take your money when I haven't a prayer of producing."

He stood there a minute, a funny succession of expressions running over his face. "Well," he bit off finally, "I suppose I owe you something for even talking to me."

"No," I said.

For another half minute, he didn't move, kept looking at my face. Finally he turned on his heel, muttered something like a surprised "Well!" and limped out.

When the outer door closed behind him, Tam came and put her head into my office. "What the hell?"

"Nut," I said.

That was three years ago, the first and only time I had ever seen David Kyle.

I HADN'T forgotten a word of it, either. But the atmosphere around banks makes me a little fidgety. And when I'm fidgety I get pretty cagey. So I wasn't broadcasting when this curly-headed ex-football player started the conversation by asking did I know a man named David Kyle. I just said I didn't seem to recall the name. He frowned, took up a long, wax-sealed manila envelope, started tapping it on the triangular, brass, desk sign that read—*Mr. Ryan—Assistant Trust Officer.*

"Well, no matter," he said finally. "He—they—seem to have heard of you. I—we—have been acting for Mr. Kyle for some years. He is a very eccentric man—or was, possibly I should say. This envelope—" he stopped tapping—"he left with us, sealed. We were instructed to deliver it to you, should anything happen to Mr. Kyle. You, in turn, are to deliver it to Miss Louise Kyle, his daughter, unopened, at the earliest possible moment. Also, you are expected to remain at their home—it's in Oakville, Pennsylvania—for not less than forty-eight hours. You are to investigate the theory of foul play, regardless of any official decision to the contrary, and endeavor to make out a case against the perpetrator. Certain conditions—"

"Wait a minute," I said. "What happened to him? Is he dead?"

"Dead? No. He's disappeared."

"When?"

"Why, why—I don't know exactly." He reached for a clip of papers, thumbed through them. He located a telegram, handed it to me. "Possibly you'd better read this."

As I glanced at the telegram I noticed it was dated that same afternoon.

Trust Department
Century Bank & Trust Co.
New York City, N.Y.

David R. Kyle, my father, missing from home. I was told some time ago to get in touch with you in this eventuality. Please advise.
Louise M. Kyle,
Oakville, Pa.

I handed it back to him. "When did you say he left these instructions with you?"

"About a year and a half ago."

"Who pays my retainer—if I take the job?"

"Eventually, the amount will come out of the estate. Temporarily, Miss Kyle has wired a thousand dollars for that purpose." He cleared his throat. "There is also a reward offered for the conviction of his murderer."

"His murderer? How do you know he's murdered?"

"We don't. I am only quoting from the instructions Mr. Kyle left. Let us say, if there is one. Five thousand dollars reward."

"And a thousand in hand."

He nodded. I held out my hand. "How do you get to this Oakville?"

"I would suggest you charter a plane. There is an emergency landing field ten miles from the town. I called the airport to find out. The trip will take around two and a half hours."

I looked at my watch. "That means I'll arrive there about nine o'clock."

"Just sign this receipt, will you?" he said. "I'll wire Miss Kyle."

THE air was hot, heavy, humid, even three thousand feet up. And the plane could have been wrapped in black velvet—for all I could see from the windows. I'd gotten myself into a dull, uneasy frame of mind. The picture I kept getting of a dead man, pulling the strings to start the manhunt for his killers, from beyond the grave, seemed kind of horrible, somehow, and the storm and the state of my stomach didn't help any.

It was six minutes to nine when the plane started to dive at an orange postage stamp of light completely framed by wet, smothering darkness. We straightened out for a little while. Then the pilot leaned forward, fumbled with a gadget, and the nose of the plane dipped. The frame of light angled up at us, grew larger and larger, was suddenly a field. It rocked once from side to side—then we hit—bumped up again—came down to stay, sped across the soggy ground, little spurts of water flying up from the wheels.

There were flare-lights around the field. Big puddles reflected the glare. We stopped fifty yards from the northeast corner of the field, where long, low sheds were dimly outlined.

I took out my handkerchief and mopped my face. Three figures, dim in the blanket of fog that was steaming up from the ground, detached themselves from the shadows and tramped toward us. I hoisted out my bag, climbed down.

Two of the men were mechanics, the third a tall man with a tan polo coat and no hat. As he came nearer, I made out a smooth, thick thatch of dark hair, and a leathery, seamed face. Then his eyes were looking into mine.

"Mr. Blue?"

I said I was. He didn't offer to shake hands. "My name's Crane—Harold Crane. Miss Kyle asked me to meet you. My car is behind the sheds."

I picked up my bag. "Fair enough."

He turned and led the way, across the lighted field and into the darkness. Around the corner of the shed, headlights were visible.

The car was a big coupé, the rumble open. I put my bag in the rumble, walked around and climbed in as he started the car. The headlights lit up a narrow, tree-lined dirt road.

"Any news of Mr. Kyle?" I asked.

He looked straight through the windshield. "Yes. In a way. You'll see when you get there."

He spoke abruptly, almost hostilely. I didn't like that. He seemed like a reasonable party. "You're a friend of the Kyles?" I asked.

"Yes."

"Mind telling me what you know about—this?"

"Mr. Kyle disappeared some time during the night. He didn't appear for breakfast, or for lunch. Miss Kyle had instructions from her father as to what to do in such a case. She wired the trust company. They informed her that money was necessary. I lent it to her. She sent it to them, and they sent you. There are other facts, of course, which you can best learn at the house."

I got out cigarettes, lit one, looked at the side of his face a couple of times. His jaw was tight, and there was lots of worry in the blue eyes he kept on the road.

"What's the matter?" I said finally. "Don't you like the idea of my being here?"

"I have no opinion on that."

"What's this latest news of Mr. Kyle?"

"A special-delivery letter, sent out from Oakville, arrived at the house an hour ago. It purports to come from David Kyle."

"You don't think it does?"

"Listen, Mr. Blue," he spoke through tight lips, "you'll find out shortly that I am suspected of being behind this disappearance. I am not going to make any statements of opinion. I am not going to place myself in the position of appearing to point out any line of investigation for you. When you have seen the situation at the house, if you want to ask me any questions I'll be glad to answer them to the best of my ability. The letter is indescribable and I will not attempt to summarize it for you."

We swung off the narrow road onto a graveled highway. The speedometer started mounting.

I let a minute or two go by. Then I tried: "Mr. Kyle was pretty wealthy, eh?"

"He was wealthy, yes."

There was finality to it. But I've handled tougher ones than Crane. "Big establishment, is it?" I said.

His eyes got a little narrower. "There is Mrs. Kyle and a son and a daughter. Besides myself there is one other guest at the moment, a young man named Menocal. He is a friend of Miss Kyle's and was a former neighbor. There are only three servants—two maids, one of whom cooks, and an outside man. It is not a large house. I would suggest that you keep the rest of your questions till later."

I let it go at that. The powerful car was eating up the miles. I'd get going at the house.

CHAPTER TWO

HOUSE OF HATE

I **T STOOD** at the top of a long, winding rise. In the fog, I couldn't be sure, but it seemed that we practically circled a hill. There was a bank of trees around the house, hut not close to it. The house itself squatted there blackly, unlovely in outline as far as I could see it, turreted and cupolaed. There was light from windows on the ground floor, and from a single pane on the second. A veranda stretched across the front, ending in three steps down to the driveway. Crane brought the car to a halt by the steps. The headlights glared into a frame two-car garage, its front set flush with the rear of the house.

"I'll run it in, if you don't mind." Crane said.

I got my bag out. He pulled forward into the garage, snapped the lights out. He swung the door of the garage to with much creaking, then emerged from the gloom, mounted the steps beside me. For a minute he hesitated, seemed about to say something, but didn't. I followed him along the veranda and he opened the door.

We passed through a vestibule and into a carpeted hall. On the left, just opposite the foot of a flight of stairs, was an arched opening. As Crane closed the door, a woman appeared in this arch.

Crane said: "This is Mr. Blue, the detective, Martha. This is Mrs. Kyle, Mr. Blue."

She looked me over searchingly. "How do you do?" she said without enthusiasm.

I said I was pleased to meet her. She was a striking-looking woman. Her eyes were dark blue—strained and red right now; her hair was coal-black. I suspected a touching-up. A soft oval face, crow's-feet around the eyes and two lines from nostrils to mouth corners. She was tall, and I got the impression of a very youthful figure. She carried herself like a queen, even in a jersey suit, unadorned with any jewelry—not even a wedding ring. Her eyes shifted to Crane.

"I think it's important that you see that letter at once, Mr. Blue," Crane said. "Its nature is such that we decided it would be best to have you see it when all of us are there. Will you step into the living room?"

I put down my hat and bag. The envelope I'd gotten at the bank was still in my topcoat, so I just kept that on. I followed him in.

I don't know why, but I'd expected a crowd. There were only two other people in the room.

Louise Kyle was about eighteen. She had curly brown hair back over her ears *à la* Garbo. Ordinarily, she would have been a dream. She had a complexion like cream satin, a soft, mobile red mouth, and big brown eyes, a slender figure. Now her eyes were hard, hostile, strained, like her mother's; her jaw was set hard, drawing the mouth into a straight little line and adding lines around the chin. She stood at the far end of a long mahogany table, one tight-clenched little hand resting on it; there was a cigarette in her other hand. She acknowledged Crane's introduction of me with a curt nod. Menocal did little better. He was a slender-hipped young Spaniard. He had black eyes and black hair, and a black double-breasted suit; an orange silk tie and black-and-white sport shoes. His skin was swarthy. He had one foot up on a chair in the corner of the room. He grunted something, made no move to shake hands.

I looked at the table. In the center of it was an ordinary sheet of notepaper that had been folded once. Crane said: "That's the letter, Mr. Blue."

I looked round the room. Four set faces were turned toward me. Four pairs of defiant eyes were on mine. There was dead silence as I stepped over and picked it up.

THE paper was heavy, porous—no fingerprints. The writing was small, crabbed, almost all angles. And it was a brutal document.

> To the Kyle family, and others:
> Seventeen years of hell on earth for me come to a close tonight— seventeen years that you've all had a hand in building, in stoking the flames. You think I'm a fool—all of you. I'm not—not such a one as you believe. I've seen it—seen you gradually closing in on me, si- lently, getting as close as you dared in your dirty hearts, to what was in your minds—to kill me—to get rid of me—to get your greedy hands on my money—to grind me out. I've read it in your eyes—in your silky voices. You all hate me—have hated me for years. Well, I hate every damned last one of you. My family—my devoted ones—that would give an eye to drive a knife into my back—if they thought they could get away with it. Well, here you are—you snarling fools—here you are—I'm finished. I'm at the end of my string. And I'm going to

snap it off myself—if I can. If I can make it in time. I'm going to kill myself—unless one of you—or that other one—happens to strike first. And the one who knows doesn't dare to tell.

I'm beating you to it. I know every one of you has it in your minds to do it—now—tonight. Even you, Crane—you'd breathe easier, wouldn't you? And you, my chaste wife—now you can have your slinking lover—if you can get him! And my son—my dutiful son—how you will enjoy throwing my money to the four winds. Do you think you'll get it?

Good news! I'm talking from the brink of hell. Another hell—a different one from that I've been in. But that one will go on too, my charming people—it's boiling under you now. And you—you fools—you think that you'll be free! What a joke! I'll watch you, from the pit as you squirm and writhe and take up the torment I've escaped. I've stood it off—protected you from it, for seventeen years. Until finally I began to have to protect myself from all of you, too—behind my back—and it's too much. I've had to watch you day and night—and all the while, being hunted by this other thing, like a wild beast. Now you can take your turn.

How you have longed to have me out of the way! How you have all tried to whip up your courage to get me—to shove me off your shoulders! And now it's done! You're free of me. I'm no more than rotting flesh now. You can follow your own will—not mine! Isn't it glorious? Well, see how you like it, you fools, see how you like it!

David Kyle.

P.S. (For Blue, the detective): Maybe I'm not going to kill myself, Blue; maybe somebody is making me write this letter. Who knows? It's up to you to find out. That's what you're paid for, isn't it? And don't forget—whatever my plans might have been, I could have been interrupted—I could have been forestalled. I had to jump before they did it. The way I have it planned is pleasant, easy. I tell you it was the only course. They were all at the point of doing it—and their ways would not be pleasant. Find out, Blue—and make them sweat blood—and watch your back. As well as anything else I left word for you to do.

D.K.

I laid down the letter, put my thumbs in my vest pockets. I didn't want to meet their eyes for a minute. A grandfather clock in the corner tick-tocked, tick-tocked.

Finally I said: "Is this Mr. Kyle's handwriting?"

"Of course it is," Louise Kyle said in a hard voice—and I saw her teeth. They were tiny, white, pointed.

I coughed politely. "I don't suppose there's anything in all this—I mean about all you people hating Mr. Kyle—"

"Of course you do!" the girl rapped out. "You suppose that every one of us loathed and detested him. And you're damned well right. We do—did. That letter—"

"Be quiet, Louise!" Menocal shot suddenly.

"That letter is practically—"

"Be quiet!" the Spaniard roared. I turned and looked at him. His eyes were blazing; his fists were clenched at his sides.

"What's the matter with you?" I said quietly. "Did you kill David Kyle—or anything?"

"No, I didn't—but understand this, Blue—we none of us relish having a cheap snooper like you wished on us to pry into our affairs. I know how your kind works—and I warn you—try any of your cheap intrigue here and you'll be sorry."

I let my eyes narrow. "I place you now. You're the friend of Mrs. Kyle's that's mentioned, eh?"

HE WENT white to the lips; his fists clenched, unclenched; he took a stumbling step toward me. "Why—why you cheap, rotten—"

"Mr. Blue—Mr. Blue!" Mrs. Kyle said suddenly, shrilly. "Wait—stop—you're making a terrible mistake, Mr. Blue. Mr. Menocal is engaged to my daughter—engaged to be—"

"The hell with that stuff!" The girl's voice cut like a knife. "Do you two think I'm blind? Tell him the truth!"

Menocal's face was livid. "Why you little hell-cat! You—"

"I'm not a fool!" the girl cut in. "Go on tell him—tell him why Martin cracked you in the jaw this morning. Tell him where—"

"Louise, Louise—that's not fair!" Mrs. Kyle blurted out. "You don't know anything about that. Martin was drunk—he misunderstood. You know Martin is—"

"Sure. I know he's a drunken swine," the girl cracked at her. "What of it? He found you—"

"That's a damned lie!" Menocal shouted.

I stepped in. "Stop it!" I rapped. "Where is this Martin Kyle?"

Menocal snarled: "Upstairs in his room—dead drunk, like the beast he is."

I looked at Crane. His eyes were on the floor. "I'd like to see this Martin Kyle," I said, "drunk or sober."

He looked up with a start, not realizing that I was talking to him. His eyes were haggard. "I—I am afraid—you see, it was necessary for me to put him to bed before we left."

"I can sober him up," the girl said harshly. "I've done it plenty of times before. Give me ten minutes." She started for the door.

"Just a minute," I said. I looked them all over. "There's something I want to say to you all. I realize—now—that none of you want me around here. I can't help that. I can understand why you don't want me—because I'm working for a man none of you like. He may be dead. It looks as though he were. But I'm going to find out if he is, and if so, how he died. And I can get the authority—in case any of you doubt it—and make it damn unpleasant if I want to. I don't want to—but I've got to have a little cooperation around here. Your private affairs are your private affairs—unless they bear on what's happened to Mr. David Kyle—then they're mine. Obviously, you're all under suspicion. Of what—I don't know, yet. I've got to make this investigation whether you like it or not.

"You've got a lot of quarrels among yourselves. That isn't necessarily important. Evidently every one of you has a reason for wanting to do harm to Mr. Kyle. I'll ask you to forget that end of it for the time. One of you must—or at least should—have seen something suspicious between the last time you saw Mr. Kyle and now. I want you yo try to remember any little detail you might have overlooked. Mrs. Kyle, I'd like you to have everybody in the house—that is everyone who was here when Mr. Kyle left—including the servants, in this room in ten minutes. I hope that we can make this the last conference of the sort. I realize that you are all upset"—I looked hard at Menocal—"and I'm willing to overlook any hasty words that might have been passed. Miss Kyle—if you'd please get your brother—" She nodded, and went out into the hall. I said: "Just one more minute," to the rest of them, and followed her. She had one foot on the stair when I called, "Miss Kyle."

She swung round on me, said nothing.

"Will you please tell me why you hate your father so?" I said quietly.

HER eyes bored into mine. There was green in them. "I'll tell you," she said in a dull voice, "but you'll never understand. Listen—if your father started when you were about five years old to refuse you every single thing you asked him for; if he started when you were about fifteen to swear at you for asking, and threatened you with whippings if you did, till you dared not ask a thing; if he never let you spend any money—not one red cent; if he insulted, carefully and calculatingly, every friend you managed to make; if he tried to keep you a prisoner—not a day or a week or a month—but day in, day out, every damned hour of your life. Then, on top of that, if he accused you of planning to kill him—planning to steal from him—over and over again—would you hate him? Would you wish him dead, too?"

I couldn't hold her eyes. I let mine drop. "I see," I said. "I see."

"You don't see," she said bitterly, "but that's how it is."

I couldn't think of anything to say for a minute. Finally I asked: "Has the sheriff been notified of this letter?"

"No. That's your business."

"Surely, but—would you mind showing me where the telephone is—or is there—"

She made an impatient sound, swung back from the stairs, went to the rear of the hall. I saw the wall instrument now. She jerked the receiver off, started to spin the crank on the side. It was that kind of phone.

I stepped back inside the living room. "That's all for now, thanks," I said.

Crane followed me out. "I'll show you to your room now, if you—"

"In a minute," I said, then to the girl, "Tell him he'd better come right over."

I turned back to Crane. He picked up my suitcase and started up the stairs. I noticed a label had come off and was sticking to the rug. I picked it up, and followed him. On the way, I happened to notice it wasn't one of the hotel labels at all. It was a druggist's—the kind they stick on bottles. It came from an Oakville drug store. I put it in my inside pocket.

As we reached the top I heard the girl swear viciously at the telephone. Crane led the way toward the front of the house, turned right. My room was apparently the lighted one I had noticed outside.

It was roomy, old-fashioned, with a fireplace and a four-poster bed. The furniture was solid, heavy. Crane put my bag on a luggage stool, went back and closed the door. I took my topcoat off, found a hanger in the closet and was just putting it on when he said suddenly: "Look here, Blue—in the letter"—his voice was clipped, almost violent—"he says about the one who knows—not daring to talk—to tell. I'm the one."

I stood still and looked at him. "Oh?"

He had his hands clasped behind him; his arms were drawn tight to his sides. There were white bumps at his jaw corners. "And I can't tell you. I don't know what conclusions you've come to. And I'm not trying to exonerate anybody of anything. All I want to tell you is this—that any explanation you may make has got to reach a long way into the past, Blue. Everything you've seen tonight— and more—is the climaxing of certain things that started from one single cause— twenty years ago. That's as far as I can go."

I looked at him searchingly. "Why can't you tell all of it?"

He put his lips together, shook his head.

"I'm not a policeman, you know," I said.

His eyes snapped back to mine. "What?"

"I'm not forced to repeat anything anyone tells me. I have the same legal privilege as a lawyer or a doctor, that way."

He eyed me hard. "Suppose you heard of a crime—committed many years ago—and in a foreign country."

"I would consider it none of my business," I said. "Unless, of course, it was directly connected with this investigation. I am only interested in David Kyle's disappearance right now."

He started to pace up and down, then stopped and looked at me half over his shoulder. "If it turns out that you have to tell my story in court, will you give your word to protect me—to withhold any clue to my identity?"

"I will—unless you're guilty of something I'm investigating." Then I added: "Or at least something that happened in this country."

He held my eye for a long minute. "All right. Listen.... Good God!"

CHAPTER THREE

BROTHERS IN BLOOD

THE SCREAM came from directly overhead; it put my teeth on edge. It was a woman's scream, high-pitched, and there was a quality to it I couldn't recognize. I sprang for the door, jerked it open.

The frantic scream came again. I saw the stairs at the end of the corridor and raced toward them. The scream suddenly died—then in its place came a peal of harsh, squealing laughter. It rose, grating and furious, again and again. I ripped open the door at the foot of the stairs, raced up them three at a time. There was a bump, just as I reached the top. On the floor, on her knees, in the doorway to a room twenty feet away was the girl, her arms over her head, great sobbing bursts of laughter racking her.

Crane was at my heels, white-faced. I called: "Look after the girl—she's hysterical!" Gun out, I hit the half-open door with the heel of my hand, slammed it back against the wall. The light was already on. I jumped inside.

Lying half on the bed, half on the floor, was a young man in golf trousers. His face was staring at me, upside down. It was black. His tongue protruded. His hands were grasping the shirt at his throat. His eyes were wide open.

I could hear feet clattering up the stairs outside. I called: "Stay out of here, everybody!" as I caught the bitter almond smell of hydrocyanic.

I hesitated myself for a minute, sniffed cautiously, saw the window was open a few inches. Most of the fumes were gone. I stepped over to the bed, grasped the boy's pulse.

The hand was cold. There was no pulse.

My eyes darted around the room. I thought of suicide—and that idea collapsed. There was a handkerchief, diagonally folded twice, its ends crumpled, lying against the wall—an improvised mask.

I thought fast I wanted to go through that room with a fine-tooth comb, and do it then, but these rural coppers are hell if they think you're against them. I didn't want the sheriff's heavy hand on me the rest of my stay in Oakville. I backed from the room and closed the door.

One of the maids was half huddled on the top of the stairs, afraid to go down, afraid to come up. From a room at the end of the hall came the sound of muffled sobbing, gasping, and the terrified voice of Mrs. Kyle. "What is it—what's happened?"

"Go on back down!" I snapped at the maid on the stairs. "Tell everybody to stay down from here! Mr. Crane!"

He came hurrying out of the room where the sobbing was taking place.

"Phone the sheriff," I clipped at him. "Martin Kyle has been killed. Tell him to bring the coroner and if he has any fingerprinting outfit in this place, to bring it too. I want the rest of the household to wait exactly where they are—every soul in this house. Go on, hurry—before anybody gets up here!"

Crane looked dazed, hesitated, then hurried down the stairs, herding the frightened maid ahead of him. There was a key on the inside of the murder-room door. A piece of ice was melting on the floor where Louise Kyle had dropped it. I took the key out using my handkerchief, and locked the door.

The sobbing lost its violence. I eased along, waited a moment outside the door of a room, which was half open. Louise Kyle said in a voice so husky and grating that I hardly recognized it: "I'm—all—right—mother, now."

I tapped on the door. "It would be better if you'd go downstairs now," I said.

They went down. I started opening doors. There were only four of them on the third floor. One other room beside Martin Kyle's was habitable. The rest were unfurnished. I found no sign of any human on the third floor.

I WENT down the steps to the second floor, walked the length of the hall till I was at the top of the front staircase leading down but could still keep the upper flight in view. I called over the banister, "Mr. Crane."

He came out of the living room hurriedly, ran halfway up the stairs, then looked up. "I caught him before he left the house—the sheriff, Mr. Blue."

"Good. Will you come up, please," I said.

He came the rest of the way. I led him along the hall and back up to the third floor.

"The house will be full of cops in a few minutes," I said. "See how fast you can tell me what you were going to tell me."

"I—yes, I've got to tell you now. But you'll keep my confidence—you'll—"

"Yes. Go on."

"It happened twenty-one years ago—in Rione. Rione is a little town near Ortona, in Italy. We—David Kyle and I—we'd been knocking around—various countries. We—well, you understand that I don't see things now as I did then. We were young, arrogant—we weren't very particular—about what we did. We were nearly penniless when we reached Rione, and pretty desperate. Somewhere we'd heard that there was a lot of money in Rione. You—you understand—money that belonged to somebody else.

"The reason we went there was to try to find it. It turned out that it was there all right—but not in the shape we expected to find it. I don't know if you know the history of Fascism in Italy."

"No," I said.

"It was a party formed partly by the army, but gaining its great strength from hundreds of local societies—secret societies, all over the country. In nineteen eleven these were all loosely knit together. These societies were a combination of trade union and radical political organization. The members were fanatical in their loyalty, both to the aims and secrecy of the organization. It served them half as a religion, half as a hope for salvation of the country.

"We know now that the treasure we sought was the secret store of wealth of the headquarters of one of these cliques. We didn't know it then. And you understand that the members of these societies were not necessarily poor people. Some of the richest men in the district belonged. They had been, for years, patiently gathering money together against the day of the party's bid for power.

"Naturally, the government spies were active, trying to ferret them out. The result was—deeper secrecy. At the time of our appearance in Rione, government activity was at its height in that district. I can only guess at the details of this—but I imagine that the treasurers of the local band had found the search too warm, and were forced to seek a hiding place for the really sizable amount of funds in their custody. They elected to open an ancient crypt in the local cemetery that had been sealed up for years, and deposit it there, then seal it up again, until the danger was past.

"The drunken stonemason that Kyle ran into—how I never did know—was the man who had been employed to open the vault, and to seal it up again. Kyle milked him of his information, got the location of the vault.

"We happened to know two brothers—their names were D'Aguido. They were stonemasons of a sort. They were not above—well, thieving—any more than we were. We induced them to help us for we had to have someone with us who could open up the place. Until the actual moment when they opened the vault for us, we managed to keep them in ignorance of what our loot was to be. Then Kyle turned his flashlight on inside the vault. By coincidence—or whatever you want to call it—the rays fell directly on a great heart-shaped ruby. The gem was called the Bloodstone. And the trail of trouble leads directly from it.

"I am sure the D'Aguidos didn't know that the treasury of the local society was where it was. But apparently every one knew that this stone was part of it. They, at least, recognized it at once. Had it been at the bottom of the chest—but no matter.

"We had made our mistake in not ascertaining whether these two were members of the society. We found out, only too terribly now. They were. And we had drawn them into committing what was, to them evidently, an unpardonable sin. They were wild with fury. They attacked us and set up a furious outcry. I managed to overcome one of them and ran to aid Kyle. There was a shot, then another. In the darkness and confusion I thought he had been hilled. But it was the other way around. He had slain the other brother.

"We escaped—somehow. Needless to say, we had no chance to steal the treasure. Literally hundreds of people had been attracted by the outcry and the fighting. They were almost on us when the shots were fired. Nevertheless we escaped, managed to make the coast, and shipped as seamen on an American boat.

"A year or two later Kyle came into a small legacy. He plunged on the Stock Exchange and made a fortune. I have patented one or two ideas that have managed to keep me.

"This—this is the part that I almost hesitate to tell you." He ran a finger inside his collar. His forehead was covered with little beads. "I am sure that I don't have to tell you that this man D'Aguido would kill us—both of us—if he found us. Personally, I have never seen nor heard of the man—except through Kyle—since the night we killed his brother.

"Kyle has told me—many times, that he has seen him. And each time Kyle has bolted, moved his whole establishment practically overnight. Twelve times, in eighteen years. Out of a clear sky, I'd get these telegrams. I got to know them for what they were. I didn't dare ignore them. I'd come—and always it was the same story.

"He'd seen D'Aguido. D'Aguido had tracked him down. All he could think of was to run—to find a new hole to hide in. He'd go—and I'd clean up after him, send his stuff to wherever he had chosen. He believed his family to be in the same danger as he was. And yet he dared not tell one of them what was behind these sudden moves, these tyrannical rules he laid down for them. He tried to keep them under cover in every way he could. You can see the result—on them. You can't see the result on him—now. He was a normal young man. Now he is a creature fit for the gutters. This fear—or conscience—or whatever the devil it is, has eaten away his mentality, his morality, and most of his body. He has made his family loathe him. He has let his diseased fancies fasten on them—you saw that letter. Maybe he has driven them to the point of murder—I don't know.

"As for myself, Mr. Blue—I have never seen D'Aguido, or heard trace of him, save from Kyle's lips. I have hired private detectives by the dozen, and I know he has, too. I have spent weeks of my own time trying to get on his trail. I have gone to every conceivable length to locate him. I—it seems impossible that the man could have absolutely vanished twelve times running from under our eyes. How he located Kyle in the first place has always been a mystery—if he ever did."

"You think Kyle just imagined him?"

"I—I don't know what to think. It isn't inconceivable. Kyle was a mortal coward, Mr. Blue. If he went about day and night, expecting to see D'Aguido, who's to say he did not conjure up his image out of a feverish brain? And now you see why I wanted to tell you this, don't you? You see what I mean—what I'm afraid of! Damn it, man—don't you understand—"

"You think it's finally been too much—that he's gone mad."

"Yes! Yes! And God knows what he'll do, with this fear and hatred cankered inside of him! He—"

The door at the foot of the stairs burst open, and heavy footsteps came up. I motioned Crane to silence. It was the sheriff and his party.

CHAPTER FOUR

FINGERPRINT STUFF

THE SHERIFF was named Marx, and he was so far out of his depth it was harrowing. He had a deeply tanned, outdoor face, thin black hair, oiled, and apprehensive blue eyes. He was about forty-five, wore blue riding breeches and boots. A heavy Colt swung at his hip. He had two deputies with him. One was a great hulk of a man, easily six foot five, with hungry blue eyes and big hands. His name was Ellison. The other was a little whiffet, with the narrowest face I'd ever seen, and tortoise-shell glasses. He hugged a big tin box under his arm. The county coroner completed the party—a Dr. Ease—believe it or not.

I introduced myself. The sheriff had read of me in the New York papers. I unlocked the door and Marx and the doctor preceded me in. The deputies waited outside.

The room was a block "L." The door to the hall was at the top of the "L"; there was a bureau in the angle. The window, open an inch or two, was between the bureau and the foot of the bed, and there was a table two feet or so out from the bed. The bed was against the outside wall. There were two whiskey bottles, one Dewar's, the other Hilltop, and a water glass on the table. The Hilltop was full. There was about an inch in the Dewar's. The coroner went to the body. The sheriff stood with his hands on his hips, watching him.

"Cyanide, eh doctor?" I asked.

"Yes, yes."

I touched the sheriff on the arm, pointed out the folded handkerchief, and he swooped down on it. "A mask, eh? A mask!"

The doctor looked round, then back again. I prowled around the room. The window was slightly open. I looked out. It was a sheer forty feet to the driveway below. No human could make it.

The doctor got up after a minute or so. He took out his watch. "This man died from a whiff of hydrocyanic acid gas. He died—let me see—between five minutes to nine and ten minutes after. That is definite, sheriff. At the time of death, he was under the influence of liquor, too far, in my opinion, to admit of suicide. The nature of the poison is such that one whiff kills instantly. That's why I can time it so closely."

There was a waste basket at the corner of the table. I went over to it. There were several crumpled pieces of paper—and a small glass bottle. I got out my handkerchief, removed the bottle. It still held the almond odor. The sheriff was at my shoulder when I straightened up. "Here's what the stuff came in," I said.

He looked stupid, put out a hand for it. "Lay off," I snapped. "Get your fingerprint man."

He walked over to the door and called, "Hayes."

I saw I'd have to do his work for him too. "And I'd send a man down to take alibis and see that nobody goes away," I said, "and have Mr. Crane out there go down, too."

I looked at my watch. It was ten minutes after ten. The sheriff tried to glare at me, but did what I said.

The doctor closed up his bag. "Go ahead," he told Marx. "I'll send for the body when you're through."

Hayes came in and put his tin box on the table. I gave him the bottle. "Try that and the doorknobs and the whiskey bottles," I said. His eyes gleamed. He went to work.

Marx stood looking expectantly at me. "How—how did it happen?" he asked. I told him part of what I knew, why I was there. He nodded nervously. "Yeah. We've been lookin' for Mr. Kyle all afternoon," he said. "There's a posse out."

I handed him the letter. "Just came about the time I arrived," I said. "That's what the first call was about. The one the girl made."

He took the letter, stood spread-legged, read it through. The color went out of his face. He finished, looked at me, licked his lips, looked back down at the letter. "Gosh," he said in a dry voice. "Gosh." Then after a minute. "What—what do you figure, Blue?"

"About the old man, or this one?"

"Well—well, they're probably both tied up, don't you think?"

"Not necessarily."

"Well, the old man's dead now, surer than hell, eh?"

I shrugged. "Mr. Crane, who's known him for years, thinks he may have gone off his head and wandered off somewhere."

"But we've looked—as good as we can in the fog, anyway—all around here. I don't see—"

There was a queer sound from Hayes. He spun around, his eyes big with pleasure. "Got him!" he said excitedly. "Got a swell print from the poison bottle, Mr. Marx."

We moved to the table together quickly. There was the full print of a man's forefinger outlined in white powder, as well as several smudged ones.

"Photograph it," I said.

Relief spread over Marx's face. "We'll print everybody in the house!"

I said: "Are you through with this room?"

"Yeah. Let's go down and get the prints."

"Suppose we move the apparatus down to the library on the second floor," I said to Hayes. "We can close this room up, and you can have the wagon come and pick the body up, Marx."

Marx said: "Sure. Hurry up, Hayes," and went out. He had an ink tablet and a bunch of cards in his hands.

Hayes started putting things back in the box, frowning. I went over and picked up the whiskey bottles—and damn near let them drop again.

From below came a hoarse, startled shout, then a banging. Then Marx's hoarse voice. "Stop! Stop—or I'll shoot!"

I RAN out the door and to the stairs, skidded halfway down, caught myself, and plunged the rest of the way. I swung around the corner into the hall, one hand on a gun, and checked myself just in time to avoid crashing into the sheriff. He stood at the bottom of the steps, his Colt in his left fist. The tablet and the cards were sprinkled all over the floor.

His hands over his head, a stocky, short man with stiff red hair stood sullenly halfway down the hall, breathing fast. "Awright," he said. "I'm here. What's the idea?"

"What's happened?" I asked Marx. "Who is this?"

"I'm the gardener here," the sullen-faced man cut in. "I come out of my room, and he bumps into me, and—"

"Where've you been?" Marx barked. "You haven't been in your room!"

"The hell I haven't." He gestured toward the half-open door at the foot of the steps. "I been sleepin'—"

I stepped forward, stooped, and ran my finger around the sole of his shoe. I held it up so the sheriff could see the wet mud. The sullen one said: "Who the hell are you?" to me.

"Sleeping, eh," the sheriff snarled, "and got mud on your shoes? Or maybe you're a sleepwalker, eh? Search him, Blue."

Marx was on more familiar ground now, and he was blossoming. I took a .44 automatic from the red-haired one's pocket. He said: "Are you Cass Blue?"

"Yes. Why?"

"I—nuthin'. What—what's all the fireworks?"

"Murder!" the sheriff rolled out. "Murder—that's what. And now let's hear where you were between five to nine and ten after."

"Who—who's murdered? David—"

"Never mind that! Where were you?"

The sullen face froze up again. He clamped his lips. "I'll do my talking later."

I went into his room. The window was open. I walked over and put my head out. The roof of the veranda was right outside. There were muddy footprints leading across it. From the light in the room I could see a coil of rope in the corner of the roof. I went back out into the hall. They were all looking at me.

"You'd better talk," I told the gardener. "You're in a tight spot."

"Maybe I'll talk, if somebody'll tell me what it's all about!"

The sheriff took a quick step toward him. I thought he was going to slam him one with the cannon. "You'll talk—you'll talk, all right! I'll—"

"Listen, Marx," I said, "you've got a clear path to an arrest if you can find anybody in this house that made the fingerprint on that bottle. This man will keep. If the prints don't click, then we can work on him. But take it from me—you've got to work fast, or there'll be more trouble!"

His jaw gaped open. "What?"

"Just get the prints," I said.

He blinked at me. "What have you found out, Blue?"

"Nothing you haven't. But for Heaven's sake—don't waste time."

Marx whirled on the red-haired man. "Get into the library, there." To Hayes he said: "Hurry up and get your stuff."

Hayes went back upstairs. I called: "Lock the door and bring the key."

He came back a minute later and we all went into the library. The little deputy was a wizard with his stuff. It took him just two minutes to say positively that the prints on the bottle were nothing like the gardener's.

Before the sheriff could get started again, I suggested he lock the gardener up and proceed with the family.

It was not till they had gone out, and were on the stairs, that my apparently ossified intelligence jerked me up. I slapped a hand to my breast pocket and with a sick feeling remembered the letter from the bank. Remembered that the scream of the girl had interrupted me before I switched it from my topcoat to my jacket. I turned and ran down the hall, burst into my room, strode across to the closet and yanked it open.

The lapel of my coat was turned back over the hanger. The manila envelope, of course, was gone.

And I remembered without pleasure the fact that the entire household had passed the open door of my room while Crane and I were upstairs with the girl. Any one of them could have taken it.

I JAMMED my hands in my pockets and cursed. I felt my confidence slipping. It had finally penetrated my thick skull that I was up against something almighty damned smart. A man who could watch his opportunities closely enough to crash in on this one was bad enough. That he was getting all the breaks as well was beginning to rankle. And I was a long way from sure that he was through. That was the real hell of it. For if there wasn't more murder in the air of this unholy household I was crazy. I set my teeth, snapped myself out of it. Outclassed or not, I was the only thing that stood between this clever butcher and the rest of the household. And he'd made one slip—or someone had. The fingerprint. I'd hang someone on that.

I went through the futile motions of looking around for the envelope. Then I went out and downstairs, and I won't say I wasn't pretty well geared up.

I kept trying to recall if the man at the trust company had said the girl would be expecting the envelope, and finally decided that he hadn't. If she asked for it—well, I hoped she wouldn't. As it turned out, she didn't. I got that much of a break anyway.

I could see the broad back of Ellison, the big deputy, in the archway as I came down. He jumped a foot when I pushed him aside and went in. Menocal, Crane, the girl, and Mrs. Kyle were standing in a semicircle around the far end of the table, staring at the fingerprint cards on the table, their arms held away from their sides. They all had ink on their fingers. Two frightened-faced maids were standing together in a door at the rear of the room, also with stained fingers. Marx was saying irritably to the red-haired man we had discovered upstairs: "All some mistake. Come on—put 'em down."

The red-haired one turned on me as I came in. "Blue—tell this guy to wake up. He wants to spend the day printing me!"

It wasn't my argument, I shrugged.

"All right—then will you tell me—is Kyle dead?"

"Martin Kyle is dead. David Kyle is still missing."

His eyes got like marbles. "Martin Kyle!"

"Come on, come on," the sheriff barked, "put—"

"Wait a minute!" The red-haired one swung on Marx. "Listen—and get this straight! My name's Pearson, and I'm an operative of the Corcoran Agency in New York, and I ain't any part of a gardener. If you'll look upstairs in my bottom bureau drawer, you'll find my shield and my papers. David Kyle had me come down here about three weeks ago. Nobody was supposed to know I was a dick. He fixed that rope stunt upstairs so's I could get in and out without nobody in the house knowin' it. And I got plenty to tell you in private. Send these people outside, and I'll give it to you."

The sheriff clamped his lips together, glared at him.

"All right," he said finally, "all right—but if you—"

"Just a minute, sheriff," I said. "While these people are together why not get them all placed between five to nine and ten after?"

"Eh? Well, yeah, yeah."

I took out my watch. "Mr. Crane picked me up at the flying field about one minute to nine. From then until after the time Miss Kyle discovered the death of her brother, he has been with me. Could he have been here at five minutes to, and at the field at one minute to?"

"How could he—"

"I'm asking you."

"Well, he couldn't. It's over ten miles and the roads are bad."

"All right," I said. "Now the rest of you speak for yourselves."

"I'll speak for them," Menocal's husky voice said nastily. "Mr. Crane left here at twenty to nine. We—Mrs. Kyle, Miss Kyle and myself, sat down right in this room, and none of us left it till you arrived."

I bored into his eyes. "You'll swear to that?"

"I don't say things I won't swear to."

I looked at Mrs. Kyle. "And you?"

"Yes."

"Miss Kyle?"

"Yes. It's true."

THAT kind of cut the ground from under my feet. I'd expected alibis, but nothing so utterly straightforward and final as this. I played with the idea that they were all lying. There was a minute's silence. Marx turned on the two frightened maids in the rear of the room.

"Where were you?"

They couldn't speak. They turned appealing eyes toward Louise Kyle.

"They were in the kitchen," the girl said, "all the time."

"How do you know?" I asked.

She took an exasperated breath, walked over and pushed the two maids aside. I saw through the door a butler's pantry, doorless, and had a clear view through that of the kitchen. There was a back staircase whose bottom end was a door, and a sink, in sight. Between them were two chairs, directly in my line of sight.

Louise Kyle pointed to a chair directly behind me. "I happened to be sitting in that chair the entire time. I could see them."

I looked back at the maids. "Could you see Miss Kyle?"

They nodded together hastily.

I threw up my hands, figuratively. It was rock-ribbed, all round. I looked at the sheriff, shrugged my shoulders.

The sheriff had kept one hand on Pearson's arm all this time. He called: "Ellison!" and the big deputy was again in the doorway. "Go up and look in the bureau in the room by the third-floor stairs. This guy says he has papers and a shield there. Bring 'em down." Ellison nodded, went out. "Now the rest of you—"

"Oh," I said, "just a minute. I'm not quite through." I looked at Menocal. "What did you do when you heard Miss Kyle scream?"

He looked me full in the eye. "I went to the foot of the front stairs, and maybe a few steps up. Then when Mr. Crane and Vokes," he nodded at one of the maids, "came down, I came back in here."

I ran my eye over the others. Crane, Miss Kyle, Mrs. Kyle—they had all come up—and one maid. I picked out the other maid. "What did you do?"

She managed to say she'd gone as far as the top of the kitchen stairs and stood there.

That was a break. I turned round and sat down in the chair Miss Kyle had said she had occupied. There were two others, close beside it. I said to Menocal: "When Miss Kyle was sitting here, were you in one of these?"

"Yes."

I looked out through the arch. The lower third of the front stairs was plainly visible. "Then," I said, still to the Spaniard, "since the time Mr. Crane went out to fetch me, the front stairs have never been out of your sight?"

He frowned. "No, they haven't."

"Has anybody come down those stairs that is not in this room?"

"What do you mean?"

"Don't waste time. You know what I mean."

"Well, no—certainly not. Nobody else came down the stairs."

"I presume you're willing to swear to that, too."

"I am."

I turned to the maid who had stood at the top of the kitchen stairs.

"Please try to think carefully. From the time Mr. Crane left the house, it seems as if you should have been in sight of the back stairs, right up till this moment. Is that right?"

She took her time to think, and I was glad of it. I was reasonably sure she'd tell the truth, and I didn't want a hurried statement. She finally said in a clear voice that she had been.

"And did anybody come down the back stairs—anybody that's not in this room now?"

"No, sir. I am sure they did not."

I turned to Marx. "The ground is soaking wet outside, sheriff," I said. "It should be pretty easy to find footprints. It's very essential to know whether anybody jumped out a second-story window, and whether more than one person used Pearson's rope exit from the top of the veranda. It's important enough so I'm asking you to check it up yourself."

He blinked at me, still not quite with me. "Well, why—"

"I'll look after things here."

He hesitated, frowning, finally acceded. He went outside. While he was gone, Ellison came down with Pearson's shield and papers.

"Hang on to them," I said. "Mr. Marx is outside."

CHAPTER FIVE

MURDER VIGIL

WE WAITED a full ten minutes. Then Marx came back in. "Only one man came down Pearson's corner and went up again," he said. "There isn't any doubt of it. And there are no fresh footprints around the house anywhere. Nobody came out of no windows here tonight."

"You're absolutely sure?" I said.

"Sure I'm sure. What of it?"

"Just this," I said. "The man that killed Martin Kyle has had no opportunity to get down from the second floor since the murder. Every means of getting down has been checked. Either one of the people in this room killed him—or else the killer is still hiding somewhere upstairs!"

"But—but—"

"On the other hand—every single person in this room has a shock-proof alibi for the time the coroner says the murder was done—except Pearson."

"I've got an alibi! I've got an alibi, too!" Pearson said anxiously. "You'll see—"

The sheriff grunted. "I bet you have."

"I'd get that rope taken away from the corner of the veranda roof," I said to Marx.

He started, went hurriedly out into the hall and called up to Hayes, the little deputy upstairs, to get the rope. Hayes wanted to know where the fingerprint cards were.

THEN Marx came back in and gathered up the white cards on the table, gave them to Ellison. "Take these up and come right back down."

Ellison handed him Pearson's stuff. "Got this in the bureau drawer," he said.

"All right." The sheriff frowned at the police card. Ellison went curt. When he came back, Marx was still trying to look judicial over the stuff.

I coughed. "Suppose everybody go to their rooms now," I said to Marx. "We can see what Pearson has to say for himself."

"Yeah." He swung round. "You can all go to your rooms—your own rooms," he amended. "Nobody is to move outside till we see what's what. That clear?"

It was. They filed out. I took a position from which I could keep an eye on both front and back stairs. Marx stood spread-legged till the room held only Ellison, Pearson, himself and myself. When the last of the others had gone, he turned on Pearson. "All right. Let's hear you talk yourself out of this."

Pearson pointed. "You've got my papers there."

"These don't mean nuthin'. Anybody c'd have these."

Pearson's eyes narrowed. He looked at me. "You going to let him frame me for this, Blue?"

"Go ahead and talk," I said impatiently. "Nobody's going to frame anybody. What'd Kyle hire you for, anyway—and when?"

"He went to the agency about three weeks ago. When I got there he said there was a Wop in the village named Ricigliano. He thought the moniker was a phony and he wanted me to find out if the real one wasn't D'Aguido. Seems this D'Aguido had a grudge against Kyle from away back, and Kyle thought he might try and bump him off. But that wasn't all. He thought somebody in his family was fixing to give it to him, too. So nobody was to know I was a dick, and he cooked up that rope stunt so's they wouldn't get wise to me coming in and going out. See what I mean?"

"Go on."

"Well, when I hear them say you're comin' out—" he looked at me—"I figure I better grab this D'Aguido—er Ricigliano—and freeze onto him. Then you and me could work on him together. See what I—"

"Where is he now?"

Pearson licked his lips. "Well, the fact of it is, he's lammed. The guy in the next house to where he was told me he seen him load up an old flivver late this afternoon, and put a trunk in it. Then clear out. The guy that told me's named Tomaso. He's a Wop, too. He's my alibi. I left here just before Crane did tonight, and—well, I got in just when you glommed onto me."

"Alibi?" the sheriff snorted. "You call that an alibi?"

"Easy," I said. "You can't afford to take a chance, Marx. You better spread the word around for that flivver."

"I never heard of any Tomaso in Oakville."

"All right, all right—but if you're going to charge this man, you'll look funny in front of a judge if you pass these things up."

He hooked thumbs in his belt, eyed Pearson hostilely a long minute. "All right," he snapped. "Ellison, take this guy and lock him up in the cellar or some place. Then go see if you can find any Wop named Tomaso in the village. He'll tell you where he's s'posed to live."

"Well, hell now—" Pearson started.

He could have saved his breath. Ellison marched him toward the back. Two lights arced across the outside of the windows, and the sound of an automobile came up the drive.

"Morgue wagon," Marx said.

"I'd get on the phone if I were you," I suggested. "That flivver might be real."

"Say—those fingerprints." Marx suddenly remembered.

"Sure. Do your phoning, and we'll go up and see."

THE white-coated boys from the county morgue came in with their grim wicker basket. I said to one of them: "See that the little fellow in the horary takes the prints of the corpse before you take it away, will you?"

"Sure. Where is it?"

"Third floor. You'll find it."

They went upstairs. Ellison reappeared. When he saw that Marx was phoning, he hung around dubiously.

"Go on," I said, "what are you waiting for?"

He mumbled something, took another look at Marx, avoided my eye and went out.

Three minutes later when the morgue boys came down Marx was still phoning, I held the door open for them, then closed and locked it. I went out and made sure the doors in the rear were locked. I came back to the hall, just as Marx hung up, mopped his face.

"He won't get far," he said, "if there is a flivver. I've got a line out for a hundred miles all round."

"Nice," I said. "Let's go see what Hayes has got."

Hayes was sitting scowling at the array of cards, behind a big library table. The bottle, a heavier coat of white powder outlining the telltale mark on it, stood in the center of them.

"Get it matched yet?" Marx asked.

Hayes grunted. "It isn't any of these."

The wind went out of Marx. He sat down suddenly. "It—it isn't any of them?" he said incredulously.

"No."

"But—hell, it must be! That bird Pearson—take another look at—"

"I did. I did."

"Well—well hell, Hayes—" He looked over at me absolutely bewildered.

I was standing just outside the doorway, where I could keep an eye on both sets of stairs—back and front. I said: "Don't get in a panic, Marx. We're no worse off than when we started."

He scrambled to his feet suddenly, "Listen—that killer must be hidden, in this house!"

"Sure. Sure. But take it easy. Stand here a minute."

I went to the juncture of the front hall and the one I was in. The flight of steps leading to the third floor was placed right beside a small window that would look down into the driveway. I tried to figure the best way to cover the house for what was left of the night.

I went back to where Marx was waiting.

"Listen," he said hoarsely, "we've got to search this house!"

"Didn't you search it when you came in?"

"Well, sure, but not the third—"

"I searched the third floor. There's no one there—at least no one you'll find by an ordinary search."

His eyes got wide. "You—you mean you think there's secret rooms?"

"I don't know. It may be. If there are, they're almighty damn well hidden. You won't find them without taking involved measurements. Everyone in this household is frightened stiff, already. They'll be of no help—and it's still possible one of them is the killer. Get them wandering around this house—knowing that they are likely to see this murderer any minute, and you'll have them jumping out windows. The one place where the three of us can watch them, is where they are now—in their own rooms.

"We've got our man bottled up here, I think. The one thing that's important is to keep him bottled up. I think his plans have miscarried somehow. I'll tell you frankly, I think there's something in Pearson's story. If we find that Italian, you'll have the key to this thing. Meanwhile—we've got to keep what advantage we've got. Turn these people out of their rooms, and there'll be so much confusion that the killer's bound to make a break for escape. And if you don't understand what that will mean, I'll tell you, it'll mean more killing, because I don't think he'll be taken alive. He's got everything to gain by killing everybody in the house, rather than that. They can only hang you once."

"But—but what'll we do?"

"One of us can stay downstairs and watch the bottom of the stairs. The other two can watch this hall. In the morning, if there's no news of this D'Aguido, or Ricigliano, you can get a posse of men here to surround this house, and we'll go through it right. I'm telling you— smoke this killer out now—even if you could—and you'll make a slaughterhouse of the place!"

Marx swallowed twice. "You think it's that bad?"

"If it isn't, we can't lose anything by preparing for it to be," I said shortly. "Has Hayes got a gun?"

"Yeah, sure, but—"

"O.K. Now, you go downstairs," I told Marx, "and get a spot where you can watch the bottom of both pairs of stairs. If anybody—anybody at all—comes down, without Hayes or me telling you it's all right—kill them—and do it fast. Don't get softhearted and start talking—or we'll bury you tomorrow."

Strong? Sure, I made it strong. But the extra set of nerves that any good dick develops was clamoring inside of me to be careful. I didn't think anybody'd get by me, but if they did—then nothing I could tell Marx would be too strong.

HE WENT downstairs. I posted Hayes with his back to the door of the third-floor stairs. I got a chair from David Kyle's room, set it against the banister right at the top step of the front stairs, opposite Menocal's room. I put cigarettes and matches and a gun on my knees, and settled down to the long wait for dawn.

Gradually, the household quieted down. And after maybe an hour my nerves relaxed a bit.

Hayes had a pipe going. I could catch an occasional whiff of smoke from around the bend of the hall. And more often, Marx's restless tread downstairs. After a while the clock in the living room boomed out hollowly, twice.

And then Menocal's door swung open a foot.

I was on my feet in a flash, swung myself aside and covered the pitch-black aperture. "Stand still!" I snapped in a low voice.

"I'm standing still," Menocal said. "Don't point your damned gun at me."

"What do you want?" I snapped.

"Nothing—nothing. Just wondered what was going on, that's all."

I cursed him. "You get the hell back inside, and stay there," I said. "You're lucky I didn't throw a bullet at you."

He said something inaudible, and closed the door.

For a minute, I stood frowning at his door, trying to figure him out. I couldn't, but I didn't like it much. I sat down again, but I wasn't relaxed any more.

I let fifteen minutes go by.

Then I started humming. Not loudly, but so that if Menocal happened to be standing with his ear against the door, he could hear it. Then I got up, and walking slowly, went casually to the turn of the hall, swung round, stopped humming, and swung right back again. I caught a glimpse of Hayes' baffled face at the end of the hall. I stood silent, waved a hand behind me to warn Hayes to silence.

And Menocal's door came slowly open again.

I'D HAVE given a lot to swing back around the corner, and watch where Menocal was trying to go, but to do it, I'd have to lose sight of the two staircases. I didn't dare do that. I've found it doesn't pay to lose sight of what your main object is. My main object at present was to keep anybody from getting down those stairs. I just stood there till Menocal stepped cautiously into the hall, and stopped in mid-stride as he saw me looking at him. His face got red.

"I thought I told you to stay in your room," I said.

"Damn your snooping soul!" he burst out surprisingly. "I'm entitled to look around and try and protect myself. I heard what you said to Marx. This killer is in this part of the house, and I'm not going to lie quietly and be murdered! Who are you to—"

"Listen—" I reversed my gun in my hand, put the butt under his nose. "How would you like that across the teeth?"

"Why—why, you—" His face got white.

"Whatever you're trying to pull, we'll investigate in the morning. Right now you get back where you belong, and if I catch you moving around any more, I'll make it good and hot for you. Now, get inside!"

He jammed his hands in his bathrobe pockets, cursed me under his breath as he turned back. I slammed the door on him and started pacing up and down the hall.

Hayes was blinking anxiously at me, each time I came in sight. I finally halted, shrugged, and grinned, to relieve his mind. He grinned back, sat down, and I turned away—and then I saw it from the corner of my eye....

Through the window behind Hayes an angry roaring sheet of flame was beating against the window pane!

He saw it the same second I did. He leaped up, his chair toppling over, and almost ran backward toward me. He swung round. His face was bloodless, his eyes wide. "Blue—Blue—fire!" he croaked wildly.

There was a queer feeling in my stomach. I rapped: "Shut up!" and ran down the hall. I slid to a stop, flung him out of my way, dropped my gun, and started to raise the window. It stuck. I jammed both palms upward again, and again. Finally it gave, slid up with a screeching sound. The flame swayed inward, but in the first glance I saw the wide sloping sill outside and the source of the fire.

Involuntarily, I'd ducked back. I sprang forward again, cursed, and shoved the wadded-up newspaper off the sill, still blazing. It fell to the driveway beneath. Then I noticed five other little balls of fire around the driveway.

I looked along the row of dark windows—the library, Menocal's, David Kyle's, Crane's. And they were all open except the library. It might have been possible to land a missile on the sill of the window where I was, from any one of them. Menocal's was the best bet. But then there was David Kyle's room, supposed to be empty and finally Crane's. Anyway whoever it was had had five misses.

Hayes was beside me. I swung round. "Phony!" I snapped. "Stay here a minute."

I scooped my gun from the floor, raced back down the hall, keeping to the small rugs which were scattered along its length. Just as I came to the corner, I heard a door close softly. I swung round, one hand on the wall angle, and I was wild. I don't relish being tricked—and I got madder when I realized that whatever it was Menocal had been trying to do, he had undoubtedly done now. I took one step toward his door and checked myself, my eyes nearly popping from my head.

CHAPTER SIX

WHAT MAD HANDS?

THE CHAIR I had been sitting on was a heavy one. Unconsciously I had placed it on one of the small rag rugs. The corner of the rug was turned back, and protruding from under it, its corner evidently held down by the leg of the heavy chair, was the manila envelope I had received from the trust company.

I had been too fast for him! He hadn't been able to retrieve the envelope from where he had hidden it when he snatched it from my pocket! And was I pleased to see it?

I dropped to one knee, tugged gently at it, found it stuck. I lifted the chair with one hand, eased the letter out with the other, took one hasty glance at the envelope and saw it was the right one. I slipped it into my side pocket, let the chair down, got up and whirled toward Menocal's door....

A black velvet hand whipped over my shoulder with the speed of a snake, smothered my mouth, jerked me off balance. I fell back against a body; the point of a long gleaming knife flashed down—and stopped—an inch from my throat.

Grunting breath was in my ear; the knife pricked me. I was as utterly helpless as a baby. My gun was useless; the safety catch on, and before I could move it anyway, the knife would be coming out between my ears. I know death when I see it, and this was no counterfeit. I froze. We stood like that for seconds, the only sound, the other's tense breathing. Then he eased his hand slowly off my mouth. Little good it did me. That knife couldn't miss by a miracle, the way he had me.

His hand slid down to my gun wrist. He took the gun from my fingers, tossed it onto the top step of the stairs where thick carpet swallowed the sound. Then he knocked my arm impatiently upward, from underneath. He had to do it twice before I got what he wanted. I wasn't even breathing till then.

I raised my hands slowly, and my nerve started coming back. By putting my throat deliberately against the knife as my arms raised, I made him let me get my balance back. My heart was going good and fast, and I was sweating all over as the knife made little pricks in my throat. I had to do something. My mind was racing, looking for a tenth of a chance, but the smooth, deadly efficiency of the devil left no opening.

Then he plunged his hand into my left coat pocket. I felt him pulling the manila envelope from my pocket. Then I came out of it.

In one motion, I hipped him, spun myself to the left. He made a muffled, furious sound, tried to drive the knife home as I whirled, but his hand, imprisoned in the pocket, jerked him just enough. There was a flaming line across my cheek as the razor-edge slashed me—and then I was around, diving for his wrist with both hands.

I caught it, threw my whole weight on it, dragged to get it down. I got the surprise of my life at his strength; he practically held me up on his forearm. His free hand snatched the knife from the imprisoned one, flashed upward. I remembered to shout. I let go his wrist suddenly, kicked his legs viciously from under him, and threw myself wildly aside. He collapsed. I caught a glimpse of flaming eyes through slits in the all-over black hood. I threw a look for my gun, saw it on the top step, and dived for it as he scrambled up. I clawed behind me for the gun, missed it, had to look again. In that second he was on one knee. A sixth sense jerked my head back round as my fingers closed on the gun. I saw flashing steel almost in my face and flopped wildly aside. The knife thudded into the wall. I couldn't catch myself. I swung my gun around, fired wildly, and plunged head foremost down the stairs, rolling, flopping, till I hit the landing with a crash.

DOORS started banging; there were screams through the house. Marx came running from below, his face white as a sheet, as I picked myself up. He cried: "Good God!" when he saw the blood streaming from my face. I roared over my shoulder: "Watch those stairs!" Then pounded back up, three steps at a time, swung round the banister—and saw Hayes appear round the corner, his gun up, his eyes just closing to take a shot at me.

I called: "Stop, you fool!" just in time. He opened his eyes in utter astonishment.

"Get out here, everybody!" I shouted. "Fast! Come on, move!"

Doors burst open. I backed to the banister at the front, both my guns in my hands. "Hurry up!" I raved.

Doors stopped opening. I ran frantic glances around. Louise Kyle stood white-faced in the opening of her door. Crane, a heavy Colt in one hand, was fumbling with a dressing-gown cord. His eyes were haggard. Mrs. Kyle, looking as though she'd seen a ghost, clung to the door jamb of her room. The two maids huddled together; one of them was sobbing.

Menocal's door was open an inch. It was black within. No one came out.

"What is it—what's happened?" Louise Kyle blurted.

"Be quiet!" I snapped.

I had my eyes on Menocal's door. "Watch them, Hayes!" I said. I stepped forward, kicked the door open. "Come out, Menocal!" I barked.

There was no movement. I stepped through, fumbled for the light switch and turned it on. There was no one else in the room, but a tremendous black cloak, fitted with a hood for the head, and a pair of black velvet gloves lay on the floor beside the leather couch. I snatched up the cloak, stretched out the arm. There was wet blood on it. My blood!

I heard a banging downstairs. I threw a quick glance around inside Menocal's room, then went out into the hall. I looked over the banister, saw Marx at the door, unlocking it. I waited long enough to see Ellison come in. I called out: "Come up, and leave him there, will you, Marx?"

He came running up, calling instructions over his shoulder. When he was at the top, I shushed him with a motion.

I called in a loud voice. "If you're hiding in one of the rooms, Menocal, you'd better come out. We're going through them, and shoot you on sight if you—"

Menocal appeared at Mrs. Kyle's door, behind her. "All right," he said sullenly. "Here I am."

"Put your hands up!"

He put his hands up.

"Come out of that."

He came. I stepped forward, held a gun against his middle, ran a hand over him. He had on pajamas and a dressing gown. There was nothing on him but a handkerchief.

"Where's the envelope?" I said.

He looked at me through narrowed eyes. "What's all this about?"

I checked myself. I had forgotten my own peculiar status in regard to that envelope. I turned to Marx. "I want to question this man alone a minute. Do you mind?"

"Well, hell—what's happened, Blue—what's—"

"I was attacked by a man wearing that hood; he gave me this." I touched my cheek. "I'll just be a minute. Get in there, you." I jabbed him with my gun. "Just keep the rest of them where they are a minute," I said to Marx.

Menocal went into his room; he eyed the hood as though he had never seen it before. I closed the door behind me.

"All right, greaseball—where's the envelope you stole from my pocket while we were scuffling?"

"Are you crazy?"

"I'm just crazy enough to give you a dose of this," I erupted, and took a step toward him. I had every intention of pistol-whipping it out of him, too.

"Wait—wait!" He backed away, real fright in his eyes. "Listen— you've got this wrong, somehow, Blue. Take your time, will you?

Listen—when you went running down the hall, I ducked into Mrs. Kyle's room. I—I had something I wanted to ask her. I was trying to get to her all evening. You—you can ask her!"

I HESITATED. And I'm damned if I wasn't even now, half convinced that he was telling the truth. I clamped my lips. "All right," I said. "You keep your mouth shut when I open this door. I'll give you a chance."

I went out into the hall, just in time to hear Hayes' voice say excitedly: "Another print! Clear as day!"

I had to look round a minute to locate him. He was crouched by the top of the stairs, a tiny flashlight in his hand, looking through a magnifying glass at the knife that had been thrown at me, imbedded in the wall.

"A print?" I said.

"Yeah. Yeah."

"Take the knife out and see if it matches any of your collection."

Marx said: "For Heaven's sakes, Blue—what happened? And listen—"

"Save it—just a minute!" I said. "I had a scuffle with a masked man. I'll go into it in a second." I turned and faced the panicky crowd. "Everybody turn their lights on and leave their doors wide open."

They did it.

I took Marx by the arm and stood him in front of Menocal's door. "Watch this bird every second. He's got a hell of a lot to explain."

Menocal's insolence was back in his face. He was sitting on his bed lighting a cigarette. "Don't waste any time looking for the real murderer, by any chance, Blue," he said bitterly, and reached for a magazine.

I figured I'd take all that out of him later. I turned and started toward Mrs. Kyle's room. Marx grabbed my arm. "Listen, Blue—"

"I'll be with you in just a second," I said, and shook clear. I said to Mrs. Kyle: "Inside, please."

I followed her in, and closed the door. Her lips were trembling; her eyes were terrified. I guess I didn't look any too sane myself, with the blood all over me. I said: "If you lie to me, Mrs. Kyle, there's going to be more trouble than you'll care to cope with. When did Menocal come into this room?"

"Just—just now," she said weakly.

"When, just now?" I rapped. "Just after the scuffle in the hall?"

"I didn't hear any scuffle. The doors are thick—"

"Did you hear me run down the hall a while ago?"

"Yes. I heard your boots on the bare floor."

"How long after that did he come in?"

"Just—just then. While you were running."

I cursed under my breath. Had she just guessed it right, or was she telling the truth? I tried a new angle. "What did he come in for?"

"He—he wanted to ask me a question," she said.

"Why didn't he ask you before?"

She swallowed. "He—he said he wasn't quite sure before that I—I hadn't anything to do with—with David's disappearance."

"What was the question?"

"He—he wanted to know if I had ever heard David—heard David mention a bloodstone."

"A what?" I almost shouted at her.

"A bloodstone."

"What did he know about a bloodstone—I mean Menocal?"

"Oh, I don't know. He didn't tell—"

I DIDN'T wait for the last of it. I jerked open the door, strode into the hall. Marx came toward me, gesturing with both hands. "Blue—listen just a minute—Ellison says there ain't any such guy as this Tomaso. The house next where this other Wop lived has been vacant for months."

That stopped me. "What?"

"This Pearson's a fake! The Wop he said would prove his alibi—Tomaso—is a fairy story. Nobody ever heard of him, and the house Pearson said he lived in has been empty for months!"

"Well, get Pearson up here and see what he says now."

"Yeah." Marx leaned over the banister and called: "Ellison!" I took two steps toward Menocal's room. The little deputy, Hayes, suddenly emerged from the library, his face alight.

"Hey, Blue—Blue—what do you think?" he said excitedly. "The prints on the knife match up!"

Marx and I spun on him. We spoke in unison. "With what?"

"With the prints on the poison bottle!"

I just gaped at him; so did Marx. Hayes stood there, looking as though he thought he was pretty bright.

Then from below came Ellison's anxious voice. "You want me, Mr. Marx."

Marx spun round impatiently. "Get Pearson up here!" he called down.

And I got an idea that I should have had hours ago. My eyes went to the door next to Menocal's. "Get your glass," I said to Hayes, "and come in here."

I had the door open and the lights on in the room, when he came hurrying back. It was a larger room than mine, more modernly fitted up. There were bookcases and a leather couch, a dark mulberry rug, a couple of heavy leather chairs, as well as a bed and dresser. "See if you can pick up the prints of the man that lives in this room," I said.

He went to work. He found a silver hairbrush, got one from the back of that, and another from a whiskey decanter. A third from a polished mahogany cigar box on the table. They were all the same.

"This is it, all right." he said.

"Take the cigar box, and try it with the poison bottle and the knife," I suggested, and we went out again.

I stopped at Menocal's door, as Hayes went back into the library. I couldn't make up my mind whether to wait and see if the prints matched, or question Menocal now. He was lying on his bed, his back turned to the door. Over his shoulder I saw a magazine. I hesitated— and there was the sound of running feet down below. Marx bent over the banister. Ellison came running halfway upstairs, panted out: "He's gone, Mr. Marx—he jerked the staple out of the door of the cellar!"

Marx made a hoarse bellow in his throat. He spun on me. "He's escaped!" he croaked. "Pearson's escaped—Blue, damn you—you made me keep him here! I would have—"

We both turned toward the library, as Hayes, his eyes flaming behind his spectacles, burst through the door. "Blue—you've got him! The prints on the cigar box match the ones on the poison bottle and the knife! Whose are they?"

I felt a chill in my stomach. "They're… David Kyle's," I said.

MARX'S face went slowly white; his jaw hung open. Hayes stared from one to the other of us.

"You—you mean—" Marx gasped.

"I don't mean anything!" I burst out. "The prints on the poison bottle and the knife belong to the missing man, David Kyle." I clipped myself short, suddenly remembering the open doors around us, but there was no sign that we had been heard by anybody. I sank my voice. "Go put out the alarm for Pearson!" I said to Marx quickly. "Whatever this mess is, we've got to have Pearson. Send Ellison up, and phone round an alarm like you did for the car. Hurry up!"

Marx licked his lips. "That letter, Blue," he said in a hoarse whisper. "David Kyle's gone mad! He's hiding in this house!"

The blood was pounding in my forehead. "Go on and phone," I roared at him.

He went down, sent Ellison up. I set Ellison between the two staircases. Then I turned to Menocal's room. My patience with the Spaniard was at an end. It was clear he knew something. The fact that he didn't trust me or Marx with his information was no longer of the slightest consequence. If I had to beat it out of him, I was prepared to do it. I stepped into his room.

"Get up, Menocal!" I rapped at him.

He made not the slightest sign that he heard me. He was still lying on his side. The magazine was no longer visible over his shoulder. I saw red. I reached the bed in two strides, grabbed him by the shoulder. Asleep, I thought. The damned nerve of… I shook him hard. "Get up, you—"

His shoulder was limp in my hand. His head flopped over toward me. His eyes were wide open; his face, putty-colored. A gasp smothered itself in my throat.

I plunged my hand under his dressing gown, felt his heart; then his pulse.

It was no use. Menocal wasn't asleep. He was dead—stone dead.

And I caught a faint whiff of bitter almonds.

I felt panic racing over me. Five minutes before Menocal had been fully, insolently, alive. Since then he had not been for one instant out of sight of either Marx or myself. He had been murdered while in plain view of either one of us!

There was sweat on my forehead. I stood staring down at the dead face, almost in a daze.

Then something glistened on his cheek. I snapped myself together, leaned down. There was a tiny piece of glass imbedded in the dead flesh.

Hastily, I lifted the corpse to a sitting position. More faint slivers of glass lined the edge of the pillow. I turned back the pillow, held my breath, and jerked my head back as a smell of the hydrocyanic came up at me. After a moment, I looked again.

It was all too apparent what had happened. Somebody had put one or more fragile glass globes of the deadly poison under Menocal's pillow-edge. As he lay down, the weight of his head was more than enough to shatter them. The amount of gas instantly released would have killed three men. Somebody had been in Menocal's room while he was in Mrs. Kyle's!

Involuntarily my eyes flew round the walls. They seemed solid, ordinary. If there were a secret entrance to this room, it was concealed with the devil's own skill.

The idea had been in my head for hours. Now, at this moment, I was driven absolutely to it—David Kyle, a raving maniac, was hidden, somewhere in the house and the disease in his brain had turned to murder madness!

But where was Pearson? Where was D'Aguido?

I laid Menocal back on the bed, walked out the door and closed it behind me. The big ox, Ellison, looked at me, and his jaw fell. I guess I was looking pretty queer. I said nothing to him, walked downstairs, and told the sheriff.

CHAPTER SEVEN

PHANTOMS OF THE FOG

IT WAS no longer possible to spare the feelings of the people in the house. We didn't tell them Menocal was dead, but we went through every room on the second floor with grim, deadly earnestness. I told Marx nothing about the manila envelope, but I followed him on the search, and if it had been in any of the places we looked, I would have found it, but it wasn't. And I didn't really expect it would be.

We found nothing. Inch by inch, we tapped the walls of Menocal's room, Kyle's and even Crane's, but nothing came of this effort. In the morning, with measuring instruments, we might do better. Tonight, till dawn, there was absolutely nothing to do but stalk silently up and down the hall, praying that no more tragedy would strike.

Five o'clock came, and with it, the coroner again. Then it was no longer possible to conceal from the others what had happened. Mrs. Kyle collapsed. Dr. Ease gave her a shot in the arm. With every ounce of will power we possessed, Marx and I fought down hysteria in that house, as the frantic fear of death turned everyone half insane.

The morgue wagon rattled up, performed its grisly function, went away again.

Then the dawn—at six o'clock. A cold, wet dawn, the fog still rolling dismally, obscuring the sun with a faint gray haze.

At ten minutes to seven the phone rang for Marx. Someone had located the flivver in which the Italian, Ricigliano was presumed to have escaped. It was turned over, wrecked in a ditch, about twenty miles the other side of Oakville. There was no sign of either occupant or trunk.

At eight the coroner called, to say he would hold an inquest on both Martin Kyle and Menocal at ten o'clock, in his office, and would we all please be there.

That finished Marx. He tried to argue with the coroner, to get him to hold off the inquest. I guess Ease made some nasty remarks about Menocal's murder, under our very noses. Anyway, he made it plain that he wanted to get the case into the hands of the county prosecutor's office as soon as possible, and that the inquest would be when he said it would, and that was all there was to it.

Marx came to the foot of the stairs and in a dull, dead voice asked me to come down, and told me about it. He sat on a chair, licked to a splinter. There was more of a problem in this than appears at first. Ellison was the only one in the house that wouldn't have to go. Marx was faced with either leaving the house in care of the one man, or else locating some new deputies by telephone—an almost impossible task at this hour. He thought it was impossible at any rate.

"But I'm afraid I'll have to do it," he said. "I guess maybe Ellison can handle it."

I went on back upstairs to my post. While I was talking to Marx, I had touched the druggist's label in my inside coat pocket. I hadn't forgotten about it, but from the time it had started seeming important, till now, there hadn't been any opportunity to check up on it. I took it out and re-examined it. It was the most important lead—the only one, as a matter of fact—that I had. There were a few figures and meaningless letters in the upper corner. It seemed a strong probability that the druggist would be able to name both the purchaser, and the contents of the container from which the label had come.

And there was no doubt in my mind as to where I had got the label. It had been lying in the rumble seat of Harold Crane's car when I had put my bag in there, and it had stuck to my bag when I took it out.

If that label should prove to have come, say, from a bottle of hydrocyanic acid, it would be something that could not be explained away. Who had bought it? Crane, was the most logical guess. Was Crane's the diseased mind behind all this wanton killing? Reluctantly, I had to admit that he could hardly have done the murder of Martin Kyle—yet that did not clear him of Menocal's death. And, like every single one of the possible suspects, he had had the opportunity to be the black-hooded one that attacked me and retrieved the trust company's envelope.

Mrs. Kyle? Louise Kyle? The maids, even? In cold hard fact, there was nothing to say that one of them had not been the person beneath the black hood, save my impression of more than normal feminine strength. And any one of them could have set the death trap for Menocal.

But every one of those people had what looked like an unshakable alibi to clear them of the death of Martin Kyle.

Any of them could have killed Menocal. None of them could have killed Martin Kyle. Any of them could have made the original theft of the trust-company letter from my pocket. Any of them might have donned the black hood, and made the attack on me, to recover the letter a second time.

Then the question rose: were both Martin Kyle and the Spaniard Menocal murdered by the same person? And the answer was: there isn't a shred of evidence to show that they were.

Allow the idea of secret rooms, secret passages in the house, and it opened up two very clear lines. Pearson, for one. For the second, that which led to a homicidal maniac, hidden in his home, slaughtering, one by one, his family, whom he hated—the line that led to David Kyle.

And then of course there was the Italian, D'Aguido. If there were secret rooms, if the bottle could be traced to the Italian—

I jammed my hands in my pockets, and went downstairs. I smelt coffee and went out into the kitchen and got a cup. There was breakfast served, a little later for those that wanted any.

AT ABOUT nine, Mrs. Kyle and Miss Kyle, their faces pasty against their black clothes, came downstairs with their suitcases. The little deputy Hayes was to drive them to the hotel in the village, where they were to stay, under his guard. Marx had decided to get them out of the house and keep them out. Marx himself was taking the two maids, and the bundle of fingerprints and other evidence. Crane seemed to be left to me. That suited me all right.

Hayes and the Kyle women left first. Then the sheriff and the maids. Then Crane and I.

Oakville was the other way from the airfield. Crane drove quickly, silently, along the sticky road. He only spoke once before we reached Oakville. "What—how are you going to handle it after the inquest?" he asked.

I said I didn't know—it was up to the sheriff.

We rolled into the outskirts of the town in about fifteen minutes. I looked at my watch. We'd made just a little too good time, for my purpose. The sheriff wouldn't have had time yet to sit down in his office. I made excuses to keep Crane driving me around for five or ten minutes. The fog was so thick we could only see the stores directly abreast of us as we passed. I had the label in my hand in my pocket, and I was squirming with impatience. I didn't want to ask Crane to drive me directly to the drugstore. If he had been the purchaser of the bottle of acid, it might give the whole show away. Finally I asked him to drive me to the sheriff's office. He seemed to know where it was.

The sheriff's car was parked in front of a grocery store. "I think it's upstairs over that store," Crane said.

I got out, and he did, too. I looked questioningly at him, was going to tell him to stay there, but he waved toward the store. "I'll get some cigars. Will you be long?"

I said I didn't think so, and we split. He went into the store and I ran up a flight of wooden steps. Marx and a couple of men I hadn't seen before were there. Marx was fussing with the evidence. A conversation stopped as I went in.

Marx said: "Hello."

I handed him the druggist's label. "Do you know the man that runs that store?"

"Sure. Charley Rouse. Why?"

"Can you phone him right now and ask him what that label was stuck on, originally? Also who bought it—whatever it was, and also whether he has sold any other—that is, any hydrocyanic acid in the last few months?"

His mouth opened. He looked respectfully at the label. "Where'd you get this?"

"Found it. Call him in a hurry, will you?"

He reached for the phone, called the number from memory. When he got an answer, he held a short conversation, read off the hieroglyphics on the label, then put one hand over the mouthpiece. "He's looking," he nodded quickly. "He says he can tell. Where did you find this?"

"At the house," I said.

"Who had it? Say, this will tie somebody into the...Hello, Charley. Yeah, Who?... Oh, yeah, yeah, I know. Crane. Sure, sure, but what was in it? Was it hydro... what? Oh, hell, wait a minute." He put his hand over the mouthpiece, looked at me disgustedly. "It was a bottle of alcohol for Crane's car."

And that cleared the boards. My last piece of evidence had blown up in my face.

I mumbled something or other to Marx, and my face was red as a beet. I backed out, closed the door behind me, went slowly down the steps, my hands in my pockets. Licked? No, I wasn't licked, but I don't mind admitting I was stumped. There wasn't a cursed thing to get your teeth in. The whole gruesome affair was like the rolling fog—melting into nothing whichever way I turned, yet full of very real and ugly menace.

CRANE emerged from the grocery store, as I crossed the sidewalk. We both consulted watches. Mine showed twenty-five past nine. We climbed in the car. Crane asked, "Coroner's office?"

I shook my head. There were still about twenty minutes before we had to start for the coroner's. "Just sit here a minute." I said.

Somewhere in my head, there was one of those ideas floating around that you can't quite put your finger on. I sat there, trying to get it. Something I had seen, or maybe heard, trying to blossom. And I couldn't quite catch it. I racked my brain to locate some angle I'd overlooked. But it just wouldn't come. I tried a dozen lines of reasoning, but they all led back inevitably to the house on the hill. Slowly, but with maddening certainty, I was backing into the theory that the house must be honeycombed with secret passages. It was a pill I didn't want to swallow, but damn it, I had to! Why didn't I like it? Well, for one reason—it smacked too much of crime plays and motion pictures.

I asked Crane: "How long have the Kyles been living here?"

He looked surprised. "About a year, I guess. Maybe a month more."

"Where were they before that?"

He mentioned an address in New Jersey.

"Did they own the house in New Jersey?"

"No, they had rented it from some people named Davidson."

I chewed on that. I didn't quite know what I was driving at, myself. "How long did they live in that house?"

"About eighteen months."

"When they came here, did Kyle have any alterations made in the house?"

Crane frowned over that one. "It seems to me he did," he said finally. "As—as I told you, he moved very suddenly. I went to New Jersey and cleaned up after him, so I'm not sure, but I believe he had Mrs. Kyle and Louise stay at the inn here for a while, while he got the house in shape."

I knew now what I was driving at. And it seemed kind of feeble at that. I asked him: "Were there any secret passages in the house in New Jersey—or secret rooms, or anything of that sort?"

His eyes widened. "Why—why, I don't know, I'm sure. I didn't see any."

"Would you have seen them, do you think, if they were there?"

He hesitated. "Well, that's hard to say. I was there alone for nearly a week, but I wasn't looking for anything like that, of course. I—well, I don't know. No, I guess."

"Is there a telegraph office near here?"

"Why, yes. We wired you from—"

"Let's go there. It's a long chance," I explained patiently, "but I'm going to wire these people Davidson and see if they found any secret construction in the house after Kyle left there. I don't know much about insane people, but I do know that they repeat themselves over and over again in things like that. It's worth the price of a telegram, anyway."

Crane located the telegraph office in the fog. We went inside. I wired my office girl, Tam Cotter, giving her the address which Crane wrote out for me, and asking her to find out if any secret chambers of any kind had been discovered in the house after Kyle had vacated it.

As we went out again Crane gave me a worried look that said as plainly as words that he thought I was slipping.

We opened the car doors together, and my eyes popped open. So did his.

On the seat lay a dirty white envelope. Scrawled in pencil was: "To the detective from New York."

I turned it over. On a plain white sheet of paper inside, in the same scrawl, I read: "If you want Frank Ricigliano, look in the old church by Marsh's corners." The note was unsigned.

CHAPTER EIGHT

SATAN'S SANCTUARY

I **FELT** a warm feeling run through me. I said, "Saved!" and handed it to Crane. I was already thinking miles ahead. A trap? Of course it was a trap! How the man who wanted to trap me had managed to drop the note in our car at the right moment was one of the things I didn't worry about. He had long since proved himself the master opportunist of all time.

When Crane read the note, he went white as a sheet. When he looked up, his eyes were saffron. "This—this must be D'Aguido," he said, hoarsely.

"Sure," I said. "Where is a hardware store—fast?"

"Wait—wait—the sheriff, Blue. We'd better get the sheriff, at once."

"Why?"

He licked his lips. "Listen, Blue," he said desperately, "if this is D'Aguido, he's—he's a dangerous man—a killer, Blue. I tell you, I know him better than—"

"Where is this church? Do you know?"

"No."

"Where can we find out? Or wait—is there a hardware store around?" My mind was racing now.

"There—there's a hardware store, yes. But—"

"Get there—in a hurry!" I snapped at him.

He started to speak, caught my eye, swallowed, and drove down the street.

The hardware store was a ramshackle ex-barn, fitted with glass show windows. There was a confectioner's on one side of it and a public garage on the other. As I sprang out I pointed to the garage. "Go and see if they know where that church is," I snapped at him.

The old man that ran the hardware store was polishing stock on a shelf. He looked at me over glasses, inquiringly.

"A box of thirty-eight automatic cartridges—blank. Pistol," I said.

He wrinkled his forehead. "Blank?"

"What I said."

He produced them.

While he was in the rear of the shop making change I took one of the two guns from under my armpits, ejected the bullets from the clip, and filled it with blanks. I dropped the gun in my side-coat pocket. The rest of the blanks I deposited in a barrel of nails by the counter. When he gave me my change I asked about the church but he was very vague about it.

Crane was still talking to the garage men as I got into the car again. I took my second gun from my armpit holster, slid it down behind the upholstery of the seat. Crane finally left the man he was talking to, came slowly toward the car.

"You get it?" I asked.

"Yes, I—yes, I got it, but—"

"Climb in."

He got in heavily, hesitated. "Damn it, Blue," he blurted, "we're supposed to go to an inquest. We'll both get into trouble—even if we don't get our heads blown off. Why, in the name of Heaven, won't you get the sher—"

"Start this car," I said grimly, "and drive to that church. Never mind any more conversation. I'll look after you."

He flushed, opened his mouth, closed it again, banged the door. He let in the clutch, swung back toward the Kyle house, put on speed, and we rolled through the fog-laden town, in silence. When we hit the gravelled highway, I said: "Step on it."

WE ROLLED and bumped over the uneven road. The speedometer steadily climbed. Crane sat tight-jawed, looking straight ahead. I sat on the edge of my seat, smoking a cigarette, a mounting excitement in my blood.

A trap! Queer as it may seem, the thought sent a warm glow through me. Why? Because it meant that I was treading on the killer's heels. There could be no other answer. Just how, I didn't know. But I had forced his hand, had forced him in some way to change his plans.

That it was his intention to murder me was beyond doubt. How, I didn't know, and I made a guess that he didn't have the details planned either. That wasn't his style. He had proved himself a Simon-pure opportunist. All right. I'd give him an opportunity he couldn't resist. I'd give him a chance to add to his murders. In short, if he wanted a crack at Cass Blue, Cass Blue would give it to him—in exchange for the one thing I had almost despaired of getting—contact with the murderer of Martin Kyle and Menocal. In the desperate frame of mind in which the note had caught me, the thousand-to-one chance it offered had seemed like a gift from the gods. Any chance would have. I wasn't fooling myself; I knew that he'd start with a deadly advantage—but whether he could hold it or not was something else. Maybe two could play at his game of opportunity.

Presently we slowed down. Crane peered to the left, looking for a side road that led to the church. We were almost by, before we saw it—an arrow sign that said: "Marsh's Corners." Crane turned in. It was a bumpy dirt road, past an occasional meadow, and an occasional clump of trees. We drove for three or four minutes. Then Crane cleared his throat. "We—we must be near it. Shall—"

"Drive within fifty yards of the church, if you can," I said, "and don't take the keys from the ignition when we get out."

We puttered along. The fog hid everything at twenty yard's distance. Finally Crane came to a sudden stop. He pointed to a footpath leading from the road. "I think—we must be here," he said in a husky voice.

I got out quietly. He hesitated, then got out too, stood with his hands in topcoat pockets, shivering. His face was almost saffron. I took the gun from my side-coat pocket. His eyes fastened on it, and he licked his lips. I said: "Come on," and started up the path. He grabbed at my arm, checked me.

"Mr. Blue—" he said desperately, "if—if that is the man I think it is, he—he's been searching for me, too—for twenty years—to kill me… I am unarmed. If—if—"

"Take it easy," I said. "All I want you to do is stay away from the car. Just do as I tell you and you won't be hurt."

We went silently up the path. I tried to peer through the rolling fog, but it was too heavy. And then suddenly the wooden frame of the long-disused church loomed out of the fog right in front of us. I stopped.

It was square, crumbling, with a pointed roof and a little belfry. Once there had been white paint on the walls, but now not much of it remained. The outside gleamed with moisture; the windows were board-covered. I said quietly to Crane: "Go round to the back. If there is a rear door, you can keep an eye on that and shout if anyone tries to get out. But whatever you do—stay where you are until I call your name. Things may happen. They don't concern you. If you feel too alarmed, go for the sheriff, but don't break in on my party. Is that clear?"

His eyes were bewildered. He nodded.

"Go on, then."

HE TURNED and groped his way out and around the church. The fog swallowed him. I waited two or three minutes, then closed in on the little building. At the top of the rotting steps was a vestibule. The outer door was closed, but the latch had long since fallen off. I went up the steps, got my fingers on the edge of the door, pried it slowly open. The inner door was closed too. I slipped inside, drew the outer one carefully to behind me, putting myself in pitch blackness. Carefully, I made the inner door, put my hand against it. It was unfastened. I eased on pressure slowly. It creaked once, then swung easily inward. I dropped to my knees, crawled carefully through into the musty church.

There wasn't a sound, and the inside was as black as the vestibule for a minute. Then my eyes got accustomed to the gloom, and I made out objects. A row of fat white pillars down the center of the church. A broken chair to my right. An accumulated pile of dirt to the left. And high up in the back of the one-room building, a faint patch of luminosity that might be an old stained-glass window.

For a long minute I crouched there motionless. I couldn't hear a sound. Then, as I started to get to my feet, someone moved, far to the right, and ahead of me.

Feet moved across the floor. I was astonished. Anything that smacked less of a trap was hard to imagine. Automatically, I was on my feet, darting noiselessly toward the front of the church, in the shadow of the pillars.

A match rasped, burst into flame, and I flattened myself. The flame moved directly toward me. Still puzzled, I sidled round the pillar to try and keep in the shadow. The flame became stationary, brighter. I risked a look.

A gaunt, stocky-looking Italian stood before the remnants of the altar, setting a candle upright in its own grease. His face was covered with a black beard, his hair was unkempt and dirty, under an old hat. There was a dirty bandanna around his neck. His eyes were wild, the candlelight catching leaping glints in them.

I couldn't make myself believe that the tip-off had been on the level. Neither could I believe that this giant was playing a part. Either way, the die was cast. There was only one thing for me to do, and I did it. I stepped silently into the aisle and rapped: "Reach, D'Aguido!"

He made a queer sound in his throat as he whirled on me, one hand diving for his waistband. I leaped forward, jammed the muzzle of my gun into his face, clamped down on his wrist, hard. "Steady!" I clipped. "I'll take it." He stared cross-eyed at the gun against his face. His grip on the knife relaxed. I whisked it out, threw it clattering into a corner. "Now get your hands up!"

I stepped back as his hands went slowly upward. "What you want?" he threw at me hoarsely.

"I want you, D'Aguido, for murder." Fire sprang into his eyes. For a second I thought he was going to jump me, and then his eyes flickered. "Come on!" I snapped. "Get going—out!"

I stepped back, to leave him room to pass me, started to gesture with my gun. And then I felt a hand suddenly snake up under my armpit, clamp up and around the back of my neck, jerking my gun muzzle skyward, and—for the second time in twenty-four hours—the razor-edge of the killer's knife was against my throat. A tense, hoarse voice hissed in my ear: "Drop the gun, Blue! Quick!"

I dropped it. D'Aguido's hands came down. He burst into a torrent of angry Italian. The black-hooded one snapped a sentence at him, and he paused. The hooded one clipped in my ear: "Raise your hands."

I raised them. The Italian burst out anew. My captor rapped a few words back at him. D'Aguido came toward me, scooped up my fallen gun, and stuck it in his waist, then searched me quickly. He collected my meagre belongings, stepped back and held them up, for inspection. They spoke a few sentences back and forth. I had my eyes on the Italian's face. This was the touchy point. If they decided to kill me here—I'd die like a dog, and there was nothing I could do about it. But they didn't. The Italian stuffed the contents of my pockets in one of his, stepped back—and his eyes winced, just a little. He might as well have written me a letter. I loosed my knee joints, relaxed my neck muscles, in the instant that the blackjack crashed down on my skull from behind.

There was a blinding flash of light in my brain. I let myself sag, sway forward, and flopped on my face and lay still, groggy, but not quite out.

I KEPT my eyes closed. D'Aguido said surprisingly in English: "What's happened? How did he—"

"Grab him—I'll explain later. There's a car at the road with the keys in the ignition; we'll use that. Get out of here as fast as you can with him. I think there's someone else around. Hurry it up!"

I felt myself lifted, swung over the Italian's shoulder like a bag of flour. As though the thing had been rehearsed a thousand times, we marched quietly, quickly to the door, out, and along the path. We came to the car in a minute or two. The hooded one opened the door, and I was pushed into the seat. A hand grabbed me and held me upright, till they got in, one on either side of me.

"Jerk the hat down over his eyes."

D'Aguido performed that function. The car started. We rolled away quietly.

"Who is this?" D'Aguido asked.

"A private detective. Blue his name is. He's the one I told you was coming."

"How in hell did he get into the church and you right behind—"

"The idiot stumbled onto something—the one thing that would give the show away. I had to get him out of the way somehow. It's bad enough as it is. I left a note where he'd see it, telling him you were hiding in the church. I knew he couldn't resist it. Then when he came in, snuck right behind him, and when he held you up, I took him. He's got to be put away—put away right now."

"You mean—" I couldn't see the Italian's gesture but I knew what it was all right.

"Yes. I've phoned for a plane. It'll be at the airfield in half an hour. There's a hornet's nest going to break open in about an hour, and we've got to get the stuff and get out. The other plans will have to go by the board."

"What's the program?"

"I'll let you off by the rock. You can dispose of this dick—put him in bed with the other one. I'll go on up the hill and get the stuff—"

"How? I thought you said—"

"The hell with what I said. I've got some nitroglycerine in my bag. If I have to, I'll blow the whole damned house to hell. Get it into your head, D'Aguido—we're on the run—due to this damned Blue. If we move like lightning, we'll be over the border in an hour, with the stuff—and then we're all in the clear. If we don't, we'll both hang. That's all there is to it. As soon as you've finished with—him—you come up and wait where the private roadway joins the highway, and I'll pick you up as I come out. And don't waste any time, understand?"

"How long will you be?"

"Not more than ten minutes in the house. I may have to shoot my way in. Here—" he handed something to the Italian—"throw that in with his body."

The car suddenly slackened speed. Then we turned to the left, slushed into trees, stopped. "Get going!" the hooded one clipped.

The Italian opened his door, dragged me out, and once more threw me over his shoulder. Without another word, he turned and started at a dog trot through high, wet grass.

The gun from behind the upholstery in the car was now resting snugly in my hip pocket.

CHAPTER NINE

THE MAN IN THE HOOD

A MINUTE later I caught the sound of running water. I had my hat worked pretty well back off my eyes by now. I took a look. We were beside the bed of a small stream. Twenty yards farther on, without any warning, D'Aguido suddenly let go of me. I nearly bit the end of my tongue off as I flopped to the ground. For a second he stood still, breathing heavily, then spat in my face and stepped over toward the stream. I opened my eyes. Where we were the stream was not more than twenty yards across. A few yards upstream there was a huge bowlder. D'Aguido made for this bowlder.

I watched, puzzled. The rock was of such size that it seemed impossible one man could budge it, but some trick of balancing made it movable. As D'Aguido put his shoulder to it, it swung out hingelike, quite easily, till a two-foot gap was opened between it and the bank.

D'Aguido looked down the crack, then wiped his forehead on a grimy sleeve. I rose silently to my feet. When he turned, he looked down the barrel of my gun. I said: "Just hold it, D'Aguido!"

For a split second, he stood as though paralyzed, one foot uplifted. Then he blurted, *"Madre!"* and with a single, lithe, twisting motion flung himself into the shelter of a tree trunk, his hand diving for his waistband. The gun flashed out—the one I had so painstakingly planted on him—and almost in the instant he leaped, it roared. Three blasting reports stammered out before he took his finger from the trigger.

I roared: "Stop it, you fool! There's nothing but blanks in it…" and with an angry snarling curse, his other hand came up and over, and I caught the flash of light on the hissing knife blade as it streaked through the air.

I threw myself awkwardly to one side. The knife flashed past; my foot slipped on the slimy grass, and I lit on my back. I roared: "Stop— or—" but there was no stopping him. When he was ten feet away—I was up on one elbow—I let him have it in the shoulder.

Thirty-eight slugs aren't heavy, but at that distance they hit like an express train. I whirled him completely around before he fell. I was on my feet in a minute. I leaped forward, slashed him with the muzzle of my gun, hard, across the head. He shrieked a curse at me. I hit him again. He groaned. I hit him once more and he lay still.

I grabbed up the gun he had dropped, jammed it into a shoulder holster and ran for one look at the crevice between the rock and the bank. I was pretty sure by now, what I should find there. And I was right. I turned away, sickened by the smell, stepped over D'Aguido— and stopped. There was a small black ball a few inches from his hand. It struck me that this was probably the object the black-hooded one had told him to drop in with my body. I picked it up. It appeared to be a length of black fishline wound on a small rubber cylinder. I had no time now to figure it out. I dropped it in my pocket, took a quick look at the ground, located the tracks we had left on the wet grass coming in, and broke into a run.

I WAS halfway across the clearing, feeling damn pleased with myself, when the silence split open with the crashing report of a gun. A red-hot cannonball burned through the fleshy part of my leg, and I dived headlong into the ground, my face plowing up a furrow. I spun like an eel, threw up my gun—and saw nothing. A stentorian voice from the fog shouted excitedly: "Drop your gun! Put your hands up!"

If I could have seen him, I would cheerfully have pumped my gun empty into his imbecile carcass, but I couldn't. I roared: "You damn fool, Pearson. This is Blue!" and he came stumbling into the clearing, a look of frightened astonishment on his bovine face.

"Blue—my God—how—where—"

"Don't stand there you fool!" I yelled in fury. "Come here! Give me your handkerchief!"

He stumbled toward me, fishing in his breast pocket. "God, Blue—I'm sorry! Cripes, listen—Blue—you know yourself Marx was out to frame me. I didn't have a chance. I bust out an' I happen to think of this place. I tailed D'Aguido here once. I been waitin' here—then I hear gunplay, and how was I to—"

I had my trouser leg rolled up; the slug had gone right through. It was painful but I can take it—when I have to. "Give me a piece of stick!" I clipped at him.

I made a combination tourniquet and bandage and tightened it around the wound. It stung like fury. I got up, walked around a little, hastily. "All right," I said, "you wait here—and watch the Dago—over there! And don't you move out of here or I'll have you lynched. You get it?"

"Yeah, yeah," he said anxiously. "But listen—I tailed this guy here—I would have caught him if you hadn't come. You'll—you'll gimme a break on the reward, huh Blue?"

I couldn't think for a moment which I'd rather do—stay here and murder this guy or go after the triple killer. I howled: "Reward! Why, you blithering fool, if I hear another peep out of you about reward, I'll jug you for obstructing justice, accessory after the fact and about a dozen other charges that'll hold you in the local can the rest of your life. You stay here—and thank God you're alive!" And I turned and ran.

He shouted after me: "Hey—where you going?" but I didn't take time to answer.

I CAME out on the gravelled highway. For just a minute I was stumped. A bank of fog ended my line of sight in both directions at about twenty yards. Then I realized the slope of the ground. It was upward to my left. I jogged along that way, found myself making a wide spiral, and gasped my relief. I was less than a quarter of a mile from the Kyle house!

It was a tough run uphill, and with a wounded leg. The bandage slipped twice but I fixed it and increased my speed to make up for it. Then, as the bulk of the house loomed, through the fog, I stopped. I saw Crane's car in the driveway, and went over and ripped the ignition wires loose. I stood there a minute, panting, till I got my breath back.

I hurried to the porch, listened. I could hear no sound. On tiptoe, I hastend along the porch to the front door. It was swinging open. And from the arched doorway of the living room, protruded a foot!

I was inside in a second. Ellison was lying unconscious on the living-room floor, blood from a scalp cut staining one side of his face. He was breathing regularly. I left him, crept to the foot of the stairs, undecided.

Then from underneath my feet came a clank, clank!

I said, "So!" to myself, and shot like a cat toward the kitchen, my rubber-soled shoes noiseless.

The door to the cellar was ajar an inch.

Carefully, I eased it fully open. The clanking sound went on for a minute, then ceased. I stood tense, my hand on one of the guns in my shoulder holsters, afraid I'd been heard. Then came a grunting sound, and a scuffling footstep from below.

I reached for the first step with a tentative foot. The scuffling continued in the cellar. I tested the top step for creaks, found none, went down another, then another. I crouched down, tried to peer between the steps of the stairs. I could see a dim filtration of light, and that was all. The furnace bulged out near the top, and that cut off my view.

Halfway down, I could just see a black foot—and the bottom of the black hood, moving in and out of view.

I was two steps from the bottom before I could actually see what was taking place. There was an immense pile of vegetables of all kinds strewn around the floor. There was dust over everything. A light shone out from a small closet-like room. The vegetable cellar, I concluded.

And on a table was a coil of insulated wire, on a small drum, and a queer plunger-like instrument that I could not identify at first. As my eyes got keener, I saw that the other end of the wire ran into the vegetable cellar. And at that moment, the man in the hood emerged from the closet-like room. In his hand was a portable electric lamp. He set it high on a window ledge and suddenly I realized what the plunger signified.

Amateur-like, he had rigged up a device similar to that used for setting off dynamite in mines! Apparently, he was going to blow the house up! And then two things checked me—the memory of his mention of nitroglycerin in the automobile—and his declaration that he was seeking certain stuff in the house and that if he had to, he would blow the house up to get it. There was only one answer to that. The "stuff," whatever it was, was imbedded under the concrete floor or in the walls of the cellar.

THE MAN in the hood had picked up the plunger, was backing toward the door that led to the yard, the wire from the drum slowly unwinding in his hand. I shot a hasty look below me, found that what I had thought was the bottom of the stairs was only a supplementary landing—the stairs turned at right angles and continued down for another few steps. There were half a dozen empty packing boxes around the foot. I started down, slowly, cautiously—and the man in the black hood turned toward me, set the plunger on the floor, fussing with it.

I didn't think he had seen me and I saw no reason to wait any longer. I grabbed a gun out of my shoulder holster, jumped lightly to the landing—my foot suddenly crunched fragile glass, lots of it, and in one flash I realized what it was.

The man in the hood, the cyanide killer, had distributed a quantity—probably all of his remaining supply of the glass globes of hydrocyanic gas—on the landing of the stairs. I had a tenth of a second to act before the fumes reached me—and I acted blindly. I leaped—as far to the right as I could—and landed squarely on a packing box that was lying upside down.

The thin wood gave way with a cracking and a rending, and I hit the floor—up to my knees in the box, but I had a gun trained on the man in the black hood. And in that moment, he leaped too.

"Raise 'em," I snapped, "I'm not fooling with you. You stand a better chance with a judge and jury and a lawyer than you do with me. Get 'em up, or—"

"Notice where I'm standing, Blue!" he cut in, coolly. I did. He was standing crouched over the plunger of the infernal machine he had rigged up. I'll give him credit. He was the fastest thinker I've ever seen. "Shoot me," he went on, "and I'll fall on this plunger—and the chances are that the whole house will come down on your ears. I've a charge of nitro in there and I'm going outside to explode it. I don't know—it may just rip out a piece of the wall. That's what I hope. But I haven't enough faith in my own judgment of the proper dose to stay here and take a chance. If you have—then shoot me! And understand— I'm desperate. There's nothing you can do to me as bad as what'll happen to me if I'm caught. You know that. I'm going through with what I say—you can bank on it. Now—throw me that gun!"

"What do you think I am—crazy?" I said, and jammed the gun into my armpit holster. I kept my hand inside my coat though.

"Throw it here—or so help me God—I'll touch this blast off! Hurry—or—" and I saw his hand close down on the handle of the plunger.

"All right, all right!" I shouted, with as much terror as I could manage to get into it. "Don't—don't—" and I sent the gun skidding across the floor. It stopped twenty yards from where he was. He made a queer sound in his throat, darted for it—and left the plunger.

His hand was closing on the butt, when my finger tightened on the trigger of my other gun—the one with real bullets in it—the one I'd switched on him when my hand was inside my coat. I shot him through the right leg. He screamed with pain; his leg buckled and he slammed back against the wooden outer wall of the vegetable cellar. His gun burst into roaring flame.

I guess he must have thought a miracle had happened when I didn't fall. I let him exhaust the blanks. Then, as his hammer clicked on an empty shell, he flung it wildly at me and dived toward the all-important plunger.

I shot his left leg from under him. He dropped like a sack of potatoes.

"Just lie there," I said quietly. "Till Ellison comes round. He'll probably make a tour of investigation when he does. I won't kill you—I'm saving you for the hangman—but I'll shoot your hands off if you try crawling. Now be quiet."

For the hell of the matter was that I was imprisoned as neatly as a fish in a net. Try jumping through the top of a thin wooden box. The damned boards go down with you, and form a nice little hedge around your legs. If you try to pull your leg up, particularly if you've got a badly sprained ankle, and I'd got one when I'd jumped—well just try it. I was wedged in properly.

So we just sat there.

AS A MATTER of fact it wasn't Ellison that came finally. It was the two strangers I had seen in Marx's office. He had been swearing them in at the moment I'd appeared to ask about the label. They arrived—it couldn't have been more than fifteen minutes afterward. The man in the black hood had lost consciousness. The knee joints are terribly painful places to be hit.

It was a blessed relief to me to hear footsteps overhead. I shouted and they came piling down the stairs.

"Careful!" I called, "there's globes of poison gas on the little landing there."

"Hell," one of them said, "it's that detective from New York. What's happened? What are you—"

"Help me out of this damned box, and I'll tell you everything," I said.

They came down, gingerly, fingering guns.

"It's all right, boys," I said, "the case is all washed up. Get me out of here and let me phone the sheriff."

They looked at each other, finally tore the box apart and let me out. I pointed to the dark blob on the floor that was the hooded man. "Just keep your eye on him," I said. "One of you can come up with me, while I phone, if you're still suspicious."

They were staring wide-eyed at the motionless figure.

"What—is it, a man?" one of them said inanely.

"Sure. It's Harold Crane—and he's got three murders against him. Come on upstairs."

I found my leg was practically numb, but I limped up, the shorter of the two helping me along.

"You know the coroner's number?" I asked him.

He did. I called it. When I got the coroner on the wire, I said, "This is Cass Blue. I've got your killer here—and the whole story. Adjourn your inquest, and bring everybody here. Send some men to pick up that detective, Pearson—and another *corpus delicti*—David Kyle— at a spot about quarter of a mile east of here on the highway. I can't locate it for you exactly, but there's a stream… Eh?"

He said he knew where I meant.

"O.K. And bring a stonecutter with you with an electric drill. You might also stop by the telegraph office and see if there's any wire happened to come in for me yet." I hung up.

The deputy was staring at me in astonishment. "David Kyle—dead?"

"Yep," I said. "Let's go back down."

We went back down. Behind the table I found what I needed—an open gladstone bag. And its contents were considerable. Crane had evidently collected everything incriminating at the last moment and dumped it into this bag.

There was a bottle of hydrocyanic acid, nearly gone. There were two more extra black hoods and cloaks, and a couple of the long, blued-steel knives, and the big Colt revolver, but it turned out to be empty—it had never been fired. And most gruesome of all—a gallon bell jar of alcohol—and floating in it, a hand, severed at the wrist— David Kyle's hand.

"You fellows will back me up that I shot this bird down and collared the evidence myself, won't you?" I said.

They said they would.

CHAPTER TEN

THE BLOODSTONE

WE STOOD or sat in the living room of the Kyle house. Crane, his legs swathed in bandages, his face the color of marble, sat on a couch, his feet on an improvised stretcher. Only in his eyes was there any sign of life. D'Aguido, surly and in handcuffs, stood between Hayes and one of the deputies by the fireplace. Marx and the other deputies stood around the room. Ellison had a bandage around his head. I had one on my leg. Dr. Ease had put in a busy hour. And in my pocket reposed the manila envelope that the trust company had given me. I had found a necessary moment to slip it out of Crane's pocket. It had been opened.

In the center of the table lay a miniature magnesium-steel safe. It had taken an expert stonemason almost an hour to cut into the concrete wall of the vegetable cellar to get it out.

I took from my pocket the manila envelope. I looked at Louise Kyle. "I was supposed to give this to you, unopened," I said, "but it has somehow become open. I hope you will forgive me. It contains only information of value to everyone in this room."

She stood right where she was. "What—what is it?"

"The combination to this safe—and a description of where it was hidden in the vegetable cellar. Also, a suggestion from your father as to what to do with—the thing inside. That you can figure out later. Shall I open the safe?"

"Yes. Yes."

I did. In a box of green lizard skin, the size of a collar box, resting on a bed of white velvet was a ruby. I've never seen anything like it. It was the shape roughly, of a heart—of perfect color, flawless, and larger than a turkey egg. Pure pigeon-blood.

"This is The Bloodstone," I said.

Marx had his mouth open. They were all gazing at the stone, fascinated. The coroner cleared his throat suddenly. "And—what has this—what is the story, Blue?"

I turned and looked at Crane. His eyes were fastened on the ruby, burning, fiery, a hungriness of twenty years in his white face. I took the ball of fishline from my pocket, tossed it up and down, till Crane's eyes shifted from the stone to it. He drew in breath sharply, then a slow, bitter smile twisted the corner of his mouth. His voice was infinitely tired.

"So you got even that, Blue," he said. "You're a very thorough young man."

"Kyle double-crossed you, didn't he?" I said.

He nodded. "Yes, he double-crossed me."

I turned to Dr. Ease. "Years ago, David Kyle and Crane went in on a plot together to steal this jewel. But Crane was under the impression that the attempt was a total failure. As a matter of fact, Kyle actually got away with it. He never gave Crane his share of it. Is that right?" I was facing Crane again.

He smiled faintly. "Yes, that's right. You needn't use your persuasive tactics, Blue. I'll save you the trouble of guessing. I'm waiting to be hanged." He moved his eyes to the coroner.

"As Blue says, Kyle cheated me of my share of this stone. He also cheated D'Aguido there—" he nodded toward the Italian—"of his share and he killed D'Aguido's brother. Mr. Blue knows the details. The story I told you, Blue was substantially true—with the exceptions you see here now. D'Aguido has spent twenty years tracking Kyle down, with the intention—not simply of taking a revenge in blood, but of recovering that ruby. If you know the value of stones, you know that one is worth anything from a hundred thousand to a quarter of a million. To make a long story short—Kyle has lived the life of a hunted man. Since he returned to this country, twenty years ago, he has lived in constant fear of D'Aguido here. For D'Aguido knew that he had the ruby. I, of course, did not.

"Each time Kyle saw, or thought he saw, D'Aguido, he would move overnight. I would come and clean up after him—send his belongings on to whatever new spot he chose to hide in. He employed private detectives by the score, and so did I, unbeknownst to him. You can understand that I too was in fear of the vengeance of this man.

"The last place in which Kyle lived was in New Jersey. It was when I went to perform my customary services there that I finally did locate this D'Aguido. I caught him as he was boarding a train to get out of town.

"**I TOOK** him back at the point of a gun to the house in which Kyle had been living, and then he told me that Kyle had had this ruby all the time, and that he, D'Aguido, wasn't worried much about his revenge—he wanted The Bloodstone.

"Then things began to dawn on me. Kyle was supposed to have been left a small legacy with which he speculated to make his fortune. I checked up, and found that this legacy was a loan he had obtained on the stone. All my life I've had only moderate means while he has had the cream of everything. And half of what he had was mine.

"I plotted with D'Aguido to kill him. I came here and did it. It was then that I found out that you, Blue, were coming. I had to stage my act well, for I didn't underestimate your talents. There was one flaw in the situation—young Martin Kyle had come in on a conference that David Kyle and I were having, the night I arrived. Frankly, I was trying to induce him to come outside. He did, later, and D'Aguido and I killed him and put his body in the place where you found it. I cut off his hand and put it in alcohol, solely for the purpose of creating the impression that he was still alive. But that you know—how I put his fingerprints on everything, and so forth.

"Anyway, there was the problem of the boy, but there was no use to take chances. He was a young rotter—a drunken, blasphemous swine anyhow, and I took rather a pleasure in killing him. As a matter of fact, I might not have done it, except that the method I used should have—save for the acumen of our friend Blue here—definitely made me the one person not suspected. For the only logical assumption that could be made was that one person had abducted Kyle, or murdered him, and had also murdered the son. By putting myself in the clear on one count, I felt that it would remove suspicion on both.

"And also, I wanted to terrorize the household so they would get out, and let me search for the ruby in peace. I knew it was here somewhere. I knew it would be very difficult to find, and still more difficult to secure. I had to be alone in the house to do it. I had a hunch where it would be, for in the basement of the Jersey house, there was a tremendous aperture left in the wall of the vegetable cellar after Kyle left.

"Before we had killed David Kyle, I had forced him to write that letter. I included my own name, so that I might appear even more innocent by divulging the secret to the authorities that the letter said I dared not reveal.

"When I heard that Blue was coming, it crystallized all my ideas. I planned and executed the murder—the perfect murder, if I do say so myself—if I had only burned that ball of fishline that Blue has there."

"I'll tell them how you did it," I interjected, "in a minute. How about Menocal—why did you kill him?"

"**BECAUSE,** if you had ever disclosed the fact that the trust-company envelope had been stolen from your pocket, and questioned everyone about it, Menocal would have given the evidence that would have betrayed me. If you remember, he ran up the stairs when Miss Kyle screamed. I had seen this envelope in your topcoat pocket downstairs, and I guessed that the reason you didn't remove your coat was that same envelope. So when you rushed out of the room, I grabbed the envelope as I followed you. Now before I had gotten out of sight of the front stairs, Menocal was standing there. He could have testified that nobody went into your room from the time I left it, till we all went downstairs. That would have branded me as the thief. It was a break for me that you didn't say anything about it. I hid the envelope under that rug, on my way downstairs a little later, for I expected, of course, that you would have the household searched. Then when I heard Menocal making those repeated attempts to get out of his room—I just made it a little easier for him by throwing that burning newspaper onto the window ledge to attract your attention. When he rushed out, as I figured he would, I ducked into his room and laid the trap for him, under his pillow. But you came back too quickly—before I could accomplish my secondary purpose—to get that letter back. I was in the shadow in the corner when you got it out for me—and I jumped you.

"The letter, as you see, mentions the hiding place of the ruby and the combination of the safe. I thought the jewel as good as in my hands when you had to go and get a hunch about a similar hiding place in the last house Kyle was in. You sent a wire requesting the information. I see you have an answer there. What does it say?"

"Just what you expected," I answered. "It tells about the hole in the vegetable cellar."

"There you are, then. I knew that when that answer came through, I was sunk—that you would beat me to the jewel. By getting you out of the way, I would prevent the information getting out for at least another couple of hours, by which time I expected to be many miles from here, but—it didn't work."

Marx could contain himself no longer. "But Martin Kyle!" he burst out. "Blue says you were with him when the boy was killed! How in the name of—"

"I'll tell you that," I said, and I produced my fishline. "Here is the murder weapon—or the most important part of it."

They looked at it in bewilderment. I looked back at Crane. "Correct me if I'm wrong.

"Martin Kyle was a drunkard. It was an easy matter for Crane to get him drunk, just before he was scheduled to start for the field to get me. He took him to his room, laid him, unconscious, with his head near the floor. You will recall that the head of the bed is only a couple of feet from the edge of the table opposite it. The waste basket is at the corner of the table.

Crane had a small vial of this hydrocyanic acid. He had it corked with a bobber cork, so that he could pull the cork almost out before the fumes would start to escape. He balanced the small bottle on the edge of the table, just over the wastebasket, and saw that Martin Kyle's head was close to it. Close enough so that as the vial spilled into the waste basket, enough of those deadly fumes would reach the boy to kill him.

"The crux of the situation was—this." I pointed once more to the fishline. "The black, thin thread was attached to the cork. Crane simply set up his arrangement, and dropped the other end of the line out the window, which was open a few inches. Then he threw the mask, the wadded handkerchief, in the corner for stage effect.

"Then when he drove me up and let me off at the steps, he drove the car into the garage, turned off the lights, and as he walked back to join me, he grabbed the end of the string that was hanging against the wall, jerked it. The cork came out of the bottle upstairs, the bottle fell into the waste basket and Martin Kyle was killed. Crane simply pulled the cork out through the window and pocketed it as he came toward me. There he was with the perfect alibi—in my sight, practically talking to me at the moment of the crime. Am I right, Crane?"

He said I was. I beckoned Miss Kyle over and showed her the bottom of her father's letter. It said that she ought to send the ruby to a certain man in Rione, Italy, as treasurer of this society he had stolen it from.

She tore the letter to bits, angrily. "Fat chance!" she said.

THE CORPSE WAS COLD

HE WAS A FIEND
INCARNATE, THAT
PHANTOM KILLER OF
GRANITE BAY. DEATH
FOLLOWED IN HIS WAKE
AND EVERY TIME HE
STRUCK THE SMELL OF
FRESH-SPILLED BLOOD
ROSE TO MINGLE WITH
THE HEADY ODOR OF
THE PINES. WHAT WAS
THE GHASTLY SECRET
OF THAT ISLAND LODGE?
WHY WERE ITS TENANTS
TERROR-MARKED FOR
DOOM?

CHAPTER ONE

THE LYON ROARS

HE WAS one of those amazing phenomena that Wall Street produces once or twice in a generation, and his name was known—and feared—three-quarters of the way round the financial globe. Born on a poverty-stricken farm in the Middle West, at eighteen he managed to get on as an oiler on the Santa Fe, where he held a succession of jobs. At thirty, he left the practical end of railroading for the financial, and went to work in a New York bucket shop. By the time he was fifty-seven he had mastered every devastating, crooked-legal trick in the stock market calendar, and added dozens of his own invention. His exploits on the Stock Exchange had made him fortunes that caused even that affluent body to gasp. He used methods in his operations that smelled to high Heaven, but an almost uncanny shrewdness guided him through as sound as a rock.

Newspapers made much of him. It was a front-page item if he so much as appeared in public, for in a way, he was picturesque. A small, red-faced, untidy figure, nearly bald, his red pate flanked by pads of pure white hair over small ears, deep-brown, gimlet eyes—he was unique in appearance. And, of course, the unsavory details of his career were not publicly aired.

He was without friends and held his family in the bondage of his purse strings. A supreme egotist, he had tried various byroads of stock market manipulation, but inevitably returned to his first love—the railroads. From his fiftieth year on, Gardner Lyon was known as the king of the railroad plungers.

Though succeeding successes increased his egomania, his vanity, they did not blunt the startling effectiveness of his razorlike shrewdness.

But the shadow of defeat did.

It was not till his fifty-seventh birthday —the Sunday before Labor Day—that the incredible happened. Gardner Lyon found himself facing what seemed inevitable, unexpected defeat. One so disastrous that it meant total financial collapse—utter, irretrievable ruin.

Yet up till the last minute, his almost fanatical faith in his own shrewdness remained. He managed to persuade everyone concerned to foregather secretly—to avoid the press—at his magnificent island lodge in Granite Bay. And there he made his last abortive attempt to bolster his fortunes.

He could not save himself—and his collapse was a terrible thing. In one moment, it seemed as if all the crushing forces of hate, of greed and fear, of treachery, that he had fostered in his fifty-seven years, suddenly caught up to him. And Gardner Lyon's vicious career culminated in a blaze of murder that converted the isolated lodge, for two days and one ugly night, into a boiling, seething inferno....

THE NIGHT before Labor Day—the little fiend's birthday night—he held the two grim conferences that touched the flame to the tinder.

The first was directly after dinner, in the magnificent high-ceilinged library. It was—with one exception—a family meeting. Apart from himself, there were five people present.

Two of them—Sarah Lyon, his sister, and Gardner Lyon, Junior—

—and the gunwale caught him across the waist.

were actual blood relatives. Two of them were his adopted children—
Paul and Estelle. The fifth—the outsider—was Murray Douglass, the
young lawyer.

The little red-faced tyrant sat at the head of the long chromium table.

Sarah Lyon, the sister, in black from toe to throat, her white hair un-fashionably knotted behind her leathered neck, was at his left. The others, all in evening dress, lined the far side of the table. Paul, the foster son, blond, a little stolid-faced—then Gardner, Junior, high forehead ruddy, mutiny in sharp brown eyes—and Estelle, radiant, blond, petite, with her hand in that of the man beyond her—Murray Douglass.

There was no one in the room that had not guessed, long before the old man started to speak, why they had been summoned to the lodge. There was no one there that did not resent it fiercely.

"There is no need for a long speech," he said when they were all assembled. "My affairs are at a crisis. I need all the money I can lay my hands on. You will recall that some years ago—at your urging—I created a trust fund of three million dollars for you people in the event of my death. Now, I want that money. It can be recovered, by each of you signing a waiver. This is Sunday. Tomorrow, as you know, is a holiday—Labor Day. I need the money the first thing Tuesday morning. I wish you to sign these papers sometime between now and tomorrow night. Paul will have the necessary papers ready." He paused, frowned. "That's all I have to say, I guess."

His abruptness was a little startling. For a full half-minute there was an electric silence.

Murray Douglass' clearing of his throat sounded like a thunderclap. "You'll excuse me, sir. I—Miss Estelle has appointed me her representative." He ran a finger inside his collar. "May I—may we inquire the purpose for which this money is—is to be surrendered?"

The old man's eyes flickered, grew dreamy. His body got smaller. "I'd suggest that you keep out of this."

"I'm sorry, sir. You are asking my client something that—"

"Oh, no," the old man corrected him softly. "I'm not asking your 'client' a damn thing. I'm telling her—and the rest of you, too! Paul here pays his way as my secretary. The rest of you—none of you—have ever earned a blasted sou. And you," he singled out Estelle, "have the gall to appoint a representative to deal with me about my own money." He sat back and his eyes got thin. "I'll have something to say to you about that later. Right now I have no more time to waste on this group. You know what I want done. Do it!" He pushed back his chair.

Douglass was on his feet; his face was crimson, dogged. "Mr. Lyon! My client has a legal right to that money, wherever it originated. If you expect her to sign it away, you'll have to tell us—her—why!"

THE LITTLE tyrant got slowly to his feet. He put his hands in the side pockets of his coat, eyed Douglass steadily. "I've had enough out of you. One more word, and I'll—"

Paul said hastily: "Pardon me for interrupting, Father, but the vital thing is to get the waivers signed." Then more quietly, "I'm sure Mr. Douglass does not understand. This is how things are, Douglass," he went on before the old man could interrupt. "There are two railroads running from New York to the citrus-fruit-growing parts of Florida. Father owns one of them. The two gentlemen who are our house guests"—he inclined his head toward the door—"own the other. Father's is the Coastal Rail; theirs—Mr. McLintock's and Mr. Bliss's— is the Florida and Eastern.

"The bulk of the business of both roads has been the carrying of citrus fruits from those parts to the Eastern cities. Each road had various growers with which they did business. This year, more or less as a surprise, we found that practically all the growers had made contracts with a new firm—the Amalgamated Citrus Shippers, a new sort of jobbing house. What it boils down to is this: in order to get any business at all, it was necessary to get it from this Amalgamated Citrus outfit. Naturally, both Father and the others tried to sew the Amalgamated up on a long-term contract, but they were clever enough to hold off.

"To secure the business for the present, at least, Father slashed his transportation prices, and, of course, had everything coming over his road. Then the Florida and Eastern countered with an even more drastic slash. It developed into a plain price-cutting war.

"It has gotten to the point where the fruit is being carried practically free. Both roads have been losing money heavily for over a year now. To be frank, the resources of both Father and his opponents have been very nearly exhausted. It has become a matter of only a few months at the outside, before one road or the other must go bankrupt. The surviving road, naturally, will be in position to dictate prices to the Amalgamated Citrus people, being the only carrier left. In two years, the survivor should easily make back all the money that has been sunk in this price-cutting battle."

Paul hesitated, looked down at the octagon gold pencil he was twisting in his fingers. "A certain, unexpected happening has thrown Father's plans askew. A private banker had advanced Father ten million dollars, against his note. Now, in the ordinary course of affairs, this banker would have been more than willing to wait indefinitely for payment of the note. However, either through accident, or through—through some one of us deliberately giving out the information, Father's rivals found out about that note. They also found out that it was—legally—due on the day after Labor Day. In other words, the day after tomorrow. They went to the private banker, and offered him a huge premium for the note, which he accepted.

"Father's rivals now hold that note. They demand payment on the date it is due. Obviously, if the note is not paid, they will throw Father into bankruptcy—and that is the end of the Coastal Rail. Now, Father has arranged the bulk of the accommodation—roughly, seven million dollars. To complete the total needed for the note, this trust money is required." For the first time Paul looked up at Douglass. "So you see, there can hardly be a question of our hesitating."

THERE was another second of tense silence that suddenly got awkward as it was prolonged. Paul's face started to flush. Gardner Lyon's lips tightened.

Murray Douglass' eyes finally lifted from the table, and locked defiantly with those of the old man. "I can only act according to my rights, Mr. Lyon. I am forced to advise my client not to sign—"

Paul burst out: "In God's name, Douglass, get out of this! We know what's best for ourselves—and you, too. Estelle, you little fool, call him off! You haven't any idea what the pair of you are stirring up!"

Douglass' voice rose. "I've got more to say. Wait—just a minute!" His eyes were on those of Gardner Lyon. The little czar stood with his hands still in his pockets. His lips were clamped, and there was a queer yellow gleam in his eyes.

"Mr. Lyon,"—Douglass' voice was almost pleading—"Estelle told me all this. I knew it this afternoon. I hoped she had it wrong—but she hadn't. Here's my point: if your resources are in such bad shape that you can't raise ten million dollars without calling on this last nest egg, it seems obvious to me that you're already beaten in your fight with Mr. Bliss and Mr. McLintock.

"If it's a matter of who can pour in money the longest—and I understand it's just that—how in the name of Heaven can you expect to go on? You are practically stripped. They—even if they haven't another cent in the world—at least will have the ten million dollars you pay them on Tuesday.

"By taking this trust money, leaving your family destitute, you will possibly stave off the collapse of your railroad a few weeks—maybe only a few days. If you had any other outside resources—any other place from which you could draw money—that would be one thing. But if you had, you wouldn't have come to the point of demanding the trust fund in the first place. Unless I've misunderstood something I've heard, I can see no positive sense or reason in throwing this good money after—"

"By Judas—that's enough!" Gardner Lyon's voice was hardly above a whisper. Bottled fury cut lines in his face. "Of all the impossible damned presumption I ever heard, this stops everything! Estelle—I'll take this out of you." He checked himself, swung, almost stooping, on the rest of them. "As for you—any of you—make any more trouble about this, and you'll feel my hand on you the rest of your miserable lives. You'll get no further talk." He hesitated deliberately, breathed deeply, before he turned back to Douglass. "You—you'll feel my hand, now."

Paul said anxiously: "Father—wait—" but the old man's hand slashed him to silence.

"Did you suppose," he asked Douglass in a voice literally trembling with anger, "that I'd let a penniless young fortune hunter into my house without having him investigated? I had your dossier before you ever crossed this threshold."

"I'm sure I don't know what you're driving at."

"Have you told my daughter you were arrested for blackmail, not more than a year ago?"

Douglass' eyes stared. "That's untrue, Mr. Lyon—and I think you know it!"

"You never heard of a Mrs. Carolyn Jackson, I suppose?"

"To my sorrow, I did. I won a case for her. She refused to pay my fee and complained to the district attorney. I talked to him for five minutes and he cleared me completely."

"Did he! Well, district attorneys in New York aren't so damned cavalier about dropping prosecutions when Gardner Lyon is interested in seeing a conviction. They can usually get them. Think that over, my smart young advisor!" He kicked back his chair. It toppled and went over, crashed to the floor. Gardner Lyon turned toward the door, clipped at Paul: "Bring the dispatch box."

Douglass was white. "Of course, you can probably frame me, Mr. Lyon, but you—"

"Don't try leaving this island, Mr. Douglass," Lyon cut in. Then, struck by a sudden thought, "In fact, by God, don't any of you leave—till those papers are signed."

He strode toward the door. Paul followed reluctantly, carrying the heavy bronze dispatch box. When the old man's hand was on the knob, Murray Douglass said desperately: "Mr. Lyon—"

Gardner Lyon jerked the door open without giving him the slightest attention, and when Paul had come through, slammed it shut, behind them.

"Find Bliss and McLintock," he told Paul. "I'll see them now, and I'll take that box."

CHAPTER TWO

MYSTERY ISLAND

THE SECOND conference took place within a few minutes of the first, on the third floor, in a room at the west side of the house that had been fitted up as an elaborate office.

Gardner Lyon sat at the ebony desk. The bronze box was on the blotting pad before him. As Paul ushered the two in, he was just closing the box; its spring lock clicked audibly. The old man said, "Sit down, gentlemen," in a perfectly expressionless voice.

The only items common to McLintock and Bliss were that they owned jointly the Florida and Eastern Railroad, and that they both had blue eyes. McLintock was a living skeleton, tall, gray-clad, gray-haired, even gray-faced, saturnine, with long, artistic hands. Bliss—just what his name implies—fat, rotund, with good nature exuding from every pore, from the sole of his number-four shoes to the top of his corn-colored hair. His reputation was almost as bad as Gardner Lyon's.

"Gentlemen," Lyon said. "I wish to ask a ninety-day extension on my note, which you hold."

McLintock and Bliss exchanged faintly surprised glances. The gray-faced one said in a smooth voice: "What is this—a joke, Lyon?"

"Not at all. Possibly I have begun at the wrong end. I was about to suggest that we get together on an agreement to maintain freight rates at a level where we can both make some money."

"Oh?"

Lyon nodded. His eyes were drawn almost lazily closed. "Consider—we are both pouring money like water into our railroads. We have both lost millions—lots of millions. The only people who are making anything are these damned Amalgamated Citrus robbers. They are selling their produce in the East at prices that are doubling and tripling the normal demand. They are profiting almost in direct ratio to what we are losing. I suggest that we close down on them, make some kind of a joint agreement on shipping, and cease being suckers. Conditional, of course, on you renewing my note."

McLintock sighed wearily. "It's your house, and you can go on talking as long as you see fit, but—I hope you don't think you're kidding anybody. We know we've got you, Lyon, where the hair is short. You started this ruinous price-slashing, and you've damned near run us both to the wall. We can go on for another six months. You can't operate for two. If you want to toss in the sponge and save us the trouble of buying your road out of the receivers' hands—transfer it to us now, and maybe we'll allow you a little something on it. I presumed that was what was in the wind when you asked us down here. Certainly, I didn't expect jokes."

Lyon nodded dreamily. "There is one other item to be considered. I think I'm safe in saying that I've shown myself to be a dangerous enemy, gentlemen—broke or not. Persist in your determination to wreck me, and I tell you solemnly I'll do the same for you—individually, and collectively, if it takes me the rest of my life."

Bliss shifted his bulk uncomfortably. "What sort of talk is this for grown men, Lyon? Particularly now?"

"You are determined to break me—no matter what I say?"

"Why be dramatic about it?"

Lyon sat back in his chair. "I see. Very well." He turned to the foster-son secretary. "We'll excuse you now, Paul."

The secretary rose and started for the door. As he was going out, Lyon said suddenly to Bliss and McLintock, "Excuse me," and got up. "Paul—just a minute."

Outside the door, out of earshot, he said: "I want you to get in touch with New York and have a detective sent out here at the earliest possible moment. You will have to drive to Trumbull Junction to meet him."

Paul said hesitantly: "Father—please don't go through with that. You'll break Estelle's—"

"Damn it, are you going to try and tell me my business too?" the old man snapped. "And another thing—see that there are no boats in commission, except the one you'll have to use. I don't want—anybody—leaving this island during the night. I'll be—I have some work to do, and I can't play watchdog. You understand?"

"I understand."

The old man went back in. Paul went down the hall to the wireless room.

THERE was, of course, no telephone line that far up-country, and they had been unable to secure a telegraph wire. Their only means of communication was a short-wave wireless set. A similar set was tuned with it, in Gardner Lyon's New York apartment. Sometimes it worked and sometimes it didn't.

Paul sent the message as ordered, but he did take it on himself to specify a private detective.

The operator at the New York end had been impressed with work I did for some people named Kyle in Oakville, Pennsylvania a while back, and that's how I happened to get the call.

The wireless went on the fritz though, before any word came through as to what they wanted a detective for.

Of course, I didn't know anything at all about the things that were happening in the lodge, until much later. I did know that Gardner Lyon was a pretty slick stock-market operator, though I didn't even know the half of that. And I was under the impression that he was fabulously rich.

When I got on the train at Grand Central under a six o'clock hazy sun, the next morning—Monday—I weighed around one-sixty. When I finally came out of a sort of brain fever at three in the afternoon to hear the conductor's, "Trumbull Junction," I was down to one-fifty. The rest had rolled off me in sweat.

That was all right with me. I can spare poundage when the bill's going to run into numbers like I was figuring on here. There's nothing wrong with the Blue Inquiry Agency, understand, but we're new, and the fact is, we run into that investigator's dream—a millionaire client—about once a magenta moon.

This was no Pullman I was on. I lugged my bags out to the vestibule in person, stood there swabbing my face as we began to rattle over switches. The country was woods—pine. The sun had gone out of business hours ago. Copper-colored clouds seemed to have formed a hot, heavy, humid blanket, across the horizon. There was plenty of thunder in the air. When the rain did come, it was going to be a honey.

When I finally swung off onto the platform of the lumber yard they called a station, Paul Lyon and a clean-looking young Scotchman in a chauffeur's uniform came over from beside a long, specially built roadster that stood in the sea of sawdust around the station shack.

"You're the detective?" Paul asked.

I said I was, and that Cass Blue was the name. He introduced himself and the chauffeur and told him to stow my bags in back. Naturally, I asked him what had happened.

"Nothing has happened," he said. "My father may wish you to take a certain—person—into custody, back to New York. Though he may change his mind."

"What for?"

"I'd rather wait till we get there, if you don't mind."

I climbed in the car. "O.K. Very far from here?"

"About a hundred and sixty miles."

I blinked. "That's some driving. You just drive down?"

"No. We left there around quarter to two last night. We were trying to beat the rain here. We got in about seven."

"A five hour trip?" I groaned inwardly. I'm not much for automobile riding.

"Five and a half, more like."

And at that he didn't tell me the worst of it. The roads were corduroy. I'll pass over that lightly.

THEY alternated in the driving. Conversation was impossible. They drove at a rate that would have literally dissolved the springs on an ordinary car. I thought I'd shake every tooth out of my head. I was bruised, bumped, shaken. If they had added one mile per hour to their speed even the expensive roadster would have left the road.

And at that, it was ten minutes to nine—almost six hours—before we struck the long incline, at which Paul began to blow the horn almost continuously. It was nearly pitch dark now. We raced downward between two tall banks of pine trees.

As we began to slow down, the trees on our left disappeared abruptly—and there was a long, shimmering, silent lake. We leveled out almost at the water's edge, topped a slight rise. Two hundred yards ahead, on the bank of the lake, in a clearing, was a flat, two-story structure, of considerable breadth. There was a light gleaming through a window.

Paul cursed in surprise. "We left that damned light on."

The chauffeur made no reply. We rolled on up, turned left, just this side of the structure—it was about a ten-car garage, on closer inspection—and cut the motor.

As though it were an echo, from across the dark lake came the hasty throb of a high-powered motor boat. I realized why Paul had been blowing the horn.

We got out. Paul said, "This way," and I followed him over ground a few yards and then our footsteps were loud, hollow, on the wood of a dock. He lit a cigarette, nodded casually toward the north end of the lake. "There's the place." And I got my first glance of the house of Gardner Lyon.

Fully three-quarters of a mile off shore, I made out the long, black, plum-pudding of an island, covered with tall pines. At the upper end, lights twinkled, vaguely outlining what seemed like an immense house to me.

Halfway between me and the island were the green and red running lights of the motor boat, nearing us rapidly. Paul walked to the outer corner of the dock, switched on a small electric lantern there, for the boat to make a landing, and we waited. Finally it came opposite, swung at a right angle, the motor racing as the speed was cut—and came in. The prow was razor-edged, graceful—a real powerboat. It shuddered alongside. A heavy-set man straightened up with the painter in his hand, literally threw himself up on the dock, bursting with words.

I've got sensitive nerves. The minute he straightened, something inside me jumped, and mentally I snapped into high gear. I was at Paul's shoulder as the heavy-set man got to his feet, and poured out: "Mr. Paul—José is still missing. Everybody's found out about it. And one of the guests was beaten unconscious during the night. I've had to sit with a gun to guard the boats—"

"Wait! You mean you couldn't find José?"

"No! No! We searched the island by inches. It's just opened and swallowed him. He couldn't swim—you know that. And Mr. Bliss— Mr. Bliss woke up in the night to find somebody in his room, and before he could make a sound, he was beaten on the head. He offered me money to take him off the island—he was willing to sleep in the garage—but you told me nobody was to leave the island, sir, and—"

In the light from the dock lamp, Paul's face was ghastly. He seemed to have frozen—and yet I knew he was thinking about what the boatman had said. I cut in with, "Let's get out there, at any rate. You can tell us as we go," and Paul started as though out of a trance.

WE PILED into the launch. I looked around for the chauffeur, saw his shadow inside the garage. "Get him here, too," I called at Paul, and he shouted, "Hayes! Hayes!" The uniformed man came running out.

When he was in, we backed out, banked, sped across the smooth water for the island. Paul told the boatman who I was, and when he heard "detective," he said, "Thank Heaven."

"Did anyone leave the island?" I got over, above the motor.

He shook his head, no. "Nobody but José—if he's gone—and he couldn't swim, and there's been no boat out. I took all the propellers off the motorboats and locked up the oars. Mr. Paul told me to."

I asked Paul: "Who's this José?"

"One of the servants. Ellton—has anyone told Mr. Lyon, Senior, about all this? Has he come downstairs, yet?"

"No, sir—you told us he wasn't to be disturbed. We've not dared go upstairs. One of the guests went up and hammered at the steel doors. He wouldn't believe us when we told him Mr. Lyon couldn't hear him. We've been waiting for you, sir."

I was getting muddled. I frowned at Paul. "What's he talking about? Is Mr. Lyon sick?"

"No. The top floor of the house is his study. He has soundproof doors to cut him off from the rest of the house. He won't be disturbed while he's working." He hesitated. "It's hard to explain. You'll see."

Lights suddenly came on, around a dock, some sixty or seventy yards down the shoreline from the house. We were hitting the calm water hard enough to send up spray into my face, and the distance melted. I could see the house plainly now. It was—at least this side of it—built on a rock, and steps led down from a wide veranda, vanished into some small pine trees on the shoreline. People were coming from a brilliantly lighted room out onto the veranda. We made for the dock, and passing into the little bay, lost sight of the house. There were two or three white figures on the dock, but the landing light was in my eyes, and I could not make them out.

I had time for one more question, before we pulled in. I asked Paul: "How long has your father been barricaded in his study?"

"I don't know. I imagine since about one o'clock last night. I made him some sandwiches and took up a bottle of milk then. He closed the doors when he let me out."

I was the first one out on the dock as we nosed in, and as I scrambled to my feet I thought I'd lost my eyesight.

I was back of the lights now. Standing directly in front of me—one of them had secured the painter—were three slant-eyed youths, dark-skinned. They were attired identically—in white trousers, white shoes, shirts, tieless, and white dickey coats—somebody told me later they were "mess" jackets. They were absolute doubles for one another—features, height, weight.

"Who—who are these?" I asked Paul.

"Most of our staff. Their name is Pennzke. That is Carlos—that is Antonio—and that one Ramon."

"How can you tell?"

"I'm used to them. It's their brother José that's missing."

"Good God! Another? What are they—quadruplets?"

Paul ignored my question. He shot at them, "You haven't found José?" and like dolls on identical clockwork, they shook their heads. He turned to me and I could see sweat gleaming on his forehead. "I—I guess you'd better see my father, first." He hesitated. "Frankly, I don't relish the responsibility of disturbing him," he blurted.

"This is the damnedest nonsense I ever heard," I said. "With all this going on, you mean to say you don't think he should be disturbed?"

"What I—or anyone else in this house, except father—thinks doesn't matter, Mr. Blue." He turned and spoke impartially to the three native boys. "Take Mr. Blue's bags to the room next Mr. McLintock," and one of them picked them up, cracked through the brush.

CHAPTER THREE

THE DOOR WITHOUT A KEY

PAUL LED the way off the dock, and along a winding, pine-needle-covered path. As he neared the steps I looked upward, said to him thickly: "Save the introductions till later."

The people on the veranda made an aisle for us to the door. They were a somber-faced lot. I made out one elderly woman and one girl, four or five men, but I didn't try to register them. They were all curiously hushed as Paul and I reached the veranda, and before they had a chance to start talking, he cut them off with, "Excuse us for a moment, please. I'll introduce Mr. Blue to you in just a few minutes," but the short, rotund man—whose face would have been jovial except for the anger in his eyes and a purple lump where his yellow hair joined his forehead—declined to be put off. He detached himself suddenly, and grabbed my arm.

"You're the detective?"

"Yes."

"I want to get the hell off this island— right away. The owner of this house has given orders to his boatman that no one is to leave, and he—the owner—has locked himself up in his rooms and won't come out. What have you got to say about that?"

I shrugged. "If you'll give me a chance to find out why I'm here, I can maybe straighten this out for you. I'll be back shortly."

"My name's Bliss."

I said, "I see," as though I did, and eased round him, followed by Paul into the living room.

The house consisted of one long wing, and a short wing dropping back from the end of it—sort of L-shaped, if the bottom bar of the L were pushed up to the top. Where we entered, the living room occupied one end of the long wing. It was an enormous room, running the full width of the house, surrounded by veranda on three sides. There were also French doors on three sides.

In the center of the fourth wall was the entrance to a hall leading toward the rear. To right and left of that hall were other, closed doors. We went down the hall. I identified the room on the right as the library—that on the left as the dining room.

As closely as I could figure, behind the dining room were the butler's pantry and then kitchens at the back of the house. The library extended back to where the hall right-angled to the right. There were doors down that short hall also, but they were closed. The stairs were exactly in the right angle, and faced a door at the rear of the hall that evidently led outdoors.

The whole place was decorated in a hashed modernistic style. The woodwork was black, the heavy carpet was black. The walls were some sort of enamel, running mostly to green and flamingo. There were any number of windows—and clocks. There were clocks literally everywhere you looked. I figured there was some sort of connection between railroads and clocks and let it go at that. Clocks never make a detective's work harder.

The second floor was two halls of closed doors. The walls were green. The carpet—as everywhere else in the whole house—was black, the woodwork black. As we turned to mount to the third story, I noticed the native boy putting my bags through the door of one of the rooms near the front—by the front I mean the end occupied by the living room on the first floor.

We reached the top of the stairs, and were on the famous third floor. We were facing the back of the house as we came up. To the right was the short hall—more closed doors. When I turned round to the left, I faced the pair of gleaming black steel doors, fitted tight across the throat of the longer hall.

Paul's rather stolid face was pale, and his blond hair was rumpled. "The whole floor is soundproofed," he told me. "He's probably in one of the rooms inside, with the door closed. I doubt if you can make him hear you. He's probably worked all night and is sleeping now."

By now I had my mind made up. "He's got to be wakened," I said. "If I have to break this door open. I don't get this stuff at all."

I HAMMERED at the door a while—without result. I took the only metal thing I could find on me—a gun—and roused some rare echoes banging with that. After about four minutes, I quit. My face was red. I said to Paul: "You mean to tell me he can't hear that?"

He shook his head. "I doubt it. He went to a lot of trouble to make it soundproof."

"All right," I said. "Get me a cold chisel and a hammer, and I'll open this door."

He started to demur. I said: "Never mind that. Get me those tools."

He went off down the stairs, worried, and I smoked a cigarette until he came back up with what I'd requested. I smashed the lock of the doors and pushed them open.

By that time, white faces were on the staircase. They might well have thought I was taking the house apart, the noise I made. Yet there was no sign, sound, or motion from the rooms of the apartment beyond the steel doors.

I handed the tools back to Paul Lyon. His face was chalk white when he answered my "Which of those doors is the office?" with, "The one on the left."

I went down the hall, till I was before the door, and knocked, hard. Paul came hesitantly after me.

When I'd knocked three times without response, I tried the door-knob. The door was locked. It was not a spring lock, but an elaborate triple-turnbolt affair. Paul had a key. I opened up and Paul snapped the light on.

It was certainly a sumptuous office. A black ebony desk, with silver desk fittings; black bookcases lining the flamingo walls; the inevitable black carpet, with a few black scatter rugs on top of it.

Directly beyond the desk from where I stood was a window. There was a hole in the glass of the window, about the size of an indoor baseball, a little lopsided. Eyeing it, I shifted my position a few inches, just enough to show me the tip of a patent-leather shoe pointed ceiling-ward, on the floor behind the desk. I literally jumped in, and around.

Gardner Lyon lay on his back in the exact center of a scatter rug. His face was striped with blood that had streamed down from two bullet holes in his temples, and caked. He had died with a contorted, snarling expression that drew his lips back from dirty teeth. Sightless, muddy eyes bulged up at the ceiling. There was blood on his shirt front and his black dressing gown. The blood was dried to a mahogany color.

DEATH is my business and it doesn't move me—usually. Yet as I went down on one knee beside him, my pulses were hammering.

Behind me, I heard Paul's gasp. "Good God, he's—what's…" and then he was staring down over my shoulder. I flung a hand back against his legs just in time to check his coming down beside me.

"Get back—back to the door!" I cracked at him. "Don't touch anything."

He stumbled back a step, then froze. His eyes came alight as they jerked round toward the desk, and he sucked in breath audibly. "The box—Mr. Blue—the bronze box—it's gone! He had it here—my father's dispatch box—his private papers! Somebody's taken it!" And then as though with horrible intuition, "Whoever—whoever did this must have...."

I got up, eased him back toward the door a little. "Stand there. Now, what about this box? What was it like? What was in it?"

"Nobody knew what was in it—but him. It was about half the size of a desk drawer—one of those down the side—but it was metal, terribly heavy metal. He had it made specially of magnesium steel, and the outside was bronze finish. He had it made fireproof and as nearly burglar-proof as he could. Mr. Blue, there must have been something in it that someone—"

"All right," I said, "I understand." I took his arm, swung him toward the door, urged him out.

Like a sea of sharks, the guests and family of Gardner Lyon had arrived, were filling the doorway. As I propelled Paul toward them he blurted: "Father's been killed—been shot to death!"

Someone gasped, "Shot! My God!" and someone else said, "Police—we should call the police!"

Paul turned suddenly round on me. "Mr. Blue—we'll have to get the sheriff. I'll go and get—"

I put iron in my voice. "Now just a minute!" I said savagely. "For the time being, I'm the law here—and all of you—understand that! I'll get things lined up in a minute. If any of you tries to leave this island before I'm satisfied you had nothing to do with this"—I jerked my head backward—"you'll find yourself in hot water."

"But—but—good God!" Paul said. "Surely I—why, I wasn't even here! I was a hundred miles away—"

"When did you leave?"

"I—I told you. At one thirty last night—this morning, rather."

"Exactly. Well, your father has been dead a good many hours. I don't see anything that says you didn't kill him before you left. And don't have a lapse of memory and forget that you told me that he closed the steel doors on you. Those doors are impossible to open without breaking the lock, and the lock was all right when I worked on it."

He fumbled for my arm, his eyes gray grapes. "Mr. Blue—for the love of Heaven—me—not me—you don't think I—"

"I don't think anything yet!" I snapped. "You—Paul—stay where you are. The rest of you—please clear out. Go somewhere—go downstairs and wait in the living room—please! At least keep clear of this floor." Then I added: "Unless one of you wants to admit doing this thing."

THEY moved off, not without hesitation. I glared from the doorway, till the crowd was at the stairs, then I swung back on the death room, and scoured it—all but the body. I was reluctant to touch it, till I found out how I was going to stand with the local law. And anyway, I figured the person who had shot the old devil would have gone over him thoroughly. If he could fire a gun and not be disturbed, he should certainly have had plenty of time to clean up evidence, at least in the obvious spots.

It was a cold, bare room—no loose papers anywhere; just desk, chairs, bookcases, rugs and carpets, the body, and an electric water cooler in one corner.

The murder gun was not in the room.

On top of the water cooler was an empty quart bottle that had held milk, and a plate of crumbs.

The room gave me exactly—nothing—except the broken window. I asked Paul:

"Was that window broken before?"

"No—no, it wasn't."

I went over and put my fist through the hole. It just went in and out without touching. It hadn't been made by the bullets that killed the old man—they were no larger than thirty-twos and would never have knocked a hole like that. And there were no glass fragments on the rug.

A hand-hole, knocked out to enable someone outside to reach the catch and raise the window. I got on my tiptoes, put my pencil flash along the ledge made where bottom and top halves of the window joined in the middle. Green paint, in spots, completely covered the crack. The window had never been opened!

I opened my mouth to throw a question over my shoulder at Paul—and almost choked on it. Something in the dark outside the window—something shadowy, at my level, and off to the right—had moved. I jumped, got my eyes against the glass between my cupped hands, stared out at the gloom, and saw—the thin, fragile, green, top spire of a pine tree! The breeze had evidently moved it.

I came to my senses with a bang. There had been no sign of a breeze when I arrived. True, one could have sprung up....

"Down!" I jabbed a finger at the window as I jerked round. "I want to get down there—outside this window—quick!" I dove at Paul in the doorway and he blinked, opened his mouth, then turned and half trotted ahead of me, as I came out on the run.

"Be quiet—and run!"

We hit the stairs, skidded down. Then around the banister and down to the first floor. We went out the back door at the rear of the hall, onto smooth, uneven rock. Paul began, "What—" and I snapped, "Quiet! Get around there!" as we shot to the right to circle the short wing of the house.

The short line of the island at this point was smooth, rounded rock, rising almost straight up out of the water. The L of the house had been designed to follow roughly the shape of the shore line. A thirty-foot ledge of rock separated house and water, all along the inner side of the L. The pine tree stood in solitary glory in a clump of moss.

Whatever I expected to find—I didn't find it. The tree stood motionless. There was no one else on the ledge of rock. I shot the beam of my pencil flash around, to no purpose.

The air was hot, sweltering, close, and there was still no slightest sign of a breeze. Someone had been at that pine tree—either climbing it, or shaking it, or—my forehead furrowed.

I turned the beam of my light into the criss-cross branches above, with their heavy load of needles; squinted up, while I made a quick circuit of the tree. The greenery was too thick. I turned back to Paul. "Can you locate a ladder in a hurry?"

"Why—yes."

WHILE he was gone, I went and stood looking up at the lighted window of the death room—and realized that I had something new to worry about. My brain had finally emerged from its fog, all right, for now I realized that the hole in the window above could only have been made in one way. Something had been thrown from the death room—through the window—almost certainly with the intention of dropping it into the water.

Fair enough.

The question was—who had been smart enough to figure it out, figure that the object thrown—whatever it was—might not have reached the water, but have lodged in the branches of the tree? If the person were not one of those that crowded in the door of the death room as I found the body, that was one thing. If it were one of them—somebody was an almighty damn fast thinker, and the fact that he had vanished at my approach was no character reference.

I was suddenly alert, my interest whetted, as Paul came back.

The tree stood only about six feet from the water's edge—the trunk, that is—but the spreading foliage practically filled the space between house and water. I braced the ladder good and firmly before I tried going up. I wasn't looking for a bath.

As I went up, I played my light around at various levels, taking my time. But I didn't see anything—had actually started down, in fact—when I got just a flash of metal on a far point of a branch, among thickly clustered needles. I couldn't reach the branch. I looked down, caught Paul's upturned face in my light.

"Can you get a stick somewhere—not less than three feet or so?"

He got a cane. I got one hand twined in the pine tree, with my flash in it, and leaned far out. The cane was a little short. I lashed at the branch, sent it bobbing up and down, missed it once and almost fell over. The foot of the ladder screeched on stone, and I grunted a curse, steadied and kept on whacking.

The metal object dropped like a plummet, pinged on the smooth rock below—and I whirled my beam of light down, spotted it. I was half afraid it might be something that would roll. Paul Lyon made a dive for it, but I called, "Let it alone!" and half jumped, half fell, down the ladder.

As I touched ground, I saw what it was—knew I hadn't wasted my time. It was a key ring, holding a large bunch of keys. As I picked it up in my handkerchief, I got a real thrill. Among many others was one queerly constructed, flat, small key—made of bronze. Bronze dispatch box—bronze key. Paul's exclamation in the dark was a gasp. "Father's key ring! Mr. Blue—that's Father's!"

A foot scraped wood, some distance the other side of the pine tree. I jammed the handkerchief and keys in my pocket, armed back the foliage of the pine tree quickly—and found I had an audience. The veranda on this side of the living room held several dark figures. Two of the French doors had been opened since I came out. Cigarette ends glowed. I could have kicked myself.

I turned back, dropped the foliage. "All right," I told Paul grimly. "That's all here."

CHAPTER FOUR

ENTER JOSÉ

WE WENT back the way we had come, back up to the third floor, and I examined the other rooms on that level. I found nothing.

The room across the hall from the death office was a long one, three-quarters the length of the house. It was filled with counters, on which reposed maps, charts, and railroad models. The room at the front—straight up over the living room on the first floor—was a master bedroom, a mammoth one. I made quick work of them, locked all the rooms up, and we went downstairs again. I was doing mental gymnastics, trying to be careful I hadn't missed anything—and guessed I hadn't.

"That chauffeur," I said to Paul on the way down, "does he live on the island?"

"No. He keeps house for himself above the garage."

"Was he on this island yesterday?"

"Lord, no." Paul's eyes got wide. "You surely don't think he—"

"I certainly don't. Where is he now?"

"At the boathouse, but—"

"We'll go there."

We went down to the boathouse, going out the back door to avoid the people in the front room. The boathouse was right beside the dock, and the chauffeur was sitting with the boatman on the dock, smoking. He said he had not been on the island for four days, and the boatman nodded confirmation, so I said: "All right. You go for the sheriff. Tell him to bring the medical examiner, and a deputy or two." I hesitated. "That should land you back here about noon tomorrow."

He blinked and Paul corrected me. "The sheriff doesn't live at Trumbull Junction, Mr. Blue. His place is only thirty-odd miles from here."

"Oh," I said. "Well, that's fine. Make the best time you can."

The pair moved off into the gloom, toward the boathouse. As Paul and I followed, I thought I saw something white at the place where the dock joined land. As we got closer I saw I wasn't mistaken.

One of the white-clad native boys was standing there, silent, erect, waiting. To Paul's "What is it?" the boy's slurred voice answered: "If you please, sir, I would like to speak to the detective."

"All right," I said. "I'm the detective."

He was silent. I could see the green glint in his eyes.

Paul started testily, "Well, go ahe..." but I cut in. "Wait for me in the living room," I said. "I'll just be a minute."

"Oh—of course," Paul muttered and crunched off.

I turned to the houseboy.

"Mr. Detective,"—this lad had been educated—"last night when Mr. Paul came to get in the boat to go to the mainland, he told us my brother José was not in the power house, where he should be. That alarmed us, but not for his safety. My brother was tired, and he resented being sent there to work all night. We thought he had gone somewhere to rest—"

"Wait a minute," I said. "I haven't gotten around to this, yet, but I'm ready to. Why did your brother resent this power-house business, and who sent him there and so forth?"

"Mr. Gardner Lyon ordered him to set the central heating plant going. Never do we do that, till the first frost. There has not yet been frost, as you know. José worked hard all day. To attend to the heating plant, he would have to work most of the night. It was unfair. Today, or tomorrow, would have done equally well, for the heat was not to be connected to the house anyway. However, that is not what I wish to tell."

I WAS getting a succession of small surprises in his tone, and his attitude. "You talk pretty freely about your employer, don't you?"

"He is not my employer. He is dead. Please do not patronize me. You are detective. I have information to give. When my brother José does not come where we are, I went up to the power house, at an hour later. He is not there. I came back and suggest to my brothers that we look for him. As we start from this boathouse, Mr. Detective, we see a man coming from the woods, and hurry in back door of large house."

"Did you recognize him?"

"No. It was dark."

"What time was this?"

"Fifteen minutes after three, or twenty after."

"Well," I said, "this is interesting. What did you do?"

He shrugged. "We do nothing. Then, we do not know that anything is wrong. It is not till we search for three hours and more that we are sure my brother is not on the island."

"I see. Anything else?"

"No."

"Well, thanks for telling me," I said inanely. He made a little ceremonial bow, and vanished around the edge of the boathouse, leaving me a little astonished. But there were too many other things worrying me to do more than shelve his story for future investigation.

I was trying hard to keep everything in hand until the locals arrived. I was moving—I'd found out certain items, even though I hadn't yet sorted them—and though I did seem to be working backwards, I was still blank on so much that I was plenty uneasy. That bronze box, for instance! I hadn't had time to speculate on that, up till now. I did, as I hurried up the woods path.

Naturally, we'd search for it when the sheriff arrived, but to do the thing up right, we'd have to go over the whole island with a spade. There were a million hiding places. And the idea was getting stronger inside me that some subtle plan was definitely going forward in this house, and that it revolved around that box— and its unknown contents. What could...

And that was the end of my speculation.

I was twenty yards from the house and had just a sixteenth of a second's warning. A twig snapped at my right. I tried desperately to throw myself backwards, automatically grabbing for the gun under my arm. My head jerked round as I tried to drop. Before I could move an inch, a whistling club flashed down at me from the trees on my right, slammed a murderous, sledgehammer blow across the side of my face. My ear went numb. Fireworks went off inside my head, and I was sent spinning over backwards. I lit, flopping, rolled over wildly twice, and banged into a tree, rebounded, and—the gun that by some miracle had gotten into my hand spurted flame.

Through rocking red mist, I saw a huge shape—it seemed huge— spring into the avenue of trees, dive for me, the club upraised once more. I tried desperately to flop myself away. My gun exploded a second time. A window in the house crashed. I tried furiously to telegraph a message to my gun hand—and couldn't. Yet its dumb reflex saved me; the gun roared again, and a fourth time. It was in my hand, but I couldn't get it pointed. The shape in front of me hopped ludicrously. I felt a tree at my left, tried to drag myself upward; the house at the end of the path was a whirling blur...

The figure in front of me suddenly froze, made a jerking motion—then jumped backwards, and my spinning eyes just made him out as he fled down the path, and vanished through the trees at the left. I fired again—and then I was on my feet, lurching, giddy, trying to pound after him, stumbling, colliding with trees.

I rocketed up to about where I thought he'd ducked off. There was a black opening between two trees. I dived through the opening savagely—and smacked head-on into a third tree in the gloom. I let out a groan, dropped my gun, sat down slowly and held my ringing head in my hands.

DOORS were banging up at the house, footsteps pounding wood. I heard someone calling my name. I swayed there, half mad with pain, but I managed to make my comeback in a matter of seconds.

I was on my feet, and in a run toward the house, when I saw Paul Lyon come charging down the steps. One of the women was at his heels—as far as the top step; a third figure blotted out light from the living-room door. I roared at Paul as I ran, "Back—get back inside that room!" and he slid to a stop at the foot of the steps, started to back up hastily, gasping: "What—what happened? I heard shots. Did you shoot some..." and then he saw the gun in my hand, and drew in breath sharply.

I hit the bottom step, shoved at him to speed him up, but he was moving of his own accord by now. "Nothing happened—just an accident," I rapped as we ran up the long flight. "Who left that room after you got back inside—or who wasn't there?" And as we came to the top, I tossed at the two dark figures there, "Inside—please!"

"We—we all went out," Paul panted. "They all—went out—my aunt at the window—she saw a body in the water—we all ran out—"

He got it all out just as I jumped through the door. And I almost tripped in checking myself on the waxed floor, as I swung back on him from the empty living room. "Body? What body? Where?"

"José—the servant—he's in the water—" He pointed to the open

French windows at the other side of the room. My teeth set, I whirled, and we took up our run again. I was wild with disappointment. I'd thought sure I could single out the murderous devil that had swung on me; this confusion banished that hope. We ran through the windows onto the veranda, and hopped the railing.

The whole group of them were huddled round the water's edge, three people kneeling, the others standing. They swung pasty faces on us as we came out, then hastily backed away. I saw the round-faced Bliss and one of the young men on the ground, just as they lifted between them the dripping, white-clad body of the fourth native boy. His face was puffed, swollen, his head lolling grotesquely, hair plastered down over one side of his face, his green eyes staring at me oblique-ly, almost merrily.

Somebody blurted in a ghastly voice at me: "It's José."

I was in among them, down beside the figure, as the two men laid him on his back. But I wished—a second later—that I hadn't been. I thought he was drowned. He wasn't.

His skull and scalp were terribly—horribly—fractured. The back of his head, right across his hair, was literally cracked open, from ear to ear, and as they inadvertently let his head flop down on the rock, the whole thing came apart.

I went green at the gills myself, then flopped sideways on my knees, spread my coat to shield the sight from those behind. "Get inside," I jerked at them. "All of you—into the living room!" They scattered like chickens. I called, "Paul Lyon!" over my shoulder, and he came up behind me as the two, who had dragged the body up, stumbled back, white-faced.

"Get a blanket or something," I told him. "You two—go on inside."

Paul came back with a black rug in a minute. During the short time I had to wait, nothing on earth could have kept me from comparing two things—the frightful gash in the boy's head, and the vicious swing of the club that had downed me, minutes ago. Though I had saved myself from the full force of it, I'd had an uneasy feeling that that club was intended to do more than just knock me down—or at least that the person behind it didn't care if it did do more. This settled it.

The body covered, I stood tight-jawed, with my hands in my coat pockets, staring down at the grim mounds under the cloth. I saw no point in making any close examination. I knew all I wanted to know about it right then. There'd be no subtle information to be found on that corpse.

My mouth was dry. The rest of me was sweating. The silent horrors of this place had begun to touch me. I was thinking fast, desperately fearful of making a wrong move at this point. Yet, at last, I did seem to have an opening to do what should have been done at first—find out who all these people were and hear what they had to say.

I swung on Paul. "I'll meet these people now. Get everybody on the island—servants, everybody—into the living room right away."

CHAPTER FIVE

THE BODY ON THE MAT

YELLOW GLOW flooded the living room from a single powerful fixture in the center of the ceiling. French windows on three sides were opened but the air was heavy, hot, wet. Moisture gleamed on the tall flamingo walls. The yellow light jaundiced faces that were white and strained enough in the first place. Paul's voice was dry and harsh as he made quick introductions, and as though by unspoken consent, the people fell instinctively into little groups.

I stood at one end of the living room, my back to a fireplace, facing them. Paul was at my right hand.

The servants fanned out at the far end of the room, on either side of the hall entrance. There were two women servants I hadn't seen—a Mrs. McMath, the cook, and a liquid-eyed, trim little French maid, Cecille. They stood at the right, by the door to the library, and the four men over to the left, before the dining room. Alters was the wireless man; he had an unlighted pipe in his mouth, and kept a little apart from the three native boys.

The seraphic-faced Bliss and his death's-head partner, McLintock, eyed me dully, silently, from a point by the veranda door at my left.

Sarah Lyon, Gardner Lyon, Junior, Estelle Lyon, and Murray Douglass grouped loosely over to the right. The florid, wasp-waisted Gardner, Junior, and the white-haired Sarah Lyon were both smoking. The old lady was seated, as was the radiant little blonde, Estelle. Douglass stood with one hand on the back of Estelle's chair, jaw set, his gray eyes defiant, his mop of hair like a bushman's.

I didn't waste time on politeness; "I want information," I said abruptly. "I want all the information any of you have, and I want it quickly. I'm trying to find the reason Mr. Lyon was shot. Some of you, besides the one that did it, must have knowledge that will help me find that reason. There is a bronze dispatch box missing. Do any of you know where it is—or do any of you know what it contains?"

There was no answer.

"All right. Then, do any of you know of a reason apart from that, that Mr. Lyon might have been killed?"

There was another silence, but it wasn't the same sort. Ignorant as I was of the wild knot into which the old man had snarled the lives of this roomful, I could feel that something was coming.

Sarah Lyon's queer husky voice said calmly: "Paul, you'd better tell it."

And Paul told it. In a husky, almost toneless voice, he jerked out everything that had happened at the sulphurous family conference of the night before. Then followed the details of the meeting between the dead man and Bliss and McLintock, and taut as I was, and avid for every word I could get, I could hardly digest the amazing situation that his rushing, short sentences revealed. When he got to the point where he had wired for me, I stopped him.

"Wait," I said. "I want to get this trust-fund business straight. When Mr. Douglass, as Miss Estelle's attorney, advised Miss Estelle not to sign away her rights in it, and gave Mr. Lyon an argument, then Mr. Lyon threatened to use his influence to rake up these old charges against Douglass and prosecute him criminally. Is that it?"

"Yes."

"Am I to assume that this three million dollar trust fund belonged equally to you, Miss Sarah, Miss Estelle and Mr. Gardner, Junior? That you all would have—as a matter of fact that you all now do get—three-quarters of a million apiece, which you would have lost if your father were alive and you had agreed to his demand?"

"Yes. He made no distinction there."

"How do you mean, distinction?"

Paul looked up, then down again. "Estelle and I are only adopted children—not blood relatives."

I STOOD tight-lipped, not meeting their eyes. My brain was flying. Motive? Here was motive for five! Ready cash!

I got that clear and started looking for anything else there might be. Some obscure line of thought moved me to single out Gardner, Junior. "Your—uh—mother—Mrs. Lyon—she's—passed on?"

His face got even darker. "That has nothing to do with this!"

"I'll judge that. Please answer me."

His eyes got furious. "You can—"

Sarah Lyon's husky voice broke in quickly, smoothly. "Don't be a fool, Gardner. No, she isn't dead. She's in South America. There was a divorce. Nothing terrible, in case that's what you're thinking. Myra—Mrs. Lyon—simply found a man she preferred to live with, and went off with him." She hesitated. "Maybe I'll save your time by giving the rest of the family history. I was living in Paris then. My brother located me, and asked me to come and take care of him," indicating Gardner, Junior. "I came. I don't think children should grow up alone. I suggested that he adopt some more. He could afford it. He did, and there they are."

I nodded. Going back to Paul, I asked: "Who inherits—whatever is left?"

"Gardner, Junior."

"No legacies? The servants—or—"

"No."

I met Gardner, Junior's heavy-lidded stare again. Actually, I wasn't thinking of him, but he got slowly furious under what he thought was my scrutiny, finally boiled over. "Well? Don't glare at me! I didn't do it. I'm about sick of this farce, anyway. I think it's time you quit being smart, and wake up. He jerked his head toward the rear of the room. "There's your damned killers—one of them—or all three of them. My God! The only thing I can't figure is why they didn't do it years ago."

"All right. Why did they kill him?"

"To get quit of him, before he killed them. I suppose your white-haired clerk, Paul there, has been so damned anxious to make trouble for me he hasn't told you that Ramon is blind in one eye from a stone my father threw at him. I suppose he hasn't told you the old devil used to whack them with his stick when they didn't suit him. I suppose you don't even know what they are! Well, I'll tell you—they're slaves! Nothing more or less—bought, by God, body and soul, for fifty dollars apiece. They—oh hell, ask the clerk there."

Paul's face was livid, white. He was literally swaying with fury. His voice was harsh, flat. "He is referring to Carlos and Ramon and

Antonio. I hope you will pay no attention to such cowardly, rotten, lying talk. It is true in a way, they were—that they belonged to my father. They are Hondurans, and my father did pay their parents—money, for them. It's not as bad as it sounds; it's not uncommon down there. The natives have large families and they live in misery—they're glad to have Americans take them as unpaid servants. The boys receive training and education, and they are free when their—purchaser dies. Then they're equipped to take advantage of American opportunities." He hesitated, and his lips tightened. "Father treated them badly—that's true enough. It's not true that they ever did or said a thing to give color to this rotten accusation. I don't think such a statement should pass. It should either be backed up or the maker should admit he's lying."

I TOOK a lightning glance at the three native boys—and I was shocked. Their eyes were actually yellow with fury. Fantastically, teeth had become visible in all their three mouths.

"Very clever!" Gardner, Junior snarled. "Very clever, clerk—your wording. No—the lice didn't say or do anything; they didn't dare to. But anybody with half a brain could look at their dirty yellow faces, week in and week out, and see—"

"Stop it!" I barked. "I understand what you mean." And to Paul, "I'm interested even in guesses, if they bring out motives. Motives are what I'm looking for." I hesitated. "I mean what I was looking for. I seem to have gotten swamped with them." I looked over the room again grimly. "You two,"—I indicated the little French maid and the cook—"seem to be the only ones without reasons to do this." I nodded at Alters. "And you, I guess. Or did you have something against him, too?"

They said anxiously that they didn't.

"I'd like to know," Bliss's voice was suddenly rasping, "just why the devil you figure we had any reason to do him in. Of all—"

"Sorry," I clipped. "I guess you're in the clear, on motive, too. If you're ready to explain that knock on the head you're supposed to have gotten in your bedroom last night, I can probably satisfy myself completely as far as you're concerned."

"Supposed to have gotten? What the devil do you mean, Brew, supposed to have? I—"

"Blue's the name."

"Blue, then. I was sleeping soundly in my bed at three o'clock and I woke up with the feeling that there was somebody in the room, and just then he hit me, and I went unconscious, and that's all there bloody well is to it, and there's no supposed to be about it. Is that clear?"

"How did you know the time if you were asleep?"

He swore. "There's a luminous clock on my bedside table. If you want to look at—"

"What was stolen from you?"

"Nothing. Not a blistering thing."

I stood silent. For some reason, I knew, as surely as I knew my own name, that he was lying. I also knew that this round-faced little man was clever enough not to lie unless he knew he was safe doing it. Who else was lying? Or was anybody else? I raked my brain. Murray Douglass, Paul, Gardner, Junior, Estelle, Sarah Lyon—and the three native boys. All with motive. And I couldn't shake clear of the idea that these two Wall Street sharpers might have something to do with it. That mysterious bronze box still loomed large. I jerked myself out of the theorizing hastily, turned once again to McLintock and Bliss.

"What time did your meeting with Mr. Lyon break up?"

"About quarter to eleven, or ten to."

I looked at Paul. "And you saw your father last—when?"

"I went up about twelve or a little after, and we talked for about an hour about this situation." He nodded vaguely at Bliss and the other. "He decided he would spend the night working out his plans, and I accompanied him down to the kitchen and made him some sandwiches and got him the milk. That was a little past one. I walked upstairs with him, and left him at the steel doors. He closed them behind me, as I went down. I went directly to the boathouse, and went for you."

"All right." I looked round the room. "Did anybody else see Mr. Lyon, either between quarter to eleven and twelve o'clock, or after one thirty?"

Murray Douglass said evenly: "Yes, I went up to his study around quarter past eleven."

"What for?"

He shrugged. "I should think that would be obvious. To try and get him not to make this trouble for me."

"Did you succeed?"

"No. He wouldn't even talk to me. I wasn't there two minutes."

I said: "Uh-huh. Well, anybody else?"

MURRAY DOUGLASS again broke the silence after it had lasted a second. "Gardner, Junior was up there. I saw him going up, right after me."

I let my eyes get narrow on the red-faced Junior. "You seem to be looking for trouble."

He grunted. "Sure, I was up there. What of it? My father was seen alive long after I left him."

"What did you want to see him about?"

"That happens to be a confidential matter, and my own private business—"

I boiled over.

I took three strides; my eyes flamed an inch from his. "I've had enough of your damn smart-alec attitude. In about two minutes, you're going to be wearing a pair of bracelets, and you'll face a judge for obstructing justice, if nothing else. There are two dead men on this island, and it's my business to find who killed them. If I say it's my business what you talked about, it is my business, and by Judas you'd better understand that! You may be important sometimes, but for the time being, you're just a suspect in a murder inquiry. Don't undertake to try and tell me my business again, understand?"

He was purple. "At any rate—at any rate, it's not all these people's business. I—"

"All right. I'll give you a chance to tell me in private in a minute, if that's what you want." I turned and looked over the room again. I couldn't think of any more to ask them and so I said: "Is there anything else that any of you know that might have a bearing on this case?" And when I got nothing but dead silence, "All right. Mr. Gardner Lyon and myself are going to step outside. The rest of you, don't leave this room, please."

The gray-faced McLintock cleared his throat. "Mr. Blue—Mr. Bliss and myself have certain matters to discuss—important matters—in private. If you have no objection, we will retire to my room upstairs. As we are not under suspicion, it would seem—"

"Who said you weren't under suspicion?" I said. But as a matter of fact, I couldn't see any further use in holding them there. In spite of my attitude, I wasn't too anxious to get into trouble with these people. They were big enough to make it damned uncomfortable for me, if they chose to, later. "I guess you don't have to stick to this room," I told the group at large. "You can all go to your rooms, or anywhere in the house, except the third floor, and—under no conditions is anyone to step outside the house. I'm not just sure what's going on here, yet, and I'm carrying a gun. I hope it won't go off at an innocent person, but it's up to you not to make any suspicious moves, if you are such. Is that clear?"

I took Gardner, Junior out to the gloom of the veranda. He hesitated. "Not here—let's get away from where that crew can listen in."

I let him do it. We went down the steps, a few yards along the path, and took a cross path that landed us just opposite the rear of the house on still a third path that led to buildings beyond. He had his self-possession back. He blew smoke calmly over my head.

"Go ahead," I said impatiently, "why did you go up to see your father?"

"With every intention in the world of killing him," he said startlingly. "I had a proposition to make, and if he refused I was going to fix him, once and for all. He wanted to get his money out of hock. All right—I was willing to help him do it, if I got my share of it—seven hundred odd thousand—in cash. The old goat had made me lose more than that, anyhow."

"What do you mean? How?"

"He told me to buy stock in that damned railroad of his. I thought I was getting inside dope, and I mortgaged my shirt—yes, and my partners' shirts, too. We're out on a limb properly right now, and unless we get some cash, we may have to fold up."

"You're not in business with your father?"

"Hell, no. I'm in with two other fellows in the brokerage business."

"What did your father say to your proposition?"

"Oh, he sold me the idea that he'd take care of me in another way in the next day or two. He wouldn't say what way."

"Did you have a gun when you went up to see him?"

"I did, and I've got it now."

THE BEAM of my flash went on, and held him in the light, and I had my own automatic half free of my pocket, too. I wasn't taking even the faintest chances. "I'll take your gun," I said, "and get it out delicately."

He handed me a blued-steel, thirty-two calibre S&W. It didn't smell of burned powder. I pocketed it. "Anything else you want to tell me?"

He shrugged.

I spent a moment in thought. It struck me that I'd forgotten to ask Paul who had signed the waivers and who hadn't—not that I knew what I could do with that when I did know it. And it was high time I got some idea of the layout of the island. The bronze box was the most important thing of all and I couldn't even try wild guesses as to where it might be, till I knew the ground. And, too, I felt that I ought to keep my eye on Paul. He was logically my chief suspect.

"All right," I said. "You go back in, and send Paul out. Tell him to come out the back door—and do it slowly so the light shines on him and I can recognize him."

He shrugged, put his hands in trouser pockets, swaggered slowly toward the back door. I let my eyes narrow on his back. I wondered if he were clever enough to adopt all this truculence and seeming frankness as a cloak for what was really in his mind. The gun episode had seemed just a little overdone.

The back door opened, he went in, and it closed. Almost simultaneously, a light appeared in one of the second-floor windows, and a figure—I couldn't distinguish whose—came over and pulled the shade. Bliss and McLintock were evidently having their conference.

I looked toward the veranda. Through the trees I could just see the front door. A bushy-haired man and a girl were silhouetted in the door, just moving away from it, back into the living room—Douglass and Estelle.

I stood and waited. The grim, silent house towered over me in the hot darkness. I shifted uncomfortably from one foot to another, my mind a riot of speculation. That bronze box! What could it contain? A multi-millionaire's strongbox, but a ruined multi-millionaire. And yet it was apparently the motive for a double murder. Gold? Money? Papers—compromising papers? Was blackmail going to show up here? Or was—

I came out of it with a start to realize that five minutes had passed, and my first reaction was a rush of anger. Then a second, chilling thought struck me—and I was hurrying toward the back door. If Gardner Lyon, Junior were in truth the one behind the ugly business in this house, I had presented him with an absolutely perfect chance to carry out—whatever he might be planning to carry out.

I was cursing myself inwardly as I opened the door and shot a quick glance down the hall toward the living room. Then my eyes suddenly narrowed. Somebody had deliberately opened the side door of the dining room and it now stood straight across, blocking the line of sight down the hall from here to the front. And then I got it. I swung round, my eyes raking the floor at my feet—and I gasped.

From under the door of a broom closet sunk in the wall of the hall by the kitchen, was seeping a thin line of red, across the inch of polished floor that flanked the carpet. I dived silently for the closet, my heart in my boots, and threw the door open.

Gardner Lyon, Junior was crumpled on his side, on a hemp-rope mat on the floor of the closet. The heavy elk's-foot handle of an immense hunting knife stuck out of his throat. The floor of the closet was a crimson, sluggish welter of blood, and the mat under him was soaked. His face was horribly contorted in an expression of excruciating pain. His hands were clutched on the handle of the knife, as though he had attempted to wrench it free. And the hands were covered with blood, too.

He was still warm, but he was dead.

CHAPTER SIX

BLUE SEES RED

FOR A full forty seconds I just stood there, shocked, staring. Then bitter, furious rage flared up inside me, had me actually trembling, white-lipped, before I could fight it down. Finally my brain struggled through to the surface, and—I saw the rag mop hanging in the closet.

I jerked my head around. Nobody was in the hall—or on the stairs. I reached in, snatched down the mop, swung it out, shot another glance down the empty corridor. Then I hastily swabbed the blood from the ribbon of floor between closet and carpet. It shone clean. I flattened the rags of the mop, just inside the door, so they blocked the stream of scarlet, then closed the door on it silently, and swung back, tense, listening.

Thoughts bombarded me. What to do? If I spread the alarm through the house—hysteria. But if I pretended I had found nothing—ignored it—I might at least puzzle whoever had done this. If I could only upset his balance, even just a little—

My teeth came together. This killer was a monster. Ice touched my spine as I wondered if it could be that, in spite of everything, I was up against that horror of a detective's life—the motiveless killer—the maniac.

Then my thoughts came back to the bronze box. Hidden in it was the motive—the heart and center of all this unbelievable butchery. The bronze box! I cursed it furiously.

Where in the name of Heaven was the sheriff? Self pity shook me. One man—with one pair of eyes—in this charnel house that was literally steaming with death; a round dozen of possible killers—triple murderers—that might, for all I knew, even at this minute be adding to their trail of blood! I couldn't watch them all!

I was suddenly furious—furious with myself—with everybody in the house. They were fools. I was suddenly convinced that they were all holding out on me. Certainly the dead man in the closet must have known more than he told me—and he was killed because of it. All right—then there was only one thing for me to do. Find that box—as fast as I could—find it—and sit on it—and let this murderous rat come to me for it. That was the only certain plan—the absolutely infallible one. Let them look after themselves—if they blanketed me in ignorance, I'd play this game my way—and to hell with them. If I could find that ghastly box, before the killer struck again, I'd have the slaughter checked—

And the maddening thought came back—I still knew nothing about the island—about where to look for the damned box. The house—yes, I knew the house—but that was the one place absolutely out of the question. Nobody but a fool would take a chance on keeping the thing in the house —and this devil was no fool.

I jammed my fists in my coat pockets, set my jaw, swung toward the living room—and stopped, cursing. My wretched policeman's conscience was up in arms. Murder had been done, right here, within minutes. I'd been free enough in telling people I was the law. The law didn't walk calmly out on murdered bodies without even a gesture of investigation! I stood there, sweating, fuming.

My eye fell on the kitchen door, a few yards up the hall, and I made up my mind. A gesture! That's what it would be, but it would be something. I let my eyes get hard as I strode for the kitchen door, opened it suddenly, and stepped inside.

THE THREE Hondurans were standing in a huddled group, in the butler's pantry, through an open door to my left. The cook and the French maid were sitting on chairs in the kitchen, close together. I said "Excuse me," harshly, and walked over, planted myself right in front of the two women, peered in through the butler's pantry. My jaws clamped. It would have been a cinch for one of the boys to have slipped out through the dining room, around into the hall, waited there, and knifed Gardner, Junior, then slipped back in again, and—

There was no use even asking! These two women would supply his alibi—and they'd be sincere about it, too. As for his brothers betraying him—I said, "Thanks," bitterly to the astonished servants, and walked out, straight on down the hall toward the living room.

I flattened the half-open dining-room door against the wall as I passed, and the bang brought Murray Douglass, alone in the living room, to his feet. He had a notebook and pencil in his hand. I frowned quickly round.

"Where's Paul?"

"I—they all went upstairs."

I turned on my heel, went back down the hall, my lips tight. The devil was certainly taking care of his own. So far, four people could have stabbed Gardner, Junior! Was it luck—or was it deadly cleverness—the ability to jockey things till they were just right—and then crash in?

As I reached the second-floor landing, I called out: "Will everybody on this floor please come to your doors!"

Doors opened. Bliss and McLintock were in one room. Sarah Lyon, Estelle Lyon and Paul each appeared before a separate portal.

"Have any of you been downstairs in the last ten minutes?"

There was no answer. "All right," I clipped grimly. "That's all. Paul, I want to see you a minute."

The other doors closed. I told Paul, "Wait here a minute," and went up the stairs to the third floor, went along the short wing to the wireless operator's room, opened the door.

Alters was lying on the bed, his eyes closed, shoes off, gently snoring!

I backed out, went on down to where Paul was waiting. "I want to get an idea of what's on this island besides this house—in a hurry," I told him. "I want you to show me around."

"Yes," he nodded. "All right." We went down the stairs, and out. He hesitated a second, then led me swiftly along the back path. I drove him to speed.

The island was the shape of a boot, roughly. The house was at the heel. We walked to the very toe, then came back. There were three other buildings on the place.

The boathouse was two-thirds of the way from heel to toe, along the bottom of the boot. The four Hondurans lived in a dormitory on the flat second floor, and the boatman, Ellton, had a room there to himself. That floor was built over the water-filled slips in which the boats were kept. There were half a dozen dinghies—two with outboard motors—and two fast-looking launches, three canoes, in the slips. The powerboat, of course, was still waiting, over at the mainland.

The other two buildings were a commissary, ten yards behind the main house, and a power house, fifty yards nearer to the toe of the island than the commissary.

IT WAS while we were on the path leading from the boathouse to the power house that I got a sudden definite suspicion that at least part of this hidden story might turn out to have its roots in the character of the dead old man—Gardner Lyon, the elder. Paul was walking a few yards ahead of me. He suddenly arced off the path to the left, then back again to the right. I couldn't see why, in the darkness, so I said, "Easy a minute," and turned on my flashlight, swung it around.

An area of about twenty square yards was fenced off with string and little sticks. In the center of it, about three feet high, stood a little maple tree, its leaves in the still air, like molded green wax. I asked Paul why it was fenced up.

"It has to do with a bet my father made a friend. The friend maintained that father couldn't grow any kind of a tree but pine on this island."

"I thought the island was all rock," I said.

He hesitated. "It was. Father had a crew of men come out and drill a big basin in the rock, and fix up irrigation of some sort. Then he had it filled with some special earth from the mainland. Naturally, the tree won't grow for very long, but he had the ground fixed up with moss and everything, so it would look like a natural phenomenon, for the time being."

"He bet money on this, you say?"

"Fifty thousand dollars."

I grunted in disgust. "A sure-thing gambler, eh?"

Paul said nothing.

"All right," I said. "Go ahead."

The power house was a large, square, windowless building of tile and brick. It was full of machinery—an electrical generator, a water-pumping system, a water-heating system, and—as the native boy had told me—a central heating system, a large oil-burning furnace. Also, at one end of the building, completely walled off, an incinerator of some sort. This had an entrance of its own.

The commissary was the same shape building, a little smaller, and it had windows. It was divided by a narrow hall down the center. It contained a tremendous electric refrigerator in which current edibles hung; a smaller, but still large, cubicle, in which game—ducks, par-tridges, bittern, and so on—were to be frozen, when shot, for the long trip back to the city; a surprisingly modern little bakery; a carpentry and cooperage shop, and a liquor vault. There was only one door to this buiding.

We were again within a few yards of the back door of the house, and through the trees I could see figures moving against the light of the living room. It had evidently been populated again.

"I guess that's all," Paul said.

I hesitated. There was a nice question here. I was only in doubt for a second, though—then I clung grimly to my policy. I wanted no company, if I were going to search for that box, chief suspect or no chief suspect. I told Paul he could go back inside.

As I stood there, my mind racing over the places I had just visited, I couldn't decide where to look. The buildings? That was the worst bet of all, to my mind. The boathouse? That had the advantage of being close to the only line of flight—but people lived there. And then—I thought of the soft earth around the little maple tree. It was the only spot on the island where a person could dig to any depth. There had been no frost yet—the ground would not be hard. It looked like a natural.

I turned round, my eyes narrow. I was within a few feet of the path that connected front and rear paths to the house. The maple tree was closer to the front path, so I started quickly down the cross alley to get on it. And as I passed within a few yards of the house, I gave it another look—and stopped dead.

I WAS directly opposite the rear window of the dining room. The window was half opened. The door to the hall was still wide open. Directly across the hall—well in my angle of sight—was the door that opened off the hall into the library. Paul Lyon stood with one hand on the library door, his eyes narrow, looking down the hall toward the living room. And in the second that I stopped, his head jerked toward the library. He was signaling somebody in the living room!

I craned hastily to see who it was—but the dark interior of the dining room blocked me. Paul repeated his gesture, and this time he turned the knob and opened the library door. It was dark inside. Paul waited, frowning, and—the gray-faced skeleton McLintock appeared at his side. His long, bony fingers hung down at his sides, spread out. The two whispered curtly. McLintock's eyes were suspicious. Then he shrugged, followed on Paul's heels into the library. As he entered, his long fingers reached to where the light switch was, just inside the door—and Paul's hand quickly grasped his sleeve. There was a second of hesitation when all I could see of them were the sleeve and the hands—then McLintock's hand dropped. The door closed.

I was tense. A conference in the dark! I whirled back, running on my toes.

I was around the house, catfooting toward the library window, in less than half a minute. I got a break here. There was a mat of moss under the window. The window was just on the far side of the pine tree. I crept round the tree on hands and knees—and the breath of whispering reached me before I was at the window. It was pitch dark inside, and it was pitch dark where I was.

McLintock's gloomy voice was unmistakable, even as a whisper. "You're mad. I've got no bronze box. If you ask me, you've got it your—"

"Don't bluff! We can't talk here indefinitely. Listen to me—it was just quarter past one last night when my father and I went down to the kitchen to get some food for him. We were there only five minutes. I walked back up with him, and left him at the steel doors. He closed them as I went down. You were in the door of your room, when I passed the second floor, and you hadn't undressed, either. Now—don't interrupt me—I'll tell you exactly what happened—

"Through some freak of memory, father left the bronze box on his desk when he went downstairs. You went up there, while we were in the kitchen. Whether you knew in advance that we weren't there is immaterial—I don't imagine you did. You found the room vacant—but the bronze box was on the desk. You knew what was in it—he'd showed it to you directly after I left that conference you were having with him around eleven. You knew the contents of the box spelled ruin for you and your partner. You stole the box, hurried down to your room, secreted it somewhere there, then came out again, intending to go back up and wait for Father, possibly make a deal with him. And you expected trouble—because I saw a gun in your dressing-gown pocket when I passed you!

"You went up—and found the steel doors closed—or maybe you didn't go up again—that doesn't matter. What does matter, is that my father went back into his apartment—and discovered his box gone. Just how long it was before he noticed it, is a question. If Bliss told that detective the truth, it must have been an hour and a half. Anyway, he found it was gone. He knew it was one of you two that took it—for you and myself are the only ones—I think—that knew what it contained. He came back, and opened the steel doors from the inside, came down with blood in his eye.

"Evidently, he picked on Bliss as being the more likely to have taken it. He went into Bliss's room, knocked him unconscious and searched his room. He didn't find the box. Then he went for you.

"Either the noise he made in Bliss's room woke you up, or else you hadn't gone to sleep at all. You were ready for him. When he walked in, you had the jump on him. You held your gun on him. You forced him to go back upstairs. You knew you couldn't get that box open without the keys. I presume you told him you wanted to talk things over, or something like that. Anyway, when you got him back up there in the office and found out where the keys were, you tried to grab them from him. He threw his keyring out the window, rather than let you get it, and—you shot him. Then you came out, closed the steel doors behind you, and—"

McLINTOCK burst out: "You're mad, I tell you! I didn't take..." And he cut himself to silence.

"Ha!" Paul's whisper whipped out. "You didn't take what?"

"I didn't do any of those things—and you know it," McLintock blustered. "You yourself probably—"

"Don't waste time. You know and I know I didn't do it. I don't mind this detective thinking so—I'll even stand for an arrest, if you want to play ball with me. They can't convict me—when they find out when the old man died, they'll realize that it was after I left the island. I'll make a fair bargain with you. As far as killing the old maniac, I owe you a vote of thanks—we all do. Turn over that box to me—at once—wherever you've hidden it—and I'll do everything in my power to keep you clear—"

"Wait! Wait!" McLintock said hoarsely. "You've got things mixed. You've got it partially right, but—by the living Judas! I know—by God, I know who did it! It just came to me—"

"You certainly do."

"No—no—listen—after we broke up that meeting around eleven, Bliss and I went downstairs for a while, down to the ground floor. I was there still when that young whelp, Gardner, Junior, came down from seeing the old man. By Heaven! Do you know what he said to me? He said, 'Hello, sucker!' It had slipped my mind absolutely! Get that? As sure as we stand here, he knew what was in that box! The old man must have told him!"

There was a second's tight silence.

Naturally, every nerve of mine was concentrated on that darkened room. I was literally holding my breath, straining not to miss a syllable. I was on hands and knees. If I hadn't been, I flatter myself I could have looked after myself.

I heard the rustle behind me—just heard it. It took a split second to switch my attention—then I tried to duck wildly. But, unconsciously, I tried to be silent, and I was seconds too late. There was a slight swish—I knew I was caught—then thunder exploded in my head and I flopped down. Then the second vicious whack got me behind the ear; my brain seemed to split; there was a fiery roaring pinwheel of light; I felt as though I were flung out into space, and—I dropped a million feet dizzily, into stone, cold darkness.

CHAPTER SEVEN

THE LITTLE DOCTOR

WHEN I came to, I was literally on fire with rage, shame, and embarrassment. There was absolute, flaming murder in my heart, even before I'd struggled up through the stabbing mists of unconsciousness. My head threatened to come off, as I made a futile attempt to spring to my feet.

I sat there, and fought it, pressing my temples between my palms. I realized, after a minute, that I was still where I had fallen—on the bed of moss—and it dawned on me that the whole damned proceedings must have been noiseless. Otherwise, I'd have been found. By the same token, I couldn't have been out long. The fury gripped me again, and I staggered to my feet, my teeth clenched—

Then, with a rush, the conversation I'd overheard came back.

It snapped me back to an effort at clarity. I stumbled over to the wall, leaned there, while the sweat rolled off me.

My head still ached like fury, but I was thinking fast again....

Memory suddenly smacked me—a sickening blow. I grabbed for my pocket, and—a furious groan dropped from my lips. My hand-kerchief was almost pulled out of my pocket, and Gardner Lyon's key ring with its bronze key, was gone!

Another two minutes, and I was steady. The giddiness passed. I strode toward the veranda, grimy, straightening my clothes.

I stepped through the French windows into the living room, si-lently, suddenly, and raked the room for any betraying movement. Murray Douglass whirled round from the front door, where he had been peering out. Estelle's face came up suddenly from her hands; there was fright in her eyes. She was sitting on a chair near the front door, and there were signs of tears on her face. Sarah Lyon's sharp old eyes peered without surprise at me, through a cloud of her inevitable cigarette smoke. Her tall body was reclined on a chaise lounge near the dining-room door. I faltered a second, irresolute, and—a monstrous thought was suddenly alight in my mind. I put my hands in my coat pockets, went over and stood looking down into Sarah Lyon's face.

"I find I'm a little short of information, Miss Lyon," I said abrupt-ly. "I'll have to ask you a question or two. First—did you open this house up this summer? I mean come up here before Mr. Lyon, Senior, and get it ready for use?"

"Of course. I run—ran the domestic end of things for him."

"May I ask why you went to Paris?"

Her eyebrows went up slightly. "Paris?"

"When you were younger—years ago, I mean. You said you were there."

"Oh, of course. Well, frankly, because I couldn't stand bigoted, dull people. Have you ever lived in an Iowa town?"

"No. Did your brother feel the same way?"

"Men don't."

"Yet you left Paris when he asked you to, and came back."

She shrugged, exhaled smoke. "He was rich. I was a flop as an artist."

I tried to see behind her long-lashed eyes as I said quietly so the others wouldn't overhear: "What became of your husband?"

"He died." The answer was fairly jolted out of her. Then her eyes got even thinner, and her lips tightened. "Where did you learn I had a husband?"

I pretended surprise. "Didn't you tell me? No, I guess not—"

Her eyes were like flint. "My husband died three months after my marriage. What possible bearing…"

I BOWED, said, "Thank you," shortly, turned and went quickly down the hall before she could finish. Halfway down I stopped. The most welcome sound I had heard since I arrived was suddenly coming through the night.

It was the sharp *putt-putt-putt* of the motor boat, out across the water.

It sent a sudden stir throughout the whole house. Up above, I heard doors opening, and snatches of conversation. I waited, my eyes narrowed on the stairs.

Paul came down first. At his heels were Bliss and McLintock. Paul caught sight of me. "I guess that's the sheriff, Mr. Blue."

I eased out breath in quick relief. His tone told me definitely that my sandbagging had indeed been silent. He was unaware that I had overheard his talk with McLintock.

I turned on my heel without a word, strode back ahead of them to the living room. I was in the door leading to the veranda, when—I suddenly whirled round on them.

Bliss, McLintock, Paul, Murray Douglass, Estelle Lyon and Sarah were in a group a few yards behind me. Alters, the sleepy-eyed wireless operator, was ambling through the hall door. I singled out Paul, but I wasn't missing a muscle's twitch of any of them. I shot savagely at Paul: "Unless you can tell me a good reason why I shouldn't—I'm putting you under arrest right now for the murder of Gardner Lyon, Senior!"

It made them jump. The whole group fell back like magic, shock and horror in their faces.

Paul's eyes flickered. He involuntarily half turned toward the two Wall Street operators, checked himself. I was watching McLintock. But it was Bliss's voice that blurted quickly: "I—I'll arrange everything like you said, Paul! Get—get you a lawyer, and—and all. Just sit tight."

"Who the hell asked you to butt in?" I rapped.

He puffed. "The boy's entitled to—"

"I'll see he gets what he's entitled to." I eyed Paul. "Well, have you anything to say?"

His lips were tight. "I'll say nothing till I see my lawyer."

Murray Douglass took a step forward. "Paul, will you let me—"

Paul's eyes jerked round, locked with those of the lawyer. "You!" he said harshly. "Hardly!"

McLintock's voice came from my left. "I presume the rest of us are free to go—to leave, then? I'm terribly sorry, but I've important business—"

I cut him off. "It's twenty-five minutes past one now," I said. "At two o'clock I want all the people that are on the island now, in this room." I thought I'd better add, "Except Gardner Lyon, Junior. The sheriff will have some questions. After that, I hope you will all be able to go home."

I turned, started out to the veranda. Paul's voice called after me. "What do I do now?"

"Nothing," I threw over my shoulder. "Nothing at all."

MY JAW was hard, but there was a light burning in my eyes, as I hiked down the little path toward the dock. The motor boat was putting into the little bay. Reinforcements? With the sheriff, his deputy and the coroner to help, I could show this killer—

I rounded onto the wooden pier, located the light switch just as the razor-prowed craft slid in toward me, motor throttled. The lights flared up, had me dazzled for a minute. Then the boat came alongside, chugging, and a rope snaked out as I blinked. I caught it automatically, turned, and slipped the bite quickly on a post. Then I turned back—and blurted a groaning curse.

There were, in the boat—Ellton the boatman, Hayes the chauffeur, and—only one other person! He was a little, blond, red-faced man without a vestige of hair above his ears. He wore an expression of frightened unhappiness. His pale blue eyes looked as though they'd leak tears any minute. Ellton cut the motor.

I blurted: "Where in God's name is the rest of your party?"

"Rest of it? Ha! There isn't any. I'm all of it—the sheriff and the coroner. Where the hell do you think I can get deputies in this Satan-begotten wilderness? Are you Cass Blue?"

"Yes, but—"

He scrambled out, chattering blandly. "You can work with me on this thing, Blue, if you've a mind to. Most private detectives—no. Crooks—chiselers—I know. But I've heard of you, and I'm willing to take a chan—" He straightened up, puffing. "Matter of fact, I'm glad of your assistance. You see, this is the first murder case I've ever—I told them they were damn fools to force both jobs on me, but seems there isn't anybody within a hundred miles that can even read. Of course, I'm not the full sheriff, y'undersrand—just a deputy sher—found anything out yet?"

I clenched my teeth, bit off at Ellton and Hayes, "Go up to the house!" To the little bald man I said bitterly: "I hope you're at least a doctor—or are you an amateur there, too?"

"By God, I resent that! Who do you think you're talk—of course I'm a doctor—a damned good one. Pitkin's my name. And by the Lord Harry, Blue, you'll take a diff—"

"You maniac!" I was so galled my voice was quivering. "Drop that stuff—there's hell boiling in this house—right now. Since I sent for you, another man's been killed—nothing to show who did it. You do as I say, understand. If you don't, you're liable to get us both killed. Killed—you hear me?" I gave him no chance to reply. "I haven't a shred of evidence against anybody, but I've got them to the point where something's got to break. If you start throwing your weight around, so help me God, if they don't kill you, I will. Now listen—if you ever listened to anything in your life!"

He'd deflated like a pricked balloon; he gulped. "I—I'm list—"

"There's a native boy out behind the house—dead. There's the old man upstairs—and a third corpse that nobody knows of but the killer and me—in a broom closet downstairs. I don't want you to waste time on the native boy, or the one in the broom closet, but I've got to have definite information from the body upstairs! Just take a glance at the others. We've got to get upstairs as fast as we can, and find the time of death."

"Yes—all right." He mopped his bald head furiously. "You—you really think there is danger? What—what's going on, anyway? Why—"

"I'll catch you up when I can. Now, move—fast!"

WE WENT up the steps. The whole family was in the living room. Pitkin halted, said solemnly, "This is a terrible thing. I can't tell you how deeply—" and my hand slammed into his back. "Straight through those French windows!" He almost stumbled, looked about to make some protest, caught my eye, and waddled on without a word. We stepped into the dark, and I used my flash while he examined the native boy, confirmed my first guess. We came back in, went through the roomful again in silence, down the hall. I took care to leave the dining-room door straight across the hall, as it had been at the time of the stabbing. My purpose was the same the killer's had been—to cut off the line of sight from those in the living room.

I hurried him in his examination of Gardner, Junior's body, as soon as I had made sure there was nothing in the pockets of value to me. I got bloody to my elbows, searching him.

The doctor was shaking his head as I led him quickly up the two flights of stairs, then down the hall of the steel doors. I used the key Paul had given me, let him precede me in. He halted, looked around.

"Other side of the desk," I said.

He went over, clucked his tongue, knelt down, then looked up. "Why, he's been dead many hours. The others now—"

"Forget them, please!" I raved. "And for God's sake tell me when this man died, quickly!"

He picked up a wrist, thumb-nailed his chin, shook his head. "No rigor mortis, yet, although I think it's beginning. If he's as healthy as he looks, that means he died somewhere around twenty-four hours ago. I'll see. At any rate, we'll have to wait for the stiffening."

"My God," I said. "There's a million other ways to tell!"

"Not in this wilderness, there isn't—with the apparatus I've got. It won't be long, though, and it's sure."

"Within what limits can you fix the time?"

"Oh—an hour or two."

"All right. Let me go through the pockets."

I searched the old man's body, quickly, put everything on the desk, then got out of the doctor's way while I examined my take. Among other things was confirmation of the old devil's wise-money bet on the tree-growing business. There was an envelope addressed to a well-known New York stockbroker. It had been sealed for mailing, but had been ripped open again. I guessed that this was the killer's work—making sure the letter contained nothing to incriminate him. Inside the envelope was a letter and a beautifully scarlet maple leaf. The letter read to the effect that enclosed was the first proof of the winning of the bet, and that further, conclusive proof would be shown the stockbroker when he arrived on a visit which had evidently been arranged for the following week.

There was, as well, a gold fountain pen and pencil; a thin platinum watch still ticking; a leather address book; a cigar case of some white metal, presumably platinum, initialed; various letters, concerning obscure and irrelevant business; two handkerchiefs, linen, also initialed.

That was all.

CHAPTER EIGHT

THE TIME EQUATION

THE DOCTOR'S voice startled me just about the time I had run through the pile. "Look—it's coming on now—the rigor," he said. "We'll just have a few minutes to wait. What's the motive—or do you know?"

"There's so damned many possible ones I'm nearly bugs trying to figure it out," I said. "There was a bronze strong box stolen, among other things." I hesitated, tight-lipped, looked down at the corpse. "I can't do anything till I know when he died. I might as well give you what they told me, while he's stiffening."

"What who told you—you mean the family?"

"Yes, and the servants, and this Bliss and McLintock, a couple of railroad—"

"Parker Bliss and Henry McLintock? Are they here?"

"Why?"

"Lord, they're big men! They own the Florida and Eastern Rail-road—that's the biggest rival of Gardner Lyon's Coastal Rail—say, maybe there's something there, Blue. I've heard rumors of some pretty keen rivalry—"

"My God! You're telling me? That's the heart and soul of this whole ugly mess. It seems those two railroads have been fighting each other to get the business of the Amalgamated Citrus Shipping Company—"

"Shippers—not Shipping Company."

I frowned. "How do you know all this?"

"I play the market a little, and I watch the news. This Amalgamated Shippers is listed on the curb. It's gone up in the past year from around a hundred to about six hundred; it's been a sensation. They seem to have been coining money. Maybe that's how—if those railroads have been price-cutting on freight rates. You hear anything about price-cutting on freight—"

"That's right," I said, and hesitated. Something I couldn't quite understand made me say: "Listen—do you mean to say that this Amalgamated outfit is owned by the public—not by any one man or group of men?"

"Hell, it's not owned by the public. Over ninety percent is owned by the man that started it—a fellow named Tripler. The remaining ten percent is owned by the public; it's that ten percent that's traded back and forth on the curb. The big fellows don't speculate; they just sit on what they've got for years. So Gardner Lyon was beating Bliss and McLintock, was he?"

"The hell he was! It was the other way round. Gardner Lyon was ruined—or at least that's what I heard. Did you hear different?"

"No, no! I just assumed—well, the fact that Gardner Lyon was killed, and those others here made me think naturally that he might have had them in a corner, and they killed him to get out of it. Of course, if it's the other way, then they haven't any motive at all, have they?"

"I'm no mind reader," I said. "But if they haven't there are plenty of others about who have." And I told him the whole set-up as well as I knew it.

"God," Pitkin said in a hoarse voice when I'd finished. "How are you ever going to pick out the right one? They all had reason... Listen, though—who had the opportunity of getting to him at the time he was... oh, now I see why you're so anxious for the time of death. But say—how about those other two bodies—aren't you going to try and find out who did..."

"The people in this house aren't natural murderers—this isn't a gangster's family," I said. "They're solid people. It seems almost incredible that even one of them could have cracked—gotten to the point of murder. It's impossible that more than one of them could have. At least I'm gambling that way. One person killed Gardner Lyon, the native boy, and Gardner, Junior—he's the one in the broom closet." I looked anxiously again at the body on the floor. "Isn't he stiff yet?"

After a second, "Not yet. Coming, though."

I SAID: "All right then, here's all the things that happened last night from ten o'clock on, as far as they've admitted them.

"From ten to ten thirty, there was a family conference in the library. From ten thirty to around eleven, Bliss and McLintock were here in this office with the old man. Murray Douglass was here, for a short while, at quarter past eleven. Gardner, Junior was here at around twenty-five past eleven.

"Paul came up just before midnight and stayed till after one. Sometime during that time he and the old man went downstairs to get some sandwiches and milk. The old man was planning to lock himself in behind those steel doors down the hall. He was going to work all night—I don't know what on. Apparently that wasn't unusual. He'd work all night, and then sleep all day.

"Paul left around one thirty, to drive to Trumbull Junction for me. Bliss claims that someone entered his room and knocked him unconscious at three o'clock. One of the native boys told me that he and two of the others saw a dark figure slipping through the woods, and entering the back door of the house just around three o'clock.

"I've got no actual proof of any of the things that happened after midnight, except that Paul took off in the motorboat and was away from the island at one thirty. Both the boatman and the chauffeur, who I peg for square lads, vouch for that. So you can see how damned important it is that you get the time exact."

The bald-headed doctor looked haggard. "By God, Blue—do you suppose this thing was planned—a long time ahead? Of all the tangled-up businesses I ever—"

I shrugged. "I think the one that did the murder had been meaning to do it for a long time, if that's what you mean," I said. "I think the plans were probably hurried up when such a golden opportunity appeared. There's a flock of possible suspects, at least ten. Although, personally, I leave the servants out of it. I don't think they'd do such a thing."

He passed a hand over his bald head, shook it from side to side. He still had one of the old man's hands in his, was kneeling on one knee. He looked up suddenly. "You said something about a bronze box. When did it disappear?"

"Paul says it was on that desk when he and the old man went down for sandwiches and milk—sometime between twelve and one. Paul didn't come past the steel doors when they came up, so he couldn't say after that. The old man closed the doors in his face."

Pitkin blinked. "What was in the bronze box? Does anybody know?"

And then—like the turning on of an electric light—an idea burst in my head. Gardner Lyon—the sure-thing gambler! Something was in that box that meant ruin to Bliss and McLintock! And something was in that box that had everybody that had seen it crazy for possession of it! I stammered. "Wait—wait—" while I tried to arrange the flood of questions and reason that was swamping me.

"Listen—" I flung at Pitkin. "Let me see that address book."

He handed it to me. In a second I was staring at the name I thought I had noticed on first inspection. It was Tripler. And underneath it had been penciled, "Pri. Phone… Long Beach 5746."

My eyes were nearly falling out; I turned on Pitkin, whipped at him: "Listen—you said a man named Tripler owns ninety percent of the stock in the Amalgamated Citrus Shippers. How do you know he does?"

"Why… why… well, to be literal, I don't—nobody actually knows. There was an article in a financial paper saying his name appeared on the registry as owning it. That's how I—"

"Wait—you mean the stock is registered in the company's books as belonging to him?"

"Yes."

"Well, my God—then it must belong to him, mustn't it?"

"No. You see a stock certificate is like a check. If I make out a check to you, then it appears in my check book with your name on—I mean on my stub. However, you might endorse it on the back and give it to your tailor, say. Then it belongs to him, and he owns the money it represents. Tripler had the stock issued to him in the first place, but there's no way of telling whether he endorsed it, and gave the certificates to somebody else."

I STOOD there, with my mouth open, literally dumbfounded. The sure-thing gambler! I was too excited to speak.

Pitkin's forehead wrinkled. "I don't see what you're driving at, yet—"

"Listen—" I could hardly get it out. "Tell me—tell me if this is possible—just possible, is all I want to know.

"Gardner Lyon determined to put his rivals out of business—to break them. He gets this man Tripler—who is really his undercover man, sort of, understand? He supplies Tripler secretly with funds to go out and organize this Amalgamated Citrus Shippers, make contracts with all the growers of citrus fruits—guarantee to sell their entire output for them, for two years ahead. They'd jump at the chance for sure money. Then—when he's got them all tied up—he starts this price-cutting on freight rates with Bliss and McLintock. Both railroads lose money right and left. But for every dollar Gardner Lyon loses on his road, he makes two on this Amalgamated Citrus Company, which he actually owns!

"Everybody thought Bliss and McLintock had him lashed to the mast. They didn't! Everybody thought he'd been losing money. He hadn't! He'd deliberately made everybody think that! He'd even gone through with this farce about needing this last three million's trust money—just to carry out the deception! He'd milked Bliss and McLintock dry—and he was in position to take their railroad away from them.

"I'll tell you what was in that bronze box—the endorsed certificates of the Amalgamated Citrus Shippers stock that was supposed to belong to Tripler. Tripler was Gardner Lyon's man of straw—his front man—his dummy! My God—do you see it?"

There was not a drop of color in Pitkin's face. His mouth hung open. "My God—he—oh, this is sensational! Blue—that stock—that stock do you know what it's worth? And it's negotiable! The person that has it can cash it in—just like money!"

"What's it worth?"

"So many millions that I wouldn't dare guess—maybe thirty or more! Oh, more—yes, more than that... I see it now—I see what happened! Lyon invited Bliss and McLintock out here to gloat over them! They thought he was going to surrender. He pretended he was, up till the last minute—and then he opened his bronze box and showed them what was there. They realized that so far from being out of money, he had enough to swamp them ten times over. They faced ruin—and they killed him and stole the box! By God, we've got him—got them, I mean! They're the ones—" He jerked to his feet. "Get handcuffs on them. Here—" He struggled with an ancient pair of bottle-neck twisters, but I slashed a hand at him.

"Cool down! That only adds them to the list. Don't forget—Gardner Lyon, Junior might well have known what was in that box. He came up here to demand money from the old man—and he came up with a gun. The old man may have shown the stock to him to pacify him—to assure him that he would be able to give him money in a day or two. Then Murray Douglass was up here. He could have walked in on the old man and caught sight of the stock certificates. And Paul Lyon was his secretary. And—any one of the ones that knew, might have told the others." I hesitated. "It's enough to drive any man silly—that much money in one little box!"

"How—then how are we going to find out which one of them?" he fairly wept. "How can we ever—"

"Snap out of it!" I rapped at him. "I'll handle this thing. You get back to your knitting—and find out what time that old man was shot!"

He almost tripped himself, whirling round. He got back down on his hunkers, snatched up the dead wrist again and almost shouted, "It's come. Look!" He could not lift the arm from the side. The whole body moved. He dropped it, sprang to his feet, whipped out his watch. He made quick calculations, went back and hastily tamped places on the body. When he got up again, his eyes were like live coals. "What time did you say Paul Lyon left this island?"

"One thirty. That's positive."

"Then we begin! You can scratch his name from the list. This man was killed between two fifteen and three o'clock—or maybe three fifteen to be exact."

"You're figuring on twenty-four hours?"

"A little less. The old man was in splendid condition—perfectly sound and normal. However, it's hot, and that speeds things up just a little."

My eyes were narrow. "I can cross Estelle off, too," I said quickly, "and Gardner, Junior, and the Hondurans. For a while I thought Junior might have done this before he was killed himself—but I don't now. There is only one killer—one rat behind them all."

"It—it's one of four—we've got it down to four—Bliss, McLintock, Sarah Lyon, or Murray Douglass. We can arrest them all! There's enough circumstantial evidence against all of them to give us a legal right, Blue! By God—we'll arrest them all—then we'll have them! Eh?"

I opened my mouth to reply—and gagged on it. Ice suddenly froze in my veins.

From a point outside the house—not far away—the night was suddenly opened by the hoarse, terror-frantic scream of a man. There were words— "Help! Murder! Help! Ahhhhhh!" and the last wordless shriek seemed to be sliced off, as though by a knife!

CHAPTER NINE

THE CORPSE WAS COLD

I FLUNG myself out and down the hall, my heart in my mouth. I had my gun out of its sheath when I hit the second floor. I literally threw myself around the banister, fell halfway down, and crashed to a carpeted floor in the ground-floor hall. But I was up and sprinting wildly down the hall toward the front in a flash. I burst through the living room. The crowd had gathered at the door, were hurrying out to the veranda. I roared, "Back—back inside—all of you!" and hurled myself through them.

As I did, someone screamed hysterically in my ear, "Down there—down by the boathouse!" and I rocketed down the steps, my flash shooting quick dancing beams ahead as I raced.

Behind me, Pitkin's thin voice called: "Wait—Blue—wait for me!" The little doctor had spunk, at that. But I couldn't wait.

I pushed pine needles wildly under my feet, desperately shooting the flash around. I roared vainly, "This is Blue—where are you?" and the silence was agonizing.

And then I saw him.

A dark huddled figure, crumpled in a heap, ten yards to the left of the path, in a tiny clump of woods. I shouted, "Doc—this way!" and ploughed my way like a maniac through the pines, dropped to one knee by the prone figure, turned him over. It was McLintock. His eyes were closed. He was white as a sheet. From his scalp, blood was flowing down over his face. I grabbed for his pulse—and thanksgiving flooded me. His heart was beating strongly.

Behind me, there was the sound of crashing. Pitkin's voice called, "Blue—where are you?" and I swung the flash around to light him in.

"Hurry up! This man's badly hurt!"

He was at my side in a second. In half a minute, he said: "He's not badly hurt. Just stunned. He's had a blow on the head—but it was a glancing one and cut the scalp. Get him up to the house."

I bent, and swung McLintock over my shoulder as if he had been a bag of meal, charged through the brush. I burst through into the path, my face stinging, and we hurried back to the house.

I snapped at the distracted doctor, "The library!" and as we pounded up the steps and back through the living room, the ghastly-faced crowd of people literally flew out of our way. The little medico ran ahead, opened the door, and I found the couch in the dark, dumped my burden then turned on the lights. "Get him round—in a hurry!"

It took him four minutes to draw a groan from the unconscious man. McLintock's eyes opened dazedly; he tried to squirm, blurting, "No—don't—I'll..." and just then he realized where he was. His eyes cleared; there was a sucking sound from his throat, and he seemed to shrink. There was fear in his eyes when he saw me.

"All right," I said. "What happened?"

"I—I don't know. I was just walking around, trying to think. Somebody jumped out at me from the dark—hit me—and I..." He put a hand to his head, got blood on it, gasped, started to shout in panic, "Doc—Doc—what—am I—" He struggled to sit up.

"You're all right," Pitkin cut at him. "And you're lying! Blue, he's lying! Make him tell—"

"Hell with that!" I clipped. "Can he get out to the living room with the rest of them?"

"Certainly, but—"

I swung on McLintock. "Outside—fast!"

Pitkin said, "Wait!" and made a quick job with gauze and sticking plaster. "All right—go out to the living room."

McLintock avoided my eye as he staggered up, and obeyed. Pitkin looked at me nervously, anxiously, "What—what are you going to do?"

I said grimly, as I strode after McLintock : "Find that damned box."

PANIC and hysteria were in the air of that living room now, definitely. Everyone there was white as a sheet. Eyes stared at me in pure, dumb terror, as I strode taut-faced through the group that had gathered round the library door.

When I was free of the crowd, I turned and looked at them with flint in my eyes as I backed the few steps to the end of the room. It was the same crowd that had come together earlier, with the exception of Gardner, Junior and the addition of Hayes and Ellton. There was no grouping together now, though. They seemed frozen where they stood, not wanting to make the effort to move around. Just as I stopped—in front of the fireplace again—Paul came in from the dining room, closing the door behind him. He, too, looked at me anxiously, fidgeted, then stayed where he was.

McLintock, evidently thinking his wound rated it, had limped over to an easy chair on the left of the room, directly in front of Paul, close to one of the French windows. And—my eyes narrowed as I saw that the light switch was just over his head. I waited, my hand in my coat pocket gripped hard on the butt of my gun, my lips compressed, till all movement ceased. Then I told them, "Those of you who don't know it—I am sorry to have to tell you—Mr. Gardner Lyon, Junior has been stabbed—by the same skulking rat that shot Gardner Lyon, Senior, and beat in the head of that poor devil, José."

Before the shock of that could really get them, I went on. "And I think I know who it is—which one of you it is."

I let that lie on the air a second, swept their faces. I was tense, on the balls of my feet, almost crouched, my gun pointed upward through the cloth of my pocket—and they all were staring at it, wild-eyed.

"First of all," I said, "most of you know, by now, that Mr. Gardner Lyon, Senior, so far from being defeated in his battle with Mr. Bliss and Mr. McLintock, had them absolutely backed into the corner. The way he did it—for those of you that don't know—was by being the owner of the Amalgamated Citrus Shippers—the company that was profiting to a fabulous amount, by the price-cutting war between the two railroads. The stock certificates, the possession of which mean practical ownership of that company to whoever has them—were in the bronze dispatch box that was stolen from the study upstairs!"

If I needed any confirmation that the one I was after was a finished actor, I got it now. Every face in that room was dazed, incredulous, at the announcement—even though I knew that at least three of them must know all about it.

"My opinion is that the person who killed Gardner, Senior was carrying out a long-laid plan. Not in detail—I don't think the plan could have been made in detail, more than a few days beforehand. Just the plan to kill. When news of this fabulous convention of a dozen of you that might have reason to do the old man to death was circulated, then I think the details were planned. Yet, even then, I don't see how the contents of the bronze dispatch box could have been known. I think the killer learned about that sometime last night. But—the killer was not the only one who learned it.

"Now, I'll tell you some of the things that happened last night—and tonight, too. Paul went up to Mr. Lyon's study just before midnight. He left the old man just before one thirty." I looked over at Paul. His eyes were anxious. He stood with his hands behind his back. "Is that right?"

HE LICKED his lips. "Yes." Then he hesitated. "If you don't mind, I don't care to say any more, till I see my lawyer."

"Forget that," I said. "You're not under arrest any more. The sheriff has determined that your father died between two fifteen and three fifteen, and your alibi has been checked. I've got to have answers to my questions, if I'm going to get anywhere."

"All—right," he said faintly. I turned back.

"Sometime between twelve o'clock and one thirty-five, Paul and Mr. Lyon were out of the third-floor apartment together. They went downstairs. It was while they were downstairs that some other person went upstairs and stole that box! For a minute, I'm going to call that person the stealer.

"All right. The stealer got the box. Unfortunately, in one way or another, he was overheard by still another individual—the hijacker. I am sorry I have to use these terms—that I can't come right out and say the names that I have in mind—but I don't care to invite lawsuits, in case I am wrong. Anyway—to get on.

"The hijacker got the box away from the stealer. Of that I am sure. What I am not sure of is this—how many of the rest of you also entered this picture? How many of you succeeded in finding out exactly what had happened to the box, and who had it? And did you, any of you, or how many of you, in turn, get your own hands on the box, and—who ended up with it at three o'clock?

"The box was stolen between twelve and one, roughly. Between then and three o'clock—I'll tell you why I say three o'clock in a minute—there must have been a terrible battle going on in this house for that box. Now, here is something else—I am almost positive that the one who killed Mr. Lyon, was actually standing beside the dead body of his victim before he realized that the box was gone. Obviously, he too would be driven to plunge into the fight to regain possession of his spoils.

"Now—here is why I say three o'clock: because I think the person who ended up with that box in their possession around three o'clock was smart enough to get it out of the house and hide it in the woods.

And—three of the native boys saw somebody come out of the woods and slip in the back door of the house, at fifteen minutes after three." I hesitated, clamping my jaws. "There is also another angle.

"We do not know exactly what time José was killed. It appears that he was at work in the power house from early evening, till the time he was killed. My idea is that he saw or heard somebody doing something suspicious out back of the house, and that he went over to investigate. He was killed for his pains and his body thrown in the lake.

"Also, Mr. Bliss was attacked in his room around three o'clock.

"I'll jump, now, from last night at three o'clock, till tonight at the time I got here. Shortly after I arrived, I found the keys to that box—a vital necessity to whoever had the box—or hoped to have it. I haven't told you this, but I've since had two vicious attacks made on me, to get those keys. The first attack was the work of a bungler. He wasn't experienced enough to kill me deliberately and he was so damned careless that he almost did it accidentally. The second attempt was a clever performance, and was done by a clever person—but one that didn't want to make any noise. The second attempt was successful.

"Now—the keys should be on the person of somebody in this room—and I believe that I can prove that after all the fighting, they are in the possession of the killer himself—or herself! I am going to conduct a search of everybody in this room, for those keys! Has anybody any objection?"

For one minute, there was dead, breathless silence. I took one step forward. Then—the sensation.

ESTELLE LYON'S little blond figure was suddenly out in front of the crowd. Her face was like a lined mask. Her arms were folded in front of her, and, "I'll save you the trouble," she said almost hysterically. "You'll never find the keys! I threw them in the lake—and the box too. I killed father. I killed José, too—and—"

"Stop! Stop it—you little fool!" Douglass's voice roared shrilly. The lawyer's big figure dived from the crowd, snatched the little blond Estelle close to him, smothering her mouth. "That's a lie, Blue—a lie—you know it's a lie! I'll admit everything—I did it—did them all—only don't, for God's sake, pay any attention to this child. You hear me—I'll confess—in private! Aunt Sarah—take her to her room—quickly—please!"

I clipped harshly: "Stand where you are—everybody! And if you damned moving-picture heroes will quit this time-wasting, maybe we'll get somewhere. Neither of you two did it. You must have a high opinion of each other, I must say—both of you suspecting the other of a thing as rotten as this. No—the rat behind this—behind all this—is a blood relative of Gardner Lyon, and the possession of those keys will definitely prove the one point I need. Now, stand back, please."

And then, so quietly and calmly that I almost didn't hear it, Sarah Lyon's harsh, husky voice croaked: "You won't find the keys, Mr. Blue. By some crazy coincidence, the child hit one thing right. The keys—and the box—are in the lake."

Her face seemed to have aged fifteen years in a minute. She stood there, her hands folded in front of her, her eyes with the light of madness in them, as she made her confession. "You call me a rat—maybe you're right. Yet you'll never know the full story. I killed my brother, yes. I had to kill the native boy. And Gardner, Junior threatened to expose me. But the box—I didn't want the box—didn't want the taint of the money on me. I'm willing to take my medicine, but I'm not—a rat—Mr. Blue. I—"

"That'll be enough of that," I said. "And if any of the rest of you plan to make phony confessions to shield some…"

And then Paul Lyon, triple killer and thief and amateur criminal with the cunning of the cleverest professional that ever walked—Paul Lyon outguessed me at the last ditch. His timing was perfect; his move the one thing I hadn't thought of.

One hand came from behind him; his eyes were on mine—blank, uncomprehending. He seemed to grope out toward McLintock's chair in front of him—then, with the speed of lightning, his other hand whipped up and over, and he dived for the light switch.

I shot him in the shoulder. It would have been his heart, but I was trying to duck the flashing arc of liquid; I flung him back—and the fiery shower of ammonia slapped me across the face. Literal hell dug into my face—my eyes—my nostrils! My gun roared again, but white-hot fingers were clawing at my eyeballs; my bullet smashed glass in a French door—and then the lights clicked out, and feet shot across the veranda, as I groped in a frantic, burning black world.

I dived blindly for the door. I dug a coat sleeve frantically across my face; I couldn't keep back the groan. I banged into the wall. Estelle was shrieking, now in hysterics. Everybody was shouting in high-pitched voices. I finally clawed my way to the door, stumbled out, tears streaming down my face. I grabbed where I thought the banister of the stairs was, missed, and went hurtling down the steps, thumped onto the path, on my side. I could hear feet crunching furiously far down the path.

I jerked myself up, went weaving, banging against trees, as I raced after. I hit my third tree, just as Paul's feet clumped in staccato far ahead across the dock, and I heard him leap into the motor boat. I was beginning to be able to see light through blurring tears. I made a furious effort, as I heard the motor of the launch suddenly roar, and as I flung onto the dock, I could vaguely see the long dark blur of it shooting away from the end of the pier. I let flame roar from my gun—twice, blindly—then from the stern of the boat there was a stabbing flame of orange, and something white-hot slammed into my shoulder, flung me off balance, and I crashed down. And then, suddenly, I could see again. I jerked to one knee, roared, "Stop—you haven't got a chance!" I gave him one split-second, and then, as other feet pounded on the dock behind me—I gave it to him—everything I had left in the clip.

He was standing erect, trying to fire again at me. My first slug jerked his head right back, slammed him against the steering wheel; he spun as the lead poured into him, then suddenly his knees gave way, and he flopped—to the left—and the gunwale of the craft caught him across the waist. It doubled him up like a jacknife, and there he hung, with the boat making thirty-five knots an hour.

Screams were still coming from the house. Pitkin's hoarse voice blurted behind me: "God in Heaven, Blue—you've killed him. He couldn't have been the right one! He couldn't have I tell you!"

My eyes were glued on the boat—it was beginning to go into a slow curve—a wide slow curve, its engine spluttering, racing. I jerked around for a second, to see Bliss and McLintock behind the doctor. Then as I swung back, I said: "He was the right one, all right. Look— he's curving—he'll hit the island at the back. We've got to be there to catch him—or we'll lose what he's got in his pockets. Come on—back around the house!"

I led the three of them in a race to the spot where the native boy's blanket-covered body still lay. I shouted, "Ramon—Carlos—and the other!" as we ran. By the time I stopped at the side of the pine tree out back, the three of them were milling around us. Estelle's screams had ceased inside. Pitkin was saying hoarsely in my ear: "How, in

God's name, could he have done it? He wasn't even on the island at two fifteen. You proved that yours…"

I clipped at him over my shoulder, "Gardner Lyon, Senior wasn't killed after two fifteen."

"What! You're crazy! I, myself—"

"You drew your conclusions from the rigor mortis. All right. Paul knew that up here in the wilderness, you'd have to draw your conclusions from that. You told me that heat speeds up the rigor. By the same token, wouldn't cold slow it down—delay it?"

"Yes, but that's absurd. The weather hasn't changed… My God, to delay it two hours, the body would have to be frozen—frozen stiff—"

"That's exactly what it was," I clipped. "It was frozen in the little room in the commissary where they freeze game for shipping. Paul Lyon killed his father shortly after twelve o'clock. He wrapped the body in a rug, took it down to the freezing room, and left it there for nearly an hour, in sub-zero temperature. Naturally, it delayed the rigor for about two hours. Or am I still crazy?"

His mouth hung open.

"Well?" I snapped.

"By God!" he said. "By God—it could be done. The body lying there in that warm air, would thaw out in about ten or twelve hours, and—there would be nothing to show it had been frozen. I think you've stumbled on it, Blue—by God, I do—"

"Stumbled!" I snarled at him. "Why, you two-bit—look—here she comes! I'll tell you the rest in a minute," I said hurriedly, as the launch, sixty yards out, was slowly arcing in. I called to the native boys, "Down about here," and we all shifted fifteen yards toward the tip of the island—the heel.

Then the boat was rushing at us. Paul's body, still swayed grotesquely over the gunwale.

It crashed head-on into the ledge of rock, and I jumped in, lost my footing, and fell. But we landed the boat.

CHAPTER TEN

A STUDY IN SCARLET

TEN MINUTES later I faced Bliss, McLintock and the bald-headed Pitkin.

The sheriff held in his hands, as though they were holy, the thick bundles of certificates I had taken from Paul's pockets—the Citrus Shippers stock.

The empty box, its key still in its lock, we had found out in the woods, thirty yards from where the last attack had been made on McLintock.

Evidently the announcement I had made, prior to the recent gathering in the living room, to the effect that they would be able to leave the island right after the meeting, had had its natural effect. The one who had hidden the box away—obviously McLintock—had gone to retrieve it, so as to have it ready to take away with him. And Paul—evidently still suspicious—had been right on his heels, had attacked him and taken the box. Being by now in possession of the keys that had been taken from me, Paul had simply unlocked the box, pocketed the contents, and thrown the box away. But—I didn't tell that to the sheriff.

The uncomfortable thought had suddenly struck me—that the case was over, the killer found, the plunder retrieved, but—my client was dead. I'd done a lot of work, taken a lot of punishment, and now, unless I moved—and moved fast—I was going to be left out in the cold. And—the idea bloomed suddenly—Bliss and McLintock, the two chiselers, were in no position to refuse me anything if I played my cards right. As for the sheriff—I could tell him anything and he'd believe it. He had his killer. If I wanted to forget some of the supplementary skulduggery that had been going on, that wouldn't be hard. So I told him enough of the truth to satisfy him.

"Paul Lyon originally planned to kill the old man because he hated him. Then when he found out last night about the bronze box, he simply added that to his original plans. He waited till everyone had finished their business with the old man, then went up and held a gun on him, tried to force him to give up the keys to the box. The old man, rather than give them up, suddenly threw them out the window.

Paul shot him, but he didn't realize at that time that the keys might not have reached the water—might have lodged in that pine tree. However, that's incidental.

"As soon as he had killed the old man—remember, those rooms are soundproof—he wrapped him in a rug, got him downstairs, and into the freezing room, and froze him. Meanwhile, he had been seen by José—so he killed José."

I hesitated. That much was truth. Now I mixed it up a little. "Then he went back upstairs, laid the body on the floor where we found it, took the box, and went out, closing the steel doors behind him. He had to leave the island right away, in order to establish his alibi, so he hid the box somewhere, and got on the boat for the mainland."

Here, I went back to the truth again. "While he was away—or maybe he had planned it all along—he realized that if Gardner, Junior were dead, the whole estate would go to Sarah Lyon. Then, instead of walking off with his plunder, he could pretend to recover it. It would become part of the estate and go to Sarah Lyon. That was why he killed Gardner, Junior."

"Wait—wait," Pitkin interrupted. "What good would it do him to have Sarah Lyon get it?"

I HESITATED. "I have a hunch that Sarah Lyon would do anything her—anything Paul told her to."

Then, somehow, I felt suddenly very sorry for the old lady. That she was the one that had blackjacked me outside the library window where I listened to the conversation between Paul and McLintock, was certain. I had heard the rustle of her dress. And she had had to hit me twice to get me out. Once would have been enough if a man were behind it. Yet—I couldn't seem to want to make any more trouble for her, so I covered her.

"He didn't, however, ask her to do anything she shouldn't—I mean she had no connection with this whole mess. Up till the last minute—there in the living room, I don't think she knew what it was all about—and then, when she finally realized that I knew it was Paul, she tried to protect him, by sacrificing herself."

"But why? Why should she do that?" Pitkin said blankly.

"Well, I'm not sure—and I wouldn't want to be, because it doesn't matter—but—I think that Paul Lyon was Sarah Lyon's son. Remember, she lived for years abroad when nobody knew what she was doing. She was married for three months. And when she did come back over here, the first thing she did was to talk the old man into adopting two more children. I think one of them was her own son. The second one was just to avoid it's being too suspicious. However, that's only speculation, and means nothing. Just say they were fond of each other and let it go at that. You've got your killer—and that's the main thing. If you want, I'll help you make out your report."

"Say—that's right—my report! By George, Blue—"

"O.K. I'll see you up in the study, in about five minutes."

"Eh?"

"I'd like to speak to Mr. Bliss and Mr. McLintock for a minute, if you don't mind."

He wavered, finally said, "Well, all right," and went back into the house.

I said to the two railroad owners: "I hope you don't think I go for that hooey about Paul hiding the box before he left the island."

I could hear them breathing. Bliss said quietly, "No?"

"No. What actually happened was that someone did go up, while Paul was down freezing the body, and take the box. That someone took the box downstairs, waited till the house quieted down, then made an ineffectual attempt to open it. All he succeeded in doing was making enough noise to rouse another certain individual. That individual made a shrewd guess as to what was going on, waited a little while longer, and went in and crowned the first person, and hijacked the box. Then this man ducked outside and hid the box in the woods.

"I might add that it was that second man that slugged me down by the boathouse later on, trying to get the keys from me."

I HESITATED again. "Both the two that I'm speaking about, could, if anyone wanted to take the trouble, be hauled up on felony charges—the first one for theft, the second for criminal assault on my well-known person. I wanted to ask you gentlemen's advice. Should I point all this out to the sheriff and have him arrest the guilty pair? Or is it worthwhile? After all, everything is pretty well cleared up. It could, I suppose, just be forgotten, and nobody would suffer much. You see, that's one of the difficulties of not having a client."

They spoke together. "What?"

"I have no client," I said. "My client was dead when I arrived. Usually, I can ask my client what he wants done about certain things, and—well, it's a rule of my agency to always respect the client's wishes if humanly possible. After all—my client is the one that pays for my work. Only—I have no client now. See what I mean?"

There was a minute of pregnant silence. Then McLintock growled: "How much?"

I said: "I don't know what you're talking about."

He blew breath through his lips. "The Florida and Eastern Railway wants to retain you on this case. How much is your fee?"

"It will be high—very high," I said. "I'll let you know later—in plenty of time to take care of it before the sheriff's report goes in. Now, if you'll excuse me—"

"Wait—just a minute." Bliss's tone was interested. "Do you mind telling me how you figured out that freezing business?" I opened my mouth—then closed it again. What to tell them? The truth? No, I decided against that. They might figure that they could have thought it out that way, themselves. So I babbled.

"It's impossible to explain. When you're used to this work, you just feel the right thing instinctively. You read a lot about clues solving crimes—it's pure fancy. Only once in a blue moon is there a clue. I don't say that every investigator has it—that ability to feel the right thing. I just felt that Paul was guilty, the minute I discovered the death of the old man. And from then on it was a question of proving it. I'm sorry I can't explain it better, but—well, there it is."

There was another moment of silence. Bliss said finally: "Have you got a couple of your business cards handy, Blue? Never can tell when something'll come up. I don't mind saying, you seem to know your business."

I mentally patted myself on the back. I'd guessed right. Men like that appreciate something they don't understand. I gave them the cards, and went inside.

If I'd told them the actual truth—that I'd found the scarlet maple leaf in the old man's pocket, inside a letter—that all the other leaves on the tree from which it was taken were still green as they could be—that the only way to change the color of a maple leaf is to freeze it—that a lot of people had told me that there had been no frost this year on the island, and so that leaf must have been inside the only place on the island where it could get frozen—the freezing plant—if I'd told them that, they wouldn't have been impressed at all, probably.

As it was, when I told them the size of the checks they had to write, later, they did it so quickly that I was amazed.

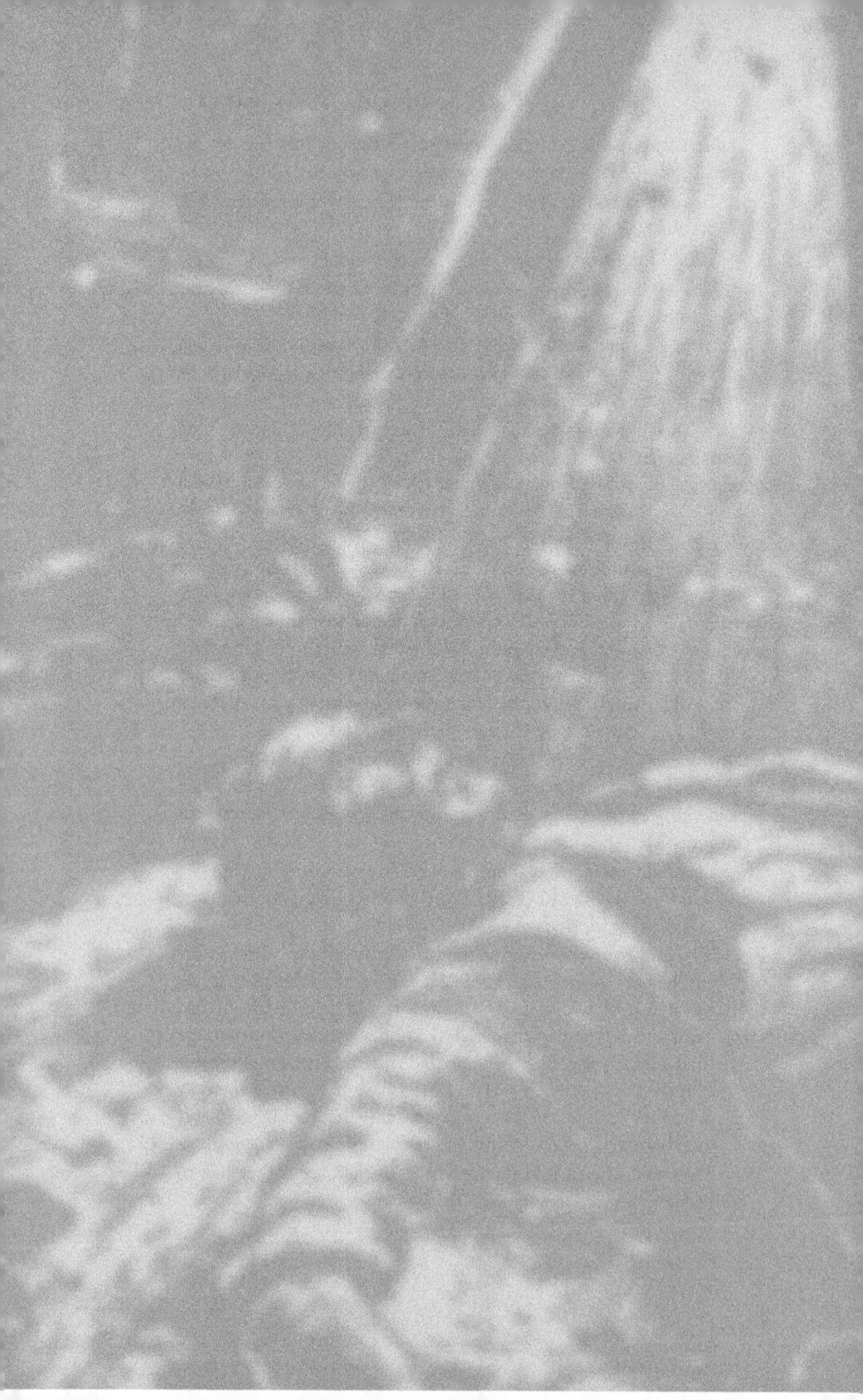

THE CORPSE CONTROL

SILENT THEY SAT AROUND THE SEANCE TABLE IN THAT PITCH-BLACK HORROR-ROOM. AND AS THE MEDIUM, CORPSE CONTROL DRONED HER MESSAGE FROM THE OTHER WORLD, MURDER FLASHED IN THIS—ON THE SHINING BLADE OF A SWORD. IT WAS THEN—AND ONLY THEN—THAT DETECTIVE BLUE GAINED AN INKLING OF THE DOOM SHADOW HOVERING OVER THE HOUSE OF CORPORAL.

CHAPTER ONE

SECONDS TO BURN

I 'D HAD the Devereux job marked down as a joke, months before. I'd almost forgotten it. It stopped being funny, the night I went to Sing Sing.

Not that I realized that what happened was part of that job—I didn't get a chance to realize anything. One minute, I was speeding along through the wet night in Ben Vick's dilapidated roadster; I certainly expected no trouble; at the moment, I thought I was on my way to do a kind act; currently, what few cases I had, had no danger in them, as far as I knew. The next, I was pitched blindly into a frantic, murderous struggle, without the slightest idea of what it was all about; by the time I finally did struggle up for air and got myself sorted out, I was almost convinced I was living in a nightmare.

It was exactly twenty-one minutes to eleven, when we thundered to the top of the slick gleaming hill, where I could see, a few miles ahead, the fuzzy glow of lights in Ossining. Rain rattled on the roof. Our headlamps were bobbing, shining pencils. Oil fumes were coming through the floorboards to mix with the hot, damp air, and with that, and Vick's whining, unending stream of questions, I felt low. As we dipped down into the black hollow, his fat face took on an expression of anguish, and I winced. He'd gotten to the point where he was groaning them out hoarsely now. "Pal—" he said desperately. "For the love of Allah. We're almost in. You don't mean to sit there and tell me nothin'—after all I've done—"

I couldn't convince him that I knew exactly what he did, and no more, about our current trip. Jack Granite, a burglar I knew, was scheduled to burn tonight for killing an actor named Steed. For some reason that was Greek to me, Granite had decided at the eleventh hour he wanted to talk to me. The cops had put it out on the radio, trying to locate me. For my sins, Vick had known where I was. He made a living snapping photos of folks and places, later to be sold to newspapers, and evidently smelt business in these doings. He had stampeded me into letting him drive me out, and had never let up on me since.

"For God's sake," I said wearily, "give me a break and lay off."

"Yeah," he nodded sarcastically. "Yeah. There you are. My pal. A mystery—maybe an A-number-one mystery, where a guy could line up a few bucks on pix, and you give me the run-around. After all I've done—"

I passed a hand over my face. "That takes the cake. My God— what's the mystery?"

"Oh," he said elaborately, "there's no mystery for you. You know what's what. But if you think I think it's perfectly natural

A cloud of wasps swarmed
out over his corpse.

when a big-time professional like Granite prowls a flat that belongs to a broken-down ham like Steed, who hasn't had a part to hiss in for over a year! And there's nothin' funny about Granite, a smarty that never packed a gun, shooting Steed to death when the actor broke in on him. And stealing nothing."

"There was nothing to steal, you dimwit. The shooting was an accident. Steed pulled the gun and started blazing away. Granite tried to take it away from him, and killed him in the fuss."

"And it was another accident when he tried to shoot it out with Lieutenant Bruckman when Bruckman ran into him outside the building, I suppose?"

"What the hell? Granite knew he was cooked. He was committing a crime when Steed went down. Naturally, he tried to smoke his way clear."

"That still doesn't explain why Granite prowled the flat in the first place—much less why Steed put on the fireworks when he had nothing to lose anyway. You want me to explain it? All right. I say the copper— Bruckman—has got the right idea. Granite did steal something— something tricky—and had a chance to hide it before he was shot down. Bruckman's been spending most of his sick leave at the prison, trying to get Granite to come across. Now—when he's lying in the dance hall, he decides to get hold of you and give you the break. And o' course, he just got your name out of a phone book."

"You ought to write movies," I said wearily. "I've known Granite for years—in a business way. He probably wants me to take a message to his folks."

"Furthermore"—he ignored me—"this Granite is on the bottom of some job you're working on—and he wants to cough before he fries. Now, go on—call me a liar."

"All right, you liar," I said dully, as we roared up the other side of the hill, topped the rise, and settled down to eat up the patch of black gloom that lay between us and Ossining. "In the first place, I haven't got a job open that amounts to a tinker's damn—certainly nothing that would interest Granite. In the second—"

We didn't get as far as the second. The rear window exploded behind my head, showered me with glass. The bullet ploughed upward into the wooden top with a ripping, cracking sound. If I hadn't been slumped deep in the seat, it would have slapped my brains all over the upholstery.

IN THE split second between the first bullet and the second, as I flung myself wildly over against the outside of the car, I don't mind saying that I had it up in my throat. Vick squealed, "Shooting! Somebody's shooting at us!" I jerked myself together. The second bullet came through the open back window and dissolved the windshield in a frantic clatter. I had one hand dragging at the gun under my arm; the other was spinning the handle on the side window furiously. The third shot from behind rang metal at the back of the car.

Vick started zig-zagging the car; it was suicide at the rate we were pounding along. I roared, "Hold it straight, you damn fool! You'll put us in the dit—" and he cut me off with a wild yelp—"Look—a side road! I'll swing down and shake them! Hold on!"

I grabbed wildly for the wheel. "You'll turn nowhere! Hold it on this road. I'll stand them off, but we haven't got time to go driving!"

Lead was rattling against the back of the coupe, as I got my back to the shattered windshield and snaked an arm through the open side window, and followed it with my head. Orange winked at me from a black hulk fifty yards behind us; the car was running without lights. I fired at the wink, as we shot past the side road.

The black bulk started to swerve, to drop back. A bullet fanned my forehead. I held steady, got a jogging bead on where their driver ought to be, and let two slugs bang.

The third one went into the sky, as our right rear tire exploded. We bounced six inches from the ground; I almost poured out onto the road. Vick wailed; the coupe went skidding wildly, yawing from side to side. I was pitched, jerked; my neck almost cracked like a whip as the car tried to get rid of me. Vick braked in spurts. We whirled round in a complete circle. The tires made a squealing sound. I thought we were going over, but we brought up rocking, my side of the car facing the enemy. I was half silly, but I fumbled desperately for the door handle under my stomach, and as my weight swung it open, I piled down to the wet cement like a ton of brick. I threw myself around to fire at those behind—and I was suddenly scrambling to my feet, gasping, as I saw them roll into the side road we had passed. I fired hastily, half ran after them.

I hit some metal part of the body once before it completely vanished behind the thick row of trees lining the side road.

Rain drenched me, as I stood there cursing. For a full moment, I was absolutely dumbfounded, as I scoured my brain for a reason for the murderous attack. It was not till Vick's plaintive wailing reached me that I thought of the time, and of the fact that unless we reached the prison before execution time, I would never talk to Granite. Somebody was trying to prevent my reaching the condemned man! For the first time, I was suddenly alive to the fact that he must have something to tell me—something of importance. I whirled back and ran for the car, my jaw hard.

Vick was mopping his face over the wheel, looking as though about to cry. "So!" he wailed. "You don't know anything! Just on an errand of mercy! Just going to—"

"Get out!" I ripped. "And get this tire changed! We've got less than twenty minutes to get there! Come on—move!"

"Hell, we haven't a chance now—"

"I'll break your fat neck," I erupted. "We've got to get there! You damn fool—that's what the shooting was for—to stop me from getting there! They must have been waiting in that damned hollow! Where's your tools?"

WE DIDN'T get there. It was ten minutes before we had the shoe changed and were back in the car, racing toward the prison. The clock said five after eleven as we hit the limits of Ossining.

It said eleven minutes after, as we skidded to take the turn into the road to the prison gates, and sent a sheet of water ten feet in the air.

I flung myself from the car as we slid to a stop before the gates, and lit running. Vick had the inspiration to bear down on his horn, till a searchlight beam from the top of the wall slapped into my face and a voice shouted: "Take it easy, there! What do you want?"

I waved a folder of credentials. "Cass Blue—private dick—Jack Granite!"

There was hasty motion behind the gates, and somebody shouted. The gates opened and a guard took a hasty glance at my stuff under a flashlight, as a second guard came running toward us.

"I think you're too late," the first one said. "Jerry—take him to the warden's office!"

We went at a trot. Then we passed close to a brick wall, and the guard slowed, stopped. From behind the wall came the sound of whirring and buzzing; the nerve-tearing song of a saw eating into something solid. The guard shrugged, spread his hands. "You're five minutes late. That's the autopsy."

My stomach sank.

THE ANTEROOM of the warden's office was crowded with men in overcoats; they had white, strained faces, most of them. The witnesses, I figured.

A reporter started squirming toward me eagerly, the minute I came in. He was a rat, a love-nest-heart-balm-torch-murder expert named Zimmerman from one of the tabs. Everybody along Broadway knew him and kept clear of him, but his youthful face and a pair of soft black eyes whose sympathy was as phony as the barbershop tan he always seemed to have, made him hot stuff on hammer murderesses. He looked about twenty—tall, slender, and I never saw him in anything but the double-breasted blue suit and blue silk tie. Apart from a sharp nose, he was a pretty good-looking guy. He'd dynamite a case for you the second he got a breath of it, whether he gave a crook a break or not. I cursed him. "Get the hell away from me. I'm busy."

"Delete that," he said in a low voice. "I'm the guy you're busy with." He swung round to block me and get his back to the room, squinted down at me. "Get this: I saw him for a few minutes before they took him through the brown door."

"So what?"

"Wake up, you chump. I've got a message for you."

"How did you get in here in the first place?"

He waved a court order at me impatiently, shot a look over his shoulder and got out rapidly in a low, clipped voice: "Listen, mastermind: Granite gave me an earful. It don't make sense to me, but it probably means plenty to you. If you want it, you'll do business with me. Tell me what it's all about and I'll give you the message."

"I'm listening," I said.

"Don't be funny. You sketch out the scenario and I'll fill it in. I'll give you my word of honor not to print anything, until you say—"

I put the back of my hand against his chest and waved him back against the wall with a jolt that shook his hair down over his eyes. "Hire a hall. You must think I'm getting simple in my old age."

The door of the warden's office opened and the quiet, subdued, gray-haired man that was the ruler of this hellhole came out.

His face was pinched, his gray eyes haggard, but he was erect, military, poised. He located me, turned his head over his shoulder. The spare, lean Indian-face of Lieutenant Bruckman—the copper who had put Granite where he was—came in sight, and his brown eyes lit on me, too. He said something to the warden, who beckoned to me. "Mr. Blue!"

I said, "Hello, Lieutenant," to Bruckman as I entered the office, and he nodded. I was surprised to see the prison chaplain, in black robes, seated in a chair by the desk.

"I blew out a tire on the way," I said to the warden. "That's why I didn't get here—in time. I can't tell you how much I regret it. I—uh—I don't suppose there's anything I can do now."

The warden cleared his throat, exchanged a glance with the chaplain, then eyed the top of his desk. "The Father wants to see you alone, Mr. Blue. You can use this office."

Bruckman came over and stood beside me, with his hands behind his back. His face was a little pale from the siege he'd put in in the hospital getting rid of Granite's bullets, but his eyes were strong and bright. He said in a husky voice: "This probably doesn't mean much to you, Blue, but I've been made a sucker of, and it's gotten my goat. Play things my way and you'll be riding high, after this is over, as far as anything I can do for you is concerned."

He didn't wait for an answer, went on out after the warden.

I STOOD fingering my hat in front of the white-haired, saintly looking chaplain till he asked me to sit down.

"I've never had anything like this to do before," he said in a worried voice. "I only hope I'm doing right. Granite called me to his cell about five minutes before his time, and asked me to repeat certain things to you—and you exclusively—should you be—too late."

He hesitated, and a shadow passed over his face. "I—I don't pretend to understand it. If you do, and I stumble, correct me where you can. It—it seems to be about some pearls."

Even then, it took me half a second to register. Then I half came out of my seat. "You—I—it wasn't black pearls, was it?"

"Yes. Black pearls."

I sat down again, thunderstruck. This was the first time I had thought of the Devereux case for six months. Black pearls! It was partly because of the unbelievable value put on the jewels the blond actress claimed to have lost, that I had laughed at the job originally. Now—if her claim were true—if the thing were real after all—a fortune that a man could hold in his hand—

He went on hesitantly: "These pearls were to be stolen from a man named Steed—" He seemed to get lost for a moment.

"Granite was executed for killing an actor named Steed," I said quickly. "Did he actually steal these pearls from Steed—and hide them, maybe?"

"No. No. Now I have it—'Corporal.' No, Steed didn't have the pearls after all. Granite tried to force him to reveal their whereabouts. That—that was when Steed drew his revolver—not at the time that was stated at the trial. Then, after the—the terrible thing had happened, Steed gasped out something that sounded like 'Corporal.' You—do you understand?"

"I—I understand what you say, Father, but it doesn't convey anything." Then, as he shook his head sorrowfully, and shrugged, I said anxiously: "That isn't all, is it?"

"I think—yes, I think so. At any rate, I can't recall anything else."

I groaned, got up, sat down again. "Father," I said quickly, "if you will keep confidential what I say, I can tell you something about those pearls that may recall some detail you've forgotten."

He nodded.

"An actress named June Devereux—through her lawyer—retained me several months ago to recover a string of black pearls that, to hear her tell it, were worth a fortune. She not only wouldn't let me check up on the actual theft, but she swore me to secrecy. I put it down as definitely a publicity stunt of some new kind. She wanted me to pass the word around to the thieves I know that I could pay a good-sized reward—and no questions asked—for its return. I did, but I haven't had any response." I looked at him anxiously. "Does that recall anything else Granite might have said?"

"No. I'm afraid not."

"He didn't mention the actress—June Devereux? Or maybe a lawyer named Nanovic?"

"No."

After a second, we got up. "If it's any interest to you, Father, somebody nearly murdered me, in preventing my getting here in time to hear that from Granite," I said, and his eyes went wide.

Outside, I told Bruckman: "On the level, Lieutenant, I've good reason to think that Granite stole nothing from Steed."

When I trotted back out to the prison gate, the guard that had let me in originally relayed the news: "That fat fellow that drove you up said he was going down to the service station to get new glass put in before he drowned. It's about three blocks that way."

CHAPTER TWO

THE GIRL IN RED

PLOWING UP the street, I came abreast of a drugstore. I hesitated a second, then went in and phoned a New York number. The storm was working on the wires, but I finally made the woman that answered—a maid—understand who I wanted. When Nanovic came to the phone, I said: "Something's come up. I want to talk to you and your client as soon as possible."

His voice got excited. "You've located—you've found the man that has Miss Devereux's—"

"I've located a man that did have it, but he's dead. I—"

"My God! Who?"

"An actor named Steed. He was ki—"

"Wait—wait—spell that name!" he said excitedly.

I spelt it out. He was so silent that for a second I thought he'd left the line. I shouted, "Hello! Hello!"

"I'm here," he said hastily. "Listen—how quickly can you get to my office?"

"A couple of hours, or more. If I can catch a train I might do better," I said. "What's biting—"

"Nothing—except that if Steed was in on this, I know who stole it! Get here as fast as you can. You'll have to tackle him—I'm not going to."

"Who?" I shot at him. "Who do I have to—"

"Don't waste a minute," he cut me off, and hung up.

I sailed out of the drugstore with fervor. I had no objection whatever to take a crack at the party that had sprayed me with lead a half hour back.

Something about the Lincoln convertible standing before the drugstore—brand new, in spite of the mud the storm had plastered it with—had a familiar look. I checked myself a minute, frowning at it, could not place it. Not till I was twenty yards west, hiking close to the building fronts, did the old memory begin to function. Then I stopped, cursing.

It belonged to Zimmerman, the wheedling reporter. I looked up and down the street hastily. I was sure he had not been in the drugstore, unless—

I trotted back hastily. Recollection of the unpleasant things my client had said would result from any publicity came into my mind. I winced with the sudden realization that the whole thing was real, after all. If Zimmerman had happened to be in one of the other booths....

I breathed again when I found the drugstore empty, the three booths the same. And as I emerged the second time, I saw the sharp-nosed reporter come around the corner two doors east, sauntering in spite of the rain. I was moving away from him before he got a chance to recognize me.

The thought that he might have been inside after all and ducked out a back door occurred to me, about the time I found the service station, but I rejected it, cursing myself for an old woman.

Ben Vick had most of his clothes drying on steam pipes in the service-station office. He pulled his bare feet off the desk with a thump and his fat jaw sagged as I came in.

"Already? Say, I'm sorry. I thought that—"

"When'll you be ready to drive back to town?"

"It'll be about twenty minutes yet, Cass. Hell, I thought you'd—"

"I'll have to go back by train, then."

He almost fell off the chair. "What?" he yelped. "You're going to walk out on me, after all I've done? That ain't fair, Cass—now looka here— "

"What time will you be back in town?"

"Well, hell—about three hours from now, if—"

A mechanic in overalls came in.

"What time does the next train leave for New York?" I asked him.

He eyed his watch. "About fifteen minutes. You can make it easy."

Vick wailed: "Why, you dirty—"

"Shut up," I said. "I'll phone you tonight."

MY BAD luck held out. The train I was on—a local that stopped at every two-by-four suburb on the line—ran into storm trouble twice and stalled on the way in, while I sweated blood. It was close to an hour and a half when I grabbed a taxi at Grand Central.

The rain had stopped by the time I reached the Wall Street section, and the moon had come out. It threw queer, slanting shadows in among the towering, silent skyscrapers. I left the cab two blocks away from the corner on which Nanovic's office building stood.

It was an old-fashioned, modest wooden building, dusty and creaky. The lobby door was unlocked, and there was no attendant in the lobby. I didn't go in at once, but circled the corner, shot careful looks in all directions. The streets were bare, silent, empty. On the second floor, at the rear, a single shaded window glowed orange.

I went back to the door and hurried in. The wooden stairs groaned under my weight, as did the boards in the hall above. Nanovic had plenty of warning that I was coming.

I tapped on the ground-glass door that bore his modest inscription and reached for the doorknob, waiting for his summons.

It didn't come. I frowned, cursed. I had noticed the absence of his car from in front but took it for granted he had used a cab. I tried the door and it was open. Then, in trying to get it open quickly and get myself into the room, I banged my head against the glass, as the door stuck against an obstruction a foot inside.

I stumbled through the foot-wide opening, almost tying my feet in a knot.

The obstruction was Nanovic, lying in a pile of scattered documents, with his throat cut open from ear to ear and blood everywhere.

For the space of five seconds, I was so flabbergasted, I just stood there gawking at the rifled office.

Then the mental fogginess that I had been unable to shake off all evening cleared. I was like a sleepy man stepping under a cold needle spray. At last I was alert, and alive. I sent swift eyes around the office—then I checked myself grimly. One look at the butchered lawyer at my feet made it devastatingly clear that the time for hit-and-miss, for blind blundering, was over. Chasing a thief is one thing; chasing a thief who kills is an entirely different one. And until I had told Nanovic something over two hours back, the name of Steed, I was certain he had not known the identity of the man he had wanted me to arrest. In that time, the butcher must have realized that the lawyer had discovered him—and struck. I was up against no fool, here.

My lips clamped, and my eyes were thin. What had Granite done since I had talked to him? Or was the killer someone close to him that had been watching for just that thing?

Hastily, I pieced things together. The killer must have known that Granite, lying in the death house, was aware that the actor Steed had had the pearls. I got a picture in my mind of the murderous rat, waiting grimly for the moment when the electric chair should have sealed the burglar's lips, forever. Waiting—to do what?

Waiting to dispose of the pearls? It seemed more than likely. That would explain why no sign of them had shown up in the underworld.

What a shock it must have been to hear that Granite had decided to talk—at the last moment—to a private detective! He must—quite logically—have been tuned in to the police broadcast, earlier in the evening. He had been waiting for me, and—my forehead suddenly wrinkled. How had he managed to get ahead of us, in order to be waiting in the hollow outside of Ossining? It was a detail—but details might be desperately important now. The wild question came into my mind—could he be a resident of Ossining—or some place near?

That failed to square with the fact that he must, almost immediately after his successful attempt to delay me getting to the death house, have been in some sort of touch with Nanovic, in order to learn that the lawyer held dangerous knowledge.

And—more immediately vital than any of that—did he know now, or would he discover, that I had had an interview with the chaplain at the prison? He had struck swiftly and ruthlessly at Nanovic when the lawyer had stumbled on vital information. Could I expect the same treatment? If he heard of my interview, it would not take much mental effort on his part to guess why the white-haired priest had been closeted with me.

Almost unconsciously, I found myself tense, listening for sound, and I cursed myself furiously. If he were out to get me, that was a sure way to help him—by developing nerves. My cue was to dig his identity out of this bloody mess, and land on him before he could reach me. But—where to start?

THE OFFICE held little hope. Thick wads of papers were everywhere. Floor, desk, and the top of a filing cabinet were covered with them. Every drawer in the place hung open, had been ransacked. And the dead man's pockets—most of them—hung inside out. There would be scant information here.

For a second, I thought of getting in touch with Nanovic's family, but that went out of my mind as soon as it came in. And with it came the obvious answer. If I could find the pearls, I could find the man I had to protect myself from. Besides that, I already had a client who would pay me money to find the pearls—the blond actress, June Devereux. Furthermore, it was barely possible that she could give me some sort of information. Certainly, if she had any, she was in danger, too. As my client, I had to protect her as well, and she could hardly hold out on me now—

It was at this point that I suddenly remembered that June Devereux was to have come to the office with Nanovic.

And simultaneously, I came out of my absorption to realize that the air in the room was heavy with perfume.

Blood started pounding at my temples. I threw another quick look at the body, noted the dark bruise on the dead man's forehead. The killer must have marched up the hall, as I had, and knocked. Expecting me, Nanovic had opened promptly, been felled and butchered. The question was—where was my client—the girl—then? And, on the heels of that one came another that suddenly eclipsed the first—where was she now? Had the killer—

I scanned the office hastily, but I could find no signs of a second struggle. Worry about that possibility faded. She must have arrived to find the lawyer dead, and fled. Where? I ran a harassed hand through my hair. The girl was my client, and possibly in danger. I wanted to swing into action on a hunt for the pearls, but it was maddeningly obvious that it was up to me to find her and assure her safety, first. Besides, she might know something—and in addition to any other trouble, she'd be in plenty of hot water if the cops turned up evidence of her presence here.

Then the harassing fact suddenly filtered into my mind—I hadn't the faintest idea where the girl lived, or where to look for her. All my dealings had been with Nanovic. I pounded a fist tensely into my palm, scoured my brain—and then hope came. She was an actress. If I used my head, it ought to be possible to trace her, fairly quickly—at least to find where she lived. I recalled a theatrical agent that lived in the same apartment building I did. If—

I half swung toward the door—almost missing the break that cracked the job wide open. I checked myself hastily, though, and swung back. Unpromising as the office looked, it was folly not to go over the ground. I snapped into action.

I found nothing in the office. I put a newspaper down to avoid kneeling in blood, and started swiftly through the dead man's clothes, just in case—

It was when I was all through, apparently without result, that I found it. His coat had been lying flattened open—from the killer's search, presumably. After I had covered the pockets, I folded the lapels over his gory shirt, and ran an exploring hand down between his right kidney and the floor. Somewhere inside, paper crackled. I found it, inside his vest, almost in the waistband of his trousers—a dirty, crumpled envelope. He must have meant to jam it into his inside coat pocket, and missed—through haste, or for some other reason. The killer, having no reason to expect anything to be on the floor under the dead man, had not put his hand on the spot I had. He must have missed it entirely.

I was flushed, as I got quickly to my feet. The letter had been through the mail, but dirt and wear had done away with the postmark. There was a limp, linen card inside, smudged and dirty. Not enough, however, to hide the message. I saw glowing eyes over the handwriting. The envelope bore the address of "M. Steed" in the West Forties. The card read tersely, "Satisfactory. Destroy this." But it was the signature that made my breath blow out. It was simply, "Corporal"— the same name that had been relayed through Steed, Granite, and the padre at the prison! Who else could it be than the man I sought? If I could locate this Corporal—

Certainly, I couldn't do it standing here. I stepped swiftly to the telephone, purely from mental habit, to call the cops. Then my eye fell on the severed ends of the cord, on the floor. On second thought, that suited me. I could do my phoning from outside, and snap directly into digging for this man that called himself "The Corporal."

Then the thought of my blond client jabbed me again. I could conscientiously do nothing, until I found her. She might well be in real trouble. After all, I had only my own guess to tell me that she had come here after the murder. If I were wrong—and she had been here when the murderer struck Nanovic down—

I clamped my jaw, swung a last swift look around the office, quickly cleaned my fingerprints from the doorknob and slipped out, closing the office behind me. The more I thought of the girl, the more uneasy I got. If—if—if—

THE HALL was the old-fashioned kind, with a deep window at the front, overlooking the street, and one at the rear that presumably overlooked the fire escape. I was halfway to the stairs, when the soft squealing of an automobile's brakes reached me from the street out in front, and I froze in my tracks.

My first thought was that it was the Corporal. (I still thought of the name as a pseudonym; it had not occurred to me that it could be anyone's real name.) The foolishness of that knocked it out instantly. Who, then? My client? The cops?

My eye fell on the front window. I shot silently toward it. The faint light that filtered through the ground glass of Nanovic's office left the hall practically in darkness. I moved the blind cautiously aside, enough to look out—and I choked on a curse.

A Lincoln convertible, new under its spattering of mud, stood at the curb opposite, disgorging a tall, slender figure. The door banged, even as I looked, and the figure sauntered diagonally toward the corner of the building in which I stood. He did not mount the sidewalk, but walked out to the center of the street. There he halted, peering up at the side of the building—the side that held the lighted window of Nanovic's office.

Lighting a cigarette, he turned and strolled back toward the lobby entrance. The match's flare made it positive. If there was one person in the world I didn't want to see now, it was Zimmerman, the nosy reporter. This was Zimmerman. I'd evidently stopped worrying much too soon about whether the tricky rat had overheard my phone call at Ossining.

I swung around, cursing viciously under my breath. I darted to the rear of the hall, jerked open the dust-covered latch of the rear window, and bent to heave it open. It screeched, stuck halfway up. I grunted, put all my strength into another jerk and sent it to the top. The lobby door down below slammed, as I dived out.

As I ran down the iron steps, feet rattled on the stairs inside. I dropped ten feet into a cement court, let my pencil flash wink for one second, till I located a gate in the wooden fence, then dived for it.

His flash, in turn, slapped down on the court, as I stumbled through the gate into an alley, and slammed it behind me. The alley was no more than a small indentation from the street. I sprinted for the street, and when I reached it, for the next one south. I swung around that corner without any sign of pursuit, settled down to a pounding walk till I'd turned the next corner, then made time for the nearest subway station.

I left the subway at Fiftieth Street, hurried toward my own apartment. My promise to Ben Vick occurred to me, and halfway there, I turned into a cigar store, rang him.

His high-pitched voice said, "Hello," anxiously, almost before the phone had started to ring. He must have been sitting waiting for my call.

I cut off his hysterical rapid-fire of complaints with, "Shut up. Have you ever heard of anybody that calls himself 'Corporal?' A crook, or anything?"

He wheezed. "A crook? A lot of people think. They had him up in the magistrates-court quiz, but they couldn't prove anything. Why?"

"What the—who is he?"

"Well, uh, a judge—an ex-judge, I mean. He lost his job when the Reform party knocked the Administration boys loose a year or so ago. There was a story around that he paid off plenty to get clear of the investigation, but that's probably all—"

"Where is he now? What's he doing?"

"Nothing—at least, I don't know. I heard he'd moved out to his country place in Grimsby to sulk."

"How quick can you get in touch with some of the newspapers you work for and get me everything—"

"How would you like to go to hell?" he exploded. "I'm fed up with being your errand boy. I'm catching me a cold as it is. That's what it gets me—a cold. And the bird. Just the bird, and—"

"You chump, your angles are just starting to break. On the level, there'll be plenty for you in this, from now on. Come on, I haven't time to get in touch with them myself."

He hesitated. "Listen, if you're handing me the—"

"Has this judge got any family?"

"Some sons and daughters, I think. I'm not sure. Say, if—"

"Where is Grimsby?"

"About—well, maybe ten miles north of Ossining, I guess. I know a deputy sheriff out there, if—"

"About—Holy Hell!" I breathed, and then, as the last of the unexplained angles of the death-house trip occurred to me: "Listen—who did you tell that you were going to drive me to Sing Sing?"

"Tell? Nobody—except the cops. I called them when I found you. They got a description of my car and broadcast it to the traffic boys on the highway so we wouldn't be stopped. We were short of time to begin with if—"

"Forget it," I said grimly. "And snap into that Corporal stuff."

As I covered the rest of the way home, I was half running. If only I could locate the girl—

WHEN I hit the lobby of my building, the combination switchboard-and-elevator boy was piloting the car in the upper stories. I fidgeted till he came down, and as he took me up I asked if this theatrical agent was in the building. He was. I said: "Get him for me in a hurry—if he's asleep, I'll make it right with him."

I unlocked my door, struggled out of my wet overcoat as I kneed it open, then held it shut behind me and groped for the light switch.

The lights blazed up. June Devereux stood rigid in front of the couch in my living room, holding one of my guns in both hands. Her black fur coat hung open. Under her red dress, her firm, round breasts were rising and falling quickly. Her deep blue eyes were wide with fright, and her rose-white skin was drained of color. Her red hat lay on the table, and her corn-colored hair was perfectly combed.

She gasped: "Oh! I was afraid it wasn't you!"

I blew out breath, and stepped over to the phone, my face grim. When I got the boy downstairs I said: "Never mind that call."

"Yassuh," he said. "I hope it was all right—lettin' yo' cousin in?"

I hung up, and looked at the girl. "My cousin, eh?"

"Oh, I had—to get in! I didn't know what to do. I knew you'd come some time—You—you've seen *him?*"

"I saw him, all right. Did you kill him?"

Her hands flew to her face. "I? Oh—you—no—no! He called me—and asked me to come in—he said you were coming. Oh, how can you—"

"All right. You got there after he was dead?"

"Yes, yes!"

"You didn't see anybody near the building?"

She shook her head.

"The man who's got your pearls killed him," I said. "Because Nanovic had discovered who he was."

She gasped, and her eyes went wide. "Who?"

"Nanovic knew—not me," I said. "I think I can find out—when you give me the whole story about those pearls."

Her eyes went wide again. "What—what do you mean?"

"My God!" I said. "We haven't time for useless questions. This is murder! We're both liable to be in the soup any minute. This bauble of yours has started out with a nice string of deaths behind it. God knows if they'll be the last. I'm chasing the tail end of the parade, a mile behind because I don't know what I'm doing. You've got to tell me everything—fast!"

"But—but I don't know anything to tell you! I swear I don't! What—do you mean, a string of—of—"

"We'll get to that later. Listen—somebody's got that necklace, that apparently doesn't care a damn how many people he butchers in order to keep it. He killed your lawyer because your lawyer knew something. He tried to kill me to prevent me from learning something. It's a cinch you know something—and there's no reason in the world why he won't go for you next."

The color left her cheeks again. "You! They—they've tried to kill you—"

"Yes, me! And if you expect me to dynamite this maniac, you'll have to give me something to work with."

"But—but I don't expect you to," she floored me. "I—you don't have to do anything but—but offer the reward, and if—"

I set my jaw. "How much did you say the pearls were worth?"

"Oh, I don't know! There—there were fifteen of them. The—Mr. Nanovic said they were about twenty grains each—they were enormous. Being matched is what made them so valuable."

"He tried to tell me they were worth more than a hundred thousand."

"Oh, more than that!" she said quickly. "I—I'm sure they're worth much more than that!"

"Then how do you expect me to get them back for fifteen thousand?"

She came to her feet, her eyes desperate. "But—but that is all I have, Mr. Blue! That is every penny I have! I can't pay more!"

"Exactly. Then your only chance is to let me nail the one that stole them. I've got to fight back at him, as things stand. As soon as—well, I think he's gunning for me. You're surely not going to let him give me the dose he gave Nanovic! Don't you see—I've got to know what's what—to have a chance."

SHE stared at me in panic, her lips parted. I drove in one more shaft. "I think you're in danger too. You'd better talk quickly," I said, "because the cops are liable to catch up to you any time now."

She gasped. "The—the cops! How—why do they want me? Oh—

no—no—they don't want me. They—they—why would they—"

"You were in Nanovic's office. When those bloodhounds start going over it with a fine-tooth comb, they're almost certain to find you were there. Furthermore, I just hiked out myself as a newspaper reporter came in, and the smell of your perfume was enough to knock a man over."

"Oh, my God!" burst from her—and this was real. "A reporter! Mr. Blue—for God's sake—you've got to help me! I've got to save that much!" She swung round and ran over to the table, snatched up her hat. "You've got to—oh, no matter what happens—nothing must get in the papers. You—you've got to—"

"Take it easy!" I said. "You can't go yet."

She was yanking the hat on in front of my mirror. "But I—I can't be found here. The—the police—and the reporter—they might come here—"

"You'll have time to tell me the story first," I said shortly. "Calm down, and start from the time the jewels were lifted."

She turned from the mirror, saw me between herself and the door. "There—there isn't anything to tell," she said desperately. "I—I had worn them to dinner. I reached the theatre late, and had to hurry into my costume. I left them in my make-up box. When I came back after the first scene—they were gone. Don't you see—anybody could have gone into my dressing room—anybody in the theatre. If you started asking questions—from all of them—they'd talk, outside. I can't—it means everything to me that nobody should know I even had them. I—I can't tell you why, but it does. Oh, it does. If—oh, I only came here to tell you I was all right—not to answer questions. I can't answer them, now. Please—nothing's changed. I still want you to keep on the way you were. I—I'll pay you more money. I—even if you can't get them back—if you could just find who has them, for certain—"

"There's another thing," I said. "I understand you're not a star. You say you've only fifteen thousand dollars in the world, yet you own these pearls worth upwards of a hundred thousand dollars. It's—you'll have to tell me where they came from."

She crimsoned. "They—they were a present. Not—not what you think. No—they weren't a present, really. They—were lent—to me."

"By whom?"

She bit her lips, twisted her handbag. "I can't tell you that under any conditions."

"But for—"

Her head came up, her eyes heavy with pleading. "Please! I've got to go now. The things—I know—wouldn't help you find my stones—really. It's just that I'm in a terrible predicament. I don't know anything to help—"

"You'll be in a worse predicament if this killer decides you do know things that have a bearing."

She shook her head tensely. "No—no, I don't."

"The murder means nothing to you?"

"Oh, yes, yes! But I can't do—anything, now."

I was licked. I didn't know any other way to make her talk without breaking with her. And I was so wrapped up in the other angle anyway that I thought I could crack it without her. I decided to believe her, temporarily at least.

"All right. Where are you going now?"

She shook her head quickly. "You must forget about me. I'll be safe. I know—I know—" as I started to speak. "I know there's danger, but—believe me—I'll be safe. I—I'll phone you tomorrow, early."

"Take my word for it—you need to watch yourself."

"Don't worry. It's impossible for them to get to me—even if they wanted to."

I let her go. I had a feeling like chewing steam, but at least the weight of her safety was off my mind, for the moment—or so I thought.

I got Vick on the phone again.

CHAPTER THREE

THE CORPORAL ON THE COMMON

I T WAS just one o'clock the next day when we turned west on the highway, and passed the signboard that read, "Grimsby—5 mi." We hit it about the same time as a train came roaring up the tracks that ran parallel to the road, and Vick stopped talking to race it to the village.

I'd learned nothing new about Corporal, save that he had two sons and a daughter—Barnaby, Max, and Dawn. Barnaby, the elder, had been married, but his wife had died. The two sons had, during their father's career in politics, held one soft spot after another on the city's payroll. Apparently neither of them had ever worked. The whole family now lived in the middle of a large estate in what they called Corporal Hall.

The train outdistanced us. It was practically at a stop in the miniature station, as we swung east, across in front of it, and I said, "Stop here," before a row of half a dozen frame stores whose backs were turned to the station. Grimsby appeared to be no more than a dusty crossroads. Apart from the stores, no other buildings were in sight. Directly ahead of us, the dirt road rose sharply between two banks of trees, to disappear over the brow of a hill. The highway we had just left, continued on north. The country was hilly, wooded beyond it.

Vick stopped before a grocery store. "What now?"

"What about your deputy friend? Where does he live?"

Vick's fat face screwed up. He pointed a pudgy finger ahead of us. "About five miles from here, that road ends in a lake. There's a footpath, turns off it, a couple hundred yards from the water and goes east a mile or so to a boys' school. My friend lives just beyond the boys' school. Only he might not be home now."

"Can you phone him?"

"Yeah. Yeah. That's the ticket."

We went into the grocery store. A bell tinkled overhead as we entered, and as Vick waddled hastily to the booth in the rear of the store, I waited at the counter to buy some smokes to appease the proprietor. It took about three minutes before an old septuagenarian shuffled out from his hidingplace and peered at me over his spectacles. By the time I had completed the purchase, Vick was in high-pitched conversation with somebody.

As he hung up, and turned to face me, the bell on the door tinkled again, and a mouselike girl came in, carrying a small suitcase and looking worried. Vick dropped his voice. "He's just left his house a few minutes back. He's comin' here. We can drive down and meet him."

I said, "Oke," and we started for the door.

Vick had his hand on the door, when the mouselike girl asked the proprietor anxiously: "Hasn't—hasn't the Corporal's chauffeur been here? He—they were supposed to meet me—on this train—"

I stopped dead. The proprietor examined the girl over the tops of his glasses leisurely. Vick's fat face turned over his shoulder. I clipped in his ear, "Go get your friend, and come back for me—fast!" and heaved him through the door, where he went stumbling down the wooden steps, to flop half over the door of his car. But out of the corner of my eye, I saw he was taking me literally, and hurrying.

"The Corporals ain't got no chauffeur," the old man said. "He quit this morning—tuk the ten-twelve to New York."

The girl gasped. "Oh. But—but hasn't anybody—"

There was the roar of mechanism outside, as Vick drove off. In almost the same second, a long, dark, maroon sedan slid into the spot he had vacated, and the sharp blasts of a horn started sounding.

The girl bent over the counter to peer out the window, said, "Oh, there—" and spun round, running.

SHE crashed into me, as I moved the wrong way. The bag in her hand burst open, and objects rained out. I didn't do it intentionally. I half tripped myself, and fell against a pyramid of salmon cans. I steadied them frantically, swung round to where she was wildly scooping the contents of her bag back inside. "I—I'm sorry—"

I almost choked on the words. What had already gone into her bag I had no idea, but in the instant that I turned, she was snatching up a white, twisted object and jamming it like lightning in the bag. Then, while I still stood frozen, my eyes bulging, she dived for the door, flinging a white frightened face for an instant over her shoulder at me—and was down the steps jerking open the door of the maroon sedan. I heard her gasp, "Oh—quickly—please—" and I got one flash of the startled face of a round, blond young man in the front seat, his amber eyes wide, as he suddenly—almost involuntarily—let in the clutch, sent the car jerking forward. I started after them—checked myself, as the car rolled away, and stood there almost doubting my own senses.

The white object had been a severed woman's hand and wrist, its hacked end brown with dried blood, its fingers drawn up into claws.

I swung round on the proprietor, ripped at him: "Who was that girl?"

He pursed his lips and shook his head. "I dunno—somebody for the Corporals. That was Max Corporal't picked her—"

"Have you got a car?"

"I got a speed wagon, but my boy's out makin' deliveries—"

"Is there—" I started. "Did you see her drop anything out of her bag?"

He shook his head mournfully. "My eyes ain't so good. I didn't notice."

I stood thinking wildly. I ran out onto the road. Both Vick's car and the maroon one had vanished over the hill. I swung back, looked round wildly for some means of conveyance. Apart from the train just vanishing down the tracks, there was none of any kind. I had to wait—

At least I knew where she was going. The Corporals'! Or would she—now? I tried to convince myself that my eyes had played a trick on me, or that what I had seen was a fake or something—but I couldn't. Her fright had been too real.

The minutes slipped away. Five—ten—fifteen—twenty—

I almost gasped with relief as I heard the hum of a car beyond the hill, and Vick's battered coupe spurted over the brow. He was fairly thundering down the hill, and I suddenly sensed something wrong.

Then I saw he was alone in the car, and as he jammed his foot on the brake viciously, I saw his fat face, drained of color. He slid to a long stop, jerked open the door and came racing around it.

"Cass—Cass—listen—the judge—Corporal—he's dead—his neck's broken—I just found him!"

I caught my breath. "What—where—where are you going?"

He ran up the steps. "Got to phone—the sheriff—and the family. Get in—I'll be right back."

He phoned, came running back out and we piled in. "Halfway across the common," he panted as we swung back toward the hill. "I saw his horse throw him—somebody shot the horse with an air gun as he was jumping the gully—"

"What common—where?"

"Nearly to the lake—there's a big common—five miles square. I was just opposite this end of it, when I saw him come cantering down towards me. Then he tried to jump the narrow end of the gully, and somebody fired this air gun from the woods. The horse nearly turned over in the air. They crashed in the gully. I swung the car right up onto the common and drove over. The judge's neck is broke—and the horse's legs. It's murder, as sure as—"

"You didn't see who did the shooting?"

"No. No. He was in the woods. I wasn't going to chase him, either."

We roared up over the hill, dropped down to rush between farms on the left and woods on the right.

"Why didn't you get your deputy friend?"

"I did. Rather—he just came along as I was coming back out to the road. He's there now."

"Did you see a maroon sedan going the same way you were?"

"Eh? No."

"Where could they have turned off?"

"Why—one of these farms—or there's the Corporal's private road turns off here into the woods, a little ways ahead. Why? Do you think—"

"Don't ask me what I think!" I lashed out suddenly. "I don't think anything! I'm through thinking—for now."

He swallowed. "Hey, listen—after all, I got to get some pix. Don't clam up on me, Cass—"

"Why didn't you get a picture of the corpse?" I snarled.

"I—oh, I got that."

WE ROARED along in silence. I saw the dark car in the rearview mirror when it was a mile behind us, but I didn't think it held any interest for me, till it suddenly started overtaking us as though we were standing still. Then I rolled down my window and looked out—just as it came abreast of our rear bumper. I purpled.

Zimmerman sat in the driver's seat of his blue Lincoln, grinning. As he caught my glance, he doffed his hat and bowed. He spurted forward till we were running abreast. "How's it, gents?" he bawled. "Out for a little drive?"

As the Lincoln dropped back, Vick enlightened me: "Hey—that's a reporter. Do you suppose he followed us out here—"

"Shut up and get to that common."

"Oh," he said suddenly. "I forgot to tell you. I didn't tell the deputy what I saw. He doesn't know it's murder yet."

"What?"

"Yeah."

"God bless you," I blew out. "That's all I need!"

The Lincoln was a hundred yards in the rear when the trees at our right dropped away. I stared across an interminable stretch of green meadow, rolling and undulating. On all sides, woods surrounded it. A few hundred yards in I saw the figures of the horse and the two men. And just as we bumped up over the shoulder of the road onto the common, the deputy sheriff shot the horse.

I threw a quick look behind as we bumped across the ground. Zimmerman's car was at rest in the roadway, his head stuck out. As I watched, his door slammed, and a second later, he came grimly bumping after us.

At a distance, the deputy sheriff—Ogilvy was his name—looked trim and smart in new whipcord and boots, a khaki shirt, with a gun belt. On closer inspection, he was a dull, red-faced Norwegian with dirty blond hair and big red hands that he kept in his belt. There was a glaze to his gray eyes.

"You call him?" he asked Vick as we came up.

Vick nodded. "This is Mr. Blue, the investigator."

Ogilvy said, "Hello," in an uninterested voice.

For the first time, I noticed that Vick had his black box under his arm. "Stand over beside the body, Og, and I'll take a snap of you for the evening papers."

"I don't just know," Ogilvy stalled while he thought it over, but he moved over.

I looked at the horse. It was a fine, sensitive animal—or had been.

A vicious, rock-filled chasm cut across the common here. Horse and rider both lay with their heads pointing back toward the way from which they had come.

Keeping out of the range of Vick's camera, I moved over and examined—from a few feet—the body of the judge. He was lying on his back, his arms out-flung. His head was turned completely around in his stock, his white hair looking startling, as it rose from the starched neckpiece where his face should have been.

Zimmerman came up rubbing his hands briskly. "How's it, Blue? Hello, Vick." He stood waiting, while the deputy looked puzzled. We growled a hello, and made no move to introduce him. He flushed, whipped a card from his pocket and held it out to the deputy. Ogilvy scowled at it, wiped his hand on his breeches before taking it.

"Zimmerman of the Echo," the reporter said. "Like to get a statement from you for tonight's edition, sheriff."

After thinking it over, Ogilvy said blankly: "A statement?"

"Sure. On the murder."

"Murder? What murder? This ain't no murder. Fell off of his horse and broke his neck."

Zimmerman blinked, looked suspiciously at me, at Vick, clamped his lips. "Oh."

For no good reason, the deputy sheriff said suddenly, "My name's Ogilvy," and spelled it out. Zimmerman had to get his pad out and take it down, while we stared stonily at him. He was at a loss, for once in his useless life.

There was a roar from the roadway. Another car—a Cadillac sedan—pulled up over the shoulder of the road and came to a stop near us. Three people got out, came toward us in a body. Vick nudged me. "The Corporals."

Zimmerman must have overheard him. He whirled suddenly toward the dead man, then grabbed the deputy's arm. "Say, is that Judge Corporal?"

"Uh-huh."

Zimmerman swung back to the body, then to us, looked over toward his car, but held his ground. Then the Corporals reached us. Ogilvy took them over and showed them the body, while we drew into the background.

BARNABY CORPORAL was a stringy, cavernous-looking, tall man. His washed-out blue eyes seemed dazed, bewildered, and his long fingers continuously stroked each other. His face was prematurely lined, and he had the air of an ascetic. His hair was blond, and he wore it long, parted on the side, a cowlick over his eye. Apart from being blond, he looked no more like the brother of Max—the one with the amber eyes that I had seen driving the maroon car—than I did. Max was quick, round, alert. He wore riding breeches—stained ones, and had a pipe in his hand. Barnaby's lank figure had tweed coat and trousers—not mates—hanging on it, and a four-in-hand tie hung out over it. Max's hair looked Prussian.

They were breathlessly solemn over the body.

Especially the girl. She was beautiful in a theatrical way, slightly under medium height, warmly curved. Her eyes were green, her skin milk white, and her dark red hair, which hung down in a long bob, was curled back over dainty ears. Her mouth was generous, and her eyes wide, questioning. She did not miss any of us, as she walked past us.

When they turned back, I eased myself into their path. Ogilvy almost ran into me. He had to introduce me.

I chose Max.

I said the proper sympathetic thing to all of them, but I was insistent on catching Max's eye meaningly while I did so. He finally developed a faint frown. I moved my head slightly to one side, and he flushed, licked his lips, glanced at the others in discomfort. I stepped out of their way and around them, caught Max's eye again, and he stopped uncomfortably. "You—you want—"

I nodded, sent an oblique look at the others, and pitched my voice so nobody else could hear it. "Excuse me if I'm out of order," I said. "I think it's time somebody realized that your—the Judge's accident might not have been an accident."

From the corner of my eye, I saw Zimmerman easing around toward us. Fortunately Vick was too smart for him, blocked him.

Max's amber eyes were wide, aghast. "You—you don't mean that he was—that somebody—"

"If I could take a closer look at him, I might confirm a certain idea I have."

"Why—why—of course," he said, suddenly intense. "You—you know something about this?" His eyes bored into mine.

"I'm a private investigator," I said. "I ought to know something about it."

"I mean this—this particularly!"

"Only what I've noticed standing here. I just happened to be passing through Grimsby when my—assistant discovered this. My presence here is pure accident, if that's what you mean."

VICK was holding the now purpling Zimmerman in play. The deputy sheriff and the other Corporal brother were talking with their eyes on the ground. The girl's green eyes were steady on me. She did not move them as I met her stare; there were lights deep inside them. Max stood with a concerned scowl on his face, as I went to one knee by the body of the horse. I was lucky enough to find the slug from the air gun embedded in the flesh above the inner part of the horse's off foreleg. I held it between my two hands and looked up at Max. His breath went in like a hiss. He whirled toward the deputy, his eyes blazing.

"Just a minute," I said hastily, and he checked himself, eyed me viciously.

"I don't want to criticize," I said in a quick low tone, "but I wouldn't say anything to Ogilvy. He's—well, he examined the ground, and overlooked this." I shrugged. "The sheriff himself is on the way. I don't know him, but he could hardly be less efficient than this—gentleman."

"He's just as bad," Max clipped. "My God—this is our police force!" Then he checked himself as I gave him a steady stare.

"It's too bad," I said. "Murder is a rotten thing. Unless you know who did this—and why—"

"My God," he said in a horrified voice. "You don't think I know!"

"The ghastly part of it is, you know who it might be. You—your brother—I've arrested men that looked like both of you in my time."

His eyes flew to the gangling Barnaby. "You—are you insinuating—" He checked himself suddenly as he realized I wasn't and clamped his jaw. "Look here—how much will you charge to—to look around and see if you can—" he stopped, but not soon enough.

I quoted my cheapest rates rapidly, and said: "I'll be more than glad to do what I can. If I don't succeed, there'll be no charge. Are you going directly home?"

"As soon as the coroner and the sheriff arrive. We have to wait for them," he said.

I nodded. "My assistant and myself will follow you home, directly we can get away."

"Are—are you going to tell Ives?"

"The sheriff?" I hesitated, frowning. "I'd rather not. He'll probably discover it himself in time. I'd as soon let it go, if you could cooperate—"

He fidgeted, looked back at the others. They were all looking at us curiously now. "Look here," Max blurted. "I—I don't know how the others will take this—I mean my getting you—"

"I'm sure you can handle that," I said. "When they know that your father—when they know what I've just shown you, they can hardly object. You'll have to tell them, of course." I pretended Vick was beckoning me, said quickly, "Excuse me. I'll see you a little later," and got away from him.

I kept away from him.

Ives, the sheriff and the county coroner, a Doctor Moench, arrived. The Corporals left.

A search of the Judge's body revealed one handkerchief, a leather cigar case, matches, money, and nothing else.

Up till the time Vick and I left, they had not discovered the slug in the horse's knee.

Vick began to complain as soon as we were in the car. Zimmerman stood eyeing us furiously as we started off. We'd completely blanked him.

"What's the idea of saying I was your assistant?" Vick raved. "I've got pix. I've got to develop them and get them to the city. I—"

"Relax," I said. "This isn't officially a murder yet. Stick with me, and I'll get you a picture of the killer to go with them. I'll get them to give you a dark room at the Hall. You can develop them there and mail them."

He gaped. "You—you know who the—the—"

"No."

"Then what they—hey, what the hell is going on, anyhow?"

"I'm looking for some pearls," I told him. "They're worth a fortune. I think they're at Corporal Hall—or will be when we get there. I may be wrong. I'll know sometime late tonight."

"How?"

"If I can't get them any other way, I'll have you hold a gun on them while I search the house."

CHAPTER FOUR

"MISS TANNER"

WHEN WE came out of the avenue of trees that lined the Corporals' private road, we were facing a miniature castle of gray brick laced with red mortar. There were little turrets, and the whole house seemed topheavy with spired, round towers. The windows of the place were red with the late afternoon sun, as we circled the round patch of green lawn that centered the gravel driveway before the house.

We parked tight against one of the sides of the circle, so as not to obstruct traffic.

For a minute we sat there. There were buildings behind the main house. A gravel drive led back, parallel to the house, evidently to a garage. The whole establishment was set in a clearing, was surrounded by trees. Climbing out of the car, I happened to glance over to the right of the house.

At a point just about even with the rear of the house was a thin clump of maple saplings, in full leaf. Behind those saplings, a gaunt, tall man in black topcoat and black hat was standing, holding a bicycle. He stood perfectly still, till we walked out of sight.

Max opened the door. His face was flushed, but his jaw was militant. He said jerkily, loudly: "Come in, sir. This is your assistant?"

"Yes. Mr. Vick."

We went into a cool, dark hall, paneled with black oak. A middle-aged, thick-ankled, thick-faced maid took our hats glumly.

Max told her, "Susan—go back to the study, now." Then to me, in clipped phrases. "I've had everybody in the house get together in one room. The servants are in another room."

"Why?" I said curiously.

"But—but," he stammered. "I—I thought you'd want to question them, I—I understood—"

"No," I said.

Embarrassment slowly reddened his face. "I—" he began, stopped, then, "Well, surely you'll want to meet them."

"If it will make you any happier," I said, then as he turned toward the double doors of the living room, "Let's have a look at the servants first."

I met the servants. Besides a chef, and two housemaids, there was the tall, gaunt man I had seen holding the bicycle outside. His name was McIlhargy, and he was the butler.

And the mouselike girl. Only she was no longer mouselike.

She had on a smart, plain black frock. Her hair, in a fashionable bob, was jet, gleaming black; her skin was smooth olive, and her eyes, now brilliant, were black, lustrous. She made not the slightest sign that she recognized me from our collision in the store. I played it that way.

Vick nudged me as we came out of the study. "Hey—what the hell are you going to do?"

"I wish I knew," I said. "I haven't figured yet. We're here—and so are the stones—I hope. I'm trying to think past that, but I haven't yet."

At the door of the living room, Max paused. "My brother Barnaby—" he began. "He—I'm afraid I haven't quite won him to the idea of having you."

"That's all right," I said, quickly. "Let's get this over with."

He opened the door. And I got the first of the series of dizzy surprises this madhouse held.

Barnaby and Dawn Corporal stood with their backs to the mantelpiece. A swarthy, starch-faced dumpy woman of forty sat on an overstuffed chair, and—

My actress client, June Devereux, sat at one end of a leather couch, smoking a cigarette.

SHE jumped a clear inch when she saw me, but her face never changed. I saw she wasn't going to recognize me, so I said nothing, though I couldn't understand why she was surprised.

Then Max said, "This—this is the detective—Mr.—" he bobbed at me embarrassingly. "I'm afraid I've forgotten your name."

"Blue," I said.

He finished: "Mr. Blue. This is my brother Barnaby, my sister Dawn, and Mrs. Murgatroyd—" that was the dumpy dark woman—"and this is my brother's—fiancée—" he indicated June Devereux, and startled me by finishing—"Miss Muriel Tanner."

We bowed.

There was a second's silence.

"The only question I have to ask you right now," I said, "is—do any of you know who fired the air gun that brought Judge Corporal's horse down in the gully on the common?"

Naturally, I got no answer.

"I may want to ask you some questions individually, as I think of them," I said, "later. If you don't mind, it would be better if no one left the house. That's all for the moment."

The dumpy Mrs. Murgatroyd rose, threw a glance at June Devereux, and my blond client got up too. They moved hesitantly toward the door. Nobody seemed to know just what to do. June Devereux paused in the doorway, said embarrassedly: "I—I may be in Mrs. Murgatroyd's room, if you want me, Mr. Blue."

The red-haired Dawn came over to me, held out a warm, white hand. "I've always wanted to meet a—"

A sonorous voice behind me said, "Dawn—if you'll excuse us a minute!" and rebellion flared in her eyes for an instant, as she jerked her head toward Barnaby.

"I'll be in my room—whenever you want me," she told me, and went out.

As the door closed, the harassed-looking Barnaby took a long breath and started: "Mr. Blue—my brother has seen fit to—"

"I said: "Just a minute, please. I have thought of a question I wanted to ask. Why did your chauffeur quit this morning?"

Barnaby's haggard blue eyes went to Max's sardonic amber ones. There was an awkward moment. Then Barnaby squared his shoulders and put his hands behind him. "He left because certain things that we were doing were beyond his cloddish mentality," he said bluntly. "And you might as well understand, Mr. Blue, that we do our thinking here a little differently than most people. Furthermore, we don't seek any gratuitous criticism for our opinions."

I blinked. "I don't get this. As long as you cooperate with me in discovering who killed your father, why should I criticize?"

"There may be more direct methods of discovering that than yours."

"Well, what gives you the idea I wouldn't like that?"

He hesitated, eyed me obliquely, licked his lips. A faint frown appeared on his forehead.

"My brother is deeply interested in spiritism, Mr. Blue," Max broke in impatiently.

The best I could do was "Oh?" to that.

Barnaby's eyes followed mine. "I suppose you laugh at such things?"

"I'm not damn fool enough to laugh at anything I don't know all about," I said. "I'm willing to learn."

Barnaby blinked and his mouth came open, "I—I must say I am pleasantly surprised." He hesitated, "If you are sincere about that, we—we—you see, Mrs. Murgatroyd is a wonderful sensitive, and—and Miss Tanner too, in a lesser way. We have planned a sitting for tonight. If you would care to join us—"

I hesitated only a second before I said: "I'll be glad to."

"I hope you may get something," he said with sudden eagerness, then quickly repressed it. He swallowed. "I'll arrange for you to be there," he said, and went out. The door opened at once and he came back in again, his forehead knotted.

"I just thought of something that might mean something to you," he said. "About a week ago, I was in Plainton. The Judge had gone out riding, like today. Just outside Plainton I saw him standing beside an Isotta car, talking to two men that looked like Italians. The odd thing was that one of them had on a silk hat— even though it was a hot day, around two or three in the afternoon. When the Judge came home, I asked him about it. He told me I was crazy, that he had not been there at all. But I know he had. Do you suppose that would have any bearing?"

Something clicked in my mind. "I certainly do," I said. "I may ask you more about that."

"Well, yes, but—that was all there was to it."

WHEN he had gone out again, I said to Max: "Where do you stand on this spiritism? Do you hold the same—"

He squirmed uncomfortably. "Oh, I don't know. It may be all right—in a way. It's cost Barnaby plenty, though."

"How?"

"The phony tips Mrs. Murgatroyd's given him on the market. It's damned near cleaned him."

"Is Miss Tanner a medium too?"

He hesitated, frowning. "Not—strictly speaking. She—she's my brother's fiancée, you know." His face suddenly clouded. "I forgot to tell you. My brother was married before. He was very devoted to Virginia—his first wife. When she died, he went all to pot." He stopped short, looked up at me anxiously. "Look here—this is confidential."

"Certainly."

"Did you ever hear of automatic writing?"

"Yes, sure."

"Barnaby met Miss Tanner at a party in New York. She was doing some of that for a stunt. You know—the people who do it just sit with a pencil in their hands and a sheet of paper in front of them and after a while it's supposed to start of its own accord—"

"I know about that."

"Well, Miss Tanner started writing for Barnaby and he swears she got a message from Virginia—in Virginia's own handwriting. Ever since then he's been—well, staying close to her. I wouldn't want this repeated, but—well, to be frank—I think the reason he wants to marry Miss Tanner is in order to keep her near to bring messages from Virginia.... What's the matter?"

"Nothing," I said. "I'm getting a headache, that's all."

Ben Vick fidgeted behind me. "Uh, Mr. Blue—about that dark room."

I got that fixed up for him, and he went down to the cellar with his boxes.

The butler, McIlhargy, was waiting in the hall. I told him where we had left our bags—in the rumble of Vick's car—and he went and got them. He led me to a pair of rooms with a bathroom between them, at the rear of the house. I told him to put Vick's bag in the back one.

I had my bag open and was digging out my spare collar when I realized he had not left, but was standing awkwardly in my doorway. "Hello. You want me?"

"Yes, I do," he said in a ringing, blurted tone, then remembered to add "sir." "I want to tell you who did this thing to the Judge, Mr. Blue—and why. I know."

"Go ahead."

"That young woman did it. She did it so that Mr. Barnaby would get the Judge's money."

"Are you talking about the actress—Miss Tanner?"

"Actress!" he ground his teeth. "You've struck it to a nicety! She wanted to marry Mr. Barnaby for his money—she's nothing but an adventuress. Then when he lost his money, she thought of the Judge's and—and killed him to get it. It's what you said, sir—she's acting. She doesn't love Mr. Barnaby any more than she does me! I—I happened to overhear a phone conversation of hers, sir. She was phoning from the den. I happened to pick up the extension in the living room, not knowing anyone was using it. I heard her tell someone, at the other end, that she was going to marry—she just said 'him' but she meant Mr. Barnaby—and that he wouldn't live forever."

"Very interesting," I said. "Is that all?"

"My God, sir!" he exploded. "Isn't it enough?"

"Hardly enough to arrest her on. You have to have evidence."

"But I'm telling you, sir—I heard—"

"It's not evidence, friend," I said. "However, I'll keep it in mind. Thanks a lot."

"You—you aren't going to—"

"Not yet," I said. "There'd have to be a lot more than that against her. Listen—is there a shortwave radio in the house?"

His teeth clicked audibly. He said gratingly: "Yes, sir. Miss Dawn has the latest model in her room." He was disgusted with me as a sleuth.

WHEN he went out, I sat down in a chair and smoked three cigarettes; my brain was spinning. I was lighting the fourth when my door burst open and Vick came hurrying in, his arms full of boxes and a manila envelope on the top. "Listen! That reporter, Zimmerman, is just coming up the steps! What do you—"

He broke off as the bell rang in the back of the house. I jumped up, hurried out into the hall, and as McIlhargy appeared from the rear I snapped: "It's a reporter. You'd better get instructions from Mr. Barnaby."

He gasped, turned and made quickly for the den at the rear of the ground floor. Barnaby's voice called to come in when he knocked.

When he emerged he marched to the front door and held it open a crack. There was a mumble from outside. McIlhargy said harshly: "I am sorry. There is no one at home."

More from outside, then, "I am sure you are mistaken. I will see," and he closed the door.

To my surprise he came up the stairs. "Mr. Blue—it's you he wants to see. Something about a man at a lawyer's office. A Mr. Nanovic. He's running away or something."

I blinked. "Running away? What the—" and then the maddening truth broke on me. Zimmerman had seen me running away from Nanovic's office. I cursed vainly, viciously, but there was no getting away from it. He could put me in a tight fix—they could take my license away for not reporting the murder. I ground my teeth.

"Listen," I said to Vick. "Get in your buggy and beat it over to Plainton. See if by any wild chance there've been two Italians or Latin men around—rich ones—one of them may be wearing a silk hat. I think they were there this afternoon. They may still be there. If they are, sandbag them or something and phone me. You can get your pictures in the mail at the same time. Make it fast!"

To the butler I said: "All right. I'll let him in."

I went down, opened up, and stepped out onto the stone porch, half closing the door behind me. "Well," I said, "what do you want?"

"Some dope on this accident. I smell something fishy. What the hell are you doing here if it's an accident?"

"Listen," I said patiently. "You followed me out from New York this morning. You know I didn't come here on account of the accident. It's just a coincidence and nothing else."

"Well, what did you come on, then?"

"Don't be foolish. You know I'm not going to tell you that."

"Is that so? Well, get this," he snarled. "I'm damn sick of being blocked off everywhere. I'm supposed to be a reporter. A fat lot I get to report when you're around. Now I've got you where I want you. I saw you duck down the fire escape and out the alley behind Nanovic's office last night. For all I know, you killed him. Now, either play ball with me, or I'll turn you in."

I hesitated, looked judicial. Finally I said: "Well, I'm willing to play ball, but I don't see anything I can do for you."

"I want some interviews with this gang. My sheet'll play up the Judge's death. He was news when they had him in the magistrates' quiz. He'll still be news."

"Oh, you just want a statement from the family."

"Sure. Anything. I've got to get some copy on the wire in the next hour—some kind of copy. That'll hold them long enough for me to get some more."

I hesitated just a minute. "Get it into your head that I'll play just so far with you," I said. "Then I'll kick your pants out of here and take my chances on what you can spill about me."

"Am I asking much?"

I LET him in, told him to wait in the living room. I walked back to Barnaby's den, and with my hand raised to knock I heard his voice talking to someone. I hesitated.

Muffled by the door I could still make out: "What… when?… But I haven't… Yes, I can do that… Well, yes, but… yes, all right, I will… I will, on my word of honor." And I realized he was phoning. I knocked. I heard him say hastily, "As near then as I can," and hang up. When he opened I stepped in.

"There's a reporter out there, Mr. Corporal," I told him. "I want you to see him—"

"A reporter!" Barnaby suddenly erupted. "I won't see any reporter!"

"Wait a minute," I said. "This is a special case—"

"I don't care what case it is!" he raved. "I hate reporters—and newspapers. They ruined my father—I won't—"

"Will you shut up for a minute," I outbawled him. "And listen to me: this bird is the slipperiest guy in the world. He smells something fishy in your father's death. He's here thinking he can drag the low-down out of you—or Max, or Dawn. He tells me all he wants is a statement about the accident, but that's a joke. Now—if we throw him out, he's only got one thing to do—go to the sheriff. If the sheriff gets here, he'll dynamite my plans—and the chances are your father's killer will never be turned up. The only way to stop him is for you to go out and answer his questions and make him think he's mistaken."

He swore again, bitterly, hesitated. "All right. What—what will I tell him?"

"Just remember that your father's fall from his horse was an accident."

I led him into the living room. Zimmerman had his personality turned on full blast as we came in. He raised his eyebrows at me. "I'd like to see you after I've seen Mr. Corporal, Mr. Blue."

That was no surprise to me. I wandered around uneasily, went back up to my room, as minutes passed and they remained behind the closed door.

There was one of Vick's masterpieces, on my bed—a photograph of the dead judge, sprawled on his back. Every vein in his wrists was clear, so sharp was the picture—and the individual hairs on his head—I could almost make out the manufacturer of his fountain pen.

The door's opening sent me hurrying down again. Zimmerman gave me a sour look, ground out: "You certainly had him coached, you double-crosser."

"What's the matter with you? If anything breaks here, you've a cinch to get an exclusive story. How can I stop you if I want to? There's nothing at all now."

"Well, I'll see the girl now."

I shook my head, looked at my watch. "You'll see nobody—till later this evening. It's nearly dinner time. You're through for now. Come back tomorrow morning."

He made a sneering noise in his throat. "Don't be funny. Listen—I'll go and file what I've got and have my dinner. I can be back in two hours—and I'm coming in when I get here—and I mean in."

I BREATHED when the door closed behind him. If he had seen June Devereux—he'd be sure to know her by sight. And that reminded me. I swung for the stairs.

Barnaby came from the living room. "You didn't spill any beans did you?" I asked.

"I certainly did not," he said proudly.

He told me where I would find Miss Tanner and I went up and knocked.

The dumpy Mrs. Murgatroyd let me in. When I said what I wanted, she came out and left me alone with my blond client, in the fantastic room. It was hung on all sides with pitch-black velvet. A black ebony table—circular—held the center of the floor. The floor was covered with black carpet, and the lighting was furnished by an indirect system that circled the room close to the floor. Only in one place was the blackness broken—in the center of the black ceiling was a gold mariners' star, showing the cardinal points.

She stared down at the table and her clasped hands as the door closed on the medium.

"Well," I said. "It looks like telling time."

She flung me a frightened glance, stared again at her hands. "I—I guess I should have—before. I don't know what you'll think of me now."

I shrugged. "You're my client. Besides that, there isn't much left for you to tell me. I've got it pretty nearly figured out for myself. If I only ask you one question, do you suppose you could tell me the truth?"

"I swear I will!" she said desperately.

"Have you got your pearls back yet?"

She jumped to her feet. "Got them back? Oh, my God, no! Whatever—"

"All right," I said. "It was either you or one other person. I think you're telling the truth. If—"

Somebody knocked at the door. Dawn Corporal stood outside when I opened. She had on a green dress that made her white skin even whiter. It was cut very low under the arms. She smiled. "Sorry to interrupt, but dinner will be served in a few minutes."

I said, "Thank you," to her, and, "Thank you, Miss Tanner," to June Devereux. I let her precede me out. Dawn put her hands in two miniature pockets in the front of her skirt and smiled at me. "I've been waiting for my turn," she said.

"I'll get to you right after dinner."

"Oh, but they're going to have the seance after dinner."

I took one look at the lights in her green eyes. They were glowing now. "I—I have to wash up," I said, and fled.

Dinner was a silent, hasty meal.

And after dinner—the seance.

CHAPTER FIVE

CORPSE CONTROL

IT WAS held in the black room. The three Corporals—Max, Barnaby and Dawn—Mrs. Murgatroyd, June Devereux, and myself formed the magic circle. Before going in, they turned all the lights out—from a switch outside the door. I almost produced my flashlight to help us get seated, but instead I tucked it under my armpit. When I sat down, its nose was pointed so that all I had to do was to press my arm against my side to spread illumination all over the table.

When the place was blocked into blackness, we hooked little fingers—the usual proposition. Then silence.

I got conscious of bodies, the warmth of them, and the perfume of the women, coming toward me. The hollow voice of the medium was resonant. "Just relax, everybody—as though you were daydreaming. Be perfectly subjective."

A dopey, eager voice spoke from the side of the table farthest from me. "Shall we sing?" I finally placed it as Barnaby's.

We sang "Rock of Ages."

It was, of course, pitch black. I was sightless. To my right, I hooked fingers with Max Corporal. To my left was Dawn. Her hand was hot and moist. My ears got tuned down so I could hear everyone breathing. The darkness started to pitch and roll.

There was a sudden sharp grunt. I almost snapped my light on. It was an effort of will not to. The grunt became a moan, became merged into labored groaning, heavy breathing. The breathing lengthened, became deep, stertorous.

The hushed voice of Barnaby came in a whisper. "She's asleep!"

I wanted to bark, "Who?" loudly and illnaturedly, but the thing was getting me. There was a queer tingling in the vicinity of my heart. My mouth was open a little and I was breathing through it—in unconscious imitation of the medium, I guess.

There was a sigh from Mrs. Murgatroyd—if she were the breather. Then suddenly she threshed in her chair, uttering a tortured, muffled cry. Her breathing took on a heavier rhythm, and there seemed, deep inside it, a trace of voice.

This, I thought, is a knockout of a performance, if phony. Then something white swam over my head.

I jerked—I'm not ashamed to admit. The fingers of Dawn on my left and Max on my right tightened reassuringly. I tried to force my brain up on top of the smothering darkness, but it had me down.

The white thing floated back over my head, toward the medium. I felt a cold breath sweep around my head. From somewhere came a faint thud.

Then Barnaby's husky, trembling voice. "Father—we are all—"

Something high overhead caught my eye. For some reason I knew it was no spook. I hugged my side.

The strong beam of my pencil flash threw the whole tableful into etched relief, and—the spot in the ceiling where the mariners' star had been. It was a gaping aperture now, and even as my light flared, a hand dived down through it—a hand that clutched a long, gold-hilted sword. I roared, "Look out—the ceiling!" and tried to kick away my chair.

LIKE a streak of light, the sword shot downward—straight for Muriel Tanner's breast. She saw it, screamed, and flung herself backward. My gun jumped into my hand, but before I could use it, thunderous roar exploded in my ear, and I jerked back, half deaf, to see Max Corporal rise from his chair, his face contorted, aiming a flat, black automatic for a second shot at the trap door above. I registered the sound of a groan from above and the patter of feet, simultaneously with the fact that Max not only had a gun, but had drawn it faster than I had mine. I hadn't exactly fumbled, either. Then I leaped, whipped open the door. The women were shrieking; the black room was bedlam. I clawed for the light switch as I passed, clicked it on, made for the stairs.

Threshing footsteps sounded on the floor above. I hit the top step, just in time to see McIlhargy stagger to the door of a room directly over the black room. His stiff face was contorted with pain. He fell back inside as my light beam hit him. I roared: "Come out, McIlhargy! I'll finish you, as sure as—"

He staggered out, one hand clapped to his streaming side.

Behind me on the stairs, I heard running feet. I roared over my shoulder, "Keep down there!" and grabbed the butler, wrenched him around to face me. As I ran quick hands over him for a weapon, I rapped: "So you tripped up finally!"

Pain-glazed eyes wandered up to mine. "Finally—sir?" he gasped out. "What—"

"Crude work!" I said contemptuously. "I'd have expected something better from you, after the way you fixed the Judge—and the others. If—"

He struggled upright, wildness in his eyes. "My God!" he shouted desperately. "You don't think that I—that I did for the Judge! I told you—it was that—that cold-blooded—murderess—"

I wrenched his hand from his wounded side as he half doubled up in sudden pain. I called back toward the stairs, "Phone for a doctor, somebody—quickly!" and I heard feet mill about below. I swung McIlhargy around quickly into the unlighted room behind him and threw my light around.

The mouselike girl lay on the floor. The skin on her forehead was broken. A wooden bludgeon lay beside her. Around her were—a pot-bellied kettle, from under whose lid, greenish, thick smoke was spilling out; a bellows; a dish of cracked ice; and—the human hand I had seen that morning. But now it was attached to the end of a long black rod. I did not wait to examine it, I felt the unconscious girl's heart. It was strong. I hurried out and flung McIlhargy's arm around my neck, carried him downstairs.

As I came to the bottom, I said to June Devereux: "Go upstairs. The medium's maid's been knocked out up there. See what you can do for her."

I was at the door of my room when Max came tumbling up the stairs. He stopped and shouted at me: "The phone's gone out of order!"

"Well, somebody go for a doctor in a car!" I raved.

From down below him came Barnaby's hysterical voice, "I'll go! I'll go!" and I heard him running toward the rear of the house. A door banged.

I LAID the butler out quickly on my bed. His eyes were closed, but his face was drawn and twitching. I worked feverishly to stop his bleeding. Finally I got the hole in his side plugged up.

McIlhargy's tortured eyes opened. His voice was a grating whisper, "Mr. Blue—I didn't have anything to do with the Judge—"

"Then where were you this afternoon?" I threw at him, "just before I arrived."

"I was—in the house," he said desperately.

"You're a liar. I saw you standing back of the trees with your bicycle. I don't think you did kill the old man, but unless you talk and talk quickly, you're going to get the credit for it."

His eyes went wide, aghast. "No—no—you've got to get her! I tried—and failed! She'll kill them all!"

"Then talk to me!" I drove. "Where were you this afternoon? It means everything to me, to know that!"

He lay back panting for a minute, his eyes closed; then he blurted out: "I was—in Plainton. The—the Judge sent me there—this morning. I had—a note for—a man I was to meet there—"

"Who?"

He moved his head feebly from side to side. Pain was sending waves across his face. "I—don't know—name. Two men—dark—Spanish—waiting for note from Judge—I—" It trailed off into sudden babbling. He started to thresh around, delirious. I roared for somebody to send me up the chef from downstairs.

I installed him as nurse, as the butler lapsed into a coma. Then I started toward the stairs—and stopped suddenly.

From the door of the seance room, a groaning, whistling sound was coming. I jumped for it, gasping.

The medium, Mrs. Murgatroyd, still sat erect, stiff in her chair. Her eyes were closed; she was still breathing heavily.

I went to the head of the stairs and called, "Miss Tanner!" and when she came up, "The medium's still in a trance—or whatever. Can you fix her up?"

She went in with a bottle of smelling salts, and when she came out the dumpy dark woman was limping with her. June Devereux looked at me appealingly. "Does she have to—"

"Yes. Get her down there. And be sure you round up all the servants."

"We—we did."

"Where is the medium's maid?"

"She—she's down there—on the couch."

CHAPTER SIX

FOUNTAIN OF JEWELS

IT WAS ten minutes later when I heard soft steps running up the stairs and I popped out of my room to see Dawn, frightened-faced coming toward me. "Mr.—Mr. Blue—something's wrong! Barnaby—Barnaby hasn't started yet."

"What!"

"We've been sitting there—waiting for the car to go past the window. Is it—is it all right if we go out and help him? He may have trouble starting—"

I flattened her against the wall as I dived past her. As I hit the bottom step I roared at her: "Switch on every light in the house—fast!"

The rear door was standing open. I tore out into the space between the garage and the house. Lights started going up in the house.

The garage door was standing open. I ran up, my flash in one hand, my gun in the other, raked the two-car space. There was no one in the solid little room.

I came out and called his name. Then I realized that there were sheds behind the garage and I ran around to the back.

From one of the sheds—a lean-to—came a terrific buzzing. I felt ice in my stomach. I heard the patter of a woman's feet coming across the gravel, and jerked back to see the red-haired Dawn coming out "Have you—is he there—"

"Go back inside!" I bawled as I reached for the door handle of the shed that contained the buzzing. I jerked it open, fanned it swiftly with light and gun. Then I yelped, stumbled backward, slamming the door shut, as what seemed like a million wasps suddenly flew wildly at me—but that didn't prevent me seeing what was inside.

Barnaby Corporal was doubled up inside, in a position that suggested he'd been thrown there. He was half lying on a crushed wasps' nest, evidently knocked from the wall in the process. There was a knife with an elk-foot handle as big as my wrist, driven straight through his throat.

Wasps stung me unmercifully. I staggered, fighting them off, ducked and ran a few steps. Dawn was frozen at the corner of the garage.

"Get back to the house!" I snarled. "Send Max out here—with some newspapers—fast!" and she stumbled away.

I was still ducking the wasps when Max's round figure came hurrying out with an armful of papers. "What—what is it?" he got out hoarsely.

"Wasps!" I grabbed the newspapers from him, twisted them into a smudge. "Barnaby's in there—stabbed to death!"

He recoiled as though I'd struck him. "Stabbed?" he shrilled. "My God—Barnaby—my God—what—who—"

I lit the smudge, jerked open the shed door and flung it inside, then ducked and ran ten yards. Half unconsciously he followed me. "Who was out of the house since the seance?" I rapped at him, as the smoke rolled out.

"I—I don't know. I—I went into Barnaby's study for a few minutes, to get myself together. I don't know what the rest of them—"

"Go on back inside—" I started, and choked on it.

The sound of an automobile was audible, coming down the private road. My teeth clicked. "Get inside!" I bit off. "Get that French chef down from upstairs, and don't let a soul out of that living room. And no matter what any of them ask, your answer is that you don't know. You understand?"

He turned and ran. I dived for the shed, had just time for one swift look. There was a welt over the dead man's ear. His pockets had been ripped inside out. He had been slugged, searched, killed and thrown in there.

I WAS sweating white fire, as I turned and ran for the house. I beat the headlights by a hair. As I ran in the back door, the car was squealing to a stop in the driveway out front. I doused the hall lights, as I ran for the panel of plate glass beside the front door, my gun in my hand, and looked out.

The reporter, Zimmerman, was coming up the steps, and behind him, his face grim, was the sheriff—Ives.

I jerked open the door before they could ring. "Come in, quickly," I said.

The sheriff plowed in. He was a dark-faced man with a completely bald, square head. "Mr. Blue," he said excitedly. "There—there seems to be some suspicion that a murder has been committed."

"Oh my God!" I blurted. "Listen, Sheriff: I'm miles ahead of you.

There've been two murders committed, and there's a man shot, upstairs. We tried to call you but the phone's been out. I was just this minute starting for you. I've—"

"Who's been—who else's been—"

"Barnaby Corporal—stabbed to death," I rattled. "The butler upstairs was shot—accidentally—we haven't been able to get a doctor yet. He may die. Will you trust me for this much—you can't lose anything by going and getting one for the poor devil. I've got everybody herded in there except the butler. I'll hold them—"

Zimmerman suddenly gasped and whirled for the door. "I'll get one," he cried excitedly over his shoulder.

I dived for him, jerked him almost off his feet. "Yes, you will, you rat! You'll get to hell in with the rest of them, till this thing's finished. Then you can tell your damned paper anything you like. Sheriff—for God's sake—"

"Wait! Wait!" he got in finally. "I've already sent Ogilvy for Doctor Moench."

"Ha!" I said. "Then let's get in here. Wait—look here—will you let me carry through on something I'm trying? None of them know Barnaby's been stabbed—except Max. If you'll let me carry on—I may be able to show you an answer to this thing that will knock your teeth out."

He looked worried. "I—I guess so."

I swung for the living-room door, opened it, and they preceded me in. The room was octagonal. I walked over so as to get the whole group in front of me. I stood with my back to one of the French windows, with my gun in my hand and flung at them suddenly: "Somebody in this room—"

The sudden sweep of headlights across the window behind me cut me short.

A car came to a stop on the driveway, then feet ran across the gravel. When the bell started ringing in jerks I waved my gun at the French chef. "See who it is."

He scuttled out. A second later Vick's fat form came pounding into the room. His face was alive with excitement. "Cass—listen—" Vick exploded. "Those two men *were* in Plainton—in an Isotta car. And that same Isotta car is parked halfway down the private road, right this minute! I just passed it!"

I gasped. "Good God—we—"

The French window behind me blew open and a hoarse, foreign voice barked: "Don't move—any of you—or we'll shoot! Drop that pistol!"

I guessed that last was for me. I dropped my gun. I couldn't have shot it out if I'd wanted to. Every bullet that missed me would have gone into the crowd behind me.

Dawn Corporal screamed and fainted.

"Quiet!" the hoarse voice rapped. "No one will be hurt—if you behave properly."

I TURNED around boldly, though nobody had told me to. I saw a thick man and a slender man in black full-face masks. They had black coats and hats on, and as they stepped through the French windows, they separated a few yards, each of them holding a gun on us.

The thick man said abruptly: "All right. Now I want my pearls." Then his glance fell on my client, June Devereux, and he gasped. "You! Then no wonder—" He checked himself and his voice got grim. "Now, young lady, you will please return my property!"

June Devereux stood up and said white-lipped: "I swear to you that I don't know where they are."

The thick man cursed under his breath. "If you do not return them at once, I will have every person in this house searched to the skin. I have been tricked long enough!"

"If you'll give me another week—" June Devereux began desperately.

"Bah! A week now! This morning, it was to be at two o'clock. Then at nine o'clock. It is now after ten—and nobody has shown up. You are a pack of thieves. Well—do we search?"

Nobody said anything. The stocky man said, "All right, we will," and they did. They searched the men with thoroughness. While they did not exactly search the women, they got a lot of handling.

No pearls were found. The stocky man was panting with rage underneath his mask. "So! Then it must be hidden—"

Far distant, came the wailing of a siren. "Listen! What's that?"

I answered him. "That's the deputy-sheriff with a dozen men," I said. "About to grab you. These pearls may be your property for all I know, but you're both facing a couple of years in jail for breaking in here and holding us up."

The stocky man snarled. "Very well. We will go. But—you—you," he nodded at June Devereux—"I will give you just twenty-four hours to get those pearls back to me. After that—" He did not say what to expect after that. "The rest of you—stay where you are. We will not hesitate to shoot if you come after us."

They backed through the French windows together, and vanished in the gloom. I let a couple of seconds go by, then dived for my gun. When nothing happened I barked at the sheriff, "Go get them, Ives—you've got them bottled up between you and Oglvy!" and he tore out.

Suddenly I heard Ben Vick come to life. "My God—what a picture!" he blurted and started for the door after them. I grabbed his sleeve. "Stay here," I whipped. "You'll get a better one."

He stood panting, eyeing me incredulously. "But—"

Zimmerman half started out, came back, his face tortured. He didn't seem to be able to make up his mind. Finally he stayed. As the roar of the sheriff's car started outside, I said to Vick quickly, "Shut the door," and we were back in the same position we had been before. Then I got a better idea. I took him aside and whispered: "Go get yourself a club and stand out there in the hall. If anybody comes out, let them have it!"

"But—but—the killers—"

"Don't be an ass," I said. "The killer—there's only one of them—is right here."

HE GULPED, waddled hastily out and closed the door behind him. "All right," I said. "While Mr. Vick is searching for the pearls, I'll say the same thing our visitors did. Somebody better produce them."

June Devereux gasped. "You—you mean someone here has them?"

"Someone here has got to have them!"

"Oh!" she burst out. "Can—can I see you alone for a minute?"

"No," I said. "You can't. It's your cold-blooded gold-digging that's caused all this—this murder and misery."

She got up, her face hard. "How dare you!"

"Sit down!" I roared at her. "You found you couldn't make the big-time on the stage, so you turned to the matrimonial racket. Then when you did land a man that looked as though he could keep you in good style, you weren't satisfied. You rang in this phony medium, to try and get him to play the market, in hopes of his making a killing.

That was your sap play. Instead of winning, he lost. Then, when it looked like he might go broke, you started playing around—on the side—with somebody else. I don't understand just yet why you didn't marry this second party—why you gold-dug him for some of his family jewels instead—but I will—just as soon as the sheriff gets back here with those amateur bandits!"

She was white as a sheet. "No—no!" she cried, "I swear—you—you've got it wrong. Carlos forced those pearls on me. I didn't want to take them. Please—you must believe me. I knew—I knew he couldn't—" She stopped and crimson flooded her cheeks.

"Oh, you knew he couldn't legally give them to you. Is that it?"

She said nothing.

"What is he—underage?" and when she refused to answer that I snarled: "Listen—if you don't answer my questions, I'll hang a murder rap on you to go with—whatever you've got coming."

That jerked her head up, her eyes terrified. "Oh—you know I didn't—"

"Then answer me."

She dropped her head. "Yes. He is underage. They were family jewels."

"But you thought you could sell them back to the family, as soon as they found out this pinhead had given 'em to you?"

Her "Yes" was barely audible.

"And instead of that, they were stolen from you. What did you do—tell the boy's old man that you could return them later—then hire me to locate them?"

She suddenly said wearily: "Yes, yes—anything you say."

"Well," I said, "maybe you'd be interested to know what happened to them. Also, maybe all of you will be interested to know that Judge Corporal stole them—because he was broke, and up against it for money. Getting out of the magistrate's investigation cost him plenty. But that wasn't what broke him. What broke him was that he was being blackmailed."

I let that sink in. "He was being blackmailed, by somebody who knew the inside of his career as a magistrate. I imagine this—person—held enough on the Judge to give the investigators a heart spasm if they ever got their hands on it. Otherwise, I can't imagine the Judge going to the lengths he did. This blackmailer sucked him dry. Then, when the Judge couldn't meet any more demands, the blackmailer probably suggested to him that he steal your damned pearls.

"The Judge hired an old actor named Steed to steal them—an actor so that he could come and go around a theater without being too conspicuous. Steed stole them from your dressing room. He delivered the pearls at once to the Judge. Unfortunately for Steed, the tip had gotten to a certain professional thief that Steed had lifted them. That thief—Jack Granite—tried to hijack them, not knowing that Steed had passed them on. It ended up in murder—and the thief, Granite, got caught and convicted for it.

"While he was in the death house for six months, the Judge and his blackmailer friend were afraid to move. They didn't know what, if anything, Granite knew about the pearls. Publicity would be disastrous for them—as the real owner of the pearls would realize what had happened, and go to the police, in which case the pearls would be too hot to handle. Then, as the day of Granite's execution got closer, they got much more confident. They made careful overtures to the real owners, preparatory to selling them back.

"The real owners realized that you had been stalling them, and probably frightened you. Anyway, you ducked out here, hoping that I could find the stones for you.

"The night of the execution, when the Judge and his blackmailing accomplice thought everything safe, Granite decided to talk—to me. That was last night.

"Naturally, the pair were frantic. They were lucky enough to have it made easy for them to lay for me, and they managed to stop me before I got to the death house. But I got the information anyhow. They didn't know that, of course.

"They arranged to return the pearls—and receive whatever price they'd agreed on—to the owners today—this afternoon. The Judge was to deliver them—in Plainton, and, probably split the proceeds with the blackmailer. The blackmailer decided at the last minute to save the Judge's share by hijacking him as he was on the way to the meeting. He lay for him out here on the common, where he knew he would have to pass, and shot the Judge's horse from under him. Unfortunately, the Judge was killed. And—twice as unfortunately from the blackmailer's point of view—my assistant happened on the scene before the pearls could be taken from the Judge.

"Later on, this blackmailer got the idea that Barnaby had the stones. When Barnaby ran out of the house, the blackmailer killed him, but—the stones weren't on Barnaby either. If they had been, the blackmailer would not be sitting here now, hoping to find them—even now."

I STOPPED suddenly, as from outside came the sudden, steady hum of automobile engines. I snapped my jaw shut. My eyes went over the ghastly, strained faces. "The question I had to solve of course was this: who would be in position to have something on the Judge, and at the same time be close enough to the theatrical world to find out all about Miss—uh—Tanner's affair with the youngster she's just been telling us about. There was only one answer, naturally—a dirty Broadway snooper—a professional keyhole artist—"

Zimmerman whipped a pistol from his pocket and fired, but he didn't have a chance. His slug went into the floor as I broke his shoulder.

There were shouts outside, and the sheriff and his deputy came rushing in, herding the two swarthy-looking men before them—one a boy hardly out of his teens, the other a stocky, proud-looking man of about fifty. It took me about five minutes to spread out the whole situation before the sheriff, and I added, "Besides all that, this rat overheard me phoning a lawyer named Nanovic. Nanovic had discovered that the Judge was connected with the actor, Steed, and Zimmerman overheard enough of my conversation with Nanovic to guess that the lawyer knew too much. He beat me in to the city and murdered him. But I'm damned if I can tell you where—" and then I stopped suddenly as the only possible conclusion forced itself through my head.

I started for the door, called Ogilvy with me. He followed me, after a quick glance at Ives, and I took him down the hall into Barnaby's den. That reminded me to explain. "I forgot to point out that the way Zimmerman got the idea of killing Barnaby Corporal for the pearls was this: Zimmerman called here this afternoon while Barnaby was on the phone. I forgot about the extension telephone in the living room and shooed Zimmerman in there. As far as I can gather—you can check this with the old Spaniard out there—the Spaniard must have been phoning just about that time to find out what was keeping the Judge. Then, under the impression that Barnaby knew about the pearls, he asked him to meet him this evening. All this, Zimmerman must have overheard, and the erroneous conclusion isn't difficult to follow."

Ogilvy swallowed. "Is—why couldn't you tell that to Ives? Is that what—"

"No, you dumb ox. I brought you in here because in a picture my assistant took of the body of the Judge, just after he was killed, there was a whopping big fountain pen in the Judge's pocket. The pen didn't show up among the Judge's effects. My assistant and you were the only ones that were alone with the body. My assistant hasn't got it. Gimme."

He reddened, started to deny it, but I grinned and he took it out of his inside pocket. "It don't work nohow," he said. "I can't get the cap off it. I never thought no one would miss it."

"They wouldn't, except for this."

I found the unscrewable part in the bottom of the dummy pen, and undid it to let out the magnificent string of pearls.

Ogilvy damned near fainted.

CALLING ALL CARS!

**THREE MILLION IN GOLD
WAS THE STAKE THAT
JEROME CREAM—MANIAC
MURDER WHOLESALER
AND LOOT KING—WAS
AFTER. AND ONLY
CASS BLUE GUESSED
HIS SUBTLE PLAN,
KNEW THAT CREAM'S
FANTASTIC SCHEME
WAS REAL ENOUGH
TO BRING FROM THE
BROADCASTING STATION
AT HEADQUARTERS THE
"30 SIGNAL" THAT'S
USED ONLY ONCE IN A
LIFETIME—CALLING ALL
CARS!**

CHAPTER ONE

ALIAS JOHN SMITH

THIS IS the story of Jerome Cream, as I know it. Nobody ever succeeded in finding out where he came from, or who he was. He was a professional criminal—yet that classification is inadequate. He was the most heartless, bloodiest, inhumanly clever monster that ever operated in my town, and, apart from my father, he was the only man that ever put actual fear in my heart.

We hooked him, in 1932, on an indictment charging eleven killings in an insurance fraud—a fraud so incredibly crafty that to this day no one can explain it—and I think the jury convicted him out of sheer panic. I know that, during the trial, as I sat day after day on the side bench with Sergeant Green and a Detroit detective named Dodge, even though I'd had a hand in everything from the start, horror did things to my stomach. As the D.A. brought out what details he could, direct, personal fear hung over every spectator in the jammed, hot courtroom like a tangible thing. At the end, when the foreman finally blurted out the verdict, he looked like a madman himself.

WHEN the judge, Roerich, asked Cream if he had anything to say, and the murderer turned his livid face toward us, my wet hands were numb with cold. Dodge and Green weren't breathing, as Cream stood there a second looking at us, tall, inhumanly thin, his narrow shoulders slightly humped, his eyes live, staring circles of orange. He was dressed from head to foot in dead black, and even in the can he had managed to stay immaculate. His scant gray hair was oiled into a toupee; some of the oil shone on his bulging forehead. His mouth extended so far back in his cheeks that it was a deformity, and save for a queer muzzle of white around his incredible lips, the skin stretched over his face was pink. He knew, of course, what we'd done to him, and his voice was husky, resonant with fury, yet he articulated carefully.

"My congratulations," he said almost in a croak, "to the three lying, perjured jackals that call themselves detectives. They've sworn me nicely—"

The judge's gavel crashed, and he came to his feet, white-faced. He sentenced him in thirty words.

Afterwards, in his chambers, Judge Roerich said to me: "The three of you ought to be indicted. Yet I'd like to give you a medal. I only hope to God he doesn't make Matteawan."

"If we have to," I said grimly, "we'll go to the sanity hearings and put the fear of God into the experts."

We did go to the sanity hearings—three months later—to watch, agonized and helpless, while criminal fools dynamited all we'd done.

He went to Matteawan in April.

The man in morning clothes
pitched from the hearse.

In November, he brained a male nurse with a piece of bedstead in the infirmary. But in faking sick to get into the infirmary in the first place, he'd weakened himself too much, and he fainted, literally on the steps to freedom, the noise rousing a guard. They slapped him on the wrist and redoubled his guard, but I knew then what was coming—that we'd have to fight him again. I didn't know I'd have to do it myself.

In February he went. He was simply there one day, and not there the next. Nobody would admit they knew how he'd gone. Nobody was hurt. If anything could have made it worse, it was that last item. For no living soul can escape Matteawan peacefully unless they have money and friends on the outside.

In June he was in New York.

A DETECTIVE saw him at the Hundred and Tenth Street station, but lost him. It took me just ten minutes to get from my office down to police headquarters when I heard it. A blockhead named Mothersill was temporarily in charge of the detective bureau, and the fool got it into his head that I was yellow—that it was my own skin I was worrying about, when I almost pleaded with him to put the heat on. I swallowed insults as long as I could, for I knew I couldn't handle it alone. Our only chance was to get him through a wire. For being the physical freak he was, it was impossible for Cream to work in the open, and he had to have help. Once he had it, he could submerge himself in a hole—and the chances of ever tracing back to him a job he directed that way, were so small that I called it impossible. The help had to come from professional thieves. That was the one spot where we might get him—if we cracked down soon enough—but I couldn't make the thick-headed flatfoot see it. It was routine to him and routine it stayed. That attitude put him back pounding a beat later, after Cream's monstrous, inconceivable scheme blew open—but that was later.

I did what I could. I practically gave up sleep. I dragged through a sieve every underworld contact I had, trying desperately to leech onto a recruit to his staff.

At the end of five weeks I knew I was lost on that angle, and that I could only wait now for him to make a play—and the fresh fear began to torture me that he might make it and I wouldn't peg it.

It was fear, and the single-track state of mind it threw me into, that gave me my only chance. Otherwise, the whole savage, unbelievable enormity might have smashed to its horrible conclusion without anyone ever knowing what had happened. Certainly no one normal would have tried to see Cream's hand behind that first murderous thrust, and if we'd muffed that, any light we ever got would have been too late.

HE STRUCK in the sixth week—at night, of course. On the surface, God knows, it was sordid and ordinary enough to seem unimportant. I got the crisp, careful report over the telephone, and the minute I had it, something touched off inside me. Not that I even suspected then the whole satanic mesh of misdirection that underlay it, and that made it, so far from the ordinary thing it seemed, a masterpiece of murder. But the one damning inconsistency was enough to send a frantic chill shooting through my veins.

This is what happened—

A little red-monkey-faced man known in the Club Chez Vous as "John Smith" entered the back door of the club around three minutes past eleven, with a companion. Smith was well under the influence of liquor and the tall, slender man who accompanied him must have practically carried him up.

The Club Chez Vous was Al Lascoine's post-Repeal effort. The shrewd little Italian had stuck to his speakeasy profits and the place was lavish. The parlor floor of the old brownstone house was divided approximately in half. The front half—the spacious, softly lighted main supper room—was a duplex, a full two stories in height. A narrow balcony circled it, where the ceiling had been. The orchestra dais fronted an ample ribbon of polished dance floor. Wide, carpeted steps led to the balcony; there was a modernistic barroom just at the top.

In the right rear corner of the room below was the most secluded spot in the maroon-draped salon. There was a door in the rear wall there, but it was marked in brass, *Private—No Admittance.* That door led into a small hall, from which ascended stairs leading to the private rooms behind the balcony. At the rear of the hall was another door, opening out into the cement-court backyard of the place. That door was fastened by an elaborate and expensive turnbolt lock.

It was through that rear door, and up that flight of stairs that Smith and his companion made their appearance, at or before three minutes past eleven.

Smith was a customer of long standing; his bright, cheerful blue eyes and the unruly shock of pure white hair framing his ruby face, were familiar to most of the staff. He had, almost since the club's opening, visited once or twice a week, paid substantial checks each time, and comported himself perfectly. Naturally, Lascoine was more than glad to observe scrupulously the old man's anonymity, and his wish to avoid notice.

To the door that led into the backyard, there were only two keys in existence. Lascoine had one; John Smith the other. The old man could let himself out, walk through a gate in the fence at the back, and be in a narrow alley. That alley ran alongside a small office building that backed up to the club; the alley eventually debouched into the street above.

By this way, also, it was Smith's habit to enter the club, proceed to Room A on the second floor, leave his things in a cupboard there, descend again, and enter the main supper room through the door whose brass sign said, *Private—No Admittance.* The extreme corner table, overhung by the balcony, was reserved for him. He usually sat there, alone, in the gloom, while the floor show was in progress. At its conclusion, he would slip upstairs again and entertain—or be entertained by—one or more members of the cast.

The show was scheduled nightly for eleven forty-five.

AL LASCOINE, summoned by a waiter, reached Room A at five minutes after eleven. Smith was propped in a corner of the divan, blinking owlishly and happily at the chandelier, his small red hands clasped over his round little stomach, apparently drunk beyond speech. The slender, tall man stood over him with his back turned to Lascoine as the latter stood in the doorway.

The tall man spoke over his shoulder. "You are the proprietor?"

"Yes. Is there—"

"He insisted on being brought here. I presume you know him?"

"Certainly. He's a fine man. He—"

"Can you get something to fix him up?"

Lascoine went down and brought from the kitchen, lemons, tomato juice, black coffee, cracked ice, and mustard.

By then, the tall man had removed Smith's coat, vest, collar and tie, and had tied a napkin around his neck. Without turning he said brusquely: "Thank you. Just leave them on the table there, if you will."

Lascoine complied. "I—uh—if there's anything else you want, ring three times. I'll come myself."

A little worried, he returned to his duties as host in the main supper room.

His worries evaporated exactly a half hour later. From his station by the front door, he saw the old man come through the brass-marked door, apparently greatly revived. He was dressed again, and presentable, save for his unruly shock of white hair. He waved sheepishly toward Lascoine as he pulled out his chair, then beckoned a waiter. He was smoking a little cigar.

The waiter said that the dapper old man, apart from reeking strongly of alcohol, was in very good shape. Smith ordered a bottle of wine, had it placed close to him, so he could pour it himself during the impending floor show. He took a swallow of wine, folded his arms on the table in front of him, and buried his chin in them—a characteristic pose.

Every light in the house went out. Floodlights slapped down on the dance floor. The first part of the floor show swung into tuneful action.

A guest, sitting five tables away—the intervening ones were empty—saw the glowing red eye of the old man's cigar as he pulled on it once, then laid it down on an ashtray.

The first part of the presentation ran fifteen minutes. At the end of that time, the lights went up. No change had taken place in the old man's position. His cigar still sent a steady stream of smoke upward. Over his crossed arms, his eyes, however, seemed to be staring uncomfortably toward the front door.

When he remained motionless for minutes, his waiter came up behind him, spoke his name respectfully.

He got no answer. Believing the old man asleep, he slapped him smartly on the shoulder, repeated his name and bent to peer into his face.

The round little body must have been poised as if on a point. The moderate shock of the blow sent him over like a tenpin. He flopped sideways, backward, carrying the tablecloth with him. He keeled over the chair cornerwise; his little legs flew up, kicking the table over in a crash of china and glass. He spun as he slid off, thudded down on his back, his arms flopping inertly, his false teeth flying from his mouth, and lay there, glaring at the ceiling.

"John Smith" was dead.

WAITERS were running toward him, long before he hit the ground, Al Lascoine at their heels.

Lascoine dived through the screen of servitors, went to one knee, and had the old man's arm almost around his neck to carry him out, before the touch of the cold flesh shocked him. Hastily, he dropped the arm, felt for a pulse, and his jaws clicked as he found none. He jerked to his feet, snapped orders.

One waiter ran to the front door; one to the back—the door into the yard. Lascoine snatched a gun from his bouncer, clipped at him, "Get the cops! There's something fishy here!" and himself dived after the man going through the brass-tagged door on a vain hunt for the tall, slender man.

The backyard door was locked firmly. The upstairs rooms were empty. The tall man was gone.

Lascoine went back in to pacify his milling guests.

Lieutenant McIlroy with a squad from homicide, a man from the M.E.'s office, and a few reporters, arrived within eleven minutes. The M.E.'s man, after ripping open the dead man's shirt, gave the verdict, "Murder, all right," and McIlroy went into action. His hat shoved back on his corrugated red hair—suspicious, oriental eyes swiveling—he cracked questions from the side of his mouth with the gymnastic twitching of his cheek muscles that he fancied.

At the end of five minutes, he said grimly: "I get it now. When the lights went out the killer sneaked in, in the dark, and either forced or persuaded the dead man to come out in the hall. He killed him, carried him back in, and beat it. All right, now let's get a description—a full description—of this tall, skinny guy!"

It was then they realized that the tall, slender man had carefully and successfully avoided showing his face to anyone. There was only one faint ray of hope. The waiter who had answered the first summons from Room A and been sent for the proprietor, had come upon the tall man as he was bent over his companion. Because of his stooping position, his trousers had been stretched up over the backs of his shoes. The waiter swore that, while the heel of the right shoe was of normal size, that on the left was a good two inches in height. The impression prevailed that the man was dark. It was that scant description that went on the police radio.

The dead man's wallet was found, empty, in the clothes closet of Room A.

The M.E. leaned back on his hunkers, pointed a shining instrument at the dead man's bare chest. "Look at this, Lieutenant."

Directly over the heart a piece of bloodstained cotton was affixed with adhesive tape. This the doctor had folded back, disclosing a small, pea-shaped, black-and-red hole. "This is what killed him. A small-caliber bullet was shot directly into his heart, stopping it instantaneously. The gun was held less than a foot away. Then somebody put dressing over the wound, to stop the blood from staining his shirt. A cool customer, I'd say."

McIlroy leaned forward, pulled a thin gold chain, broken in the center, from around the dead man's neck. "What's this?"

Lascoine answered. "He kept the key to my back door on that."

The M.E. packed up, told McIlroy to go ahead, and the homicide man made his search. Then the sensational truth came out.

Papers in the old man's pockets ripped away the "John Smith" cognomen. McIlroy stared at his find with bulging eyes. "Lovely! This guy—this is Bernays Van Ryn—the multimillionaire—the one who has the big house on the Drive! My God—how did he—hey, come back here!" This, as the reporters in a body, broke away and sprinted for phones. McIlroy swung a purple face on Lascoine. "Did you know who he was?"

"Sure. I knew for over a year. I was just going to tell you, but—"

"But what? You damned little chiseler, you're in on this! You're the one had a chance to see the killer—and you're covering him! Get this—you better talk, and talk fast, or you'll spend the night downtown! I want a full description—and I want to know who that guy was. You and that damned waiter of yours—where is he?—you're going to come across, if I have to break every bone in your heads—"

"What the hell would I have a killing in my own drum for? Besides, I was in sight of a hundred people every min—"

"So you're a dummy!" McIlroy's big hand closed on the Italian's jacket, spun him back against the wall in the corner. He dropped him into a seat, cursing furiously. "Get around this crowd!" he snapped to the men. "This whole story may be phony. Find out what anybody and everybody knows!"

The M.E.'s man said quietly: "Better get hold of his family." McIlroy growled and frowned around for a phone.

He called the Van Ryn home and got the butler. The butler said the only relative living was Kyle Van Ryn, a brother, and McIlroy's heavy eyes narrowed. He got the brother's phone number. As he called it, he said grimly to one of the newspaper men: "The only relative—and old Van Ryn worth millions! Wouldn't it be funny if this here Kyle Van Ryn was tall and skinny and had one leg shorter than the—"

The reporter pointed out that the number McIlroy was calling was in Ozone Park, the other side of Brooklyn, and that with the fastest possible transport known to man, if Kyle Van Ryn had been here and killed his brother, he could not possibly reach home for another half hour yet.

"Sure," McIlroy said, "I know that. But if he ain't home and don't answer—"

He did answer. Slightly dampened, McIlroy urged him to come right over and hung up. On a sudden inspiration, he called the Van Ryn home again and asked the stammering butler for the name and phone number of Bernays Van Ryn's lawyer. When he reached him, McIlroy said bluntly: "He's been murdered. I suppose this brother Kyle inherits everything?"

"On the contrary," the lawyer said. "He inherits nothing. Charities and museums get it all."

McIlroy was chewing his lip when he hung up a second time.

A second reporter had joined the first. He said: "Hey, Lieutenant, I know this Kyle Van Ryn—the brother."

"What's he look like?"

"A little fat guy with a bald head—built like his brother. Sort of sappy looking. Dresses like a tramp cyclist. If you're trying to mark him down as this slender killer—forget it."

CHAPTER TWO

COPPER-FACED KILL

I **GOT** word of the crime two hours after it happened—over the phone from a reporter who had been there. Before he was halfway through I started to get a cold feeling in my stomach. By the time I hung up, I was as certain—utterly without reason—that Cream had engineered that murder somehow, as I was of my own name. I got over to the club as fast as I could move, but everything had been cleared away; the place was closed. A cop on guard wouldn't let me in.

I went home and burnt cigarettes till the extras came out. Then I sweated over every inch of the accounts.

Three phone calls brought me as much about the Van Ryns—the dead man and his brother—as I could expect to find out. They were the grandsons of the original Van Ryn who thought up the idea of using steel for railroad tracks. Their father had built the Van Ryn foundry and made a name for himself as the first man to employ actual criminals to break his strikes. He had also founded the firm of Van Ryn & Co., metal and mining brokers.

The sons—Kyle and Bernays—had sold the foundry and everything but the brokerage firm, at the old man's death. From what I gathered, they had since let the brokerage firm pretty well fizzle out, although they were still actually in business, and had an office on Pine Street.

At the time of the 1929 panic, there was some talk of them having taken heavy speculative losses, and for a while there was some worry about their solvency. That had cleared away now and they rated AAA.

The impression was that they were two vague, not too intelligent little middle-aged guys, who weren't entirely sure what it was all about.

Bernays was supposed to be an expert on his hobby, antique jewelry, and had made lavish gifts to the Metropolitan Museum.

Any part of which might mean anything—but left me without a single tangible item to jump on. Eventually, I went to bed with a headache—and nothing else—to dream the thing over again as I had heard it.

My office girl woke me with a phone call at eleven o'clock. "Pratt of the World-Over wants to see you down at Centre Street."

That was important business and brought me out of bed quickly enough. "When? What's happened?"

"One o'clock. He didn't say. Did you see about Bernays Van Ryn being killed?"

She went on to tell me a few more details. "The old boy did his dissipating on the sly. His servants were under the impression he went to bed every night at ten o'clock. He had his house arranged so he could slip out and in without them knowing it. Why don't you drop by there and see what you can do? They say he has a lot of antique jewelry that's worth looking at."

"Where's the angle?" I said bewilderedly.

"I don't know," she confessed. "But I've always been curious about that big house on the drive—I mean what it looks like inside. It's so perfectly ugly—"

I made disgusted noises in my throat and hung up.

I searched the morning editions going downtown. Nowhere did I see so much as a theory as to why the old man had been killed. There was no news of the killer. The police had several important clues, and so forth. Still I had nothing—could find nothing. Only my hunch, that here, somewhere, was a connection with my man.

PRATT, of the World-Over Indemnity, was the man who attended to the policing of the clients of that organization. He had a big staff of sleuths of his own, naturally, but he hired privates from time to time, and I'd been canvassing him regularly. This looked like my break. He was a thin, stooped, sharp-nosed, sharp-eyed man with a pinched, purple, bony face. He wore thick horn-rimmed spectacles. He always had one shoulder hunched up, his hand in his trouser pocket, as though about to wince from a blow. Whether a pose or not, he gave the impression of being the most harassed man in the world. I found him with Inspector Oleson, of the robbery detail. He stopped in mid-gesture as I came in, fixed a lowering glance on me. "You, eh?" To Oleson he said: "I'm putting Blue on this, too."

Oleson nodded wearily. He and I had no quarrel. He was mopping the yellow-fringed bald dome of his head. He wasn't a squarehead—his temples bulged—but his spade chin was narrow. One of his china-blue eyes had slipped a cog and was forever motionless. He could see out of it, but it would not swivel.

"He thinks I'm simple," Pratt raved. "Listen, Blue—this morning I'm sitting at my desk. The phone rings. A man's voice says, 'We're going to knock you over for a couple of million dollars. It's going to mean plenty of killing. You wouldn't want to lay half that on the line, and let everything be serene, would you?' I said, 'Are you crazy?' and he sighed. 'I didn't think it would do any good,' he said, 'but I prom-ised to try it. I can't say I blame you—it does sound kind of goofy, doesn't it?' I was having the call traced, see what I mean? So I said, 'Wait a minute—let me get this straight. Just what sort—' Then he cut me off with, 'It's all right, Pratt—I knew it was foolish to mention it, but I had to. It's going to be good. When you find out where we're going to whack you, you'll laugh yourself sick.' Then he hung up, and my secretary came in with the number he was calling from. Where do you suppose?"

"Where?" I stooged.

"The Public Library on Forty-second Street!"

That brought on a second's silence. I looked at Oleson, but I don't know whether he was looking at me or not. I ran a finger inside my collar. "I—uh—it sounds kind of like a nut."

"Oh, does it!" Pratt climbed on me. "Well, I'm a specialist on nuts! I get more nut calls in a day than anybody, else in a year. I'm telling you this guy was in dead earnest—and I know! The World-Over insures all those public buildings. There's manuscripts and one thing an' another in the library that're worth plenty of money. It's the last place in the world anyone'd think of robbing—so that may be just what this pup's going to do. Now do you want the job or don't you?"

"Sure I do," I said hastily. "But I—uh—just because he called from the library doesn't mean they're going to boost—"

"I know that! But it's significant! Dig around! Anybody planning that size job anywhere is sure to start a ripple. You talk big about your sources of information, when you're looking for business. Now let's see you do something!"

"Well, sure," I said. "All right, Mr. Pratt—I'll try."

I felt plenty queer as I closed the door behind me. Any job from the World-Over meant a lot, but,—what a job!

I WAS rounding the dingy marble stairs near the front door when Iaccarino, the squat little Italian mouthpiece, sailed out from the other side, his huge mass of black hair falling almost to his shoulders, his chin up, as ever, and went out ahead of me. I threw a curious glance in his wake to see which of the public enemies he worked for was getting sprung. I was mildly surprised to see Al Lascoine, the little proprietor of the Club Chez Vous.

He was a sad sight.

His tuxedo was battered and baggy, his stiff collar wilted, as was his stiff shirt. His usually swarthy face was the color of dough, and there was a bruise on his cheekbone. His eyes were red-rimmed, and he walked bent over, his hands crammed in his jacket pockets, plodding dully, surlily ahead. When I spoke to him, he swung wary, dull eyes at me, then stared ahead again, as I fell in at his side.

"Hello, pal," he gave me the inevitable greeting.

"Tough breaks, Al," I commiserated with him.

"Thousands of dollars," he blurted savagely. "This'll cost me thousands. That lunkhead McIlroy—" He erupted more words I can't print.

I nodded sympathetically. Al was a pretty square guy. I was sure he wouldn't mix in a killing—at least not in his own place. I lowered my voice. "Hey, just between the two of us," I said. "Those keys now—to your back door—I read about. Is that on the level, about there being just the two of them?"

We were out in the sunlight. The flat, intricate, gold key he dug from his vest flashed like fire. "Pal—so help me, this and the one the old man had, are the only two keys to that lock. He made me swear there'd be no duplicates. He wore his round his neck. There isn't a chance anybody could have got it and had one made."

I handed it back as we reached the bottom of the steps. "I'd sure like to hear the real inside on that killing," I started.

"God Almighty!" he raved wildly, "Don't you think I would?"

I watched him shamble off, into a taxi, and roll away.

I spotted another taxi, a few cars up the curb, and moved toward it. I was less than ten feet away when its door opened silently—no clicking of the latch—and a chunky, copper-faced lad in a gray suit and dark shirt and tie, with a wild look in his eyes, slipped out. He pulled his peak cap lower as he came toward me.

"Blue?" His voice was choked, husky. "You're Blue—aren't you?"

One look at the twitching muscles around his mouth and I knew I was talking to a scared man. Words rattled at me, as he grabbed my cuff, tried to lead me. "Blue—listen—if you're working for Al Lascoine, I can tell you—can give you the lowdown—only you've got to take care—"

I disengaged my cuff. "Be your age. I can listen here."

"No—I can't here—you've got to see for yourself! You'd think I was crazy if I told you! It's—it's insane—the biggest thing ever pulled off in this town. They'll get millions! But I can't sleep for thinking— I can't—go—through—" His voice dried up with emotion.

He never had time to draw a fresh breath.

The next second, in the full glare of the afternoon sun, the long flight of steps to headquarters behind us, parked cars lining the curb and half a hundred pedestrians within yards, I felt the contact of Cream's new organization.

THE COPPER-FACED lad had stepped in front of me; his hands were pawing my forearms. He stood so as to block my view of the cars at the curb. Even so, I got one swift glance at the black-gloved hand that darted round the back of a Buick, holding a heavy revolver. But I never had a chance to save the boy; flame and roar erupted seemingly in my very face, before my hand was a quarter the way to my own gun. It smashed the informer's skull; it must have gone right through his head, for it ticked my hat, and as I tried desperately to fling myself aside, a great gout of blood smacked me square in the face, and for an instant I was crimson-blind.

I heard the gun roar again as I jerked back from the boy; wind fanned my cheek. A motor in the roadway roared. I stumbled in and toward the line of parked cars, trying wildly to get out of range, wiping frantically at my searing eyes, as the gun thundered again—and again. Fire creased my arm, and I dived to the cement; half a dozen police whistles shrilled. Chips spurted from the sidewalk as I threshed over and over. I spun off the curb, into the gutter, raking my face on the running board of a car, before the shots stopped.

I heard the motor in the roadway roar—this time in motion. My streaming eyes functioned again hazily and I twisted on my stomach, got a foot against the curb and sent myself flopping out toward the road. My head got clear just in time to see a black sedan, racing down the street, crowd a model-T Ford up onto the curb. Before I could whip my gun arm out, the sedan vanished in among traffic.

I SCRAMBLED to my feet, ran back around the car, mopping my face, bolstering my useless gun. There was noise, a converging crowd, shouting, pounding feet everywhere. A hysterical woman was screaming down the street. Police uniforms sprouted. Two coppers suddenly dived at me.

"Go away," I bit at them. "It was me they were shooting at!" I jerked out my folder of credentials, waved it in their face as I charged into the press.

The body of the gray-shirted lad was lying on its back on the pavement, blood streaming from his head. As I broke through one side of the mob, Sergeant Erskine, of homicide, broke through the other and went to one knee by the dead man. I clipped my story to him in five sentences as a uniformed man tried to push me back, and Erskine looked up from his quick search of the body to snap: "Let him alone."

He pulled from the bloody clothes a letter or two, a little change, a pocketknife, a union card that showed the dead man had once—four years back—been an electrician in Chicago, a package of cigarettes and a paper of matches. My eyes froze on the matches. They bore the name of the Croton Arms Hotel, and its little insignia. They were the type that are broadcast everywhere, but hotels usually stock their own. At least it was a chance—and faint as it was, the vein in my temple started to pulse swiftly.

I stood up, as Erskine did. The noise of shouting around us was deafening, as the cops struggled for order. I stepped quickly around to Erskine's side, and clipped in his ear: "You know all I know. You know where to get me if you want me. I've got an idea—and I've got to hit it fast!" and before he could decide to delay me, I was slipping through the jam, as swiftly as I could, toward a cab. My eyes were burning, as the things that had crammed into my mind straightened themselves out.

The stoolie had thought I was working for Lascoine! That must mean the Van Ryn murder! Yet he had attempted to spill something that echoed plainly of Pratt's pipe dream!

As I pounded northward in the cab my hands were cleaning off my clothes as best I could. Question after question burned in my head. The most vital one of all was: who was the target of that first shot? And then, suddenly I realized that it didn't matter much. Whether they had shot my would-be informer to keep him from telling me anything, or whether this was an attempt to murder me, the result was the same—except for the cold stiff body of the electrician, bleeding on the sidewalk back there. Even if they had not been after me before, they were now. They had to be. No possible way existed for them to know how much the lad had gotten across to me before he went down. And the last five shots had certainly been thrown my way.

That was one way of adding it up. The other—equally pleasant—was simply that they had been after me right along, and had caught up with me at a most opportune time—for them. And I knew of nobody who wanted to kill me at the moment except Cream. Both these things must tie in with him! The wild-sounding job Pratt had handed me. And the Van Ryn murder!

WE SLID to a stop across the street from the Croton Arms. It was a showy, orange-lighted little apartment hotel. I threw a bill to the driver and said: "Sit here till I decide what to do,"

"Now, listen, mister—" he started sourly.

"Shut up," I snapped, as a large black sedan stopped at the corner above us, and two men slid out. The car went on down the side street. The two men came toward the entrance to the Croton Arms. Their hats were low on their faces, light topcoats around their shins, and they walked swiftly. They disappeared in the Croton.

Break one! I had figured they would hardly dare come directly home from the shooting—if these were indeed the shooters. I had beaten them here. It took me just a split second to do my thinking. Then I was out of the cab, drifting across toward the Croton entrance. I had a gun in my jacket pocket, and a hand on it, though I didn't expect to use it. Even assuming that I ran into the folks I sought, they would hardly go for gunplay in their own bailiwick. Whatever this insane project was, it was being handled by professionals—and smart ones.

I almost got inside too soon. A crowded elevator was just closing, directly across the lobby from me. The second it was shut, I shot across toward the vacant one beside it, snapped at the uniformed colored boy, "Those two men in topcoats just came in—you know them?" and gave him a flash at my badge.

His eyes showed white. "Yes—yassah. They in Twelve A—"

"Beat them up there," I clipped, and slammed his door closed. "Come on, come on!"

We ate up twelve floors in a swoop. "Keep your mouth shut," I told him as I stepped off, "or I'll have you electrocuted."

I made the shadows of a stairway, just a fraction of an instant before the other elevator door slid open, and the two men in topcoats got off. I shrank back, half a flight up on the carpeted steps, as they strode toward me. One of them growled, half under his breath, and the other nodded, turned in at a door and knocked in cadence. It was opened immediately, and he went in.

The first man marched on up to the room almost at the front corner of the building, turning down his coat collar, and as he halted before it and tapped with the back of his hand, I got a view of his face. He thumbed back his hat while he waited, to give me further assistance. Even then I didn't place him, till he sniffed. In doing that, he contracted all one side of his dirt-furrowed face, baring tobacco-stained teeth. He was "Sniffler" Franklin, of Chicago, supposed to be a yegg, a fast worker, without a conviction against him. As the door opened before him, he sent shiny little green eyes over his shoulder, dancing down the hall. But he failed to look in my direction, thank God, for recognition of the shirt-sleeved man inside the room had me momentarily gaping.

Razor cheekbones, gaunt cheeks, burning, luminous black eyes, his thick, curly, black hair oiled, Vance Didrickson was the last man in the world I expected to see here. Ten years ago, he had beat it out of New York a jump ahead of rivals' bullets, who had got to him before he'd perfected his plans to get up as a gangster. He wasn't the type, anyway. Long back, I'd pegged him as too clever for any strong-arm racket.

THE DOOR closed and almost at the same instant the one down the hall—the one that had swallowed Franklin's companion—opened, and a slight pockmarked man in black chauffeur's livery ran out, pulling on a topcoat as he went toward the elevator. He left the door open behind him, and before someone closed it profanely, I bent over and caught a picture of the noisy and tobacco-haze-filled room. It was crammed with men, and echoed to the rattle of poker chips, and the clink of glasses. As the lights were on, that must mean the blinds were drawn. It was still daylight outside.

That door closed, too. The man in chauffeur's uniform went down on the elevator.

It took me about ten churning minutes to decide that, whatever mad schemes I might have in my head, now, of all times, was no place to go off half cocked. I hadn't done badly—and I hadn't tipped my hand. That might be worth plenty. That the assorted underlings in the rooms along this hall would be able to give me a line on Cream was something I didn't even consider. Whatever the set-up, he would never be trapped that simply. One man would have to know—I thought of the killer with the two-inch heel—but I couldn't see any of this crew as the one. I could take a plant—until somebody spotted me—or I could let things lie and go chase down the other angles buzzing in my head. Or, of course, I could wangle my way in to one of the rooms and try my luck at juggling fifteen armed thugs around while I trapped them into confessing murder or the like. I couldn't see much in that—except maybe an ounce of lead in my foolish face.

I went up the rest of the flight, and took the elevator down.

CHAPTER THREE

THE MEN FROM THE MORGUE

THE AFTERNOON sun was low and red, as I rode a taxi toward the Van Ryn house.

I could see a hearse standing near the portico before the house when we were only a block away. I stopped my cab and got out, paid off, tried to get my speech ready by the time I reached McIlroy, whose white-gray felt hat I made out, just inside the front gate of the place.

It was a huge, rectangular, red-and-brown house, a gloomy fortress of a place, set in a tilted square of barbered lawn that comprised a block, facing on Riverside Drive. The back end was high, the front low. The narrow side streets came down at a sharp incline to the Drive, and the Drive itself seemed to bow as it went by—to rise up again abruptly just beyond the south corner of the spiked iron fence that enclosed the grounds.

There were gates in the fence at front and side and cement walks led from the gates to rococo portico entrances, at front and side of the house, each with its few black-brown steps. At the side portico two bluecoats stood talking, the red sun flashing from their buttons. A mournful-faced detective named Khowles was camped with one foot on the front steps. McIlroy was at the bottom of the front walk, just inside the gate. I walked down toward the gate under the inimical stare of his lowering, dark eyes. The oriental-looking pads of flesh over them seemed heavier than usual; his eyes were tired, almost closed. There was none of his usual belligerency in the twitching in his cheek as he rolled out of the corner of his mouth: "Well—what do you want?"

"Like to see the family, if I could," I said. "I—"

"Well, you can't. The body's just come back from the morgue." He nodded at the empty hearse. "Come around some other time."

"Hell, Lieutenant, I'm not going to—"

He blinked suddenly. "What's your interest here, anyway?"

"World-Over Indemnity Company."

He blew breath through his nose in disgust. "You damned jackals! What's the matter? Don't you believe he's dead?" Then he blinked. "Who's the beneficiary? I didn't know he carried life insurance."

"I didn't either," I said. "Oh—the Rockefeller Institute. Have you found out what was stolen from his wallet yet?"

"No. Buzz off. You can't see anybody now. Try tomorrow."

"What would you say if I told you I knew where you could find out?"

His heavy stare switched from one of my eyes to the other. "Where?"

I shrugged. "I didn't say I knew. I might rack my brains for a suggestion though if I got a little cooperation around here."

He gestured impatiently. Bernays' body just came in from the morgue. You can't bust in on the poor guy now. What've you got on this wallet gag?"

"I'd have to get inside to know," I said. "And I don't guess anybody's feelings are going to get hurt by my going in. Kyle Van Ryn hasn't been living with the dead man for at least two or three years, has he? They couldn't have been so damned fond of each other that he'd be overcome now."

He frowned, pulled at his nostrils in indecision. "Well," he said uncomfortably, "I'll see, as soon as he's alone. But if you pull any boners—"

THE DOOR of the house opened and two stupid-looking, horse-faced young men in the ill-fitting mourning clothes that undertaker's assistants invariably effect, came out. One walked solemnly toward the street.

I looked at McIlroy. "How about now?"

He said, "I'll see," and turned toward the house. When the long-faced lad in mourning clothes opened the gate for the hearse to come through, I stepped calmly inside, stood with my hands in my hip pockets, ignoring his worried glance.

Subconsciously I heard the hinges squeak, heard the undertaker's man go back up the sidewalk behind me, and heard them both climb aboard The motor purred into activity. McIlroy was halfway to the front steps—

If I needed more proof that I had jumped into the thick of some monstrous, obscure plan—or that that plan was definitely and swiftly moving forward now—I got it then.

The door at the top of the front steps of the house suddenly opened a foot, waved closed, then opened again. Kyle Van Ryn, on hands and knees, crawled through it. He was coughing violently, horribly. He reached the stoop, and one hand went to his throat—then he collapsed, came tumbling down, head over heels.

I heard McIlroy's gasp as the big cop broke into a run; my hands jerked from my pockets and I started after him. Then my brain functioned again. I almost tripped, trying to check myself and whirl around toward the now moving dead wagon—and I saved my life.

One of the horse-faced youths stood in the rear of the moving vehicle. He was using one hand to hold one folding door open. With the other he was drawing a bead on me with a heavy blue revolver. I threw myself to the turf at my right—just as the gun exploded.

He fired a second time, as my belly hit the ground, but before he could get a third one out I had an automatic from under my arm—and this time I used it, I jerked the trigger home viciously—and held it there—no pot-shooting. Flame and roar spurted from my hand, and the kick of the gun drove my elbow in a furrow along the turf. I poured a stream of leaden death into the banging doors of the now-racing hearse. The man with the revolver staggered back. Another gun flamed from the darkness inside, plowed earth in my face. I switched aim slightly, raked the other side, ran for the shelter of the portico. There was a scream from within—the driver, I guessed, for the car gave a sudden jerk.

Then, like a shot out of a gun, one of the horse-faced youths was catapulted out through the doors. His shout was lost in the motor roar. He whipped over in an arc—and whacked head first into the pavement. I was up, and racing for the gate, but I winced as his head squashed. His heels whipped over, slammed pavement, then the whole arched body slumped slowly sideways as the hearse went through the gates.

My gun roared again at the flying hearse—and once more. Then they pounded around one of the bends in the Drive. I dived out to the outer rim of the Drive—but the upward slope and trees blocked my view. I heard the furious roar of their motor disappearing around a corner above as I swung back toward the crumpled mass of meat in the driveway.

McILROY was pounding up, his gun in one red fist, his eyes wild. "What—who—what—" he shouted shrilly.

"Phonies, in the hearse—tried to gun me!" I clipped. For a split second, the gruesome sight of the man in mourning clothes had me dazed. I jerked myself out of it, grabbed McIlroy and spun him toward the house. "Come on, you jackass!" I raved, "Don't you realize you've had a robbery? What was in the house to steal?"

"Robbery!" he gasped. "I—" His teeth clicked and he drove for the house. The two uniformed guards had come halfway round the house, stood fingering their guns, gaping, as we sprinted up to the steps. McIlroy snarled one of them out to look after the body, the other back to his post, and roared at Knowles, bent over Van Ryn: "Bring the old man inside—carry him!"

We both cleared the front steps at a leap; slammed back the front door, and were in a long hall. Doors opened from each side. McIlroy was grim-faced, as he dived through one at his right. I followed him into a cream-and-gold living room, through it and into a library behind, done in red leather and black oak. McIlroy's breath whistled through his teeth.

A silver-handled coffin sat in the middle of the floor. A huge, black, roll-top desk stood against one wall, at the end of a wide leather couch. Packed like three sardines on the couch were a huge man with bull-dog jowls and pomaded gray hair, in the livery of a butler—a buxom woman in a black dress—and a dull-faced younger woman. Their eyes were closed; they were breathing heavily. McIlroy dived to one knee beside them—then jerked out: "By God—chloroformed!"

McIlroy jumped to the coffin, as I reached it. The undersized little body inside was lying on its side, jammed against the wall of the coffin, seemingly lost in the wide expanse of white satin. McIlroy jerked him back to position. From the resemblance—in spite of startling differences of hair, teeth and expression—I knew this was Kyle Van Ryn's brother all right. I jerked my eyes away—and saw the desk.

From the rear of it—what should have been a smooth side—projected a small drawer. The drawer was splintered; smashed—and radiating out from it, on the side of the desk, were deep, long scratches; McIlroy jerked round to follow my glance, dived toward the desk. "By God! A secret drawer." Then, "It's empty!"

"That was what they were after, then?"

He jumped suddenly, wheeled and ran for the door. "The hell it is! Downstairs!"

Knowles was staggering into the cream-and-gold sitting room, the groaning old man like a sack of meal, on his shoulder, as we pounded through. McIlroy snapped: "On the couch there—bring him around as fast as you can!"

As we ran toward the back of the house he raved over his shoulder: "A steel vault—private museum for the old man's antiques! Damn them! They told me it was empty!"

We ran down a flight of steps from the kitchen to the cellar, and were in an oblong chamber about one-third the size of the cellar. The wall ahead of us was of riveted steel plates, holding a small door. McIlroy's handkerchief jerked around his hand as he dived for the small knob, on the door, and rattled it desperately. It was locked.

He looked at me anxiously, the sweat shining on his face, and I pulled a case of keys and instruments from my pocket and shoved him aside, took a quick look at the lock. I flipped open my case. The lock was a good commercial type but for a strong room it was a joke. I worked an instrument something like half a hairpin into the keyhole.

An electric shock knocked me flat on my back. Simultaneously, a gong began hammering violently in the upper part of the house, spinning McIlroy around in his tracks. "Good God! What's that?"

"A burglar alarm," I said, as I picked myself up, and snatched my hanging instrument case free. The gong stopped. "Not a bad trick. Put the wrong key in and get the works. And they put an easy-looking lock on just for temptation."

He swayed back and forth between stairs and door. "You—can't you open it?"

"Not me. Maybe Kyle Van Ryn's got the right key."

"It—it doesn't look as though anybody'd been in there, does it?" he panted hopefully as we ran up again. I didn't answer that one.

WHEN we ran into the cream-and-gold room, the butler, white-faced was swaying in the library door, saying in a husky voice to Knowles: "Mr.—Mr. Van Ryn and I were in the library when they came in with the coffin. They dropped it and covered us with pistols. Then one of them hit me with a blackjack and I went unconscious."

Van Ryn's weak voice added: "Then they hit me. I tried to duck, but they knocked me down—then the chloroform. I held my breath—then everything went black and dizzy. I heard wood crack and heard them running around. When I couldn't hear them any more, I crawled to the door to try and warn you—"

McIlroy cut in with: "Can either of you open the vault downstairs?"

There was a blank silence. McIlroy cursed under his breath. "Then do either of you know what was in the secret drawer of that big black desk in there?"

They didn't. Van Ryn said: "I didn't know there was one."

I drove one at them. "Can either of you think of anything, part of which might have been in Bernays' wallet last night, and part in the desk?"

There was another silence. Then, all of a sudden, it was broken by a deafening, shrieking, wailing of police sirens—it sounded like a hundred of them. McIlroy started to disregard it, then his mouth hung open as the screaming noise rose to an incredible crescendo. He looked at me, and we both turned and hurried out into the hall.

Through the half-open door, still ajar, I saw men in the uniform of the Vigilant Patrol—a private-watchman service—already running through the front gate, carrying shotguns and pistols. I flung the door open. No less than six police cruisers were screaming to a halt and vomiting blue-coats, on the two sides of the house I could see.

The leader of the Vigilant men roared at me, as he came up, "Put your hands high—you!" and pointed a shotgun at my middle.

I raised my hands, and backed into the hall, as he drove the gun into my stomach, without decreasing his speed. "Hey—wait a minute!" I gasped. "Where did you people come from?"

The leader bent to peer at my face sharply, as others ran in. "Blue! Say, what the—listen—somebody must be trying to burgle a vault downstairs—it's loaded with jewelry, or something—"

"It was me—trying to pick the lock," I said loudly, and calmed the turmoil. "How did you get here so fast?"

"We're using the cops' system—a shortwave radio and a cruiser in the sections where we got heavy business. What the hell are you doing picking the—"

Cops had crowded in. McIlroy started shouting fretfully at them that everything was all right, as I made hasty explanation to the Vigilant man. Finally crowds of men went out cursing. I held onto my man till the hall emptied. "Listen—can your people open that vault downstairs?"

He blinked. "How the hell do I know?"

I hurried him into the cream-and-gold room, pointed at the door of the library. "There's a phone in there. Find out—like a good guy— and don't get excited over the people in the room."

He shrugged. "O.K."

When he was at the door I called as an afterthought: "And see if they know exactly what's in the museum, right now."

As he vanished, the butler's hoarse voice said: "There's nothing in it, sir—nothing at all."

"How do you know?"

Then, as he started to answer, the phone in the library rang.

THE BUTLER half rose. From inside we heard the Vigilant man calmly answering the call. Then his tread as he came to the door. "Hey—there's an undertaker on the phone. Says his hearse was stolen or something—"

"Tell him we know all about it. I'll call him in a minute," McIlroy said.

I swung back on the butler. "How do you know there's nothing in the vault?"

"Mr. Van Ryn told me two or three weeks ago that he was sending everything up to the museum—the Metropolitan, sir. About twelve days ago, I was unable to sleep, and just before dawn I thought I heard someone moving in the grounds. I went into a room on this side of the house and saw two men carrying packing cases out to a truck at the curb, and the master directing them. I watched till they finished and drove off."

"He cleared it out in the middle of the night?" I said incredulously.

"Yes, sir."

"Why?"

The butler looked pained. "I—it's difficult to explain, sir. Mr. Van Ryn often did business late at night. It's not for me to say, sir—you understand it's only a presumptuous guess on my part—"

"Spit it out."

He swallowed, glanced at Kyle Van Ryn. "Some of the items—that is—he would not want anyone to know he had bought them, possibly. He—he was a collector, sir. Some—some of the rare bits, I dare say, have a questionable title."

McIlroy grunted. "Damn right. Half the stuff these collectors buy is hot. They don't seem to have no sense of right and wro—"

"How many boxes were there?"

"I saw them load eight or nine, sir. There may have been more. It was dark. I asked Mr. Van Ryn about them next morning and he told me he had sent them off to the Metropolitan."

The Vigilant man came out of the library. "O.K. They're sending a man up to open the vault. I have to get back to the job. He'll be here."

As he went out, I said to McIlroy: "Better check to see if those boxes reached the museum."

"Yes, by God!" He hurried into the library.

Now, if ever, I thought, was my chance to snatch the information I had come for. I tossed at the butler: "I understand you people didn't know Mr. Van Ryn was slipping out to that cabaret he was killed in."

"No, sir. I—you see, Mr. Van Ryn was in the habit of receiving people at the side door—people he did not wish to see. Hence, he had this wing completely isolated. We never knew his movements. He slept down here. We had our rooms on the opposite side, up-stairs—have you been over the house?"

"No."

"Well, if—"

McIlroy came back in. "They got there, all right. Ten of them. Stuff they'd been expecting. It's not unusual for him to send stuff at dawn."

I asked him if it was all right for the butler to show me over the house and he assented sourly.

WE COVERED it swiftly. The third floor was completely closed. The second floor had a lot of bedrooms and bathrooms on the north wing. The south wing was closed.

The north wing of the ground floor was closed. On the south wing, from front to rear, were the cream-and-gold sitting room; the library; a den, with a small bathroom, where on a day bed, the murdered man had done most of his sleeping; a small dining room and kitchen, from which stairs led to the cellar. Between den and library, a transverse hall ran, opening to the side door. It did not join the main hall, but was blocked up at the former juncture.

When I asked him the arrangements of the cellar, he got so complicated that I said: "Draw me a picture—and one of the ground floor, too."

He did. As he handed them to me, he said: "There's supposed to be a private entrance to the museum in the basement, but only Van Ryn knew it."

I stared at the diagram in my hand. "You mean a trick entrance?"

"Yes, sir."

"Do you know how the alarm system is arranged, in the basement?"

"I don't think Mr. Van Ryn trusted any living soul with that information, sir."

I let him go, stood alone in the hall, trying to make something of the picture.

Then I got my break.

I hardly heard the drawing-room door open. I looked up to see the frightened face of Kyle Van Ryn send a swift look up and down the hall. He slid out, closing the door behind him, and fixed deep-sunk eyes on me. "Mr. Blue"—his voice was a husk—"I want to hire—to hire your services. There's—there's something—it's the whole reason for all this terrible horror. I must see you somewhere—away from the police. I'm going mad—I don't know what to do. Where can I see you?"

I thought I was dreaming. "When?"

"Right away—as soon as humanly possible! As soon as we can slip away from this—this morgue! Will you come to my office?"

"Where is your office?"

He told me the number on Pine Street. "Van Ryn and Company."

The door of the drawing room disgorged McIlroy, just as I clipped: "O.K."

When the Vigilant manager arrived, the museum was found completely empty.

CHAPTER FOUR

TWO-INCH HEEL

THE BUILDING on Pine Street was small and square, of dingy red brick, almost surrounded by towering new skyscrapers. It was fully dark by the time I halted across the street, and peered over at its sickly lighted, narrow, marble lobby.

My eyes were sharp as I eased into a doorway and spent a minute searching the street. The last batch of home-hurrying employees from the buildings nearby crowded the sidewalks. I was almost certain that I had not been followed down, but I wasn't sure. And the grim knowledge overhung me every minute that—whatever was going on—I was staying alive only so long as they failed to catch me napping. Every shadow might well hold my finish, and, assuming that Kyle Van Ryn had nothing to do with his brother's death—yes, I was suspicious of everybody at this point—I didn't want to turn the spotlight on the fact that he was in touch with me privately.

I crossed over, one hand on the gun in my pocket, my eyes alert.

On the bulletin board in the musty little lobby, Van Ryn & Co. were listed on the third floor. I rode up on the creaking elevator, and the stooped old gaffer that ran it directed me to the end of the hall.

I held my gun in my hand, with my hat over it, my thumb clamping its brim, as I knocked on the ground-glass door. It was opened by a tall, thin woman with a shrewd, mirthless, square face, dressed in a severely tailored suit and plain black hat. She looked me over through wide green eyes. I said: "I have an appointment with Mr. Van Ryn—Mr. Kyle Van Ryn."

"What about?" she asked in a deep, calm voice. "The firm's business?"

"Oh, yes," I said.

She stood aside, inviting me tacitly to enter the green-carpeted office. "You may feel at liberty to discuss it with me, if you wish. I am the senior partner of this firm." She closed the door behind me.

I blinked. "Is that so? Miss—"

"Whitlaw's my name."

"—Whitlaw. I—if you don't mind. I'd rather wait."

She hesitated, looked at a cheap wristwatch, finally shrugged her shoulders. "Suit yourself. But you'll have to wait outside. I'm damned if I'll wait around for Van Ryn to appear. If—"

The door opened behind us, and Kyle Van Ryn anxious-faced and with a desperate look in his eyes, hurried in. His breath went out in relief. He said, "Miss Whitlaw," awkwardly.

"Gentleman for you," she said, and turned to pick up a square purse that lay on the wooden railing.

"I'll lock up," Van Ryn said, and held open the gate in the railing. "If you'll just step into my office—" I moved through the opening.

Miss Whitlaw's heavy voice said, "Good night," coldly, as she went out the door. I turned to say good night—and the words stuck in my throat. Just as the door swung to behind her, I happened to look at her feet.

Her left heel was a good inch and a half higher than her right one!

VAN RYN had gone on ahead and was holding the door of the little corner office open. For a second I stood stock-still, breathless, as one possible answer to a mystery flashed into my mind. I shot at Van Ryn:

"How long has that woman been working for you—or with you?"

"How long? I—ever since—she was my father's secretary."

Another second, then I followed him in, tight-lipped. He had been nerving himself. Behind his desk, he took a long breath and blew out in a tortured voice: "I've got to ask you. What is my brother's death to you?"

"A place to find a lead," I told him promptly. "I've got to nail a certain criminal. I think he's working out a scheme. I think your brother's death is one of the parts of it.

"I—if—" He swallowed, then blurted: "Do you have to—would you feel you had to tell the police—what I might tell you?"

"No. What have you done?"

He wiped his bald head with a handkerchief from his sleeve. "I—God help me—I don't know just what I've done," he said hoarsely. "I—I'll tell you everything—"

He dropped into his chair and stared at his clenched hands on the blotter. To make you understand—I'll have to go into my personal affairs. When my father died, he left this business to Miss Whitlaw, my brother, and myself. She had ten percent—we divided the rest. At the time of the bull market in Twenty-eight, I was speculating in stocks. It seemed—really it seemed as if I couldn't lose. I—but you've heard plenty of fools tell that story. I induced my brother to speculate with the firm's funds. That—that's not illegal, or anything. For a time, everything went perfectly—we rode a rising market. Then my brother—urged by Miss Whitlaw, I don't doubt—wanted to sell out. I thought he was mad. We compromised this way: the greater part of the capital of Van Ryn and Company was then in stocks. We divided everything up, in the proportions of our relative shares in the business. Miss Whitlaw sold her share of the stocks out, the moment she got them. My brother, influenced by her, sold his also, but later influenced by me, bought some of them back again.

"Then the crash came. I was worse than wiped out—I was sunk in debt. Bernays took severe losses, but, thanks to Miss Whitlaw's urging, he had saved a good deal of his capital. I had to have money. He offered to buy my shares in Van Ryn and Company from me, for many times what they were worth—that was his way of helping me out of my hole. I sold him all but ten percent. He installed me as general manager of the firm—at a large salary. It was ridiculous. Miss Whitlaw was up in arms. He had to pacify her—and I think he did it by promising her first option on any of his stock in Van Ryn and Company that he ever planned to sell. And all on my account—to provide me with a decent livelihood.

"That was one side of it. The other side of it was this—for the first time in his life, my brother began to show some of the traits of my father. Father was a hard man, and a very—he thought very highly of money. I worked in his office once, and I recall—but never mind that. The point is he thought of little but money.

"There doesn't seem to be any of that in me. I wish to God there were. Nor had Bernays shown any of it—until this time when he lost so much through my advice. I think Miss Whitlaw had a good deal to do with what happened. I imagine she reminded him constantly that I had caused him his loss. She has always thought of me as a nincompoop.

"At any rate, this loss seemed to prey on his mind, and one evening he flew into a rage—without any immediate provocation—and flung the most violent reproaches at me, about the money. Naturally, I could make no defense. Then, as suddenly as it started, his anger cooled, and he was desperately, wildly penitent.

"If that had been all, it would have been forgotten. But it wasn't. Something had changed inside him. This tirade began to be repeated—more often and more often—till my life became unbearable. I had to move away from him. He agreed that it was best. He was as miserable as I was, but he could not seem to control himself. I moved over to Ozone Park, where I have a little house that suits me perfectly."

HE LICKED his lips, let his eyes flicker to mine, back to his hands. "I—my position as general manager here was purely a sinecure. I know nothing of the business. I rarely come near the office. So, when my brother called me on the phone, two weeks ago, and told me he had some business of great importance that he wished me to transact for him, I was astonished. It appeared that he had received an anonymous letter." He ran a finger inside his collar, swallowed. "A—a certain unknown person, who had recently inherited a house from his father, in the suburbs, claimed that he had, in looking over the house, found a disused room, in which was stored—this sounds incredible, I know—bars of gold, a hoard of them. This unknown, knowing that we were metal and mining brokers, made the not unnatural mistake of thinking we handled transactions such as he suggested.

"He was, naturally, uncertain as to his exact position with the government. He wanted to turn the gold in, but he was afraid of legal consequences. He begged us to approach the treasury and negotiate for the sale of it at scrap prices—and if we were successful—to act as his intermediary. You—you understand?"

"Yeah," I said. "You and your brother were hoarding a little gold."

He erupted to his feet. "Damn it, sir, how—"

"Sit down. Never mind that. I'm after bigger game than gold-hoarding."

"But I—"

"Forget it," I snapped. "Let's hear the rest."

He swallowed, sat down, stretched out pink palms. "As God is my witness, Mr. Blue, I don't know if you're right or not. Will you believe me when I say that I had never seen or heard of the gold before? That apart from Bernays saying this letter had been postmarked in Rynton, New York, I knew absolutely nothing except that he was in touch with it—and wanted me to do the talking at the sub-treasury?"

I nodded, "I'll believe that. What did the treasury people say?"

"They were very decent. They agreed to buy it at scrap prices, and make no trouble for anybody. I told Bernays that, a week or more ago. He went out of town. I never saw him or heard from him again—alive.

Do you see the desperate position I am in? This gold must be tied up with this horrible murder—yet I dare not breathe a word of it to the police. It would be their duty to arrest all of us—regardless of what the treasury people might say! And—that is not the worst of it, Mr. Blue. There is one more thing." He hesitated, licked his lips. "This morning I phoned my housekeeper. She—she told me the phone company men had been there. My telephone had been tapped, Mr. Blue—and the tap was only removed late last night!"

"Then they may have overheard whatever part of the plans you discussed over the phone?"

"My God—we did all the planning over the phone!"

I tilted my chair back. "You certainly make it easy for thieves. Haven't you any idea where the gold is now?'

HE PUT his palms to his bald head, rocked it. "If I knew that—I would know everything! I think it was in Rynton—and I think he went there to get it. But I don't know! We have a small farm there. I phoned this morning. There are supposed to be two Swedes on the place. I could get no answer to my calls. I called a neighbor. I was told nobody had seen the Swedes since last week. My guess is that he had them truck the gold into town, then gave them money to go away. But that's only a guess, too. If he did bring it into town—God only knows where he put it. We rent space from two warehouses. I've tried them both—and our vaults are empty. Miss Whitlaw has spent the day canvassing the town to find if he had rented space anywhere else. And we've found out nothing. My God—with the vaults in his own house empty—why wouldn't he store it there, where an army couldn't get it?"

"Maybe he took space under an assumed name," I said.

"Maybe he did. If so—God only knows if we'll ever find it! And if I don't make good at the treasury, God knows what they'll do."

"How much of the gold was there?"

He said in a hollow voice, "Five—thousand—pounds!"

My chair crashed to the ground and I was on my feet. "Holy hell!" I blurted. "How much is gold worth?"

"Thirty-two dollars an ounce."

"My God! I didn't realize you were talking about millions!"

"I was," he said desperately. "Missing millions now!"

More than two and a half million dollars. No wonder they were prepared to murder—and murder again and again—on the chance of finding where it was hidden! And yet—the phone call warning Pratt of the World-Over! What could that mean but that they knew where it was—that it was in some place insured by the World-Over! I cursed inwardly as I echoed Kyle's sentiments. If only Bernays had hidden it in his own vault—in his own house! I had seen one startling, absolutely conclusive proof of its impregnability—even against an army—I checked that line of thought viciously as being fruitless.

Then an incredible idea popped into my head. I threw at Van Ryn suddenly: "Listen—has your brother been mixed up with any girl in the last two or three years?"

"Lord, no! He thought of nothing but his antiques. He didn't even—"

"You're positive? He couldn't have concealed it? Did you know he was making visits to cabarets?"

"I—well, no. I see what you mean. I—I guess I don't know."

"Can you give me Miss Whitlaw's address—fast?"

He choked. "My God, man—she—you don't think she—"

"Never mind the questions," I snapped quickly. "Get me the address." And as he led me out into the outer office, "And you stay near a telephone till you hear from me."

"You—you've discovered something?" he asked breathlessly.

I left him with a grunt to decipher.

CHAPTER FIVE

SNIFFLER SET-UP

NINE TWENTY showed on my watch when I left the real-estate office on Sheridan Square. The crumpled slip in my hand bore Miss Whitlaw's Gay Street address and apartment number. My disguised question to the real-estate agent had brought the information that her window could be seen from the street.

It was a narrow, black little canyon, as I turned in from Christopher, save for the squares of orange light staggered here and there over the fronts of the quaint four-story houses that crowded the cobblestones. I walked to the middle of the block, found a dark entrance at street level, directly opposite the number on my slip, backed into it, and scanned her window.

I cursed silently as it proved to be dark. After a few debating minutes, I went to the other end of the block—Waverly Place, and phoned from the drugstore there. I thought I could catch Lieutenant McIlroy at the Van Ryn house, but he had gone. The detective still on duty—Knowles—urged me to call downtown, advised me that nothing new had developed, and that the funeral took place next day. McIlroy felt he had to wait till after that.

There seemed no point in calling him there so I left the booth, bought a couple of paper-wrapped sandwiches at the soda counter, and went back to my doorway.

I cursed softly.

She must have come in while I was away. The light was on now in her window.

I felt something was going to happen as I stood and wolfed my sandwiches, yet even when I had finished, I stood silently there in the doorway, watching, while I fought my thoughts into order. Miss Whitlaw appeared suddenly in the window, evidently taking something from a drawer just out of sight. She must have been all of fifty, but she was smoking a cigarette and she was half undressed. She wore a pair of shorts and an undershirt like mine. They looked odd with the silk stockings on her skinny legs. She went out of sight.

I suddenly developed indecision. I started forward, then checked myself, cursed, and froze, as a curtained roadster turned in at the

Waverly Place end of the block, and coasted silently toward me. The driver parked in the nearest open space, and got out. For a second he ran his eye over the houses opposite, then came silently toward my doorway, and halted—exactly in front of me, looking up. He was so close that by bending my knees slightly I could gauge the spot at which he peered. He was examining Miss Whitlaw's room.

And then he sniffed, lengthily, and I tightened my lips. Sniffler Franklin!

His elbow came back so swiftly that only by a breathless jerking in of my stomach did I avoid it. I peered down to see what he was doing. Something glinted dully as he took it from his hip pocket. He held it in front of him as he crossed the street, entered the unlocked door of Miss Whitlaw's apartment house.

Miss Whitlaw came again into my line of sight, to squash the cigarette in the same place she had used before. She looked up, evidently at a mirror, turned her head sideways and frowned at what she saw—and then stiffened. Her head snapped around away from me. One hand shot out for a wrapper, evidently hanging on the wall, and she hastily struggled into it, going away from the window. I slid out, and took one quick look in the curtained roadster, before I crossed the street. It was empty.

I was into the vestibule in time to hear a door close upstairs.

I REACHED the front door of her apartment and laid my ear against it. Needless to say, I had a gun in my hand. I heard a man's vicious monotone.

By straining I got the words "—post-office box that Bernays Van Ryn had under a phony name. The phony name is the same one he used to rent space in warehouses for his damned antiques. We know you always collected the letters for him, from that box—and we know you got some now. We think he rented a spot over near Bellevue Hospital, but we ain't sure. We're goin' to be sure, sweetheart, when you produce them letters, because he gets bills every month from them places, and this is about the time they come in. Now—get them letters!"

Her voice was harsh. "You must be insane. I know nothing whatever—"

"Can that!" Franklin's voice rapped warningly. "You know everything about them guys. He rented the lower corner of a warehouse over there—this is our tip—and had it sheathed in steel, the same as he done in his house. He had them cut a door to the outside, so he could bring stuff in without them even knowing about it. And the only guy that could get in was him. He had the doors from the inside blocked up, so he had kind of a private building within a building. If it took a key to get in—he had it. If it was some trick arrangement like a combination—he was the only one that knew it, except maybe you."

There was a curse. Miss Whitlaw said contemptuously: "You can put that gun away and get out any time. I never heard such gammon in my—"

"Shut up! We're knocking the joint over at midnight tonight and the boss figured it wouldn't do no harm to make an extra check. Just take a good look at this—" I heard him take a step—"now—are you going to talk or am I going to beat it—"

Sock!

"Why you cat!" Franklin roared. "Ow!" There was the sound of metal crashing on stone, another fist hit flesh. "Damn you! Try this!" For a second there was a scuffle, the sound of gasping blows, then a groan and a heavy fall.

It took me just that long to discover that he had left the door unlocked behind him. Then I was in. I barked: "Freeze! Right where you are—or I'll gun you!"

The woman was on the floor, moaning, one hand at her head. He was crouched over her, his hand upraised. In the hand was a blackjack, the same kind I use.

I rapped, "Drop it! Get up—with your hands high!" and he got slowly to his feet. His gun was lying on the stone hearth of the fireplace. His face was purple, his eyes furious; he was panting.

The woman groaned, rolled her head from side to side, opened her eyes. I clipped, "Miss Whitlaw—if you possibly can—please get up," and she pulled herself to a sitting posture, stared at me through hazy eyes. She stood up. I whipped my credentials from my pocket, held them out to her, without taking my eyes from Franklin. "I'm a detective." I made the words sharp, trying to clear her head.

"The dirty little rat hit me with a blackjack," she said. "He forced—"

"I heard most of it," I said quickly, as I scooped up the gun and blackjack. "Come here, you!" I pocketed his gun, shoved the blackjack up my sleeve, and went over him swiftly. He had no other weapons. I booted him in an arc, so he dived headfirst onto a couch.

"Sit down there!" I snapped at him. "One move and I'll kill you."

I kept my eyes on him, while I told the girl: "This rat's boss is a mass murderer, Miss Whitlaw. He had your—had Bernays Van Ryn killed. I've been after him for years—and if you can help me now, I've got him! If he's going to bat tonight—and if what the rat here said is true—I can dynamite the bunch of them!"

"How can I help you?"

"Have you got any mail—Mr. Van Ryn's mail—under that alias? Can you tell me where that warehouse is, exactly?"

She hesitated only a second, then, "I don't know where the warehouse is. I have got some mail from the box. Shall I get it?"

"As fast as you can."

She went through a door into the back room, and I heard her footsteps as she strode toward the back of the house. If she only had something—I looked Franklin over, tight-lipped, and stepped over to him. "Stand up!"

He stood up. I poked his jaw and slammed him down again. He cried out.

"Shut up," I snarled. "I'm going to beat the truth out of you by inches. I've got about three minutes that I can spare on you—and I'm going to show you what hell's like—unless you loosen up. Where is this warehouse?"

He blurted desperately: "That's all I know—I swear it is—it's near Bellevue—"

"Have you guys got the key? Or the combination?"

"The—the boss has."

"The alarm system—have yoy got that cooled?"

"No—no—that's what I'm here after—the alarm system. Honest to God! I—"

Fire was in my eyes. The end of the trail. Till that minute I had not realized how much it meant to me to cage Cream.

I told Franklin to shut up as hurrying footsteps came through the rooms behind me. I backed over toward the door, trying to bring a telephone into my line of sight without looking away from the treacherous little thug. I said over my shoulder: "Your telephone—where is it, Miss Whitlaw?"

A small, cold circle of steel bored into my neck, and a harsh voice said: "You won't need it! Drop that gun!"

The voice was Vance Didrickson's.

For one second I almost lost my head. I was trembling like a leaf from galling, bitter shame, that I should have let the girl get me this way. I had made the ghastly mistake of deciding that the two-inch heel business was a put-up job on her. And now—my finish. Nothing but a miracle could—I got hold of myself desperately. My gun dropped; my hands went up.

"Turn around."

I turned and faced Didrickson's gaunt face. "Not a bad little act at that, eh friend?" His fingers ripped over me, tossing Franklin's gun back to him. He found my blackjack in my hip pocket; that also went to Franklin. "For a while you gave us heart failure when you went to the drugstore to phone. Wait now, Sniffler!"

I heard Franklin scramble up and run toward me. He raved: "Try that, you louse!" and kicked me. My knees sagged. I went numb from the hips down.

Didrickson roared: "Stop it, you damn little—"

"By God!" Franklin panted, "He gave me the works. I'm not go—"

"Stop!" Didrickson tried to dive past me and catch his arm, but he was too late. Franklin blackjacked me into unconsciousness and I went down.

CHAPTER SIX

BB GETAWAY

I **WAS** lying on the floor of the tonneau of a speeding car when I came to. I started to speak—only to find adhesive tape covered my mouth. Cords were on my wrists and handcuffs on my ankles. I heard a whistle blow mournfully nearby. We were driving close to a waterfront.

Franklin's voice asked: "Why not bump the rat and drop him out here?"

Didrickson growled: "I told you before he was wanted alive."

"Why?" Franklin insisted disgustedly. "Why would anyone want a live dick? That's what I can't—"

"What you can't understand would fill a library. My orders are to get him alive if possible—and that's that. Shut up."

"Orders from who?"

"Drop it," Didrickson said. "Your orders are from me. You get your dough from me."

The driver of the car turned back and said: "This here is Ozone Park. I never been to this place before. How far is it from Van Ryn's house?"

"In the block behind. It backs right up to it. I thought you were one of the guys ran that phone tap in," Didrickson said.

"That was me brother. He's an electrician. He's the one that's inside—"

"Shut your face!"

We drove another fifteen minutes. Cold sweat was on my body and my head was pounding.

Finally we turned in at a driveway, drove straight into a garage, and one of the two men in the front seat got out and closed the door behind us. The whole party got out of the car and Didrickson said: "Carry him—you two. Put him in the vegetable cellar."

Franklin gasped. "For God's sakes! Are you crazy? That's where—"

"Do what you're told!"

We crossed cement to the side door of a house. In the moonlight it showed as a modest, two-story residence of red brick, with a white veranda. The side door put us on a landing, halfway down a flight of stairs. Those above were painted; those leading down were rough board. My porters took me down, and a sick electric bulb came on as we hit the cement floor below. Gray dust was everywhere. They carried me across the stone room, into a passage at the far side that ended ten yards along in an iron door. Franklin, carrying my feet, was cursing under his breath, as he had to open it with his foot. We went down three steep steps, into blackness. Franklin said, "Here," and they dropped me. The other thug threw a flashlight around the room. There was a little broom closet in one corner. Otherwise, the room was bare.

They left me in the dark and the iron door clanged; a bolt thudded home. All this came through the gagging dizziness I was fighting.

My hands were in front of me and I tore the adhesive from my mouth, painfully. The dizziness went away and left me bathed in cold sweat.

Minutes went by, while I got myself together. I thought of the stone steps. The big pulse in my forehead was out like a whipcord, as I rolled, and dragged myself across the gritty floor. If I could find a sharp-edged stone step—

The steps were smooth and rounded. The only sharp spot was a point at one corner, worth exactly nothing as a rope cutter.

I SAT there with my brain chasing itself around like a squirrel in a cage. The door. It would be impassable, of course—but there might be some projection on it. I reached up my shackled hands for the top step to pull myself erect—and my heart missed a beat as I felt something in my armpit. For a second, I sat frozen. I tried to feel what it was—then I got it. Sniffler Franklin's blackjack that I had stuffed up my sleeve on Gay Street!

When I raised my hands under Didrickson's gun, it must have slipped up to my armpit, nestled there while they cut me down and tied me up! The same style as mine, they believed they had retrieved it when they took mine! If—

I lay down on my back, raised my bound hands straight up above me and shook, flopped. The jack rolled out onto my chest—and in the same instant there was a sound from the broom closet in the corner that almost made me forget the lead-and-leather club.

The noise was a faint tinkle, and it brought me sitting bolt upright. A telephone! My mouth sagged open.

I grabbed round for the steps, remembered to snatch up the jack, heaved myself to my feet.

In five long hops I reached the broom closet, was inside, and slid down to my knees, my hands weaving around. The first thing I found was a smooth square object, with a little switchboard key projecting from its top. The second thing was a handset telephone.

The churning in my head moved over to make room for a little sense. It was incredible that those above would leave me in the room with a working telephone. I lifted the handset to my face. The wire was dead.

I contacted the one-legged switchboard, groped till I pressed the key over, and listened. There was no sound on the wire. I pressed the key the other way. A faint humming was in my ear. My throat went dry. A girl's voice said: "Number, please?"

This, I thought, is a little fancy baiting from upstairs, but I could lose nothing. "New York police headquarters," I clipped. "Murder!"

The girl gasped, and I heard a quick clacking of wires. If this were phony, it was good. I was holding my breath when I got an answer and snapped, "McIlroy—fast!" and when the cracked-voice homicide man came on, I knew that somehow the miracle was real. I snapped: "Mac—Cass Blue. There's a robbery at a warehouse near Bellevue Hospital at midnight tonight. An army of crooks is hitting it. There's three million in gold inside. You hear me? Get men—lots of them down there fast! And for—"

"Wait! Wait!" he cut in wildly. "I've had eight tips tonight—all on different warehouses—"

"Forget them! They're blinds to pull you away. This is real—and I know! And for God's sake send a squad to rescue me. I'm in—"

Spat! It sounded like a pistol shot.

I called, "Mac! Mac!" It took me five seconds to realize that the line had gone.

I SQUATTED there, breathing heavily through my mouth, blood pounding in my head. I grabbed for the key, switched it back and forth. My hands were unsteady as I finally recradled the phone, and stood up.

Feet pounded the floor above me, milling about, and my head jerked round. The milling died away. I looked down at my wrists, at my blackjack. I thought of trying to smash the phone and getting a piece to cut my bonds. Somehow the idea of using rubber as a saw didn't panic me. The door. I hadn't explored it.

I kangarooed across the floor, up the steps, felt hastily over the iron surface. It was rusted. There was no projection of any kind. There was a square opening the size of my head five feet from the ground, for ventilation. Through it I heard the rumble of voices from above. A door slammed. Feet started down.

But the feet didn't come to the cellar. I heard a door—apparently the one through which I'd entered the house—open and close. Another pair of feet came down the steps, and went out.

I thought wildly of hiding just inside the door and trying to sap whoever came for me. I could rip the telephone loose and have two clubs—two clubs, my hands and feet bound, to attack a houseful of armed men! Or even one armed man. My teeth clamped. Yet—I had to do something. A blackjack, a telephone—

Then the brainwave.

One second, I stood there with the idea sending ripples over me.

Then the sound of more feet—two pairs this time—sounded on the stairs outside, and the raised, angry voices of arguing men. I swung myself round, and hopped as fast as I could down the steps, but I could not miss the few floating words: "—damned if I'll stay here and guard the rat while you guys—" Franklin's voice.

Then I was covering the ground back to the phone. I reached it, caught the cradle between my feet, and ripped the handset from its moorings. As I went back toward the steps, I hefted it. It wasn't a war club, but it would do for one blow. I sat down on the steps, laid the phone beside me, and grabbed the blackjack in both hands. With the back of one hand, I discovered the spot where the cement had drawn out to a point on the step corner. I swung the blackjack—hard. My aim was good.

I swung it again—and again—whacking it against that point. I was drenched with sweat and still it didn't split.

I went to work again, this time standing back and almost falling as I brought the jack down—and lead shot spurted out. Hastily, I cupped my hands around it.

I spread the cracked leather. The lead BB shot poured into my palms, a heaping handful. I knelt, and spread a layer of the tiny lead pellets almost solidly over the center step. I had enough left over to make a thinner layer for the bottom step, and it was while I was working on the bottom step that I heard an automobile's engine suddenly warm into life, somewhere outside the house. Almost immediately the side door opened and I heard the sound of the car's engine diminishing as it drove away. The door slammed. Sniffler Franklin's voice bit off one raving, vicious curse. There was an instant of silence, then—hard heel thumps hit the stairs, coming down.

I flung the empty leather pouch into a corner, took two long and what I hoped were silent leaps back to the spot where they had dropped me, and crumpled down to the ground. The phone was hidden in my crotch. I had my legs drawn up, my toes turned under, ready to hoist myself erect. If—

LIGHT glared in the square opening of the door, sent a throb into my head as it struck my eyes. I sat upright, my eyes staring straight at it, a scowl on my face. The light stayed on me, while I heard a bolt shoot back outside. Then the door swung open, past the light, and the light was still on me. Franklin was cursing steadily under his breath. I saw the nozzle of his gun just under the flash.

He snarled: "All right, you stinking louse. You've handed it out plenty. Let's see how you can—"

He stepped down, without moving the light beam from my face. His right foot came down on the shot.

Threshing light beam, gun roar and the man's cries blended into a wild kaleidoscope. His right foot shot out from under him as though greased; he screamed as he wrenched himself. His gun exploded at the ceiling. His right foot came down on the second layer of shot, and wrenched him again. The flashlight was whirling. His gun went off again. He was using the same words now but he was praying for relief from the anguish of his strained groin as he went whirling over backward, over the side of the steps, to crash onto the cement in a groaning, frantic tangle. I made my jump.

I put on my bent toes. The flash had rolled into a corner, was miraculously still shining. In the radiance I could see to aim my knees at his stomach as I fell. The phone was up over my head. My knees hit—then I gave it to him.

The phone lasted twice as long as I expected. I smashed him once across the bridge of the nose, once square on the temple—and it fell to pieces in my hand.

He had both a clasp knife—a vicious-looking instrument with a blade seven inches long—and the key to my handcuffs on him. He looked dead when I left him, but I had no time to find out. I raced out into the corridor, with his gun in one fist and my own—recovered—in the other, reached the stairs, crouched there, listening. I heard no sound above. I let the caution go, and took the steps four at a time, burst into a kitchen. I ran through an empty house, found a phone in the front room. It was out of order.

I went out the front door at a run. In the pale moonlight, the nearest house that had lights on was two doors down, across the street. I ran for the house. It was a bungalow with a three-step-up veranda. I landed—from the street—square in front of the door, hammered a gun muzzle against the door panel. "Open up!" I shouted. "Police!"

A mouse-like little man with a walrus mustache and lobster eyes, clad in trousers, galluses and winter undershirt stared at me with his mouth open as I shouldered the door wide, sending him back against the wall. I snapped, "Telephone!" and he swallowed, pointing a shaking finger at a wall instrument.

Ice touched my stomach as I stared at a clock over the phone registering five minutes to eleven, just as I heard McIlroy's voice on the wire.

"Blue again," I whipped. "I'm in Brooklyn. Have a squad car meet me at Times Square subway station—and wait for me!"

"But my God—what—where—"

I threw the receiver at the hook as I ran for the door again, rapping at the man: "Where's the subway—fast?"

He stammered out directions. I had a run of two blocks to the nearest station. I was lucky enough to jam my shoulder between the closing doors of an express, and wriggle in.

I lived a lifetime in that journey. My stomach was a hard knot. The payoff! The battle at the warehouse—when it came—would be history in the making.

CHAPTER SEVEN

"CALLING ALL CARS!"

THE CLOCK showed five minutes to twelve when I raced up the steps of the Forty-second Street Station. Even as I sprinted across toward Seventh Avenue, ducking the curious crowd by taking the gutter, I remembered Kyle Van Ryn's alibi. If he had been home half an hoar after his brother's shooting, he was forever in the clear.

I ran out from the crowded sidewalks, till I saw the radio car parked there beside the Times Building. I damned them viciously as I sprinted, for being headed north when I wanted to go south. I plunged into the crowd at the corner of Times Square, scattered them, shot across the street. Then I was on the far side, running toward the car. I landed on the running board. "Turn around!" I cracked at them. "We're going downtown—not up! Fast, you tub of lard—"

Sergeant Tromper, at the wheel—the fattest man on the force—lunged forward to release the handbrake. New, an acting-sergeant said excitedly, "What's it all ab—" and the shrill peeping of the radio cut him short. Tromper sent the car shooting across, whirling at right angles to the streaming traffic, gave a blast of his siren, and cut it to get the announcement—and we almost ran into the radiator of a touring car. The touring car backed hastily, as we all almost pitched through the windshield. Then, like a machine gun came the police announcer's voice—the only time in history, I guess, that he ever gasped:

"Calling all cars!"

He ripped it out. Words fairly tumbled over each other—yet they were all as clear as a pistol shot. "A bomb has just been thrown at a corner of the warehouse on First Avenue just south of Bellevue Hospital. A gang of armed men reported to be storming it. The warehouse reported to contain hoarded gold. All cars with the exception of"—he rattled off a list of half a dozen cars—"proceed at once to the warehouse as quickly as possible! Shoot to kill!"

Signal 30! The dynamite call!

Tromper jammed down on the siren. His face in the green glow was taut and hard, as the car jumped through the stalled traffic. Clinging to the running board, I was whip-cracked, jerked out to the length of my arms, as I clung to the top. I was staring straight across our tail into the touring car that had backed up for us, and was now trying to slide past behind us. And in that instant, I suddenly went watery inside.

The touring car was crammed to bursting with men. As it swerved abaft us, I caught the driver's face. It was Vance Didrickson.

I was almost flung from my perch as Tromper whirled the car southward. I roared hoarsely, "Wait—wait! For God's sake—there's something wrong!"

Tromper choked: "Wait? You damn fool, we can't wait—"

"Turn around!" I raved. "God Almighty! There they go—north—"

"I can't turn around! Don't you hear that call? Are—"

"Then let me off!"

Tromper braked wildly. "You're crazy! Get off then!"

I pitched out in the middle of Forty-second, flung forward, almost slammed to my face—and dived white-faced for a northbound cab. I leaped in the wrong side, shouted at the driver, "There's a touring car half a block ahead—a Chandler—catch it and there's fifty bucks in it for you!" and he nodded excitedly, sent his cab forward.

He was an expert.

We roared up Broadway after the touring—and caught it within ten blocks.

I snapped: "Keep back—follow it!"

WE SWEPT past Columbus Circle, and as we did, I became aware for the first time of distant police sirens wailing, in all directions. My stomach was ice. Urged by me, McIlroy had spread the warning, and now—with the bomb as confirmation of my accuracy—the huge wave of patrol cars was sweeping southward. And the thugs' car was speeding northward—into the vacated part of town.

I was half standing in the rear of the cab, one hand gripping the driver's partition, my eyes haggard on the speeding car ahead. If I could get to a phone—correct the disastrous mistake—but I couldn't! I dare not lose the car ahead! I found my gun clutched in my fist and groaned at the idiocy of the gesture. For no more than a third of the men I had seen at the Croton could at best be jammed into the car ahead. There must be others—converging at some focal point.

Galling fury boiled inside me as I realized how I had been tricked—how the whole long chain of subtle hints had been deftly funneled into my mind. They figured crudeness wouldn't trick me. They had nudged me gently forward till I had thought I had discovered something for myself. And the whole build-up was all for this moment. The phone, apparently left accidentally in my cell in Ozone Park, was a deliberate plant. They had listened in on me, till I had relayed my phony tip to McIlroy—then snipped the wire!

And the staged scene at the Whitlaw woman's apartment. They were even smart enough to figure that I would peg the two-inch heel on the woman as all part of the frame-up and that I would trust her. They must have broken into her apartment, and been hiding there before she arrived. Then they played out their farce, trapping me, and, I guess, the woman too. I wondered if they had killed her—or just left her tied up in the apartment.

We darted up Broadway, through the Fifties, the Sixties. At Seventy-second, the touring car wheeled to the left, shot over to the Drive. We were eighty yards in the rear, holding it. There were only a few cars on the Drive, and the pavements were slick and gleaming from the rain, but the touring was making time.

Then suddenly, its exhaust gave a startled roar as it passed around the bend ahead of us. I snapped, "Quick—step on it!" and the driver jammed down the throttle, swearing. We leaped forward, whirled around the bend, and my driver swore furiously, jammed on brakes.

Two huge trucks of the Black Star Oil Company—the mammoth kind that hold thousands of gallons of oil—were maneuvering into a filling station. They blocked the road completely for the time it took the cumbersome vehicles to straighten out in line with the runways of the station. The touring car's spurt had been in time to get it around them. They were gone.

It was only a few seconds that we were held up, but it almost drove me crazy until we shot around them at last.

We fairly left the asphalt as the driver got going—and then—God only knows why I hadn't realized our destination—we were suddenly a block south of the Van Ryn house. Even as I gasped, in belated realization, there came the nerve-racking, vicious hammering of a submachine gun's echoing reports. I shouted wildly, "Slow down—stop!" as we shot toward the top of the hill that overlooked the Van Ryn grounds. The driver braked, and we skidded, narrowly missed sideswiping a coupe parked on the very lip of the hill.

TWO men, dragging a screaming woman, suddenly raced up as we stopped, turned almost sideways to the hill. I got the whole scene below in one glance.

The house blazed with lights. Three vehicles were drawn up in line close to the side gate, and from these—a truck and two touring cars—men were swarming. Already some of them were inside the gate, and even as I looked I saw sharp, darting stabs of flame spit from the shadows close to the house. Knowles—and the coppers. Then the nightmare. Three of the attackers opened up with submachine guns at once. The night racked and hammered as they raked the house with death. They fired for no more than half a minute, yet there was no more chance of the police—or anybody else close to the house—being alive than of the house falling down. Somebody blew a whistle. The guns stopped. Plainly I could hear a man screaming.

The owner of the parked coupe that stood near us had evidently left his radio on, and it was out of order. A shrill, unpleasant whine came from it, sounding like a flute blown interminably on one note. I was out of the car, afire with rage and horror at the incredible scene. My driver cried hoarsely, "For God's sake, mister—don't go down there! It's a robbery!" and grabbed me.

I stood with ice in my veins, my gun in my hand. Suddenly, the side door of the house flew open, and light streamed out. A man with two guns in his hand stood on the threshold—beckoning the raiders in. And in the beam of light that ran down the sidewalk, I saw a stream of men, running toward the door, each pushing ahead of him a hand truck.

Almost at the same minute there was a dull boom from inside the house, and the burglar alarm started hammering out its frantic clanging. My driver was clinging to me, saying: "For God's sakes, mister— you can't do nothing down there—"

I dived back for the cab. "Get us back to that filling station we just passed, and make it fast!"

He jerked the cab backward, whirled us the rest of the way round, and gunned southward again. The trucks were still in the runways as I flung out of the cab, roared at the attendant: "Police! Where's your phone?"

In the little office I raved, "Police headquarters!" at the girl, and "McIlroy!" at the desk man when he came on. When the cracked voice answered wildly, I ripped out: "Blue: The warehouse was a phony—another phony! The whole gang of them are up at the Van Ryn house! They're taking it to pieces! For God's sake, send out a broadcast to those radio cars to get up here like greased—"

"I can't!" he shrilled wildly. "Somebody's turned on half a dozen broadcasting sets throughout the city—all the same wave length as ours. It's thrown every radio car out of commission! We can't reach them—they're all down at that damned warehouse, and we can't—"

"Call Bellevue!" I raved. "Get somebody to run and tell them. For God's sake do something, or these devils will get away. They've killed Knowles and the others. It's a slaught—"

"Can you hold them—for five minutes?" he gasped hoarsely, then to somebody he roared, "Get me Bellevue Hospital," and back to me, "If you can stand them off for five minutes, I'll have a hundred men there—"

"Hell!" I almost screamed at him. "There's twenty of them—armed with machine guns! How the devil can I—"

And then something seemed to explode inside my head.

I jerked at McIlroy, "Get the cars up here, and I'll do what I can!" I jammed down the receiver and ran out. I jabbed a finger at the truck drivers. "You—you two—are those trucks full?"

"Sure."

"Get up on the seats! I'm buying all your oil," I roared. "Follow me!"

"Hey, this oil's bought—"

I flashed badge and gun on them together. "This is police business. I'll square it with everybody. Get driving fast!"

They chorused, "O.K.," and ran for their seats.

I shouted, "Follow my taxi," and dived back inside. To my driver I shot hoarsely: "I want to circle round and come up on the back of that house—east of it—it takes a whole block. Go over two blocks before you turn north!"

He shot the cab forward and we swung over east. We had to pound uphill for the whole two blocks—from the Drive, past West End, and up to Broadway. We spun north, raced the eight blocks, and my driver said: "Listen—"

Directly below us sounded the crackle of shots. I shouted, "Stop here!" when we were at the corner that was above the southern edge of the Van Ryn grounds. The two trucks pulled in behind the cab, as I flung out. I looked down the narrow, sloping, side street. Less than a hundred yards separated me from the two touring cars and the truck. The pavement was wet and slippery. I snapped at the tank-truck drivers: "Park at the top of this hill and open up every spigot on your trucks! Fast! I want every drop of oil you've got to run down this hill—on the right-hand side if possible. It'll collect in a pool at the bottom!"

They ran to do what I said.

BROADWAY was filling rapidly with excited, running figures. They clustered around us, like bees on a hive, shouting excited questions. I swung a gun round on them, roared them back, while the drivers got their trucks in position, then the spigots went on.

Oil spurted out of the taps in a rushing, surging flood, into the gutter, but the gutter would not hold it. It spread, as thousands of gallons went down the hill, into a wide, swirling fan. The tumbling stream had reached the bottom of the hill, before the trucks were drained. I shouted at them, "Get your trucks away—fast!"

Even as they backed, I grabbed a box of matches from my pockets and lit them one after another, tossed them into the stream of oil. Flames sprang up, started to spread. Faster and faster, the ever-growing flames raced down the hill. By the time they reached the corner of West End, they were sheets of fire ten feet high. By the time they reached the first touring car, they enveloped it.

Wild, disorganized shouts were coming from the thugs down below. I saw the first touring car start to slip backward, heard it crash into the truck as the drivers deserted them, and the flood of oil under the wheels destroyed the traction of their tires on the slanting street. I didn't wait to see them slide, flaming, down the hill into the corner. I was sprinting wildly for a drugstore across the street. I got McIlroy again.

"Where in God's name are those cars? I've delayed them—but it may be only for minutes!"

"They're on their way!" he shouted. "Hey—wait a minute—what the hell—listen—you're sure it's the Van Ryn house? Sergeant Green's talking to Kyle Van Ryn on the phone now. He said he was at home and everything was O.K."

"You bloody chump!" I roared. "Kyle Van Ryn is working with Cream. It was Kyle that killed his brother! Trace that call and nab him!"

"But—but he had an alibi—"

"The hell he did," I rapped. "I was just in the house behind his a while ago. There was a miniature switchboard there. They had his line tapped, and run into the switchboard. When you called him after the murder, the call went into that switchboard, and was connected to another line that probably led back to New York. He talked from New York, through Brooklyn, and back to New York again. Do you get it?"

He gasped, "My God! Wait!" I heard him roar at somebody. Then, "Why would he kill—why would he be in New York?"

"Because Bernays Van Ryn was never in a cabaret in his life. Because Kyle Van Ryn, for over a year, with the aid of a wig and a little grease paint has been building up a Mr. Hyde character for his brother. Last night he managed to get Bernays out of the house, where these thugs crowned him. They poured alcohol down his throat so he would seem drunk, and if he looked a little different than usual people wouldn't notice it. Then Kyle and some slender guy carried Bernays in through the back door of the club, hid him somewhere—in the clothes closet probably—while Kyle played drunk, and let himself be seen—with his wig on and everything.

"They murdered Bernays up in that room with a small-caliber silenced pistol, pasted the bandage over the wound to stop the bleeding. Then Kyle went down and sat in the dining room till the lights went off, slipped out, took the body from his accomplice and sat it down. Then they both took a powder out. Kyle threw away his wig and props, and the slender guy threw away his phony two-inch heel—"

"Hey—what's that? Phony? You—"

"That was a gag to throw suspicion on a dame named Whitlaw that's one of their firm. She has a high heel."

"Why did they kill him? They don't stand to gain nothing by it—"

"They killed him to get Kyle Van Ryn into the house. He and his brother quarreled—badly enough so Bernays kicked Kyle out. He gave me a story about it, but I think he was lying. Anyway, Bernays kicked him out. Kyle was smart enough to let on he was satisfied. Maybe he was for a time. Then this gold came into the—"

"This what?" McIlroy roared.

I EXPLAINED. "Bernays was hoarding gold. That's what this whole thing's about. He had it at his country house. Now that the price is way up, he decided to sell it. He was going to let Kyle hold the bag—send him to the treasury people to talk it over. Kyle knew his brother well enough to guess what was what. Or maybe Bernays told him the whole thing. Anyway, Bernays brought the gold in from the country in the middle of the night, getting his two Swedes to do the carting. They carried it into the house in small crates—I don't know how many of them. They took the gold out of the boxes, put antiques in instead and shipped them up to the museum."

"But God Almighty! Where's the gold now? That museum was empty—"

"That's what the thugs are lifting. When that butler told us there was a secret passage, we neither of us stopped to think that that must mean stairs, and space of some sort. That gold must have been piled either on the stairs, or in whatever space there is in that secret entrance. I'm sure of that."

"Why?"

"That undertaker gag. Those hoods hijacked the body of Bernays today. You remember what a little guy he was and how he was crushed up against the side of the coffin? That was because some other guy was in that coffin with him when they carried it in. They knocked the people in the house out, ripped open that desk drawer as a blind, and put this third guy in the secret passage so he'd be there to open doors for them when they came back tonight for the—say, for God's sake, where are those cars?"

"Aren't they there? They must be!"

"Is the radio still out?"

"Hell, yes! Listen—I'll put my receiver to the phone."

There was a clack, and then—my knees sagged. For over the phone came a shrill, maddening whine—sounding like a mammoth flute blown on one note.

I made a queer sound in my throat, dropped the receiver and was out, sprinting down the street—and from a few blocks distant came the rising wail of a dozen police sirens. I roared at my cabby, who was staring down the hill, "Hey—get in—fast!" and as he jumped aboard, "Go back down to where we first pulled up—down there on the edge of that hill! And for God's sake hurry!"

I realized I'd made the most terrible blunder of all! The man in the coupe! The man parked calmly overlooking the whole frightful business—with his radio tuned to the police broadcast—who could it be? My head went on fire. Who but the arch-devil, Cream himself—unable to resist watching his masterpiece? And I had been within yards of him and missed him! I groaned aloud, as we thundered down toward the Drive—and then suddenly I caught my breath.

A roadster with one green-shaded parking light shot like a streak directly across in front of us and I roared, "There—there he goes!"

We almost left the ground. Taking the turn south I thought we were gone; we literally ran on two wheels for half a block. I shouted, "Catch him!" hoarsely, frantically.

Sirens wailed, screamed, on West End and Broadway, as the police cars sliced the night. Unconsciously I knew that they were in time— that the swarming murderers at the house were trapped. But it meant less than nothing to me, if the maniac ahead of me escaped.

Then—five blocks along—we saw him.

The taillight of the flying roadster was three blocks ahead of us. My driver's voice cracked as he yelled, "There—there!" and I cut him off as I plunged head and arm through the window. My gun flamed, thundered. I shattered the glass in the roadster's rear window—and for a second it faltered, wobbled. Then it sprang ahead again—this time with a screaming exhaust. We clipped the last curve on the Drive, straightened out to the long, perfectly straight ten blocks—and my heart leaped!

Five hundred yards away three police cars were tearing up the Drive toward us, sirens wide open, their red headlamps bathing the cement in ruby light! For a second, I saw Cream's roadster jerk, as he faltered, then, with a wild burst, he dived for a side street.

My driver gasped: "I can't beat the—"

"I'll murder you if you don't!" I thundered. "Step on it!" For a second, it looked as though we would crash head-on into a police car—then we whirled, and as we zoomed up the slight rise, they screamed past behind us.

The roadster was halfway up the block, and even as I swung out my window to fire again, I realized that he was cornered. A steady stream of sirens wailed on West End, a steady stream, now, on the Drive below!

He swung into the curb, fifty yards ahead of us; brakes squealed. Then he was out, and racing for the door of a small brick house. I fired once, as he threw himself against the front door, but my aim was wobbly. I started to shout my driver to a halt, but he flung us into a grinding stop before I got my mouth open and I plunged out. I heard my man fling himself again and again against the door—and then, with a crash it went open, and he dived into a lighted hall—but he had taken too long. I had a foot on the veranda as he plunged forward, and as he caught himself on a stair banister, his horrible, starch-white face whipped over his shoulder. I held my gun down at my side, waiting for a split second with my teeth chattering—and then he turned—and his hands shot above his head. His orange eyes glowed into mine. "All right," he said. "You've got me. I'll go quietly."

My free hand whipped to my hip. I flung Franklin's revolver to the floor. I heard my own voice gasping from a great distance: "I'm counting three. Then I murder you where you stand. One—" Before the "one" was out of my mouth he dived. I gasped out "two-three" like a fool, and he fired from the floor—and so did I.

My left side went white-hot. One of his eyes became a red socket. He seemed to freeze for a split second, crouched over there. His mouth sagged open, then he simply sat down on the floor, but something snapped in my brain. I fired again, and again, into that long wolf-like face, blasting the flesh into blackness until my gun clicked empty three times.

Then the door filled with charging blue-coats. I threw them my gun, and went down.

www.ingramcontent.com/pod-product-compliance
Lightning Source LLC
Chambersburg PA
CBHW061519020726
47502CB00006B/2137